W9-BPK-788

THE PALE HORSEMAN

≋

SHARPE'S GOLD
Richard Sharpe and the Destruction of Almeida,
August 1810

SHARPE'S ESCAPE★
Richard Sharpe and the Bussaco Campaign,
1810

SHARPE'S BATTLE★
Richard Sharpe and the Battle of Fuentes de
Onoro, May 1811

SHARPE'S COMPANY
Richard Sharpe and the Siege of Badajoz, January
to April 1812

SHARPE'S SWORD
Richard Sharpe and the Salamanca Campaign,
June and July 1812

SHARPE'S ENEMY
Richard Sharpe and the Defense of Portugal,
Christmas 1812

SHARPE'S HONOUR
Richard Sharpe and the Vitoria Campaign,
February to June 1813

SHARPE'S REGIMENT
Richard Sharpe and the Invasion of France, June
to November 1813

SHARPE'S SIEGE
Richard Sharpe and the Winter Campaign, 1814

SHARPE'S REVENGE
Richard Sharpe and the Peace of 1814

SHARPE'S WATERLOO
Richard Sharpe and the Waterloo Campaign,
15 June to 18 June 1815

SHARPE'S DEVIL★
Richard Sharpe and the Emperor, 1820–21

The Grail Quest Series

THE ARCHER'S TALE
VAGABOND
HERETIC

The Nathaniel Starbuck Chronicles

REBEL
COPPERHEAD
BATTLE FLAG
THE BLOODY GROUND

The Warlord Chronicles

THE WINTER KING
THE ENEMY OF GOD
EXCALIBUR

Other Novels

REDCOAT
A CROWNING MERCY
STORMCHILD
SCOUNDREL
GALLOWS THIEF
STONEHENGE, 2000 B.C.: A NOVEL

★ Published by HarperCollins*Publishers*

THE PALE HORSEMAN

Bernard Cornwell

HarperLargePrint

An Imprint of HarperCollins*Publishers*

THE PALE HORSEMAN. Copyright © 2006 by Bernard Cornwell. All rights reserved. Printed in the United States of America. No part of this book may be used or reproduced in any manner whatsoever without written permission except in the case of brief quotations embodied in critical articles and reviews. For information, address HarperCollins Publishers, 10 East 53rd Street, New York, NY 10022.

HarperCollins books may be purchased for educational, business, or sales promotional use. For information, please write: Special Markets Department, HarperCollins Publishers, 10 East 53rd Street, New York, NY 10022.

Originally published in Great Britain in 2004 by HarperCollins Publishers.

FIRST HARPER LARGE PRINT EDITION

Printed on acid-free paper

Library of Congress Cataloging-in-Publication Data
Cornwell, Bernard.
    The pale horseman / Bernard Cornwell—1st. ed.
      p. cm.
    Sequel to: The last kingdom.
    ISBN 0-06-087892-4 (Large Print)
    ISBN 0-06-078712-0 (Hardcover)
  1. Great Britain—History—Alfred, 871–899—Fiction.
2. Alfred, King of England, 849–899—Fiction. 3. Vikings—Fiction. I. Title.
  PR6053.O75P35   2006
  823'.914—dc22   2005046290

06 07 08 09 10 BVG/RRD 10 9 8 7 6 5 4 3 2 1

This Large Print Book carries the
Seal of Approval of N.A.V.H.

THE PALE HORSEMAN

is for

George MacDonald Fraser,

in admiration.

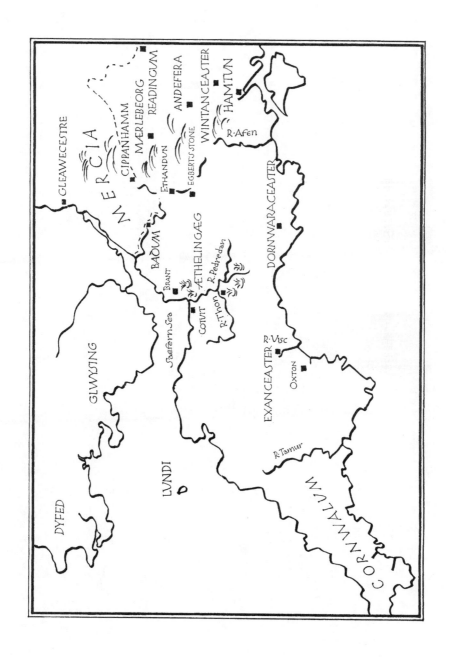

Ac her forþ berað; fugelas singað, gylleð
græghama.

For here starts war, carrion birds sing,
and gray wolves howl.
(From **The Fight at Finnsburh**)

PLACE-NAMES

The spelling of place-names in Anglo-Saxon England was an uncertain business, with no consistency and no agreement even about the name itself. Thus London was variously rendered as Lundonia, Lundenberg, Lundenne, Lundene, Lundenwic, Lundenceaster, and Lundres. Doubtless some readers will prefer other versions of the names listed below, but I have usually employed whatever spelling is cited in the **Oxford Dictionary of English Place-Names** for the years nearest or contained within Alfred's reign, A.D. 871–899, but even that solution is not foolproof. Hayling Island, in 956, was written as both Heilincigae and Hæglingaiggæ. Nor have I been consistent myself; I have preferred the modern England to Englaland and, instead of Norðhymbralond, have used Northumbria to avoid the suggestion that the boundaries of the ancient kingdom coincide with those of the modern county. So this list, like the spellings themselves, is capricious.

Æsc's Hill	Ashdown, Berkshire
Ætheling Aeg	Athelney, Somerset
Afen	River Avon, Wiltshire
Andefera	Andover, Wiltshire
Baðum (pronounced Bathum)	Bath, Avon
Bebbanburg	Bamburgh Castle, Northumberland
Brant	Brent Knoll, Somerset
Bru	River Brue, Somerset
Cippanhamm	Chippenham, Wiltshire
Cracgelad	Cricklade, Wiltshire
Cridianton	Crediton, Devon
Cynuit	Cynuit Hillfort, near Cannington, Somerset
Contwaraburg	Canterbury, Kent
Cornwalum	Cornwall
Dærentmora	Dartmoor, Devon
Defereal	Kingston Deverill, Wiltshire
Defnascir	Devonshire
Dornwaraceaster	Dorchester, Dorset
Dreyndynas	"Fort of thorns," fictional, set in Cornwall

Dunholm	Durham, County Durham
Dyfed	Southwest Wales, mostly now Pembrokeshire
Dyflin	Dublin, Eire
Eoferwic	York (also the Danish Jorvic, pronounced Yorvik)
Ethandun	Edington, Wiltshire
Exanceaster	Exeter, Devon
Exanmynster	Exminster, Devon
Gewæsc	The Wash
Gifle	Yeovil, Somerset
Gleawecestre	Gloucester, Gloucestershire
Glwysing	Welsh kingdom, approximately Glamorgan and Gwent
Hamptonscir	Hampshire
Hamtun	Southampton, Hampshire
Lindisfarena	Lindisfarne (Holy Island), Northumberland
Lundene	London
Lundi	Lundy Island, Devon
Mærlebeorg	Marlborough, Wiltshire
Ocmundtun	Okehampton, Devon
Palfleot	Pawlett, Somerset
Pedredan	River Parrett
Penwith	Land's End, Cornwall
Readingum	Reading, Berkshire
Sæfern	River Severn
Sceapig	Isle of Sheppey, Kent
Scireburnan	Sherborne, Dorset

Place-Names

Sillans	The Scilly Isles
Soppan Byrg	Chipping Sodbury, Gloucestershire
Sumorsæte	Somerset
Suth Seaxa	Sussex (South Saxons)
Tamur	River Tamar
Temes	River Thames
Thon	River Tone, Somerset
Thornsæta	Dorset
Uisc	River Exe
Werham	Wareham, Dorset
Wilig	River Wylye
Wiltunscir	Wiltshire
Winburnan	Wimborne Minster, Dorset
Wintanceaster	Winchester, Hampshire

THE PALE
HORSEMAN

ONE

These days I look at twenty-year-olds and think they are pathetically young, scarcely weaned from their mothers' tits, but when I was twenty I considered myself a full-grown man. I had fathered a child, fought in the shield wall, and was loath to take advice from anyone. In short I was arrogant, stupid, and headstrong. Which is why, after our victory at Cynuit, I did the wrong thing.

We had fought the Danes beside the ocean, where the river runs from the great swamp and the Sæfern Sea slaps on a muddy shore, and there we had beaten them. We had made a great slaughter and I, Uhtred of Bebbanburg, had done my part. More than my part, for at the battle's end, when the great Ubba Lothbrokson, most feared of all the Danish leaders, had carved into our shield wall with his great war ax, I had faced him, beaten him, and sent him to join the **einherjar,** that army of the dead who feast and swive in Odin's corpse hall.

What I should have done then, what Leofric told me to do, was ride hard to Exanceaster where Alfred, King of the West Saxons, was besieging Guthrum. I should have arrived deep in the night, woken the king from his sleep, and laid Ubba's battle banner of the black raven and Ubba's great war ax, its blade still crusted with blood, at Alfred's feet. I should have given the king the good news that the Danish army was beaten, that the few survivors had taken to their dragon-headed ships, that Wessex was safe, and that I, Uhtred of Bebbanburg, had achieved all of those things.

Instead I rode to find my wife and child.

At twenty years old I would rather have been plowing Mildrith than reaping the rewards of my good fortune, and that is what I did wrong, but, looking back, I have few regrets. Fate is inexorable, and Mildrith, though I had not wanted to marry her and though I came to detest her, was a lovely field to plow.

So, in that late spring of the year 877, I spent the Saturday riding to Cridianton instead of going to Alfred. I took twenty men with me and I promised Leofric that we would be at Exanceaster by midday on Sunday and I would make certain Alfred knew we had won his battle and saved his kingdom.

"Odda the Younger will be there by now," Leofric warned me. Leofric was almost twice my age, a warrior hardened by years of fighting the Danes. "Did you hear me?" he asked when I said nothing. "Odda the Younger will be there by now," he said again, "and he's a piece of goose shit who'll take all the credit."

"The truth cannot be hidden," I said loftily.

Leofric mocked that. He was a bearded squat brute of a man who should have been the commander of Alfred's fleet, but he was not well born and Alfred had reluctantly given me charge of the twelve ships because I was an ealdorman, a noble, and it was only fitting that a high-born man should command the West Saxon fleet even though it had been much too puny to confront the massive array of Danish ships that had come to Wessex's south coast. "There are times," Leofric grumbled, "when you are an earsling." An earsling was something that had dropped out of a creature's backside and was one of Leofric's favorite insults. We were friends.

"We'll see Alfred tomorrow," I said.

"And Odda the Younger," Leofric said patiently, "has seen him today."

Odda the Younger was the son of Odda the Elder who had given my wife shelter, and the son did not like me. He did not like me because he wanted to plow Mildrith, which was reason enough for him to dislike me. He was also, as Leofric said, a piece of goose shit, slippery and slick, which was reason enough for me to dislike him.

"We shall see Alfred tomorrow," I said again, and next morning we all rode to Exanceaster, my men escorting Mildrith, our son, and his nurse, and we found Alfred on the northern side of Exanceaster where his green-and-white dragon banner flew above his tents. Other banners snapped in the damp wind, a colorful array of beasts, crosses, saints, and weapons announcing that the great men of Wessex were with their king. One of those banners showed a black stag, which confirmed that Leofric had been right and that Odda the Younger was here in south Defnascir. Outside the camp, between its southern margin and the city walls, was a great pavilion made of sailcloth stretched across guyed poles, and that told me that Alfred, instead of fighting

Guthrum, was talking to him. They were negotiating a truce, though not on that day, for it was a Sunday and Alfred would do no work on a Sunday if he could help it. I found him on his knees in a makeshift church made from another poled sailcloth, and all his nobles and thegns were arrayed behind him, and some of those men turned as they heard our horses' hooves. Odda the Younger was one of those who turned and I saw the apprehension show on his narrow face.

The bishop who was conducting the service paused to let the congregation make a response, and that gave Odda an excuse to look away from me. He was kneeling close to Alfred, very close, suggesting that he was high in the king's favor, and I did not doubt that he had brought the dead Ubba's raven banner and war ax to Exanceaster and claimed the credit for the fight beside the sea. "One day," I said to Leofric, "I shall slit that bastard from the crotch to the gullet and dance on his offal."

"You should have done it yesterday."

A priest had been kneeling close to the altar, one of the many priests who always accompanied Alfred, and he saw me and slid backward as unobtrusively as he could until he was able to stand and hurry toward me. He had red hair, a squint, a palsied left hand, and an expression of astonished joy on his ugly face. "Uhtred!" he called as he ran toward our horses. "Uhtred! We thought you were dead!"

"Me?" I grinned at the priest. "Dead?"

"You were a hostage!"

I had been one of the dozen English hostages in Werham, but while the others had been murdered by Guthrum, I had been spared because of Earl Ragnar who was a Danish war-chief and as close to me as a brother. "I didn't die, father," I said to the priest, whose name was Beocca, "and I'm surprised you did not know that."

"How could I know it?"

"Because I was at Cynuit, father, and Odda the Younger could have told you that I was there and that I lived."

I was staring at Odda as I spoke and Beocca caught the grimness in my voice. "You were at Cynuit?" he asked nervously.

"Odda the Younger didn't tell you?"

"He said nothing."

"Nothing!" I kicked my horse forward, forcing it between the kneeling men and thus closer to Odda. Beocca tried to stop me, but I pushed his hand away from my bridle. Leofric, wiser than me, held back, but I pushed the horse into the back rows of the congregation until the press of worshippers made it impossible to advance farther, and then I stared at Odda as I spoke to Beocca. "He didn't describe Ubba's death?" I asked.

"He says Ubba died in the shield wall," Beocca said, his voice a hiss so that he did not disturb the liturgy, "and that many men contributed to his death."

"Is that all he told you?"

"He says he faced Ubba himself," Beocca said.

"So who do men think killed Ubba Lothbrokson?" I asked.

Beocca could sense trouble coming and he tried to calm me. "We can talk of these things later," he said, "but for now, Uhtred, join us in prayer." He used my name rather than calling me lord because he had known me since I was a child. Beocca, like me, was a Northumbrian, and he had been my father's priest, but when the Danes took our country he had come to Wessex to join those Saxons who still resisted the invaders. "This is a time for prayer," he insisted, "not for quarrels."

But I was in a mood for quarrels. "Who do

men say killed Ubba Lothbrokson?" I asked again.

"They give thanks to God that the pagan is dead." Beocca evaded my question and tried to hush my voice with frantic gestures from his palsied left hand.

"Who do you think killed Ubba?" I asked, and when Beocca did not answer, I provided the answer for him. "You think Odda the Younger killed him?" I could see that Beocca did believe that, and the anger surged in me. "Ubba fought me man on man," I said, too loudly now, "one on one, just me and him. My sword against his ax. And he was unwounded when the fight began, father, and at the end of it he was dead. He had gone to his brothers in the corpse hall." I was furious now and my voice had risen until I was shouting, and the distracted congregation all turned to stare at me. The bishop, whom I recognized as the bishop of Exanceaster, the same man who had married me to Mildrith, frowned nervously. Only Alfred seemed unmoved by the interruption, but then, reluctantly, he stood and turned toward me as his wife, the pinch-faced Ælswith, hissed into his ear.

"Is there any man here," I was still shouting,

"who will deny that I, Uhtred of Bebbanburg, killed Ubba Lothbrokson in single combat?"

There was silence. I had not intended to disrupt the service, but monstrous pride and ungovernable rage had driven me to defiance. The faces gazed at me, the banners flapped in the desultory wind, and the small rain dripped from the edges of the sailcloth awning. Still no one answered me, but men saw that I was staring at Odda the Younger and some looked to him for a response, but he was struck dumb. "Who killed Ubba?" I shouted at him.

"This is not seemly," Alfred said angrily.

"This killed Ubba!" I declared, and I drew Serpent-Breath.

And that was my next mistake.

In the winter, while I was mewed up in Werham as one of the hostages given to Guthrum, a new law had been passed in Wessex, a law which decreed that no man other than the royal bodyguards was to draw a weapon in the presence of the king. The law was not just to protect Alfred, but also to prevent the quarrels between his great men becoming lethal and, by drawing Serpent-Breath, I had unwittingly broken the

law so that his household troops were suddenly
converging on me with spears and drawn swords
until Alfred, red-cloaked and bare-headed,
shouted for every man to be still.

Then he walked toward me and I could see
the anger on his face. He had a narrow face with
a long nose and chin, a high forehead, and a
thin-lipped mouth. He normally went clean-
shaven, but he had grown a short beard that
made him look older. He was not lived thirty
years yet, but looked closer to forty. He was
painfully thin, and his frequent illnesses had
given his face a crabbed look. He looked more
like a priest than the king of the West Saxons, for
he had the irritated, pale face of a man who
spends too much time out of the sun and poring
over books, but there was an undoubted authority in his eyes. They were very light eyes, as gray
as mail, unforgiving. "You have broken my
peace," he said, "and offended the peace of
Christ."

I sheathed Serpent-Breath, mainly because
Beocca had muttered at me to stop being a
damned fool and to put my sword away, and now
the priest was tugging my right leg, trying to
make me dismount and kneel to Alfred, whom
he adored. Ælswith, Alfred's wife, was staring at

me with pure scorn. "He should be punished," she called out.

"You will go there," the king said, pointing toward one of his tents, "and wait for my judgment."

I had no choice but to obey, for his household troops, all of them in mail and helmets, pressed about me and so I was taken to the tent where I dismounted and ducked inside. The air smelled of yellowed, crushed grass. The rain pattered on the linen roof and some leaked through onto an altar that held a crucifix and two empty candleholders. The tent was evidently the king's private chapel and Alfred made me wait there a long time. The congregation dispersed, the rain ended, and a watery sunlight emerged between the clouds. A harp played somewhere, perhaps serenading Alfred and his wife as they ate. A dog came into the tent, looked at me, lifted its leg against the altar, and went out again. The sun vanished behind a cloud and more rain pattered on the canvas, then there was a flurry at the tent's opening and two men entered. One was Æthelwold, the king's nephew, and the man who should have inherited Wessex's throne from his father except he had been reckoned too young and so the crown had gone to his uncle instead.

He gave me a sheepish grin, deferring to the second man who was heavyset, full-bearded, and ten years older than Æthelwold. He introduced himself by sneezing, then blew his nose into his hand and wiped the snot onto his leather coat. "Call it springtime," he grumbled, then stared at me with a truculent expression. "Damned rain never stops. You know who I am?"

"Wulfhere," I said, "Ealdorman of Wiltunscir." He was a cousin to the king and a leading power in Wessex.

He nodded. "And you know who this damn fool is?" he asked, gesturing at Æthelwold who was holding a bundle of white cloth.

"We know each other," I said. Æthelwold was only a month or so younger than I, and he was fortunate, I suppose, that his uncle Alfred was such a good Christian or else he could have expected a knife in the night. He was much better looking than Alfred, but foolish, flippant, and usually drunk, though he appeared sober enough on that Sunday morning.

"I'm in charge of Æthelwold now," Wulfhere said, "and of you. And the king sent me to punish you." He brooded on that for a heartbeat. "What his wife wants me to do," he went on, "is pull the guts out of your smelly arse and feed them to the pigs." He glared at me. "You know what the penalty is for drawing a sword in the king's presence?"

"A fine?" I guessed.

"Death, you fool, death. They made a new law a month ago."

"How was I supposed to know?"

"But Alfred's feeling merciful." Wulfhere ignored my question. "So you're not to dangle off a gallows. Not today, anyhow. But he wants your assurance you'll keep the peace."

"What peace?"

"His damned peace, you fool. He wants us to fight the Danes, not slice each other up. So for the moment you have to swear to keep the peace."

"For the moment?"

"For the moment," he said tonelessly, and I just shrugged. He took that for acceptance. "So you killed Ubba?" he asked.

"I did."

"That's what I hear." He sneezed again. "You know Edor?"

"I know him," I said. Edor was one of Ealdorman Odda's battle chiefs, a warrior of the men of Defnascir, and he had fought beside us at Cynuit.

"Edor told me what happened," Wulfhere said, "but only because he trusts me. For God's sake stop fidgeting!" This last shout was directed at Æthelwold who was poking beneath the altar's linen cover, presumably in search of something valuable. Alfred, rather than murder his nephew, seemed intent on boring him to death. Æthelwold had never been allowed to fight, lest he make a reputation for himself; instead he had been forced to learn his letters, which he hated, and so he idled his time away, hunting, drinking, whoring, and filled with resentment that he was not the king. "Just stand still, boy," Wulfhere snarled.

"Edor told you," I said, unable to keep the outrage from my voice, "because he trusts you? You mean what happened at Cynuit is a secret? A thousand men saw me kill Ubba!"

"But Odda the Younger took the credit," Wulfhere said, "and his father is badly wounded and if he dies then Odda the Younger will become one of the richest men in Wessex, and he'll lead more troops and pay more priests than you can ever hope to do, so men won't want to offend him, will they? They'll pretend to believe him, to keep him generous. And the king already believes him, and why shouldn't he? Odda arrived here with Ubba Lothbrokson's banner and war ax. He dropped them at Alfred's feet, then knelt and gave the praise to God, and promised to build a church and monastery at Cynuit, and what did you do? Ride a damned horse into the middle of mass and wave your sword about. Not a clever thing to do with Alfred."

I half smiled at that, for Wulfhere was right. Alfred was uncommonly pious, and a sure way to succeed in Wessex was to flatter that piety, imitate it, and ascribe all good fortune to God.

"Odda's a prick," Wulfhere growled, surprising me, "but he's Alfred's prick now, and you're not going to change that."

"But I killed . . ."

"I know what you did!" Wulfhere interrupted me. "And Alfred probably suspects you're telling the truth, but he believes Odda made it possible. He thinks Odda and you both fought Ubba. He may not even care if neither of you did, except that Ubba's dead and that's good news, and Odda brought that news and so the sun shines out of Odda's arse, and if you want the king's troops to hang you off a high branch, then you'll make a feud with Odda. Do you understand me?"

"Yes."

Wulfhere sighed. "Leofric said you'd see sense if I beat you over the head long enough."

"I want to see Leofric," I said.

"You can't," Wulfhere said sharply. "He's being sent back to Hamtun where he belongs. But you're not going back. The fleet will be put in someone else's charge. You're to do penance."

For a moment I thought I had misheard. "I'm to do what?" I asked.

"You're to grovel." Æthelwold spoke for the first time. He grinned at me. We were not exactly friends, but we had drunk together often enough and he seemed to like me. "You're to dress like a girl," Æthelwold continued, "go on your knees and be humiliated."

"And you're to do it right now," Wulfhere added.

"I'll be damned . . ."

"You'll be damned anyway," Wulfhere snarled at me, then snatched the white bundle from Æthelwold's grasp and tossed it at my feet. It was a penitent's robe, and I left it on the ground. "For God's sake, lad," Wulfhere said, "have some sense. You've got a wife and land here, don't you? So what happens if you don't do the king's bidding? You want to be outlawed? You want your wife in a nunnery? You want the church to take your land?"

I stared at him. "All I did was kill Ubba and tell the truth."

Wulfhere sighed. "You're a Northumbrian," he said, "and I don't know how they did things up there, but this is Alfred's Wessex. You can do anything in Wessex except piss all over his church, and that's what you just did. You pissed, son, and now the church is going to piss all over you." He grimaced as the rain beat harder on the tent. Then he frowned, staring at the puddle spreading just outside the entrance. He was silent a long time, before turning and giving me a strange look. "You think any of this is important?"

I did, but I was so astonished by his question that had been asked in a soft, bitter voice, that I had nothing to say.

"You think Ubba's death makes any difference?" he asked, and again I thought I had misheard. "And even if Guthrum makes peace," he went on, "you think we've won?" His heavy face was suddenly savage. "How long will Alfred be king? How long before the Danes rule here?"

I still had nothing to say. Æthelwold, I saw, was listening intently. He longed to be king, but he had no following, and Wulfhere had plainly been appointed as his guardian to keep him from making trouble. But Wulfhere's words suggested the trouble would come anyway. "Just do what Alfred wants," the ealdorman advised me, "and afterward find a way to keep living. That's all any of us can do. If Wessex falls we'll all be looking for a way to stay alive, but in the meantime put on that damned robe and get it over with."

"Both of us," Æthelwold said, and he picked up the robe and I saw he had fetched two of them, folded together.

"You?" Wulfhere snarled at him. "Are you drunk?"

"I'm penitent for being drunk. Or I was drunk, now I'm penitent." He grinned at me, then pulled the robe over his head. "I shall go to the altar with Uhtred," he said, his voice muffled by the linen.

Wulfhere could not stop him, but Wulfhere knew, as I knew, that Æthelwold was making a mockery of the rite. And I knew Æthelwold was doing it as a favor to me, though as far as I knew he owed me no favor. But I was grateful to him, so I put on the damned frock and, side by side with the king's nephew, went to my humiliation.

I meant little to Alfred. He had a score of great lords in Wessex while across the frontier in Mercia there were other lords and thegns who lived under Danish rule but who would fight for Wessex if Alfred gave them an opportunity. All of those great men could bring him soldiers, could rally swords and spears to the dragon banner of Wessex, while I could bring him nothing except my sword, Serpent-Breath. True, I was a lord, but I was from far-off Northumbria and I led no men and so my only value to him was far in the future. I did not understand that yet. In time, as the rule of Wessex spread northward, my value grew, but back then, in 877, when I was an angry twenty-year-old, I knew nothing except my own ambitions.

And I learned humiliation. Even today, a lifetime later, I remember the bitterness of that penitential grovel. Why did Alfred make me do it? I had won him a great victory, yet he insisted on shaming me, and for what? Because I had disturbed a church service? It was partly that, but only part. He loved his god, loved the church, and passionately believed that the survival of Wessex lay in obedience to the church and so he would protect the church as fiercely as he would fight for his country. And he loved order. There was a place for everything and I did not fit and he genuinely believed that if I could be brought to God's heel then I would become part of his beloved order. In short he saw me as an unruly young hound that needed a good whipping before it could join the disciplined pack.

So he made me grovel.

And Æthelwold made a fool of himself.

Not at first. At first it was all solemnity. Every man in Alfred's army was there to watch, and they made two lines in the rain. The lines stretched to the altar under the guyed sailcloth where Alfred and his wife waited with the bishop and a gaggle of priests. "On your knees," Wulfhere said to me. "You have to go on your knees," he insisted tonelessly, "and crawl up to the altar. Kiss the altar cloth, then lie flat."

"Then what?"

"Then God and the king forgive you," he said, and waited. "Just do it," he snarled.

So I did it. I went down on my knees and I shuffled through the mud, and the silent lines of men watched me, and then Æthelwold, close beside me, began to wail that he was a sinner. He threw his arms in the air, fell flat on his face, howled that he was penitent, shrieked that he was a sinner, and at first men were embarrassed and then they were amused. "I've known women!" Æthelwold shouted at the rain. "And they were bad women! Forgive me!"

Alfred was furious, but he could not stop a man making a fool of himself before God. Perhaps he thought Æthelwold's remorse was genuine? "I've lost count of the women!" Æthelwold shouted, then beat his fists in the mud. "Oh God, I love tits! God, I love naked women. God, forgive me for that!" The laughter spread, and every man must have remembered that Alfred, before piety caught him in its clammy grip, had been notorious for the women he had pursued. "You must help me, God!" Æthelwold cried as we shuffled a few feet farther. "Send me an angel!"

"So you can hump her?" a voice called from the crowd and the laughter became a roar.

Ælswith was hurried away, lest she hear something unseemly. The priests whispered together, but Æthelwold's penitence, though extravagant, seemed real enough. He was weeping. I knew he was really laughing, but he howled as though his soul was in agony. "No more tits, God!" he called. "No more tits!" He made a fool of himself, but, as men already thought him a fool, he did not mind. "Keep me from tits, God!" he shouted, and now Alfred left, knowing that the solemnity of the day was ruined, and most of the priests left with him, so that Æthelwold and I crawled to an abandoned altar where Æthelwold turned in his mud-spattered robe and leaned against the table. "I hate him," he said softly, and I knew he referred to his uncle. "I hate him," he went on, "and now you owe me a favor, Uhtred."

"I do," I said.

"I'll think of one," he said.

Odda the Younger had not left with Alfred. He seemed bemused. My humiliation, which he had surely thought to enjoy, had turned into laughter and he was aware that men were watching him, judging his truthfulness, and he moved closer to a huge man who was evidently one of his body-guards. That man was tall and very broad about the chest, but it was his face that commanded attention for it looked as though his skin had been stretched too tight across his skull, leaving his face incapable of making any expression other than one of pure hatred and wolfish hunger. Violence came off the man like the stench of a wet hound and when he looked at me it was like a beast's soulless stare, and I instinctively understood that this was the man who would kill me if Odda found a chance to commit murder. Odda was nothing, a rich man's spoiled son, but his money gave him the means to command men who were killers. Then Odda plucked at the tall man's sleeve and they both turned and walked away.

Father Beocca had stayed by the altar. "Kiss it," he ordered me, "then lie flat."

I stood up instead. "You can kiss my arse, father," I said. I was angry, and my anger frightened Beocca who backed away.

But I had done what the king wanted. I had been penitent.

The tall man beside Odda the Younger was named Steapa. Steapa Snotor, men called him, or Steapa the Clever. "It's a joke," Wulfhere told me as I ripped off the penitent's frock and pulled on my mail coat.

"A joke?"

"Because he's dumb as an ox," Wulfhere said. "He's got frog spawn instead of a brain. He's stupid, but he's not a stupid fighter. You didn't see him at Cynuit?"

"No," I said curtly.

"So what's Steapa to you?" Wulfhere asked.

"Nothing," I said. I had asked the ealdorman who Odda's bodyguard was so that I could learn the name of the man who might try to kill me, but that possible murder was none of Wulfhere's business.

Wulfhere hesitated, wanting to ask more, then deciding he would fetch no better answer. "When the Danes come," he said, "you'll be welcome to join my men."

Æthelwold, Alfred's nephew, was holding my two swords and he drew Serpent-Breath from her scabbard and stared at the wispy patterns in her blade. "If the Danes come," he spoke to Wulfhere, "you must let me fight."

"You don't know how to fight."

"Then you must teach me." He slid Serpent-Breath back into the scabbard. "Wessex needs a king who can fight," he said, "instead of pray."

"You should watch your tongue, lad," Wulfhere said, "in case it gets cut out." He snatched the swords from Æthelwold and gave them to me. "The Danes will come," he said, "so join me when they do."

I nodded, but said nothing. When the Danes came, I thought, I planned to be with them. I had been raised by Danes after being captured at the age of ten and they could have killed me, but instead they had treated me well. I had learned their language and worshipped their gods until I no longer knew whether I was Danish or English. Had Earl Ragnar the Elder lived I would never have left them, but he had died, murdered in a night of treachery and fire, and I had fled south to Wessex. But now I would go back. Just as soon as the Danes left Exanceaster I would join Ragnar's son, Ragnar the Younger, if he lived. Ragnar the Younger's ship had been in the fleet that had been hammered in the great storm. Scores of ships had sunk, and the remnants of the fleet had limped to Exanceaster where the boats were now burned to ash on the riverbank beneath the town. I did not know if Ragnar lived. I hoped he lived, and I prayed he would escape Exanceaster and then I would go to him, offer him my sword, and carry that blade against Alfred of Wessex. Then, one day, I would dress Alfred in a frock and make him crawl on his knees to an altar of Thor. Then kill him.

Those were my thoughts as we rode to Oxton. That was the estate Mildrith had brought me in marriage and it was a beautiful place, but so saddled with debt that it was more of a burden than a pleasure. The farmland was on the slopes of hills facing east toward the broad sea-reach of the Uisc and above the house were thick woods of oak and ash from which flowed small clear streams that cut across the fields where rye, wheat, and barley grew. The house—it was not a hall—was a smoke-filled building made from mud, dung, oak, and rye straw, and so long and low that it looked like a green, moss-covered mound from which smoke escaped through the roof's central hole. In the attached yard were pigs, chickens, and mounds of manure as big as the house. Mildrith's father had farmed it, helped by a steward named Oswald who was a weasel, and he caused me still more trouble on that rainy Sunday as we rode back to the farm.

I was furious, resentful, and vengeful. Alfred had humiliated me, which made it unfortunate for Oswald that he had chosen that Sunday afternoon to drag an oak tree down from the high woods. I was brooding on the pleasures of revenge as I let my horse pick its way up the track through the trees and saw eight oxen hauling the great trunk toward the river. Three men were goading the oxen, while a fourth, Oswald, rode the trunk with a whip. He saw me and jumped off and, for a heartbeat, it looked as if he wanted to run into the trees, but then he realized he could not evade me and so he just stood and waited as I rode up to the great oak log.

"Lord," Oswald greeted me. He was surprised to see me. He probably thought I had been killed with the other hostages, and that belief had made him careless.

My horse was nervous because of the stink of blood from the oxen's flanks and he stepped backward and forward in small steps until I calmed him by patting his neck. Then I looked at the oak trunk that must have been forty feet long and as thick about as a man is tall. "A fine tree," I said to Oswald.

He glanced toward Mildrith who was twenty paces away. "Good day, lady," he said, clawing off the woolen hat he wore over his springy red hair.

"A wet day, Oswald," she said. Her father had appointed the steward and Mildrith had an innocent faith in his reliability.

"I said," I spoke loudly, "a fine tree. So where was it felled?"

Oswald tucked the hat into his belt. "On the top ridge, lord," he said vaguely.

"The top ridge on my land?"

He hesitated. He was doubtless tempted to

claim it came from a neighbor's land, but that lie could easily have been exposed and so he said nothing.

"From my land?" I asked again.

"Yes, lord," he admitted.

"And where is it going?"

He hesitated again, but had to answer. "Wigulf's mill."

"Wigulf buys it?"

"He'll split it, lord."

"I didn't ask what he will do with it," I said, "but whether he will buy it."

Mildrith, hearing the harshness in my voice, intervened to say that her father had sometimes sent timber to Wigulf's mill, but I waved her to silence. "Will he buy it?" I asked Oswald.

"We need the timber, lord, to make repairs," the steward said, "and Wigulf takes his fee in split wood."

"And you drag the tree on a Sunday?" He had nothing to say to that. "Tell me," I went on, "if we need planks for repairs, then why don't we split the trunk ourselves? Do we lack men? Or wedges? Or mauls?"

"Wigulf has always done it," Oswald said in a surly tone.

"Always?" I repeated and Oswald said

nothing. "Wigulf lives in Exanmynster?" I guessed. Exanmynster lay a mile or so northward and was the nearest settlement to Oxton.

"Yes, lord," Oswald said.

"So if I ride to Exanmynster now," I said, "Wigulf will tell me how many similar trees you've delivered to him in the last year?"

There was silence, except for the rain dripping from leaves and the intermittent burst of bird-song. I edged my horse a few steps closer to Oswald, who gripped his whip's handle as if readying it to lash out at me. "How many?" I asked.

Oswald said nothing.

"How many?" I demanded, louder.

"Husband," Mildrith called.

"Quiet!" I shouted at her and Oswald looked from me to her and back to me. "And how much has Wigulf paid you?" I asked. "What does a tree like this fetch? Eight shillings? Nine?"

The anger that had made me act so impetuously at the king's church service rose again. It was plain that Oswald was stealing the timber and being paid for it, and what I should have done was charge him with theft and have him arraigned before a court where a jury of men would decide his guilt or innocence, but I was in no mood for such a process. I just drew Serpent-Breath and kicked my horse forward. Mildrith screamed a protest, but I ignored her. Oswald ran, and that was a mistake, because I caught him easily, and Serpent-Breath swung once and opened up the back of his skull so I could see brains and blood as he fell. He twisted in the leaf mold and I wheeled the horse back and stabbed down into his throat.

"That was murder!" Mildrith shouted at me.

"That was justice," I snarled at her, "something lacking in Wessex." I spat on Oswald's body that was still twitching. "The bastard's been stealing from us."

Mildrith kicked her horse, leading the nurse who carried our child uphill. I let her go. "Take the trunk up to the house," I ordered the slaves who had been goading the oxen. "If it's too big to drag uphill, then split it here and take the planks to the house."

I searched Oswald's house that evening and discovered fifty-three shillings buried in the floor. I took the silver, confiscated his cooking pots, spit, knives, buckles, and a deerskin cloak, then drove his wife and three children off my land. I had come home.

TWO

My anger was not slaked by Oswald's killing. The death of a dishonest steward was no consolation for what I perceived as a monstrous injustice. For the moment Wessex was safe from the Danes, but it was only safe because I had killed Ubba Lothbrokson and my reward had been humiliation.

Poor Mildrith. She was a peaceable woman who thought well of everyone she met, and now she found herself married to a resentful, angry warrior. She was frightened of Alfred's wrath, terrified that the church would punish me for disturbing its peace, and worried that Oswald's relatives would demand a wergild from me. And so they would. A wergild was the blood price that every man, woman, and child possessed. Kill a man and you must pay his price or else die yourself, and I had no doubt that Oswald's family would go to Odda the Younger, who had been named the Ealdorman of Defnascir because his father was too badly wounded to continue as ealdorman, and Odda would instruct the shire reeve to pursue me and place me on trial, but I did not care. I hunted boar and deer, I brooded and waited for news of the negotiations at Exanceaster. I was expecting Alfred to do what he always did, which was to make peace with the Danes and so release them, and when he did I would go to Ragnar.

And as I waited I found my first retainer. He was a slave and I discovered him in Exanmynster on a fine spring day. There was a hiring fair where men looked for employment through the busy days of hay-making and harvest, and like all fairs there were jugglers, storytellers, stilt walkers, musicians, and acrobats. There was also a tall, white-haired man with a lined, serious face, who was selling enchanted leather bags that turned iron into silver. He showed us how it was done, and I saw him place two common nails into the bag and a moment later they were pure silver. He said we had to place a silver crucifix in the bag and then sleep one night with it tied around our necks before the magic worked and I paid him three silver shillings for one bag, and it never worked. I spent months searching for the man, but never found him. Even these days I come across such men and women, selling sorcerous pouches or boxes, and now I have them whipped and run off my land, but I was only twenty then and I believed my own eyes. That man had attracted a large crowd, but there were even more people gathered by the church gate where shouts erupted every few minutes. I pushed my horse into their rear ranks, getting dirty looks from folk who knew I had killed Oswald, but none dared accuse me of the murder for I carried both Serpent-Breath and Wasp-Sting.

A young man was by the church gate. He was stripped to the waist, barefooted, and had a rope round his neck, and the rope was tied to the gatepost. In his hand was a short, stout stave. He had long unbound fair hair, blue eyes, a stubborn face, and blood all over his chest, belly, and arms. Three men guarded him. They, too, were fair-haired and blue-eyed, and they shouted in a strange accent. "Come and fight the heathen! Three pennies to make the bastard bleed! Come and fight!"

"Who is he?" I asked.

"A Dane, lord, a pagan Dane." The man tugged off his hat when he spoke to me, then turned back to the crowd. "Come and fight him! Get your revenge! Make a Dane bleed! Be a good Christian! Hurt a pagan!"

The three men were Frisians. I suspected they had been in Alfred's army and, now that he was talking to the Danes rather than fighting them, the three had deserted. Frisians come from across the sea and they come for one reason only, money, and this trio had somehow captured the young Dane and were profiting from him so long as he lasted. And that could have been some time, for he was good. A strong young Saxon paid his three pence and was given a sword with which he hacked wildly at the prisoner, but the Dane parried every blow, wood chips flying from his stave, and when he saw an opening he cracked his opponent around the head hard enough to draw blood from his ear. The Saxon staggered away, half stunned, and the Dane rammed the stave into his belly and, as the Saxon bent to gasp for breath, the stave whistled around in a blow that would have cracked his skull open like an egg, but the Frisians dragged on the rope so that the Dane fell backward. "Do we have another hero?" a Frisian shouted as the young Saxon was helped away. "Come on, lads! Show your strength! Beat a Dane bloody!"

"I'll beat him," I said. I dismounted and pushed through the crowd. I gave my horse's reins to a boy, then drew Serpent-Breath. "Three pence?" I asked the Frisians.

"No, lord," one of them said.

"Why not?"

"We don't want a dead Dane, do we?" The man answered.

"We do!" someone shouted from the crowd. The folk in the Uisc valley did not like me, but they liked the Danes even less and they relished the prospect of watching a prisoner being slaughtered.

"You can only wound him, lord," the Frisian said. "And you must use our sword." He held out the weapon. I glanced at it, saw its blunt edge, and spat.

"Must?" I asked.

The Frisian did not want to argue. "You can only draw blood, lord," he said.

The Dane flicked hair from his eyes and watched me. He held the stave low. I could see he was nervous, but there was no fear in his eyes. He had probably fought a hundred battles since the Frisians captured him, but those fights had been against men who were not soldiers, and he must have known, from my two swords, that I was a warrior. His skin was blotched with bruises and laced by blood and scars, and he surely expected another wound from Serpent-Breath, but he was determined to give me a fight.

"What's your name?" I asked in Danish.

He blinked at me, surprised.

"Your name, boy," I said. I called him "boy," though he was not much younger than I.

"Haesten," he said.

"Haesten who?"

"Haesten Storrison," he said, giving me his father's name.

"Fight him! Don't talk to him!" a voice shouted from the crowd.

I turned to stare at the man who had shouted and he could not meet my gaze, then I turned fast, very fast, and whipped Serpent-Breath in a quick sweep that Haesten instinctively parried so that Serpent-Breath cut through the stave as if it was rotten. Haesten was left with a stub of wood, while the rest of his weapon, a yard of thick ash, lay on the ground.

"Kill him!" someone shouted.

"Just draw blood, lord," a Frisian said,

"please, lord. He's not a bad lad, for a Dane. Just make him bleed and we'll pay you."

I kicked the ash stave away from Haesten. "Pick it up," I said.

He looked at me nervously. To pick it up he would have to go to the end of his tether, then stoop, and at that moment he would expose his back to Serpent-Breath. He watched me, his eyes bitter beneath the fringe of dirty hair, then decided I would not attack him as he bent over. He went to the stave and, as he leaned down, I kicked it a few inches farther away. "Pick it up," I ordered him again.

He still held the stub of ash and, as he took a further step, straining against the rope, he suddenly whipped around and tried to ram the broken end into my belly. He was fast, but I had half expected the move and caught his wrist in my left hand. I squeezed hard, hurting him. "Pick it up," I said a third time.

This time he obeyed, stooping to the stave, and to reach it he stretched his tether tight and I slashed Serpent-Breath onto the taut rope, severing it. Haesten, who had been straining forward, fell onto his face as the hide rope was cut. I put my left foot onto his back and let the tip of

Serpent-Breath rest on his spine. "Alfred," I said to the Frisians, "has ordered that all Danish prisoners are to be taken to him."

The three looked at me, said nothing.

"So why have you not taken this man to the king?" I demanded.

"We didn't know, lord," one of them said. "No one told us," which was not surprising because Alfred had given no such order.

"We'll take him to the king now, lord," another reassured me.

"I'll save you the trouble," I said. I took my foot off Haesten. "Get up," I told him in Danish. I threw a coin to the boy holding my horse and hauled myself into the saddle where I offered Haesten a hand. "Get up behind me," I ordered him.

The Frisians protested, coming at me with their swords drawn, so I pulled Wasp-Sting from her scabbard and gave it to Haesten who had still not mounted. Then I turned the horse toward the Frisians and smiled at them. "These people," I waved Serpent-Breath at the crowd, "already think I am a murderer. I'm also the man who met Ubba Lothbrokson beside the sea and killed him there. I tell you this so you may boast that you killed Uhtred of Bebbanburg."

I lowered the sword so it pointed at the nearest man and he backed away. The others, no more eager to fight than the first, went with him. Haesten then pulled himself up behind me and I spurred the horse into the crowd that parted reluctantly. Once free of them I made Haesten dismount and give me back Wasp-Sting. "How did you get captured?" I asked him.

He told me he had been on one of Guthrum's ships caught in the storm, and his ship had sunk, but he had clung to some wreckage and been washed ashore where the Frisians had found him. "There were two of us, lord," he said, "but the other died."

"You're a free man now," I told him.

"Free?"

"You're my man," I said, "and you'll give me an oath, and I'll give you a sword."

"Why?" he wanted to know.

"Because a Dane saved me once," I said, "and I like the Danes."

I also wanted Haesten because I needed men. I did not trust Odda the Younger, and I feared Steapa Snotor, Odda's warrior, and so I would have swords at Oxton. Mildrith, of course, did not want sword Danes at her house. She wanted plowmen and peasants, milkmaids and servants, but I told her I was a lord, and a lord has swords.

I am indeed a lord, a lord of Northumbria. I am Uhtred of Bebbanburg. My ancestors, who can trace their lineage back to the god Woden, the Danish Odin, were once kings in northern England, and if my uncle had not stolen Bebbanburg from me when I was just ten years old, I would have lived there still as a Northumbrian lord safe in his sea-washed fastness. The Danes had captured Northumbria, and their puppet king, Ricsig, ruled in Eoferwic, but Bebbanburg was too strong for any Dane and my uncle Ælfric ruled there, calling himself Ealdorman Ælfric, and the Danes left him in peace so long as he did not trouble them, and I often dreamed of going back to Northumbria to claim my birthright. But how? To capture Bebbanburg I would need an army, and all I had was one young Dane, Haesten.

And I had other enemies in Northumbria. There was Earl Kjartan and his son Sven, who had lost an eye because of me, and they would kill me gladly, and my uncle would pay them to do it, and so I had no future in Northumbria, not then. But I would go back. That was my soul's wish, and I would go back with Ragnar the

Younger, my friend, who still lived because his ship had weathered the storm. I heard that from a priest who had listened to the negotiations outside Exanceaster and he was certain that Earl Ragnar had been one of the Danish lords in Guthrum's delegation. "A big man," the priest told me, "and very loud." That description convinced me that Ragnar lived and my heart was glad for it, for I knew that my future lay with him, not with Alfred. When the negotiations were finished and a truce made the Danes would doubtless leave Exanceaster and I would give my sword to Ragnar and carry it against Alfred, who hated me. And I hated him.

I told Mildrith that we would leave Defnascir and go to Ragnar, that I would be his man and that I would pursue my blood feud against Kjartan and against my uncle under Ragnar's eagle banner, and Mildrith responded with tears and more tears.

I cannot bear a woman's crying. Mildrith was hurt and she was confused and I was angry and we snarled at each other like wildcats and the rain kept falling and I raged like a beast in a cage and wished Alfred and Guthrum would finish their talking because everyone knew that Alfred would let Guthrum go, and once Guthrum left

Exanceaster then I could join the Danes and I did not care whether Mildrith came or not, so long as my son, who bore my name, went with me. So by day I hunted, at night I drank and dreamed of revenge, and then one evening I came home to find Father Willibald waiting in the house.

Willibald was a good man. He had been chaplain to Alfred's fleet when I commanded those twelve ships, and he told me he was on his way back to Hamtun, but he thought I would like to know what had unfolded in the long talks between Alfred and Guthrum. "There is peace, lord," he told me. "Thanks be to God, there is peace."

"Thanks be to God," Mildrith echoed.

I was cleaning the blood from the blade of a boar spear and said nothing. I was thinking that Ragnar was released from the siege now and I could join him.

"The treaty was sealed with solemn oaths yesterday," Willibald said, "and so we have peace."

"They gave each other solemn oaths last year," I said sourly. Alfred and Guthrum had made peace at Werham, but Guthrum had broken the truce and murdered the hostages he had been holding. Eleven of the twelve had died, and only I had lived because Ragnar was there to protect me. "So what have they agreed?" I asked.

"The Danes are to give up all their horses," Willibald said, "and march back into Mercia."

Good, I thought, because that was where I would go. I did not say that to Willibald, but instead sneered that Alfred was just letting them march away. "Why doesn't he fight them?" I asked.

"Because there are too many, lord. Because too many men would die on both sides."

"He should kill them all."

"Peace is better than war," Willibald said.

"Amen," Mildrith said.

I began sharpening the spear, stroking the whetstone down the long blade. It seemed to me that Alfred had been absurdly generous. Guthrum, after all, was the one remaining leader of any stature on the Danish side, and he had been trapped, and if I had been Alfred there would have been no terms, only a siege, and at its end the Danish power in southern England would have been broken. Instead Guthrum was to be allowed to leave Exanceaster. "It is the hand of God," Willibald said.

I looked at him. He was a few years older than I was, but always seemed younger. He was earnest, enthusiastic, and kind. He had been a good chaplain to the twelve ships, though the poor man was ever seasick and blanched at the sight of blood. "God made the peace?" I asked skeptically.

"Who sent the storm that sank Guthrum's ships?" Willibald retorted fervently. "Who delivered Ubba into our hands?"

"I did," I said.

He ignored that. "We have a godly king, lord," he said, "and God rewards those who serve him faithfully. Alfred has defeated the Danes! And they see it! Guthrum can recognize divine intervention! He has been making enquiries about Christ."

I said nothing.

"Our king believes," the priest went on, "that Guthrum is not far from seeing the true light of Christ." He leaned forward and touched my knee. "We have fasted, lord," he said, "we have prayed, and the king believes that the Danes will be brought to Christ, and when that happens there will be a permanent peace."

He meant every word of that nonsense and, of course, it was sweet music to Mildrith's ears. She was a good Christian and had great faith in Alfred, and if the king believed that his god would bring victory, then she would believe it, too. It seemed madness to me, but I said nothing as a servant brought us barley ale, bread, smoked mackerel, and cheese. "We shall have a Christian peace," Willibald said, making the sign of the cross above the bread before he ate, "sealed by hostages."

"We've given Guthrum hostages again?" I asked, astonished.

"No," Willibald said. "But he has agreed to give us hostages. Including six earls!"

I stopped sharpening the spear and looked at Willibald. "Six earls?"

"Including your friend, Ragnar!" Willibald seemed pleased by this news, but I was appalled. If Ragnar was not with the Danes, then I could not go to them. He was my friend and his enemies were my enemies, but without Ragnar to protect me I would be horribly vulnerable to Kjartan and Sven, the father and son who had murdered Ragnar's father and who wanted me dead. Without Ragnar, I knew, I could not leave Wessex.

"Ragnar's one of the hostages?" I asked. "You're sure?"

"Of course I'm sure. He will be held by Ealdorman Wulfhere. All the hostages are to be held by Wulfhere."

"For how long?"

"For as long as Alfred wishes, or until Guthrum is baptized. And Guthrum has agreed that our priests can talk to his men." Willibald gave me a pleading look. "We must have faith in God," he said. "We must give God time to work on the hearts of the Danes. Guthrum understands now that our god has power!"

I stood and went to the door, pulling aside the leather curtain and staring down at the wide sea-reach of the Uisc. I was sick at heart. I hated Alfred, did not want to be in Wessex, but now it seemed I was doomed to stay there. "And what do I do?" I asked.

"The king will forgive you, lord," Willibald said nervously.

"Forgive me?" I turned on him. "And what does the king believe happened at Cynuit? You were there, father," I said, "so did you tell him?"

"I told him."

"And?"

"He knows you are a brave warrior, lord," Willibald said, "and that your sword is an asset to Wessex. He will receive you again, I'm sure, and he will receive you joyfully. Go to church, pay your debts, and show that you are a good man of Wessex."

"I'm not a West Saxon," I snarled at him. "I'm a Northumbrian!"

And that was part of the problem. I was an outsider. I spoke a different English. The men of Wessex were tied by family, and I came from the strange north and folk believed I was a pagan, and they called me a murderer because of Oswald's death, and sometimes, when I rode about the estate, men would make the sign of the cross to avert the evil they saw in me. They called me Uhtredærwe, which means Uhtred the Wicked, and I was not unhappy with the insult, but Mildrith was. She assured them I was a Christian, but she lied, and our unhappiness festered all that summer. She prayed for my soul, I fretted for my freedom, and when she begged me to go with her to the church at Exanmynster I growled at her that I would never set foot in another church all my days. She would weep when I said that and her tears drove me out of the house to hunt, and sometimes the chase would take me down to the water's edge where I would stare at **Heahengel**.

She lay canted on the muddy foreshore, lifted

and dropped repeatedly by the tides, abandoned. She was one of Alfred's fleet, one of the twelve large warships he had built to harry the Danish boats that raided Wessex's coast, and Leofric and I had brought **Heahengel** up from Hamtun in pursuit of Guthrum's fleet and we had survived the storm that sent so many Danes to their deaths and we had beached **Heahengel** here, left her mastless and without a sail, and she was still on the Uisc's foreshore, rotting and apparently forgotten.

Archangel. That was what her name meant. Alfred had named her and I had always hated the name. A ship should have a proud name, not a sniveling religious word, and she should have a beast on her prow, high and defiant, a dragon's head to challenge the sea or a snarling wolf to terrify an enemy. I sometimes climbed on board **Heahengel** and saw how the local villagers had plundered some of her upper strakes, and how there was water in her belly, and I remembered her proud days at sea and the wind whipping through her seal-hide rigging and the crash as we had rammed a Danish boat.

Now, like me, **Heahengel** had been left to decay, and sometimes I dreamed of repairing her, of finding new rigging and a new sail, of finding men and taking her long hull to sea. I wanted to be anywhere but where I was, I wanted to be with the Danes, and every time I said that Mildrith would weep again. "You can't make me live among the Danes!"

"Why not? I did."

"They're pagans! My son won't grow up a pagan!"

"He's my son, too," I said, "and he will worship the gods I worship." There would be more tears then, and I would storm out of the house and take the hounds up to the high woods and wonder why love soured like milk. After Cynuit I had so wanted to see Mildrith, yet now I could not abide her misery and piety and she could not endure my anger. All she wanted me to do was till my fields, milk my cows, and gather my harvest to pay the great debt she had brought me in marriage. That debt came from a pledge made by Mildrith's father, a pledge to give the church the yield of almost half his land. That pledge was for all time, binding on his heirs, but Danish raids and bad harvests had ruined him. Yet the church, venomous as serpents, still insisted that the debt be paid, and said that if I could not pay then our land would be taken by monks, and every time I went to Exanceaster I could sense the priests and monks watching me and enjoying the prospect of their enrichment. Exanceaster was English again for Guthrum had handed over the hostages and gone north so that peace of a sort had come to Wessex. The fyrds, the armies of each shire, had been disbanded and sent back to their farms. Psalms were being sung in all the churches and Alfred, to mark his victory, was sending gifts to every monastery and nunnery. Odda the Younger, who was being celebrated as the champion of Wessex, had been given all the land about the place where the battle had been fought at Cynuit and he had ordered a church to be built there, and it was rumored that the church would have an altar of gold as thanks to God for allowing Wessex to survive.

Though how long would it survive? Guthrum lived and I did not share the Christian belief that God had sent Wessex peace. Nor was I the only one, for in midsummer Alfred returned to Exanceaster where he summoned his witan, a council of the kingdom's leading thegns and churchmen, and Wulfhere of Wiltunscir was one of the men summoned and I went into the city one evening and was told the ealdorman and his followers had lodgings in The Swan, a tavern by the east gate. He was not there, but Æthelwold,

Alfred's nephew, was doing his best to drain the tavern of ale. "Don't tell me the bastard summoned you to the witan?" he greeted me sourly. The "bastard" was Alfred who had snatched the throne from the young Æthelwold.

"No," I said. "I came to see Wulfhere."

"The ealdorman is in church," Æthelwold said, "and I am not." He grinned and waved to the bench opposite him. "Sit and drink. Get drunk. Then we'll find two girls. Three, if you like. Four, if you want?"

"You forget I'm married," I said.

"As if that ever stopped anyone."

I sat and one of the maids brought me ale. "Are you in the witan?" I asked Æthelwold.

"What do you think? You think that bastard wants my advice? 'Lord king,' I'd say, 'why don't you jump off a high cliff and pray that God gives you wings.'" He pushed a plate of pork ribs toward me. "I'm here so they can keep an eye on me. They're making sure I'm not plotting treason."

"Are you?"

"Of course I am." He grinned. "Are you going to join me? You do owe me a favor."

"You want my sword at your service?" I asked.

"Yes." He was serious.

"So it's you and me," I said, "against all Wessex. Who else will fight with us?"

He frowned, thinking, but came up with no names. He stared down at the table and I felt sorry for him. I had always liked Æthelwold, but no one would ever trust him for he was as careless as he was irresponsible. Alfred, I thought, had judged him right. Let him be free and he would drink and whore himself into irrelevance. "What I should do," he said, "is go and join Guthrum."

"Why don't you?"

He looked up at me, but had no answer. Maybe he knew the answer, that Guthrum would welcome him, honor him, use him, and eventually kill him. But maybe that was a better prospect than his present life. He shrugged and leaned back, pushing hair off his face. He was a startlingly handsome young man, and that, too, distracted him for girls were attracted to him like priests to gold. "What Wulfhere thinks," he said, his voice slurring slightly, "is that Guthrum is going to come and kill us all."

"Probably," I said.

"And if my uncle dies," he said, not bothering to lower his voice even though there were a score of men in the tavern, "his son is much too young to be king."

"True."

"So it'll be my turn!" He smiled.

"Or Guthrum's turn," I said.

"So drink, my friend," he said, "because we're all in the cesspit." He grinned at me, his charm suddenly evident. "So if you won't fight for me," he asked, "how do you propose to pay back the favor?"

"How would you like it paid?"

"You could kill Abbot Hewald? Very nastily? Slowly?"

"I could do that," I said. Hewald was abbot at Winburnan and famous for the harshness with which he taught boys to read.

"On the other hand," Æthelwold went on, "I'd like to kill that scrawny bastard myself, so don't do it for me. I'll think of something that won't make my uncle happy. You don't like him, do you?"

"No."

"Then we'll brew up some mischief. Oh God." This last imprecation was because Wulfhere's voice was suddenly loud just outside the door. "He's angry at me."

"Why?"

"One of the dairy maids is pregnant. I think he wanted to do it himself, but I churned her first." He drained his ale. "I'm going to the Three Bells. Want to come?"

"I have to speak to Wulfhere."

Æthelwold left by the back door as the ealdorman ducked through the front. Wulfhere was accompanied by a dozen thegns, but he saw me and crossed the room. "They've been reconsecrating the bishop's church," he grumbled. "Hours upon damned hours! Nothing but chanting and prayers, hours of prayers just to get the taint of the Danes out of the place." He sat heavily. "Did I see Æthelwold here?"

"Yes."

"Wanted you to join his rebellion, did he?"

"Yes."

"Damned fool. So why are you here? Come to offer me your sword?" He meant swear my allegiance to him and so become his warrior.

"I want to see one of the hostages," I said, "so I seek your permission."

"Hostages." He sat down opposite me and snapped his fingers for ale. "Damned hostages. I've had to make new buildings to house them. And who pays for that?"

"You do?"

"Of course I do. And I'm supposed to feed them, too? Feed them? Guard them? Wall them in? And does Alfred pay anything?"

"Tell him you're building a monastery," I suggested.

He looked at me as if I was mad, then saw the jest and laughed. "True enough, he'd pay me then, wouldn't he? Have you heard about the monastery they're building at Cynuit?"

"I hear it's to have an altar of gold."

He laughed again. "That's what I hear. I don't believe it, but I hear it." He watched one of the tavern girls cross the floor. "It's not my permission you need to see the hostages," he said, "but Alfred's, and he won't give it to you."

"Alfred's permission?" I asked.

"They're not just hostages," he said, "but prisoners. I have to wall them in and watch them day and night. Alfred's orders. He might think God brought us peace, but he's made damn sure he's got high-born hostages. Six earls! You know how many retainers they have? How many women? How many mouths to feed?"

"If I go to Wiltunscir," I said, "can I see Earl Ragnar?"

Wulfhere frowned at me. "Earl Ragnar? The

noisy one? I like him. No, lad, you can't, because no one's allowed to see them except a damned priest who talks their language. Alfred sent him and he's trying to make them into Christians, and if you go without my permission then Alfred will hear you've been there and he'll want an explanation from me. No one can see the poor bastards." He paused to scratch at a louse under his collar. "I have to feed the priest, too, and Alfred doesn't pay for that, either. He doesn't even pay me to feed that lout Æthelwold!"

"When I was a hostage in Werham," I explained, "Earl Ragnar saved my life. Guthrum killed the others, but Ragnar guarded me. He said they'd have to kill him before they killed me."

"And he looks like a hard man to kill," Wulfhere said, "but if Guthrum attacks Wessex that's what I'm supposed to do. Kill the lot of them. Maybe not the women." He stared gloomily into the tavern's yard where a group of his men were playing dice in the moonlight. "And Guthrum will attack," he added in a low voice.

"That's not what I hear."

He looked at me suspiciously. "And what do you hear, young man?"

"That God has sent us peace."

Wulfhere laughed at my mockery. "Guthrum's in Gleawecestre," he said, "and that's just a half day's march from our frontier. And they say more Danish ships arrive every day. They're in Lundene, they're in the Humber, they're in the Gewæsc." He scowled. "More ships, more men, and Alfred's building churches! And there's this fellow Svein."

"Svein?"

"Brought his ships from Ireland. Bastard's in Wales now, but he won't stay there, will he? He'll come to Wessex. And they say more Danes are joining him from Ireland." He brooded on this bad news. I did not know whether it was true, for such rumors were ever current, but Wulfhere plainly believed it. "We should march on Gleawecestre," he said, "and slaughter the lot of them before they slaughter us, but we've got a kingdom ruled by priests."

That was true, I thought, just as it was certain that Wulfhere would not make it easy for me to see Ragnar. "Will you give a message to Ragnar?" I asked.

"How? I don't speak Danish. I could ask the priest, but he'll tell Alfred."

"Does Ragnar have a woman with him?" I asked.

"They all do."

"A thin girl," I said, "black hair. Face like a hawk."

He nodded cautiously. "Sounds right. Has a dog, yes?"

"She has a dog," I said, "and its name is Niht-genga."

He shrugged as if he did not care what the dog was called. Then he understood the significance of the name. "An English name?" he asked. "A Danish girl calls her dog Goblin?"

"She isn't Danish," I said. "Her name is Brida, and she's a Saxon."

He stared at me, then laughed. "The cunning little bitch. She's been listening to us, hasn't she?"

Brida was indeed cunning. She had been my first lover, an East Anglian girl who had been raised by Ragnar's father and who now slept with Ragnar. "Talk to her," I said, "and give her my greetings, and say that if it comes to war . . ." I paused, not sure what to say. There was no point in promising to do my best to rescue Ragnar, for if war came then the hostages would be slaughtered long before I could reach them.

"If it comes to war?" Wulfhere prompted me.

"If it comes to war," I said, repeating the

words he had spoken to me before my penance, "we'll all be looking for a way to stay alive."

Wulfhere stared at me for a long time and his silence told me that though I had failed to find a message for Ragnar, I had given a message to Wulfhere. He drank ale. "So the bitch speaks English, does she?"

"She's a Saxon."

As was I, but I hated Alfred and I would join Ragnar when I could, if I could, whatever Mildrith wanted, or so I thought. But deep under the earth, where the corpse serpent gnaws at the roots of Yggdrasil, the tree of life, there are three spinners, three women who make our fate. We might believe we make choices, but in truth our lives are in the spinners' fingers. They make our lives, and destiny is everything. The Danes know that, and even the Christians know it. Wyrd bið ful āræd, we Saxons say, fate is inexorable, and the spinners had decided my fate because, a week after the witan had met, when Exanceaster was quiet again, they sent me a ship.

The first I knew of it was when a slave came running from Oxton's fields saying that there was a Danish ship in the estuary of the Uisc and I pulled on boots and mail, snatched my swords from their peg, shouted for a horse to be saddled, and rode to the foreshore where **Heahengel** rotted.

And where, standing in from the long sand spit that protects the Uisc from the greater sea, another ship approached. Her sail was furled on the long yard and her dripping oars rose and fell like wings and her long hull left a spreading wake that glittered silver under the rising sun. Her prow was high, and standing there was a man in full mail, a man with a helmet and spear, and behind me, where a few fisherfolk lived in hovels beside the mud, people were hurrying toward the hills and taking with them whatever few possessions they could snatch. I called to one of them. "It's not a Dane!"

"Lord?"

"It's a West Saxon ship," I called, though they did not believe me and hurried away with their livestock. For years they had done this. They would see a ship and they would run, for ships brought Danes and Danes brought death, but this ship had no dragon or wolf or eagle's head on its prow. I knew the ship. It was the **Eftwyrd**, the best named of all Alfred's ships that otherwise bore pious names like **Heahengel** or **Apos- tol** or **Cristenlic**. **Eftwyrd** meant judgment day, which, though Christian in inspiration, accurately described what she had brought to many Danes.

The man in the prow waved and, for the first time since I had crawled on my knees to Alfred's altar, my spirits lifted. It was Leofric, and then the **Eftwyrd**'s bow slid onto the mud and the long hull juddered to a halt. Leofric cupped his hands. "How deep is this mud?"

"It's nothing!" I shouted back. "A hand's depth, no more!"

"Can I walk on it?"

"Of course you can!" I shouted back.

He jumped and, as I had known he would, he sank up to his thighs in the thick black slime, and I bent over my saddle's pommel in laughter, and the **Eftwyrd**'s crew laughed with me as Leofric cursed, and it took ten minutes to extricate him from the muck, by which time a score of us were plastered in the stinking stuff, but then the crew, who were mostly my old oarsmen and warriors, brought ale ashore, and bread and salted pork, and we made a midday meal beside the rising tide.

"You're an earsling," Leofric grumbled, looking at the mud clogging up the links of his mail coat.

"I'm a bored earsling," I said.

"You're bored?" Leofric said. "So are we." It seemed the fleet was not sailing. It had been given into the charge of a man named Burgweard who was a dull, worthy soldier whose brother was Bishop of Scireburnan, and Burgweard had orders not to disturb the peace. "If the Danes aren't off the coast," Leofric said, "then we aren't."

"So what are you doing here?"

"He sent us to rescue that piece of shit," he nodded at **Heahengel**. "He wants twelve ships again, see?"

"I thought they were building more?"

"They were building more, only it all stopped because some thieving bastards stole the timber while we were fighting at Cynuit, and then someone remembered **Heahengel** and here we are. Burgweard can't manage with just eleven."

"If he isn't sailing," I asked, "why does he want another ship?"

"In case he has to sail," Leofric explained, "and if he does, then he wants twelve. Not eleven, twelve."

"Twelve? Why?"

"Because," Leofric paused to bite off a piece of bread, "because it says in the gospel book that Christ sent out his disciples two by two, and that's how we have to go, two ships together, all holy, and if we've only got eleven, then that means we've only got ten, if you follow me."

I stared at him, not sure whether he was jesting. "Burgweard insists you sail two by two?"

Leofric nodded. "Because it says so in Father Willibald's book."

"In the gospel book?"

"That's what Father Willibald tells us," Leofric said with a straight face, then saw my expression and shrugged. "Honest! And Alfred approves."

"Of course he does."

"And if you do what the gospel book tells you," Leofric said, still with a straight face, "then nothing can go wrong, can it?"

"Nothing," I said. "So you're here to rebuild **Heahengel**?"

"New mast," Leofric said, "new sail, new rigging, patch up those timbers, caulk her, then tow her back to Hamtun. It could take a month!"

"At least."

"And I never was much good at making

things. Good at fighting, I am, and I can drink
ale as well as any man, but I was never much
good with a mallet and wedge or with adzes.
They are." He nodded at a group of a dozen men
who were strangers to me.

"Who are they?"

"Shipwrights."

"So they do the work?"

"Can't expect me to do it!" Leofric protested.
"I'm in command of the **Eftwyrd**!"

"So," I said, "you're planning to drink my ale
and eat my food for a month while those dozen
men do the work?"

"You have any better ideas?"

I gazed at the **Eftwyrd**. She was a well-made
ship, longer than most Danish boats and with
high sides that made her a good fighting platform. "What did Burgweard tell you to do?" I
asked.

"Pray," Leofric said sourly, "and help repair
Heahengel."

"I hear there's a new Danish leader in the
Sæfern Sea," I said, "and I'd like to know if it's
true. A man called Svein. And I hear more ships
are joining him from Ireland."

"He's in Wales, this Svein?"

"That's what I hear."

"He'll be coming to Wessex then," Leofric said.

"If it's true."

"So you're thinking . . ." Leofric said, then stopped when he realized just what I was thinking.

"I'm thinking that it doesn't do a ship or crew any good to sit around for a month," I said, "and I'm thinking that there might be plunder to be had in the Sæfern Sea."

"And if Alfred hears we've been fighting up there," Leofric said, "he'll gut us."

I nodded upriver toward Exanceaster. "They burned a hundred Danish ships up there," I said, "and their wreckage is still on the riverbank. We should be able to find at least one dragon's head to put on her prow."

Leofric stared at the **Eftwyrd**. "Disguise her?"

"Disguise her," I said, because if I put a dragon head on **Eftwyrd** no one would know she was a Saxon ship. She would be taken for a Danish boat, a sea raider, part of England's nightmare.

Leofric smiled. "I don't need orders to go on a patrol, do I?"

"Of course not."

"And we haven't fought since Cynuit," he said wistfully, "and no fighting means no plunder."

"What about the crew?" I asked.

He turned and looked at them. "Most of them are evil bastards," he said. "They won't mind. And they all need plunder."

"And between us and the Sæfern Sea," I said, "there are the Britons."

"And they're all thieving bastards, the lot of them," Leofric said. He looked at me and grinned. "So if Alfred won't go to war, we will?"

"You have any better ideas?" I asked.

Leofric did not answer for a long time. Instead, idly, as if he was just thinking, he tossed pebbles toward a puddle. I said nothing, just watched the small splashes, watched the pattern the fallen pebbles made, and knew he was seeking guidance from fate. The Danes cast runesticks, we all watched for the flight of birds, we tried to hear the whispers of the gods, and Leofric was watching the pebbles fall to find his fate. The last one clicked on another and skidded off into the mud and the trail it left pointed south toward the sea. "No," he said, "I don't have any better ideas."

And I was bored no longer, because we were going to be Vikings.

We found a score of carved beasts' heads beside the river beneath Exanceaster's walls, all of them part of the sodden, tangled wreckage that showed where Guthrum's fleet had been burned and we chose two of the least scorched carvings and carried them on board **Eftwyrd**. Her prow and stern culminated in simple posts and we had to cut the posts down until the sockets of the two carved heads fitted. The creature at the stern, the smaller of the two, was a gape-mouthed serpent, probably intended to represent Corpse-Ripper, the monster that tore at the dead in the Danish underworld, while the beast we placed at the bow was a dragon's head, though it was so blackened and disfigured by fire that it looked more like a horse's head. We dug into the scorched eyes until we found unburned wood, and did the same with the open mouth, and when we were finished the thing looked dramatic and fierce. "Looks like a fyrdraca now," Leofric said happily. A fire-dragon.

The Danes could always remove the dragon or beast heads from the bows and sterns of their ships because they did not want the horrid-looking creatures to frighten the spirits of friendly lands and so they only displayed the carved monsters when they were in enemy waters. We did the same, hiding our fyrdraca and serpent head in **Eftwyrd**'s bilges as we went back downriver to where the shipwrights were beginning their work on **Heahengel.** We hid the beast heads because Leofric did not want the shipwrights to know he planned mischief. "That one," he said as he jerked his head toward a tall, lean, gray-haired man who was in charge of the work, "is more Christian than the pope. He'd bleat to the local priests if he thought we were going off to fight someone, and the priests will tell Alfred and then Burgweard will take **Eftwyrd** away from me."

"You don't like Burgweard?"

Leofric spat for answer. "It's a good thing there are no Danes on the coast."

"He's a coward?"

"No coward. He just thinks God will fight the battles. We spend more time on our knees than at the oars. When you commanded the fleet we made money. Now even the rats on board are begging for crumbs."

We had made money by capturing Danish

ships and taking their plunder, and though none of us had become rich we had all possessed silver to spare. I was still wealthy enough because I had a hoard hidden at Oxton, a hoard that was the legacy of Ragnar the Older, and a hoard that the church and Oswald's relatives would make their own if they could, but a man can never have enough silver. Silver buys land, it buys the loyalty of warriors, it is the power of a lord, and without silver a man must bend the knee or else become a slave. The Danes led men by the lure of silver, and we were no different. If I was to be a lord, if I was to storm the walls of Bebbanburg, then I would need men and I would need a great hoard to buy the swords and shields and spears and hearts of warriors, and so we would go to sea and look for silver, though we told the shipwrights that we merely planned to patrol the coast. We shipped barrels of ale, boxes of hard-baked bread, cheeses, kegs of smoked mackerel, and flitches of bacon. I told Mildrith the same story, that we would be sailing back and forth along the shores of Defnascir and Thornsæta. "Which is what we should be doing anyway," Leofric said, "just in case a Dane arrives."

"The Danes are lying low," I said.

Leofric nodded. "And when a Dane lies low you know there's trouble coming."

I believed he was right. Guthrum was not far from Wessex, and Svein, if he existed, was just a day's voyage from her north coast. Alfred might believe his truce would hold and that the hostages would secure it, but I knew from my childhood how land-hungry the Danes were, and how they lusted after the lush fields and rich pastures of Wessex. They would come, and if Guthrum did not lead them then another Danish chieftain would gather ships and men and bring his swords and axes to Alfred's kingdom. The Danes, after all, ruled the other three English kingdoms. They held my own Northumbria, they were bringing settlers to East Anglia, their language was spreading southward through Mercia, and they would not want the last English kingdom flourishing to their south. They were like wolves, shadow-skulking for the moment, but watching a flock of sheep fatten.

I recruited eleven young men from my land and took them on board **Eftwyrd**, and brought Haesten, too, and he was useful for he had spent much of his young life at the oars. Then, one misty morning, as the strong tide ebbed westward, we slid **Eftwyrd** away from the river's bank, rowed her past the low sand spit that guards the Uisc and so out to the long swells of the sea. The oars creaked in their leather-lined holes, the bow's breast split the waves to shatter water white along the hull, and the steering oar fought against my touch. I felt my spirits rise to the small wind and I looked up into the pearly sky and said a prayer of thanks to Thor, Odin, Njord, and Hoder.

A few small fishing boats dotted the inshore waters, but as we went south and west, away from the land, the sea emptied. I looked back at the low dun hills slashed brighter green where rivers pierced the coast, and then the green faded to gray, the land became a shadow, and we were alone with the white birds crying. It was then that we heaved the serpent's head and the fyrdraca from the bilge and slotted them over the posts at stem and stern, pegged them into place, and turned our bow westward.

The **Eftwyrd** was no more. Now the **Fyrdraca** sailed, and she was hunting trouble.

THREE

The crew of the **Eftwyrd** turned **Fyrdraca** had been at Cynuit with me. They were fighting men and they were offended that Odda the Younger had taken credit for a battle they had won. They had also been bored since the battle. Once in a while, Leofric told me, Burgweard exercised his fleet by taking it to sea, but most of the time they waited in Hamtun. "We did go fishing once, though," Leofric admitted.

"Fishing?"

"Father Willibald preached a sermon about feeding five thousand folk with two scraps of bread and a basket of herring," he said, "so Burgweard said we should take nets out and fish. He wanted to feed the town, see? Lots of hungry folk."

"Did you catch anything?"

"Mackerel. Lots of mackerel."

"But no Danes?"

"No Danes," Leofric said, "and no herring, only mackerel. The bastard Danes have vanished."

We learned later that Guthrum had given orders that no Danish ships were to raid the Wessex coast and so break the truce. Alfred was to be lulled into a conviction that peace had come, and that meant there were no pirates roaming the seas between Kent and Cornwalum and their absence encouraged traders to come from the lands to the south to sell wine or to buy fleeces. The **Fyrdraca** took two such ships in the first four days. They were both Frankish ships, tubby in their hulls, and neither with more than six oars a side, and both believed the **Fyrdraca** was a Viking ship for they saw her beast heads, and they heard Haesten and me speaking Danish and they saw my arm rings. We did not kill the crews, but just stole their coins, weapons, and as much of their cargo as we could carry. One ship was heaped with bales of wool, for the folk across the water prized Saxon fleeces, but we could only take three of the bales for fear of cluttering the **Fyrdraca**'s benches.

At night we found a cove or river's mouth, and

by day we rowed to sea and looked for prey, and each day we went farther westward until I was sure we were off the coast of Cornwalum, and that was enemy country. It was the old enemy that had confronted our ancestors when they first came across the North Sea to make England. That enemy spoke a strange language, and some Britons lived north of Northumbria and others lived in Wales or in Cornwalum, all places on the wild edges of the isle of Britain where they had been pushed by our coming. They were Christians. Indeed, Father Beocca had told me they had been Christians before we were and he claimed that no one who was a Christian could be a real enemy of another Christian. But nevertheless the Britons hated us. Sometimes they allied themselves with the Northmen to attack us. Sometimes the Northmen raided them. Sometimes they made war against us on their own. In the past the men of Cornwalum had made much trouble for Wessex, although Leofric claimed they had been punished so badly that they now pissed themselves whenever they saw a Saxon.

Not that we saw any Britons at first. The places we sheltered were deserted, all except one river mouth where a skin boat pushed offshore and a half-naked man paddled out to us and held up some crabs, which he wanted to sell to us. We took a basketful of the beasts and paid him two pennies. Next night we grounded **Fyrdraca** on a rising tide and collected fresh water from a stream, and Leofric and I climbed a hill and stared inland. Smoke rose from distant valleys, but there was no one in sight, not even a shepherd. "What are you expecting," Leofric asked, "enemies?"

"A monastery," I said.

"A monastery!" He was amused. "You want to pray?"

"Monasteries have silver," I said.

"Not down here, they don't. They're poor as stoats. Besides."

"Besides what?"

He jerked his head toward the crew. "You've got a dozen good Christians aboard. Lots of bad ones, too, of course, but at least a dozen good ones. They won't raid a monastery with you." He was right. A few of the men had showed some scruples about piracy, but I assured them that the Danes used trading ships to spy on their enemies. That was true enough, though I doubt either of our victims had been serving the Danes. But both ships had been crewed by foreigners and, like all Saxons, the crew of the **Fyrdraca** had a healthy dislike of foreigners, though they made an exception for Haesten and the dozen crewmen who were Frisians. The Frisians were natural pirates, bad as the Danes, and these twelve had come to Wessex to get rich from war and so were glad that the **Fyrdraca** was seeking plunder.

As we went west we began to see coastal settlements, and some were surprisingly large. Cenwulf, who had fought with us at Cynuit and was a good man, told us that the Britons of Cornwalum dug tin out of the ground and sold it to strangers. He knew that because his father had been a trader and had frequently sailed this coast. "If they sell tin," I said, "then they must have money."

"And men to guard it," Cenwulf said drily.

"Do they have a king?"

No one knew. It seemed probable, though where the king lived or who he was we could not know, and perhaps, as Haesten suggested, there was more than one king. They did have weapons because, one night, as the **Fyrdraca** crept into a bay, an arrow flew from a cliff top to be swallowed in the sea beside our oars. We might never have known that arrow had been shot except I happened to be looking up and saw it, fledged with dirty gray feathers, flickering down from the sky to vanish with a plop. One arrow, and no others followed, so perhaps it was a warning, and that night we let the ship lie at its anchor and in the dawn we saw two cows grazing close to a stream and Leofric fetched his ax. "The cows are there to kill us," Haesten warned us in his new and not very good English.

"The cows will kill us?" I asked in amusement.

"I have seen it before, lord. They put cows to bring us on land. Then they attack."

We granted the cows mercy, hauled the anchor, and pulled toward the bay's mouth. A howl sounded behind us and I saw a crowd of men appear from behind bushes and trees. I took one of the silver rings from my left arm and gave it to Haesten. It was his first arm ring and, being a Dane, he was inordinately proud of it. He polished it all morning.

The coast became wilder and refuge more difficult to find, but the weather was placid. We captured a small eight-oared ship that was returning to Ireland and relieved it of sixteen pieces of silver, three knives, a heap of tin ingots, a sack of goose feathers, and six goatskins. We were hardly becoming rich, though **Fyrdraca**'s belly was becoming cluttered with pelts, fleeces, and ingots of tin. "We need to sell it all," Leofric said.

But to whom? We knew no one who traded here. What I needed to do, I thought, was land close to one of the larger settlements and steal everything. Burn the houses, kill the men, plunder the headman's hall, and go back to sea. But the Britons kept lookouts on the headlands and they always saw us coming, and whenever we were close to one of their towns we would see armed men waiting. They had learned how to deal with Vikings, which was why, Haesten told me, the Northmen now sailed in fleets of five or six ships.

"Things will be better," I said, "when we turn the coast." I knew Cornwalum ended somewhere to the west and we could then sail up into the Sæfern Sea where we might find a Danish ship on its voyage from Ireland, but Cornwalum seemed to be without end. Whenever we saw a headland that I thought must mark the end of the land, it turned out to be a false hope, for another cliff would lie beyond, and then another, and sometimes the tide flowed so strongly that even when we sailed due west we were driven back east. Being a Viking was more difficult than I thought, and then one day the wind freshened from the west and the waves heaved higher and their tops were torn ragged and rain squalls hissed dark from a low sky and we ran northward to seek shelter in the lee of a headland. We dropped our anchor there and felt **Fyrdraca** jerk and tug like a fretful horse to her long rope of twisted hide.

All night and all the next day the weather raged past the headland. Water shattered white on high cliffs. We were safe enough, but our food was getting low, and I had half decided we must abandon our plans to make ourselves rich and sail back to the Uisc where we could pretend we had only been patrolling the coast, but on our second dawn under the lee of that high cliff, as the wind subsided and the rain dropped to a chill drizzle, a ship appeared about the eastern spit of land.

"Shields!" Leofric shouted, and the men, cold and unhappy, found their weapons and lined the ship's side.

The ship was smaller than ours, much smaller. She was squat, high-bowed, with a stumpy mast holding a wide yard on which a dirty sail was furled. A half dozen oarsmen manned her, and the steersman was bringing her directly toward **Fyrdraca**, and then, as she came closer and as her small bow broke the water white, I saw a green bough had been tied to her short mast. "They want to talk," I said.

"Let's hope they want to buy," Leofric grumbled.

There was a priest in the small ship. I did not know he was a priest at first, for he looked as ragged as any of the crewmen, but he shouted that he wished to speak with us, and he spoke Danish, though not well, and I let the boat come up on the flank protected from the wind where her crewmen gazed up at a row of armed men holding shields. Cenwulf and I pulled the priest over our side. Two other men wanted to follow, but Leofric threatened them with a spear and they dropped back and the smaller ship drew away to wait while the priest spoke with us.

He was called Father Mardoc and, once he was aboard and sitting wetly on one of **Fyr-draca**'s rowing benches, I saw the crucifix about his neck. "I hate Christians," I said, "so why should we not feed you to Njord?"

He ignored that, or perhaps he did not know that Njord was one of the sea gods. "I bring you a gift," he said, "from my master," and he produced, from beneath his cloak, two battered arm rings.

I took them. They were poor things, mere ringlets of copper, old, filthy with verdigris, and of almost no value, and for a moment I was tempted to toss them scornfully into the sea, but reckoned our voyage had made such small profit that even those scabby treasures must be kept. "Who is your master?" I asked.

"King Peredur."

I almost laughed. King Peredur? A man can expect a king to be famous, but I had never heard of Peredur, which suggested he was little more than a local chieftain with a high-sounding title. "And why does this Peredur," I asked, "send me miserable gifts?"

Father Mardoc still did not know my name and was too frightened to ask it. He was surrounded by men in leather, by men in mail, and by shields and swords, axes and spears, and he believed all of us were Danes for I had ordered any of **Fyrdraca**'s crew who wore crosses or crucifixes to hide them beneath their clothes. Only Haesten and I spoke, and if Father Mardoc thought that strange, he did not say anything of it. Instead he told me how his lord, King Peredur, had been treacherously attacked by a neighbor called Callyn, and Callyn's forces had taken a high fort close to the sea and Peredur would pay us well if we were to help him recapture the fort that was called Dreyndynas.

I sent Father Mardoc to sit in the **Fyrdraca**'s bow while we talked about his request. Some things were obvious. Being paid well did not mean we would become rich, but that Peredur would try to fob us off with as little as possible and, most likely, having given it to us he would then try to take it back by killing us all. "What we should do," Leofric advised, "is find this man Callyn and see what he'll pay us."

Which was good enough advice except none of us knew how to find Callyn, whom we later learned was King Callyn, which did not mean much, for any man with a following of more than fifty armed men called himself a king in Corn-walum, and so I went to the **Fyrdraca**'s bow and talked with Father Mardoc again, and he told me that Dreyndynas was a high fort, built by the old people, and that it guarded the road east-ward, and so long as Callyn held the fort, so long were Peredur's people trapped in their lands.

"You have ships," I pointed out.

"And Callyn has ships," he said, "and we can-not take cattle in ships."

"Cattle?"

"We need to sell cattle to live," he said.

So Callyn had surrounded Peredur and we represented a chance to tip the balance in this little war. "So how much will your king pay us?" I asked.

"A hundred pieces of silver," he said.

I drew Serpent-Breath. "I worship the real gods," I told him, "and I am a particular servant of Hoder, and Hoder likes blood, and I have given him none in many days."

Father Mardoc looked terrified, which was sensible of him. He was a young man, though it was hard to tell for his hair and beard were so thick that most of the time he was just a broken nose and pair of eyes surrounded by a greasy black tangle. He told me he had learned to speak Danish when he had been enslaved by a chieftain called Godfred, but that he had managed to escape when Godfred raided the Sillans, islands that lay well out in the western sea-wastes. "Is there any wealth in the Sillans?" I asked him. I had heard of the islands, though some men claimed they were mythical and others said the islands came and went with the moons, but Father Mardoc said they existed and were called the Isles of the Dead.

"So no one lives there?" I asked.

"Some folk do," he said, "but the dead have their houses there."

"Do they have wealth as well?"

"Your ships have taken it all," he said. This was after he had promised me that Peredur would be more generous, though he did not know how generous. He said the king was willing to pay far more than a hundred silver coins for our help, and so we had him shout to his ship that they were to lead us around the coast to Peredur's settlement. I did not let Father Mardoc go back to his ship for he would serve as a hostage if the tale he had told us was false and Peredur was merely luring us to an ambush.

He was not. Peredur's home was a huddle of buildings built on a steep hill beside a bay and protected by a wall of thorn bushes. His people lived within the wall. Some were fishermen and some were cattle herders and none was wealthy. The king himself, however, had a high hall where he welcomed us, though not before we had taken more hostages. Three young men, all of whom we were assured were Peredur's sons, were delivered to **Fyrdraca** and I gave the crew orders that the three were to be killed if I did not return, and then I went ashore with Haesten and Cenwulf. I went dressed for war, with mail coat and helmet polished, and Peredur's folk watched with frightened eyes as the three of us passed. The place stank of fish and shit. The people were ragged and their houses mere hovels that were built up the side of the steep hill that was crowned with Peredur's hall. There was a church beside the hall, its thatch thick with moss and its gable decorated with a cross made from sea-whitened driftwood.

Peredur was twice my age, a squat man with a sly face and a forked black beard. He greeted us from a throne, which was just a chair with a high back, and he waited for us to bow to him, but none of us did and that made him scowl. A dozen men were with him, evidently his courtiers, though none looked wealthy and all were elderly except for one much younger man who was in the robes of a Christian monk, and he stood out in that smoke-darkened hall like a raven in a clutch of gulls for his black robes were clean, his face close shaven, and his hair and tonsure neatly trimmed. He was scarcely older than I, was thin and stern-faced, and that face looked clever. It also carried an expression of marked distaste for us. We were pagans, or at least Haesten and I were pagans, and I had told

Cenwulf to keep his mouth shut and his crucifix hidden, and so the monk assumed all three of us were heathen Danes. The monk spoke Danish, far better Danish than Father Mardoc. "The king greets you," he said. He had a voice as thin as his lips and as unfriendly as his pale green eyes. "He greets you and would know who you are."

"My name is Uhtred Ragnarson," I said.

"Why are you here, Uhtred Ragnarson?" the priest asked.

I contemplated him. I did not just look at him, but I studied him as a man might study an ox before killing it. I gave him a look that suggested I was wondering where to make the cuts, and he got my meaning and did not wait for an answer to his question, an answer that was obvious if we were Danes. We were here to thieve and kill, of course. What else did he think a Viking ship would be doing?

Peredur spoke to the monk and they muttered for some time and I looked around the hall, searching for any evidence of wealth. I saw almost nothing except for three whalebones stacked in a corner, but Peredur plainly had some treasure for he wore a great heavy torque of bronze about his neck and there were silver rings on his grubby fingers, an amber brooch at the neck of his cloak, and a golden crucifix hidden in the cloak's lice-ridden folds. He would keep his hoard buried, I thought, but I doubted any of us would become rich from this alliance; in truth we were not becoming rich from our voyage either, and at least Peredur would have to feed us while we haggled.

"The king," the monk interrupted my thoughts, "wishes to know how many men you can lead against the enemy."

"Enough," I said flatly.

"Does that not depend," the monk observed slyly, "on how many enemy there are?"

"No," I said. "It depends on this," and I slapped Serpent-Breath's hilt. It was a good, arrogant reply, and probably what the monk expected. And, in truth, it was convincing for I was broad in the chest and a giant in this hall where I was a full head taller than any other man. "And who are you, monk?" I demanded.

"My name is Asser," he said. It was a British name, of course, and in the English tongue it meant a he-ass, and ever after I thought of him as the Ass. And there was to be a lot of the ever after for, though I did not know it, I had just met a man who would haunt my life like a louse. I had met another enemy, though on that day in Peredur's hall he was just a strange British monk who stood out from his companions because he washed. He invited me to follow him to a small door at the side of the hall and, motioning Haesten and Cenwulf to stay where they were, I ducked through the door to find myself standing beside a dung heap, but the point of taking me outside had been to show me the view eastward.

I stared across a valley. On the nearer slope were the smoke-blackened roofs of Peredur's settlement. Then came the thorn fence that had been made along the stream that flowed to the sea. On the stream's far side the hills rose gently to a far-off crest and there, breaking the skyline like a boil, was Dreyndynas. "The enemy," Asser said.

A small fort, I noted. "How many men are there?"

"Does it matter to you?" Asser asked sourly, paying me back for my refusal to tell him how many men I led, though I assumed Father Mardoc had made a count of the crew while he was on board **Fyrdraca** so my defiance had been pointless.

"You Christians," I said, "believe that at death you go to heaven. Isn't that right?"

"What of it?"

"You must surely welcome such a fate?" I asked. "To be near your god?"

"Are you threatening me?"

"I don't threaten vermin," I said, enjoying myself. "How many men are in that fort?"

"Forty? Fifty?" He plainly did not know. "We can assemble forty."

"So tomorrow," I said, "your king can have his fort back."

"He is not my king," Asser said, irritated by the assumption.

"Your king or not," I said, "he can have his fort back so long as he pays us properly."

That negotiation lasted until dark. Peredur, as Father Mardoc had said, was willing to pay more than a hundred shillings, but he feared we would take the money and leave without fighting and so he wanted some kind of surety from me. He wanted hostages, which I refused to give, and after an hour or more of argument we had still not reached an agreement, and it was then that Peredur summoned his queen. That meant nothing to me, but I saw the Ass stiffen as though he were offended, then sensed that every other man in the hall was strangely apprehensive. Asser made a protest, but the king cut him off with an abrupt slice of his hand and then a door at the back of the hall was opened and Iseult came to my life.

Iseult. Finding her there was like discovering a jewel of gold in a midden. I saw her and I forgot Mildrith. Dark Iseult, black-haired Iseult, huge-eyed Iseult. She was small, thin as an elf, with a luminous face and hair as black as a raven's feathers. She wore a black cloak and had silver bands about her neck and silver bracelets at her wrists and silver rings at her ankles and the jewelry clinked gently as she walked toward us. She was maybe two or three years younger than I, but somehow, despite her youth, she managed to scare Peredur's courtiers, who backed away from her. The king looked nervous, while Asser, standing beside me, made the sign of the cross, then spat to ward off evil.

I just stared at her, entranced. There was pain on her face, as if she found life unbearable, and there was fear on her husband's face when he spoke to her in a quiet, respectful voice. She shuddered when he talked and I thought that perhaps she was mad, for the grimace on her face was awful, disfiguring her beauty, but then she calmed and looked at me and the king spoke to Asser.

"You will tell the queen who you are and what you will do for King Peredur," Asser told me in a distant, disapproving voice.

"She speaks Danish?" I asked.

"Of course not," he snapped. "Just tell her and get this farce over."

I looked into her eyes, those big, dark eyes, and had the uncanny suspicion that she could see right through my gaze and decipher my innermost thoughts. But at least she did not grimace when she saw me, as she had when her husband spoke. "My name is Uhtred Ragnarson," I said, "and I am here to fight for your husband if he pays what I am worth. And if he doesn't pay, we go."

I thought Asser would translate, but the monk stayed silent.

Iseult still stared at me and I stared back. She had flawless skin, untouched by illness, and a strong face, but sad. Sad and beautiful. Fierce and beautiful. She reminded me of Brida, the East Anglian who had been my lover and who was now with Ragnar, my friend. Brida was as full of fury as a scabbard is filled with blade, and I sensed the same in this queen who was so young and strange and dark and lovely.

"I am Uhtred Ragnarson," I heard myself say as I spoke again, though I had scarcely been aware of any urge to talk, "and I work miracles."

Why I said that I do not know. I later learned that she had no idea what I had said, for at that time the only tongue she spoke was that of the Britons, but nevertheless she seemed to understand me and she smiled. Asser caught his breath. "Be careful, Dane," he hissed. "She is a queen."

"A queen," I asked, still staring at her, "or the queen?"

"The king is blessed with three wives," the monk said disapprovingly.

Iseult turned away and spoke to the king. He nodded, then gestured respectfully toward the door through which Iseult had come. She was evidently dismissed and she obediently went to the door, but paused there and gave me a last, speculative look. Then she was gone.

And suddenly it was easy. Peredur agreed to pay us a hoard of silver. He showed us the hoard that had been hidden in a back room. There were coins, broken jewelry, battered cups, and three candleholders that had been taken from the church, and when I weighed the silver, using a balance fetched from the marketplace, I discovered there was three hundred and sixteen shillings' worth, which was not negligible. Asser divided it into two piles, one only half the size of the other. "We shall give you the smaller portion tonight," the monk said, "and the rest you will get when Dreyndynas is recovered."

"You think I am a fool?" I asked, knowing that after the fight it would be hard to get the rest of the silver.

"You take me for one?" he retorted, knowing that if he gave us all the silver then **Fyrdraca** would vanish in the dawn.

We agreed in the end that we would take the one-third now and that the other two-thirds would be carried to the battlefield so that it was easily accessible. Peredur had hoped I would leave that larger portion in his hall, and then I would have faced an uphill fight through his dung-spattered streets, and that was a fight I would have lost, and it was probably the prospect of such a battle that had stopped Callyn's men from attacking Peredur's hall. They hoped to starve him, or at least Asser believed that.

"Tell me about Iseult," I demanded of the monk when the bargaining was done.

He sneered at that. "I can read you like a missal," he said.

"Whatever a missal is," I said, pretending ignorance.

"A book of prayers," he said, "and you will need prayers if you touch her." He made the sign of the cross. "She is evil," he said vehemently.

"She's a queen, a young queen," I said, "so how can she be evil?"

"What do you know of the Britons?"

"That they stink like stoats," I said, "and thieve like jackdaws."

He gave me a sour look and, for a moment, I thought he would refuse to say more, but he swallowed his British pride. "We are Christians," he said, "and God be thanked for that great mercy, but among our people there are still some old superstitions. Pagan ways. Iseult is part of that."

"What part?"

He did not like talking about it, but he had raised the subject of Iseult's evil and so he reluctantly explained. "She was born in the springtime," he said, "eighteen years ago, and at her birth there was an eclipse of the sun, and the folk here are credulous fools and they believe a dark child born at the sun's death has power. They have made her into a"—he paused, not knowing the Danish word—"a **gwrach**," he said, a word that meant nothing to me. **"Dewines,"** he said irritably and, when I still showed incomprehension, he at last found a word. "A sorceress."

"A witch?"

"And Peredur married her. Made her his shadow queen. That is what kings did with such girls. They take them into their households so they may use their power."

"What power?"

"The skills the devil gives to shadow queens, of course," he said irritably. "Peredur believes she can see the future. But it is a skill she will retain only so long as she is a virgin."

I laughed at that. "If you disapprove of her, monk, then I would be doing you a favor if I raped her." He ignored that, or at least he made no reply other than to give me a harsh scowl. "Can she see the future?" I asked.

"She saw you victorious," he said, "and told the king he could trust you, so you tell me?"

"Then assuredly she can see the future," I said.

Brother Asser sneered at that answer. "They should have strangled her with her own birth cord," he snarled. "She is a pagan bitch, a devil's thing, evil."

There was a feast that night, a feast to celebrate

our pact, and I hoped Iseult would be there, but she was not. Peredur's older wife was present, but she was a sullen, grubby creature with two weeping boils on her neck and she hardly spoke. Yet it was a surprisingly good feast. There was fish, beef, mutton, bread, ale, mead, and cheese, and while we ate Asser told me he had come from the kingdom of Dyfed, which lay north of the Sæfern Sea, and that his king, who had an impossible British name that sounded like a man coughing and spluttering, had sent him to Cornwalum to dissuade the British kings from supporting the Danes.

I was surprised by that, so surprised that I looked away from the girls serving the food. A harpist played at the hall's end and two of the girls swayed in time to the music as they walked. "You don't like Danes," I said.

"You are pagans," Asser said scornfully.

"So how come you speak the pagan tongue?" I asked.

"Because my abbot would have us send missionaries to the Danes."

"You should go," I said. "It would be a quick route to heaven for you."

He ignored that. "I learned Danish among many other tongues," he said loftily, "and I speak the language of the Saxons, too. And you, I think, were not born in Denmark?"

"How do you know?"

"Your voice," he said. "You are from Northumbria?"

"I am from the sea," I said.

He shrugged. "In Northumbria," he said severely, "the Danes have corrupted the Saxons so that they think of themselves as Danes." He was wrong, but I was scarcely in a position to correct him. "Worse," he went on, "they have extinguished the light of Christ."

"Is the light of Thor too bright for you?"

"The West Saxons are Christians," he said, "and it is our duty to support them, not because of a love for them, but because of our fellow love for Christ."

"You have met Alfred of Wessex?" I asked sourly.

"I look forward to meeting him," he said fervently, "for I hear he is a good Christian."

"I hear the same."

"And Christ rewards him," Asser went on.

"Rewards him?"

"Christ sent the storm that destroyed the Danish fleet," Asser said, "and Christ's angels destroyed Ubba. That is proof of God's power. If we fight against Alfred then we range ourselves against Christ, so we must not do it. That is my message to the kings of Cornwalum."

I was impressed that a British monk at the end of the land of Britain knew so much of what happened in Wessex, and I reckoned Alfred would have been pleased to hear Asser's nonsense, though of course Alfred had sent many messengers to the British. His messengers had all been priests or monks and they had preached the gospel of their god slaughtering the Danes, and Asser had evidently taken up their message enthusiastically. "So why are you fighting Callyn?" I asked.

"He would join the Danes," Asser said.

"And we're going to win," I said, "so Callyn is sensible."

Asser shook his head. "God will prevail."

"You hope," I said, fingering Thor's hammer. "But if you are wrong, monk, then we'll take Wessex and Callyn will share the spoils."

"Callyn will share nothing," Asser said spitefully, "because you will kill him tomorrow."

The Britons have never learned to love the Saxons. Indeed they hate us, and in those years when the last English kingdom was on the edge of destruction, they could have tipped the balance by joining Guthrum. Instead they held back their sword arms, and for that the Saxons can thank the church. Men like Asser had decided that the Danish heretics were a worse enemy than English Christians, and if I were a Briton I would resent that, because the Britons might have taken back much of their lost lands if they had allied themselves with the pagan Northmen. Religion makes strange bedfellows.

So does war, and Peredur offered Haesten and myself two of the serving girls to seal our bargain. I had sent Cenwulf back to **Fyrdraca** with a message for Leofric, warning him to be ready to fight in the morning, and I thought perhaps Haesten and I should retreat to the ship, but the serving girls were pretty and so we stayed, and I need not have worried for no one tried to kill us in the night, and no one even tried when Haesten and I carried the first third of the silver down to the water's edge where a small boat carried us to our ship. "There's twice as much as that waiting for us," I told Leofric.

He stirred the sack of silver with his foot. "And where were you last night?"

"In bed with a Briton."

"Earsling," he said. "So who are we fighting?"

"A pack of savages."

We left ten men as ship guards. If Peredur's men made a real effort to capture **Fyrdraca** then those ten would have had a hard fight, and probably a losing fight, but they had the three hostages who may or may not have been Peredur's sons, so that was a risk we had to take, and it seemed safe enough because Peredur had assembled his army on the eastern side of the town. I say army, though it was only forty men, and I brought thirty more, and my thirty were well armed and looked ferocious in their leather. Leofric, like me, wore mail, as did half a dozen of my crewmen, and I had my fine helmet with its faceplate so I, at least, looked like a lord of battles.

Peredur was in leather, and he had woven black horsetails into his hair and onto the twin forks of his beard so that the horsetails hung down wild and long and scary. His men were mostly armed with spears, though Peredur himself possessed a fine sword. Some of his men had shields and a few had helmets, and though I did not doubt their bravery I did not reckon them formidable. My crewmen were formidable. They had fought Danish ships off the Wessex coast and they had fought in the shield wall at Cynuit and

I had no doubt that we could destroy whatever troops Callyn had placed in Dreyndynas.

It was afternoon before we climbed the hill. We should have gone in the morning, but some of Peredur's men were recovering from their night's drinking, and the women of his settlement kept pulling others away, not wanting them to die, and then Peredur and his advisers huddled and talked about how they should fight the battle, though what there was to talk about I did not know. Callyn's men were in the fort. We were outside it, so we had to assault the bastards. Nothing clever, just an attack, but they talked for a long time, and Father Mardoc said a prayer, or rather he shouted it, and then I refused to advance because the rest of the silver had not been fetched.

It came, carried in a chest by two men, and so at last, under the afternoon sun, we climbed the eastern hill. Some women followed us, shrieking their battle screams, which was a waste of breath because the enemy was still too far away to hear them.

"So what do we do?" Leofric asked me.

"Form a wedge," I guessed. "Our best men in the front rank and you and me in front of them, then kill the bastards."

He grimaced. "Have you ever assaulted one of the old people's forts?"

"Never."

"It can be hard," he warned me.

"If it's too hard," I said, "we'll just kill Peredur and his men and take their silver anyway."

Brother Asser, his neat black robes muddied about their skirts, hurried over to me. "Your men are Saxons!" he said accusingly.

"I hate monks," I snarled at him. "I hate them more than I hate priests. I like killing them. I like slitting their bellies. I like watching the bastards die. Now run off and die before I cut your throat."

He ran off to Peredur with his news that we were Saxons. The king stared at us morosely. He had thought he had recruited a crew of Danish Vikings, and now he discovered we were West Saxons and he was not happy, so I drew Serpent-Breath and banged her blade against my lime-wood shield. "You want to fight this battle or not?" I asked him through Asser.

Peredur decided he wanted to fight, or rather he wanted us to fight the battle for him, and so we slogged on up the hill, which had a couple of false crests so it was well into the afternoon before we emerged onto the long, shallow summit and could see Dreyndynas's green turf walls on the skyline. A banner flew there. It was a triangle of cloth, supported on its pole by a small cross-staff, and the banner showed a white horse prancing on a green field.

I stopped then. Peredur's banner was a wolf's tail hung from a pole. I carried none though, like most Saxons, mine would have been a rectangular flag. I only knew one people who flew triangular banners and I turned on Brother Asser as he sweated up the hill. "They're Danes," I accused him.

"So?" he demanded. "I thought you were a Dane, and all the world knows the Danes will fight anyone for silver, even other Danes. But are you frightened of them, Saxon?"

"Your mother didn't give birth to you," I told him, "but farted you out of her shriveled arsehole."

"You've taken Peredur's silver," Asser said, "so you must fight."

"Say one more word, monk," I said, "and I'll cut off your scrawny balls." I was gazing uphill, trying to estimate numbers. Everything had changed since I had seen the white horse banner because instead of fighting against half-armed British savages we would have to take on a crew of lethal Danes, but if I was surprised by that, then the Danes were equally surprised to see us. They were crowding Dreyndynas's wall, which was made of earth fronted with a ditch and topped with a thorn fence. It would be a hard wall to attack, I thought, especially if it was defended by Danes. I counted over forty men on the skyline and knew there would be others I could not see, and the numbers alone told me this assault would fail. We could attack, and we might well get as far as the thorn palisade, but I doubted we could hack our way through, and the Danes would kill a score of us as we tried, and we would be lucky to retreat down the hill without greater loss.

"We're in a cesspit," Leofric said to me.

"Up to our necks."

"So what do we do? Turn on them and take the money?"

I did not answer because the Danes had dragged a section of the thorn fence aside and three of them now jumped down from the ramparts and strolled toward us. They wanted to talk.

"Who the hell is that?" Leofric asked.

He was staring at the Danish leader. He was a huge man, big as Steapa Snotor, and dressed in a mail coat that had been polished with sand until it shone. His helmet, as highly polished as his mail, had a faceplate modeled as a boar's mask with a squat, broad snout, and from the helmet's crown there flew a white horsetail. He wore arm-rings over his mail, rings of silver and gold that proclaimed him to be a warrior chief, a sword Dane, a lord of war. He walked the hillside as if he owned it, and in truth he did own it because he possessed the fort.

Asser hurried to meet the Danes, going with Peredur and two of his courtiers. I went after them and found Asser trying to convert the Danes. He told them that God had brought us and we would slaughter them all and their best course was to surrender now and yield their heathen souls to God. "We shall baptize you," Asser said, "and there will be much rejoicing in heaven."

The Danish leader slowly pulled off his helmet and his face was almost as frightening as the boar-snouted mask. It was a broad face, hardened by sun and wind, with the blank, expressionless eyes of a killer. He was around thirty years old and had a tightly cropped beard and a scar running from the corner of his left eye down across his cheek. He gave the helmet to one of his men and, without saying a word, hauled up the skirt of his mail coat and began pissing on Asser's robe. The monk leaped back.

The Dane, still pissing, looked at me. "Who are you?"

"Uhtred Ragnarson. And you?"

"Svein of the White Horse." He said it defiantly, as though I would know his reputation, and for a heartbeat I said nothing. Was this the same Svein who was said to be gathering troops in Wales? Then what was he doing here?

"You're Svein of Ireland?" I asked.

"Svein of Denmark," he said. He let the mail coat drop and glared at Asser, who was threatening the Danes with heaven's vengeance. "If you want to live," he told Asser, "shut your filthy mouth." Asser shut his mouth. "Ragnarson." Svein looked back to me. "Earl Ragnar? Ragnar Ravnson? The Ragnar who served Ivar?"

"The same," I said.

"Then you are the Saxon son?"

"I am. And you?" I asked. "You're the Svein who has brought men from Ireland?"

"I have brought men from Ireland," he admitted.

"And gather forces in Wales?"

"I do what I do," he said vaguely. He looked

at my men, judging how well they would fight. Then he looked me up and down, noting my mail and helmet, and noting especially my arm rings, and when the inspection was done he jerked his head to indicate that he and I should walk away a few paces and talk privately.

Asser objected, saying anything that was spoken should be heard by all, but I ignored him and followed Svein uphill. "You can't take this fort," Svein told me.

"True."

"So what do you do?"

"Go back to Peredur's settlement, of course."

He nodded. "And if I attack the settlement?"

"You'll take it," I said, "but you'll lose men. Maybe a dozen?"

"Which will mean a dozen fewer oarsmen," he said, thinking, and then he looked past Peredur to where two men carried the box. "Is that your battle price?"

"It is."

"Split it?" he suggested.

I hesitated a heartbeat. "And we'll split what's in the town?" I asked.

"Agreed," he said, then looked at Asser who was hissing urgently at Peredur. "He knows what we're doing," he said grimly, "so a necessary deception is about to happen." I was still trying to understand what he meant when he struck me in the face. He struck hard, and my hand went to Serpent-Breath and his two men ran to him, swords in hand.

"I'll come out of the fort and join you," Svein said to me softly. Then, louder, "You bastard piece of goat-dropping."

I spat at him as his two men pretended to drag him away. Then I stalked back to Asser. "We kill them all," I said savagely. "We kill them all!"

"What did he say to you?" Asser asked. He had feared, rightly, as it happened, that Svein and I had made our own alliance, but Svein's quick display had put doubts in the monk's mind, and I fed the doubts by raging like a madman, screaming at the retreating Svein that I would send his miserable soul to Hel, who was the goddess of the dead. "Are you going to fight?" Asser demanded.

"Of course we're going to fight!" I shouted at him. Then I crossed to Leofric. "We're on the same side as the Danes," I told him quietly. "We kill these Britons, capture their settlement, and split everything with the Danes. Tell the men, but tell them quietly."

Svein, true to his word, brought his men out

of Dreyndynas. That should have warned Asser and Peredur of treachery, for no sensible man would abandon a fine defensive position like a thorn-topped earth wall to fight a battle on open ground, but they put it down to Danish arrogance. They assumed Svein believed he could destroy us all in open battle, and he made that assumption more likely by parading a score of his men on horseback, suggesting that he intended to tear our shield wall open with his swords and axes and then pursue the survivors with spear-armed cavalry. He made his own shield wall in front of the horsemen, and I made another shield wall on the left of Peredur's line, and once we were in the proper array we shouted insults at each other. Leofric was going down our line, whispering to the men, and I sent Cenwulf and two others to the rear with their own orders, and just then Asser ran across to us.

"Attack," the monk demanded, pointing at Svein.

"When we're ready," I said, for Leofric had not yet given every man his orders.

"Attack now!" Asser spat at me, and I almost gutted the bastard on the spot and would have saved myself a good deal of future trouble if I had, but I kept my patience and Asser went back to Peredur, where he began praying, both hands held high in the air, demanding that God send fire from heaven to consume the pagans.

"You trust Svein?" Leofric had come back to my side.

"I trust Svein," I said. Why? Only because he was a Dane and I liked the Danes. These days, of course, we are all agreed that they are the spawn of Satan, untrustworthy pagans, savages, and anything else we care to call them, but in truth the Danes are warriors and they like other warriors, and though it is true that Svein might have persuaded me to attack Peredur so that he could then attack us, I did not believe it. Besides, there was something I wanted in Peredur's hall and, to get her, I needed to change sides.

"**Fyrdraca!**" I shouted, and that was our signal, and we swung our shield wall around to the right and went at it.

It was, of course, an easy slaughter. Peredur's men had no belly for a fight. They had been hoping that we would take the brunt of the Danish assault and that they could then scavenge for plunder among Svein's wounded, but instead we turned on them, attacked them, and cut them down, and Svein came on their right, and Peredur's men fled. That was when Svein's horsemen kicked back their heels, leveled their spears, and charged.

It was not a fight, it was a massacre. Two of Peredur's men put up some resistance, but Leofric swatted their spears aside with his ax and they died screaming, and Peredur went down to my sword, and he put up no fight at all, but seemed resigned to his death that I gave him quickly enough. Cenwulf and his two companions did what I had ordered them to do, which was to intercept the chest of silver, and we rallied around them as Svein's riders chased down the fugitives. The only man to escape was Asser, the monk, which he managed by running north instead of west. Svein's horsemen were ranging down the hill, spearing Peredur's men in the backs, and Asser saw that only death lay that way and so, with surprising quickness, he changed direction and sprinted past my men, his skirts clutched up about his knees, and I shouted at the men on the right of the line to kill the bastard, but they simply looked at me and let him go. "I said kill him!" I snarled.

"He's a monk!" one of them answered. "You want me to go to hell?"

I watched Asser run slantwise into the valley and, in truth, I did not much care whether he lived or died. I thought Svein's horsemen would catch him, but perhaps they did not see him. They did catch Father Mardoc and one of them took off the priest's head with a single swing of his sword, which made some of my men cross themselves.

The horsemen made their killing, but Svein's other Danes made a shield wall that faced us, and in its center, beneath the white horse banner, was Svein himself in his boar-mask helmet. His shield had a white horse painted on its boards and his weapon was an ax, the largest war ax I had ever seen. My men shifted nervously. "Stand still!" I snarled at them.

"Up to our necks in it," Leofric said quietly.

Svein was staring at us and I could see the death light in his eyes. He was in a killing mood, and we were Saxons, and there was a knocking sound as his men hefted shields to make the wall, and so I tossed Serpent-Breath into the air. Tossed her high so that the big blade whirled about in the sun, and of course they were all wondering whether I would catch her or whether she would thump onto the grass.

I caught her, winked at Svein, and slid the blade into her scabbard. He laughed and the killing mood passed as he realized he could not afford the casualties he would inevitably take in fighting us. "Did you really think I was going to attack you?" he called across the springy turf.

"I was hoping you would attack me," I called back, "so I wouldn't have to split the plunder with you."

He dropped the ax and walked toward us, and I walked toward him and we embraced. Men on both sides lowered weapons. "Shall we take the bastard's miserable village?" Svein asked.

So we all went back down the hill, past the bodies of Peredur's men, and there was no one defending the thorn wall about the settlement so it was an easy matter to get inside, and a few men tried to protect their homes, but very few. Most of the folk fled to the beach, but there were not enough boats to take them away, and so Svein's Danes rounded them up and began sorting them into the useful and the dead. The useful were the young women and those who could be sold as slaves, the dead were the rest.

I took no part in that. Instead, with all of my men, I went straight to Peredur's hall. Some Danes, reckoning that was where the silver would be, were also climbing the hill, but I reached the hall first, pushed open the door, and saw Iseult waiting there.

I swear she was expecting me for her face showed no fear and no surprise. She was sitting in the king's throne, but stood as if welcoming me as I walked up the hall. Then she took the silver from her neck and her wrists and her ankles and held it mutely out as an offering and I took it all and tossed it to Leofric. "We divide it with Svein," I said.

"And her?" He sounded amused. "Do we share her, too?"

For answer I took the cloak from about Iseult's neck. Beneath it she wore a black dress. I still had Serpent-Breath drawn and I used the bloodied blade to slash at the cloak until I could tear a strip from its hem. Iseult watched me, her face showing nothing. When the strip was torn away I gave her back the cloak, then tied one end of the cloth strip about her neck and tied the other end to my belt. "She's mine," I said.

More Danes were coming into the hall and some stared wolfishly at Iseult, and then Svein arrived and snarled at his men to start digging up the hall floor to search for hidden coins or silver. He grinned when he saw Iseult's leash. "You can have her, Saxon," he said. "She's pretty, but I like them with more meat on the bone."

I kept Iseult with me as we feasted that night. There was a good deal of ale and mead in the settlement and so I ordered my men not to fight with the Danes, and Svein told his men not to fight with us, and on the whole we were obeyed, though inevitably some men quarreled over the captured women and one of the boys I had brought from my estate got a knife in his belly and died in the morning.

Svein was amused that we were a West Saxon ship. "Alfred sent you?" he asked me.

"No."

"He doesn't want to fight, does he?"

"He'll fight," I said, "except he thinks his god will do the fighting for him."

"Then he's an idiot," Svein said. "The gods don't do our bidding. I wish they did." He sucked on a pork bone. "So what are you doing here?" he asked.

"Looking for money," I said, "the same as you."

"I'm looking for allies," he said.

"Allies?"

He was drunk enough to speak more freely than he had when we first met, and I realized this was indeed the Svein who was said to be gathering men in Wales. He admitted as much, but added that he did not have enough warriors. "Guthrum can lead two thousand men to battle, maybe more! I have to match that."

So he was a rival to Guthrum. I tucked that knowledge away. "You think the Cornishmen will fight with you?"

"They promised they would," he said, spitting out a shred of gristle. "That's why I came here. But the bastards lied. Callyn isn't a proper king, he's a village chief! I'm wasting my time here."

"Could the two of us beat Callyn?" I asked.

Svein thought about it, then nodded. "We could." He frowned suddenly, staring into the hall's shadows, and I saw he was looking at one of his men who had a girl on his lap. He evidently liked the girl for he slapped the table, pointed to her, beckoned, and the man reluctantly brought her. Svein sat her down, pulled her tunic open so he could see her breasts, then gave her his pot of ale. "I'll think about it," he told me.

"Or are you thinking of attacking me?" I asked.

He grinned. "You are Uhtred Ragnarson," he said, "and I heard about the fight on the river where you killed Ubba."

I evidently had more of a reputation among my enemies than I did among my so-called friends. Svein insisted I tell the tale of Ubba's death, which I did, and I told him the truth, which was that Ubba had slipped and fallen, and that had let me take his life.

"But men say you fought well," Svein said.

Iseult listened to all this. She did not speak our language, but her big eyes seemed to follow every word. When the feast was over I took her to the small rooms at the back of the hall and she used my makeshift leash to pull me into her wood-walled chamber. I made a bed from our cloaks. "When this is done," I told her in words she could not understand, "you'll have lost your power."

She touched a finger to my lips to silence me and she was a queen so I obeyed her.

In the morning we finished ravaging the town. Iseult showed me which houses might have something of value and generally she was right though the search meant demolishing the houses, for folk hide their small treasures in their thatch. So we scattered rats and mice as we hauled down the moldy straw and sifted through it, and afterward we dug under every hearth, or wherever else a man might bury silver, and we collected every scrap of metal, every cooking pot or fishhook, and the search took all day. That night we divided the hoard on the beach.

Svein had evidently thought about Callyn and, being sober by the time he did his thinking, he had decided that the king was too strong. "We can easily beat him," he said, "but we'll lose men."

A ship's crew can only endure so many losses. We had lost none in the fight against Peredur, but Callyn was a stronger king and he was bound to be suspicious of Svein, which meant that he would have his household troops ready and armed. "And he's got little enough to take," Svein said scornfully.

"He's paying you?"

"He's paying me," Svein said, "just as Peredur paid you."

"I split that with you," I said.

"Not the money he paid you before the fight," Svein said with a grin, "you didn't split that."

"What money?" I asked.

"So we're even," he said, and we had both done well enough out of Peredur's death, for Svein had slaves and we each now possessed over nine hundred shillings' worth of silver and metal, which was not a fortune, especially once it was divided among the men, but it was better than I had done so far on the voyage. I also had Iseult.

She was no longer leashed to me, but she stayed beside me and I sensed that she was happy about that. She had taken a vicious pleasure in seeing her home destroyed and I decided she must have hated Peredur. He had feared her and she had hated him, and if it was true that she had been able to see the future, then she had seen me and given her husband bad advice to make that future come true.

"So where do you go now?" Svein asked. We were walking along the beach, past the huddled slaves who watched us with dark, resentful eyes.

"I have a mind," I said, "to go into the Sæfern Sea."

"There's nothing left there," he said scornfully.

"Nothing?"

"It's been scoured," he said, meaning that Danish and Norse ships had bled the coasts dry of any treasure. "All you'll find in the Sæfern Sea," he went on, "are our ships bringing men from Ireland."

"To attack Wessex?"

"No!" He grinned at me. "I've a mind to start trading with the Welsh kingdoms."

"And I have a mind," I said, "to take my ship to the moon and build a feasting hall there."

He laughed. "But speaking of Wessex," he said, "I hear they're building a church where you killed Ubba."

"I hear the same."

"A church with an altar of gold."

"I've heard that, too," I allowed. I hid my surprise that he knew of Odda the Younger's plans, but I should not have been surprised. A rumor of gold would spread like couch grass. "I've heard it," I said again, "but I don't believe it."

"Churches have money," he said thoughtfully, then frowned, "but that's a strange place to build a church."

"Strange? Why?"

"So close to the sea? An easy place to attack?"

"Or perhaps they want you to attack," I said, "and have men ready to defend it?"

"A lure, you mean?" He thought about that.

"And hasn't Guthrum given orders that the West Saxons aren't to be provoked?" I said.

"Guthrum can order what he wants," Svein said harshly, "but I am Svein of the White Horse and I don't take orders from Guthrum." He walked on, frowning as he threaded the fishing nets that men now dead had hung to dry. "Men say Alfred is not a fool."

"Nor is he."

"If he has put valuables beside the sea," he said, "he will not leave them unguarded." He was a warrior, but like the best warriors he was no madman. When folk speak of the Danes these days they have an idea that they were all savage pagans, unthinking in their terrible violence, but most were like Svein and feared losing men. That was always the great Danish fear, and the Danish weakness. Svein's ship was called the **White Horse** and had a crew of fifty-three men, and if a dozen of those men were to be killed or gravely wounded, then the **White Horse** would be fatally weakened. Once in a fight, of course, he was like all Danes, terrifying, but there was always a good deal of thinking before there was any fighting. He scratched at a louse, then gestured toward the slaves his men had taken. "Besides, I have these."

He meant he would not go to Cynuit. The slaves, once they were sold, would bring him silver and he must have reckoned Cynuit was not worth the casualties.

Svein needed my help next morning. His own ship was in Callyn's harbor and he asked me to take him and a score of his men to fetch it. We left the rest of his crew at Peredur's settlement. They guarded the slaves he would take away, and they also burned the place as we carried Svein east up the coast to Callyn's settlement. We waited a day there as Svein settled his accounts with Callyn, and we used the time to sell fleeces and tin to Callyn's traders and, though we received a poor enough price, it was better to travel with silver than with bulky cargo. The **Fyrdraca** was glittering with silver now and the crewmen, knowing they would receive their proper share, were happy. Haesten wanted to go with Svein, but I refused his request. "I saved your life," I told him, "and you have to serve me longer to pay for that." He accepted that and was pleased when I gave him a second arm ring as a reward for the men he had killed at Dreyndynas.

Svein's **White Horse** was smaller than **Fyrdraca**. Her prow had a carved horse's head and her stern a wolf's head, while at her masthead was a wind vane decorated with a white horse. I asked Svein about the horse and he laughed. "When I was sixteen," he said, "I wagered my father's stallion against our king's white horse. I had to beat the king's champion at wrestling and sword play. My father beat me for making the wager, but I won! So the white horse is lucky. I ride only white horses." And so his ship was the **White Horse** and I followed her back up the coast to where a thick plume of smoke marked where Peredur had ruled.

"Are we staying with him?" Leofric asked, puzzled that we were going back west rather than turning toward Defnascir.

"I have a mind to see where Britain ends," I said, and I had no wish to return to the Uisc and to Mildrith's misery.

Svein put the slaves into the belly of his boat. We spent one last night in the bay, under the thick smoke, and in the morning, as the rising sun flickered across the sea, we rowed away. As we passed the western headland, going into the wide ocean, I saw a man watching us from the cliff's top and I saw he was robed in black and, though he was a long way off, I thought I recognized Asser. Iseult saw him, too, and she hissed like a cat, made a fist, and threw it at him, opening her fingers at the last moment as if casting a spell at the monk.

Then I forgot him because **Fyrdraca** was back in the open sea and we were going to the place where the world ended.

And I had a shadow queen for company.

FOUR

I love the sea. I grew up beside it, though in my memories the seas off Bebbanburg are gray, usually sullen, and rarely sunlit. They are nothing like the great waters that roll from beyond the Isles of the Dead to thunder and shatter against the rocks at the west of Britain. The sea heaves there, as if the ocean gods flexed their muscles, and the white birds cry endlessly, and the wind rattles the spray against the cliffs. **Fyrdraca**, running before that bright wind, left a path in the sea and the steering oar fought me, pulsing with the life of the water and the flexing of the ship and the joy of the passage. Iseult stared at me, astonished by my happiness, but then I gave her the oar and watched her thin body heave against the sea's strength until she understood the power of the oar and could move the ship, and then she laughed. "I would live on the sea," I told her, though she did not understand me. I had given her an arm ring from Peredur's hoard and a silver toe ring and a necklace of monster's teeth, all sharp and long and white, strung on a silver wire.

I turned and watched Svein's **White Horse** cut through the water. Her bow would sometimes break from a wave so that the forepart of her hull, all green and dark with growth, would rear skyward with her horse's head snarling at the sun, and then she would crash down and the seas would explode white about her timbers. Her oars, like ours, were inboard and the oar holes plugged, and we both ran under sail. **Fyrdraca** was the faster ship, which was not because she was more cunningly built, but because her hull was longer.

There is such joy in a good ship, and a greater joy to have the ship's belly fat with other men's silver. It is the Viking joy, driving a dragon-headed hull through a wind-driven sea toward a future full of feasts and laughter. The Danes taught me that and I love them for it, pagan swine though they might be. At that moment, running before Svein's **White Horse**, I was as happy as a man could be, free of all the churchmen and laws and duties of Alfred's Wessex, but then I gave orders that the sail was to be lowered and a dozen men uncleated the lines and the big yard scraped down the mast. We had come to Britain's ending and I would turn about, and I waved to Svein as the **White Horse** swept past us. He waved back, watching the **Fyrdraca** wallow in the long ocean swells.

"Seen enough?" Leofric asked me.

I was staring at the end of Britain where the rocks endured the sea's assault. "Penwith," Iseult said, giving me the British name for the headland.

"You want to go home?" I asked Leofric.

He shrugged. The crew was turning the yard, lining it fore and aft so it could be stowed on its crutches while other men were binding the sail so it did not flap. The oars were being readied to take us eastward and the **White Horse** was getting smaller as it swept up into the Sæfern Sea.

I stared after Svein, envying him. "I need to be rich," I said to Leofric.

He laughed at that.

"I have a path to follow," I said, "and it goes north. North back to Bebbanburg. And Bebbanburg has never been captured, so I need many men to take it. Many good men and many sharp swords."

"We have silver," he said, gesturing into the boat's bilge.

"Not enough," I answered sourly. My enemies had money and Alfred claimed that I owed the church money, and the courts of Defnascir would be chasing me for wergild. I could only go home if I had enough silver to pay off the church, to bribe the courts, and to attract men to my banner. I stared at the **White Horse** that was now little more than a sail above the wind-fretted sea and I felt the old temptation to go with the Danes. Wait till Ragnar was free and give him my sword arm, but then I would be fighting against Leofric and I would still need to make money, raise men, go north, and fight for my birthright. I touched Thor's hammer and prayed for a sign.

Iseult spat. That was not quite true. She said a word that sounded like someone clearing their throat, spitting and choking all at the same time, and she was pointing over the ship's side and I saw a strange fish arcing out of the water. The fish was as big as a deerhound and had a triangular fin. "Porpoise," Leofric said.

"**Llamhydydd**," Iseult said again, giving the fish its British name.

"They bring sailors luck," Leofric said.

I had never seen a porpoise before, but suddenly there were a dozen of the creatures. They were gray and their backs glistened in the sun and they were all going north.

"Put the sail back up," I told Leofric.

He stared at me. The crew was unlashing the oars and taking the plugs from the oar holes. "You want the sail up?" Leofric asked.

"We're going north." I had prayed for a sign and Thor had sent me the porpoise.

"There's nothing in the Sæfern Sea," Leofric said. "Svein told you that."

"Svein told me there was no plunder in the Sæfern Sea," I said, "because the Danes have taken it all, so that means the Danes have the plunder." I felt a surge of happiness so intense that I punched Leofric's shoulder and gave Iseult a hug. "And he told me that their ships are coming from Ireland."

"So?" Leofric rubbed his shoulder.

"Men from Ireland!" I told Leofric. "Danes coming from Ireland to attack Wessex. And if you brought a ship's crew from Ireland, what would you bring with you?"

"Everything you possess," Leofric said flatly.

"And they don't know we're here! They're sheep, and we are a fire-dragon."

He grinned. "You're right," he said.

"Of course I'm right! I'm a lord! I'm right and I'm going to be rich! We're all going to be rich! We shall eat off gold plates, piss down our enemies' throats, and make their wives into our whores." I was shouting this nonsense as I walked down the boat's center, casting off the sail's lashings. "We'll all be rich with silver shoes and golden bonnets. We'll be richer than kings! We'll wallow in silver, shower our whores with gold, and shit lumps of amber! Tie those oars up! Plug the holes, we're going north, we're going to be rich as bishops, every man of us!" The men were grinning, pleased because I was roaring my enthusiasm, and men like to be led.

They did have qualms about going north, for that would take us out of sight of land, and I had never been that far from the shore, and I was frightened, too, for Ragnar the Older had often told me tales of Norsemen who had been tempted out into the sea wastes, to sail ever farther westward, and he said there were lands out there, lands beyond the Isles of the Dead, lands where ghosts walked, but I am not sure if he told the truth. I am sure, though, that he told me that many of those ships never returned. They voyage into the dying sun and they go onward because they cannot bear to turn back and so they sail to where the lost ships die at the world's dark ending.

Yet the world did not end to the north. I knew that, though I was not certain what did lie northward. Dyfed was there, somewhere, and Ireland, and there were other places with barbarous names and savage people who lived like hungry dogs on the wild edges of the land, but there was also a waste of sea, a wilderness of empty waves, and so, once the sail was hoisted and the wind was thrusting the **Fyrdraca** northward, I leaned on the oar to take her somewhat to the east for fear we would otherwise be lost in the ocean's vastness.

"You know where you're going?" Leofric asked me.

"No."

"Do you care?"

I grinned at him for answer. The wind, which had been southerly, came more from the west, and the tide took us eastward, so that by the afternoon I could see land, and I thought it must

be the land of the Britons on the north side of
the Sæfern, but as we came closer I saw it was an
island. I later discovered it was the place the
Northmen call Lundi, because that is their word
for the puffin, and the island's high cliffs were
thick with the birds that shrieked at us when we
came into a cove on the western side of the island that was an uncomfortable place to anchor
for the night because the big seas rolled in. And
so we dropped the sail, took out the oars, and
rowed around the cliffs until we found shelter on
the eastern side.

I went ashore with Iseult and we dug some
puffin burrows to find eggs, though all were
hatched, so we contented ourselves with killing a
pair of goats for the evening meal. There was no
one living on the island, though there had been
because there were the remains of a small church
and a field of graves. The Danes had burned
everything, pulled down the church, and dug up
the graves in search of gold. We climbed to a high
place and I searched the evening sea for ships,
but saw none, though I wondered if I could see
land to the south. It was hard to be sure for the
southern horizon was thick with dark cloud, but
a darker strip within the cloud could have been

hills and I assumed I was looking at Cornwalum or the western part of Wessex. Iseult sang to herself.

I watched her. She was gutting one of the dead goats, doing it clumsily for she was not accustomed to such work. She was thin, so thin that she looked like the ælfcynn, the elf-kind, but she was happy. In time I would learn just how much she had hated Peredur. He had valued her and made her a queen, but he had also kept her a prisoner in his hall so that he alone could profit from her powers. Folk would pay Peredur to hear Iseult's prophecies and one of the reasons Callyn had fought his neighbor was to take Iseult for himself. Shadow queens were valued among the Britons for they were part of the old mysteries, the powers that had brooded over the land before the monks arrived, and Iseult was one of the last shadow queens. She had been born in the sun's darkness, but now she was free and I was to find she had a soul as wild as a falcon. Mildrith, poor Mildrith, wanted order and routine. She wanted the hall swept, the clothes clean, the cows milked, the sun to rise, the sun to set, and for nothing to change, but Iseult was different. She was strange, shadow-born, and full of mystery. Nothing she said to me those first days made any sense, for we had no language in common, but on the island, as the sun set and I took the knife to finish cutting the entrails from the goat, she plucked twigs and wove a small cage. She showed me the cage, broke it, and then, with her long white fingers, mimed a bird flying free. She pointed to herself, tossed the twig scraps away, and laughed.

Next morning, still ashore, I saw boats. There were two of them and they were sailing to the west of the island, going northward. They were small craft, probably traders from Cornwalum, and they were running before the southwest wind toward the hidden shore where I assumed Svein had taken the **White Horse**.

We followed the two small ships. By the time we had waded out to **Fyrdraca**, raised her anchor, and rowed her from the lee of the island, both boats were almost out of sight, but once our sail was hoisted we began to overhaul them. They must have been terrified to see a dragon ship shoot out from behind the island, but I lowered the sail a little to slow us down and so followed them for much of the day until, at last, a blue-gray line showed at the sea's edge. Land. We hoisted the sail fully and seethed past the two small, tubby boats, and so, for the first time, I came to the shore of Wales. The Britons had another name for it, but we simply called it Wales, which means "foreigners," and much later I worked out that we must have made that landfall in Dyfed, which is the name of the churchman who converted the Britons of Wales to Christianity and had the westernmost kingdom of the Welsh named for him.

We found a deep inlet for shelter. Rocks guarded the entrance, but once inside we were safe from wind and sea. We turned the ship so that her bows faced the open sea, and the cove was so narrow that our stern scraped stone as we slewed **Fyrdraca** about, and then we slept on board, men and their women sprawled under the rowers' benches. There were a dozen women aboard, all captured from Peredur's tribe, and one of them managed to escape that night, presumably sliding over the side and swimming to shore. It was not Iseult. She and I slept in the small black space beneath the steering platform, a hole screened by a cloak, and Leofric woke me there in the dawn, worried that the missing woman would raise the country against us. I shrugged. "We won't be here long."

But we stayed in the cove all day. I wanted to ambush ships coming around the coast and we saw two, but they traveled together and I could not attack more than one ship at a time. Both ships were under sail, riding the southwest wind, and both were Danish, or perhaps Norse, and both were laden with warriors. They must have come from Ireland, or perhaps from the east coast of Northumbria, and doubtless they traveled to join Svein, lured by the prospect of capturing good West Saxon land. "Burgweard should have the whole fleet up here," I said. "He could tear through these bastards."

Two horsemen came to look at us in the afternoon. One had a glinting chain about his neck, suggesting he was of high rank, but neither man came down to the shingle beach. They watched from the head of the small valley that fell to the cove and after a while they went away. The sun was low now, but it was summer, so the days were long. "If they bring men—" Leofric said as the two horsemen rode away, but he did not finish the thought.

I looked up at the high bluffs either side of the cove. Men could rain rocks down from those heights and the **Fyrdraca** would be crushed like an egg. "We could put sentries up there," I suggested, but just then Eadric, who led the men who occupied the forward steorbord benches, shouted that there was a ship in sight. I ran forward and there she was.

The perfect prey.

She was a large ship, not so big as **Fyrdraca**, but large all the same, and she was riding low in the water for she was so heavily laden. Indeed, she carried so many people that her crew had not dared raise the sail for, though the wind was not heavy, it would have bent her leeward side dangerously close to the water. So she was being rowed and now she was close inshore, evidently looking for a place where she could spend the night and her crew had plainly been tempted by our cove and only now realized that we already filled it. I could see a man in her bows pointing farther up the coast and meanwhile my men were arming themselves, and I shouted at Haesten to take the steering oar. He knew what to do and I was confident he would do it well, even though it might mean the death of fellow Danes. We cut the lines that had tethered us to the shore as Leofric brought me my mail coat, helmet, and shield. I dressed for battle as the oars were shipped, then pulled on my helmet so that suddenly the edges of my vision were darkened by its faceplate.

"Go!" I shouted, and the oars bit and the

Fyrdraca surged out. Some of the oar blades struck rock as we pulled, but none broke, and I was staring at the ship ahead, so close now, and her prow was a snarling wolf, and I could see men and women staring at us, not believing what they saw. They thought they saw a Danish ship, one of their own, yet we were armed and we were coming for them. A man shouted a warning and they scrambled for their weapons, and Leofric yelled at our men to put their hearts into the oars, and the long shafts bent under the strain as **Fyrdraca** leaped across the small waves and I yelled at the men to leave the oars, to come to the bows, and Cenwulf and the twelve men he commanded were already there as our big bows slammed through the enemy oars, snapping them.

Haesten had done well. I had told him to steer for the forward part of the ship, where her freeboard was low, and our bows rode up across her strakes, plunging her low in the water, and we staggered with the impact, but then I jumped down into the wolf-headed ship's belly. Cenwulf and his men were behind me, and there we began the killing.

The enemy ship was so loaded with men that they probably outnumbered us, but they were bone weary from a long day's rowing, they had not expected an attack, and we were hungry for wealth. We had done this before and the crew was well trained, and they chopped their way down the boat, swords and axes swinging, and the sea was slopping over the side so that we waded through water as we clambered over the rowers' benches. The water about our feet grew red. Some of our victims jumped overboard and clung to shattered oars in an attempt to escape us. One man, big-bearded and wild-eyed, came at us with a great sword and Eadric drove a spear into his chest and Leofric struck the man's head with his ax, struck again, and blood sprayed up to the sail that was furled fore and aft on its long yard. The man sank to his knees and Eadric ground the spear deeper so that blood spilled down to the water. I half fell as a wave tilted the half-swamped ship. A man screamed and lunged a spear at me. I took it on my shield, knocked it aside, and rammed Serpent-Breath at his face. He half fell, trying to escape the lunge, and I knocked him over the side with my shield's heavy boss. I sensed movement to my right and swung Serpent-Breath like a reaping scythe and struck a woman in the head. She went down like a felled calf, a sword in her hand. I kicked the sword away and stamped on the woman's belly. A child screamed and I shoved her aside, lunged at a man in a leather jerkin, raised my shield to block his ax blow, and then spitted him on Serpent-Breath. The sword went deep into his belly, so deep that the blade stuck and I had to stand on him to tug it free. Cenwulf went past me, his snarling face covered in blood, sword swinging. The water was up to my knees, and then I staggered and almost fell as the whole ship lurched and I realized we had drifted ashore and struck rocks. Two horses were tethered in the ship's belly and the beasts screamed at the smell of blood. One broke its tether and jumped overboard, swimming white-eyed toward the open sea.

"Kill them! Kill them!" I heard myself shouting. It was the only way to take a ship, to empty her of fighting men, but she was now emptying herself as the survivors jumped onto the rocks and clambered away through the sucking backwash of blood-touched water. A half dozen men had been left aboard **Fyrdraca** and they were fending her off the rocks with oars. A blade stabbed the back of my right ankle and I turned to see a wounded man trying to hamstring me with a short knife. I stabbed down again and again, butchering him in the weltering water, and I think he was the last man to die on board, though a few Danes were still clinging to the ship's side and those we cut away.

The **Fyrdraca** was seaward of the doomed ship now, and I shouted at the men aboard to bring her close. She heaved up and down, much higher than the half-sunk ship, and we threw our plunder up and over the side. There were sacks, boxes, and barrels. Many were heavy, and some clinked with coin. We stripped the enemy dead of their valuables, taking six coats of mail and a dozen helmets and we found another three coats of mail in the flooded bilge. I took eight arm rings off dead men. We tossed weapons aboard **Fyrdraca**, then cut away the captured ship's rigging. I loosed the remaining horse that stood shivering as the water rose. We took the ship's yard and sail, and all the time her survivors watched from the shore where some had found a precarious refuge above the sea-washed rocks. I went to the space beneath her sleeping platform and found a great war-helm there, a beautiful thing with a decorated faceplate and a wolf's head molded in silver on the crown, and I tossed my old helmet onto **Fyrdraca** and donned the new one, and then passed out sacks of coin. Beneath the sacks was what I thought must be a small shield wrapped in black cloth and I half thought of leaving it where it was, then threw it into **Fyrdraca** anyway. We were rich.

"Who are you?" a man shouted from onshore.

"Uhtred," I called back.

He spat at me and I laughed. Our men were climbing back on board **Fyrdraca** now. Some were retrieving oars from the water, and Leofric was pushing **Fyrdraca** away, fearful that she would be caught on the rocks. "Get on board!" he shouted at me, and I saw I was the last man, and so I took hold of **Fyrdraca**'s stern, put a foot on an oar, and heaved myself over her side. "Row!" Leofric shouted, and so we pulled away from the wreck.

Two young women had been thrown up with the plunder and I found them weeping by **Fyrdraca**'s mast. One spoke no language that I recognized and later we discovered she was from Ireland, but the other was Danish and, as soon as I squatted beside her, she lashed out at me and spat in my face. I slapped her back, and that made her lash out again. She was a tall girl, strong, with a tangled mass of fair hair and bright blue eyes. She tried to claw her fingers through the eyeholes of my new helmet and I had to slap her again, which made my men laugh. Some were shouting at her to keep fighting me, but instead she suddenly burst into tears and leaned back against the mast root. I took off the helmet and asked her name, and her only answer was to wail that she wanted to die, but when I said she was free to throw herself off the ship she did not move. Her name was Freyja, she was fifteen years old, and her father had been the owner of the ship we had sunk. He had been the big man with the sword, and his name had been Ivar and he had held land at Dyflin, wherever that was, and Freyja began to weep again when she looked at my new helmet, which had belonged to her father. "He died without cutting his nails," she said accusingly, as if I was responsible for that ill luck, and it was bad fortune indeed because now the grim things of the underworld would use Ivar's nails to build the ship that would bring chaos at the world's end.

"Where were you going?" I asked her.

To Svein, of course. Ivar had been unhappy in Dyflin, which was in Ireland and had more Norsemen than Danes and also possessed savagely unfriendly native tribes, and he had been lured by the prospect of land in Wessex and so he had abandoned his Irish steading, put all his goods and wealth aboard his ships, and sailed eastward.

"Ships?" I asked her.

"There were three when we left," Freyja said, "but we lost the others in the night."

I guessed they were the two ships we had seen earlier, but the gods had been good to me for Freyja confirmed that her father had put his most valuable possessions into his own ship, and that was the one we had captured, and we had struck lucky for there were barrels of coins and boxes of silver. There was amber, jet, and ivory. There were weapons and armor. We made a rough count as the **Fyrdraca** wallowed offshore and we could scarce believe our fortune. One box contained small lumps of gold, roughly shaped as bricks, but best of all was the wrapped bundle that I had thought was a small shield, but, when we unwrapped the cloth, proved to be a great silver plate on which was modeled a crucifixion. All about the death scene, ringing the plate's heavy rim, were saints. Twelve of them. I assumed they were the apostles and that the plate had been the treasure of some Irish church or monastery before Ivar had captured it. I showed the plate to my men. "This," I said reverently, "is not part of the plunder. This must go back to the church."

Leofric caught my eye, but did not laugh.

"It goes back to the church," I said again, and some of my men, the more pious ones, muttered that I was doing the right thing. I wrapped the plate and put it under the steering platform.

"How much is your debt to the church?" Leofric asked me.

"You have a mind like a goat's arsehole," I told him.

He laughed, then looked past me. "Now what do we do?" he asked.

I thought he was asking what we should do with the rest of our charmed lives, but instead he was gazing at the shore where, in the evening light, I could see armed men lining the cliff top. The Britons of Dyfed had come for us, but too late. Yet their presence meant we could not go back into our cove, and so I ordered the oars to be manned and for the ship to row eastward. The Britons followed us along the shore. The woman who had escaped in the night must have told them we were Saxons and they must have been praying we would seek refuge on land so they could kill us. Few ships stayed at sea overnight, not unless they were forced to, but I dared not seek shelter and so I turned south and rowed away from the shore, while in the west the sun leaked red fire through rifts in the cloud so that the whole sky glowed as if a god had bled across the heavens.

"What will you do with the girl?" Leofric asked me.

"Freyja?"

"Is that her name? You want her?"

"No," I said.

"I do."

"She'll eat you alive," I warned him. She was probably a head taller than Leofric.

"I like them like that," he said.

"All yours," I said, and such is life. One day Freyja was the pampered daughter of an earl and the next she was a slave.

I gave the coats of mail to those who deserved them. We had lost two men, and another three were badly injured, but that was a light cost. We had, after all, killed twenty or thirty Danes and the survivors were ashore where the Britons might or might not treat them well. Best of all, we had become rich and that knowledge was a consolation as night fell.

Hoder is the god of the night and I prayed to

him. I threw my old helmet overboard as a gift to him, because all of us were scared of the dark that swallowed us, and it was a complete dark because clouds had come from the west to smother the sky. No moon, no stars. For a time there was the gleam of firelight on the northern shore, but that vanished and we were blind. The wind rose, the seas heaved us, and we brought the oars inboard and let the air and water carry us for we could neither see nor steer. I stayed on deck, peering into the dark, and Iseult stayed with me, under my cloak, and I remembered the look of delight on her face when we had gone into battle.

Dawn was gray and the sea was white-streaked gray and the wind was cold, and there was no land in sight, but two white birds flew over us and I took them for a sign and rowed in the direction they had gone, and late that day, in a bitter sea and cold rain, we saw land and it was the Isle of Puffins again where we found shelter in the cove and made fires ashore.

"When the Danes know what we've done—" Leofric said.

"They'll look for us." I finished the sentence for him.

"Lots of them will look for us."

"Then it's time to go home," I said.

The gods had been good to us and, next dawn, in a calming sea, we rowed south to the land and followed the coast toward the west. We would go around the wild headlands where the porpoises swam, turn east, and so find home.

Much later I discovered what Svein had done after we parted company and, because what he did affected my life and made the enmity between me and Alfred worse, I shall tell it here.

I suspect that the thought of a gold altar at Cynuit had gnawed into his heart, for he carried the dream back to Glwysing where his men gathered. Glwysing was another kingdom of the Britons in the south of Wales, a place where there were good harbors and where the king welcomed the Danes, for their presence prevented Guthrum's men from raiding across the Mercian border.

Svein ordered a second ship and its crew to accompany him and together they attacked Cynuit. They came in the dawn, hidden by a mist, and I can imagine their beast-headed ships appearing in the early grayness like monsters from nightmare. They went upriver, oars splashing, then grounded the boats and the crews streamed ashore, men in mail and helmets, spear Danes, sword Danes, and they found the half-built church and monastery.

Odda the Younger was making the place, but he knew it was too close to the sea and so he had decided to make it a fortified building. The church's tower was to be of stone, and high enough for men to keep a watch from its summit, and the priests and monks were to be surrounded by a palisade and a flooded ditch, but when Svein came ashore none of the work was finished and so was indefensible, and besides, there were scarce forty troops there and those all died or fled within minutes of the Danes landing. The Danes then burned what work had been done and cut down the high wooden cross that customarily marked a monastery and had been the first thing the builders had made.

The builders were monks, many of them novices, and Svein herded them together and demanded they show him where the valuables were hidden and promised them mercy if they told the truth. Which they did. There was not much of value, certainly no altar of gold, but supplies and timber needed to be purchased and so the monks had a chest of silver pennies, which was reward enough for the Danes, who then pulled

down the half-constructed church tower,
wrecked the unfinished palisade, and slaughtered some cattle. Then Svein asked the monks
where Ubba was buried and was met by sullen
silence, and the swords were drawn again and
the question asked a second time, and the monks
were forced to confess that the church was being
built directly over the dead chieftain's grave.
That grave had been an earth mound, but the
monks had dug it up and thrown the body into
the river, and when the Danes heard that story
the mercy fled from their souls.

The monks were made to wade in the river
until some bones were found, and those bones
were placed on a funeral pyre made from the
timbers of the half-constructed buildings. It was,
by all accounts, a huge pyre, and when it was lit,
and when the bones were at the heart of a fur-
nace blaze, the monks were thrown onto the
flames. While their bodies burned the Danes selected two girls, captured from the soldiers' shelters, raped them, and then strangled them,
sending their souls to be company for Ubba in
Valhalla. We heard all this from two children who
survived by hiding in a nettle patch, and some
folk from the nearby town who were dragged to
see the end of the funeral pyre. "Svein of the

White Horse did this," they were told, and made to repeat the words. It was a Danish custom to leave some witnesses to their horror, so that the tales would spread fear and make cowards of other folk who might be attacked, and sure enough the story of the burned monks and murdered girls went through Wessex like a high wind through dry grass. It became exaggerated, as such tales do. The number of dead monks went from sixteen to sixty, the raped girls from two to twenty, and the stolen silver from a chest of pennies to a hoard worthy of the gods. Alfred sent a message to Guthrum, demanding to know why he should not slaughter the hostages he held, and Guthrum sent him a present of gold, two captured gospel books, and a groveling letter in which he claimed that the two ships had not been from his forces, but were pirates from beyond the sea. Alfred believed him and so the hostages lived and the peace prevailed, but Alfred commanded that a curse should be pronounced on Svein in every church of Wessex. The Danish chieftain was to be damned through all eternity, his men were to burn in the fires of hell, and his children and his children's children were all to bear the mark of Cain. I asked a priest what the mark was, and he explained that Cain was the son of Adam and Eve and the first murderer, but he did not know what mark he had carried. He thought God would recognize it.

So Svein's two ships sailed away, leaving a pillar of smoke on the Wessex shore, and I knew none of it. In time I would know all of it, but for now I was going home.

We went slowly, sheltering each night, retracing our steps that took us past the blackened hillside where Peredur's settlement had stood, and on we went, under a summer's sun and rain, until we had returned to the Uisc.

The **Heahengel** was afloat now and her mast was stepped, which meant Leofric could take her and the **Eftwyrd**, for the **Fyrdraca** was no more, back to Hamtun. We divided the plunder first and, though Leofric and I took the greater share, every man went away wealthy. I was left with Haesten and Iseult, and I took them up to Oxton where Mildrith wept with relief because she had thought I might be dead. I told her we had been patrolling the coast, which was true enough, and that we had captured a Danish ship laden with wealth, and I spilled the coins and gold bricks onto the floor and gave her a bracelet of amber and a necklace of jet, and the gifts distracted her from Iseult who watched her with wide, dark eyes, and if Mildrith saw the British girl's jewelry she said nothing.

We had come back in time for the harvest, though it was poor for there had been much rain that summer. There was a black growth on the rye, which meant it could not even be fed to the animals, though the straw was good enough to thatch the hall I built. I have always enjoyed building. I made the hall from clay, gravel, and straw, all packed together to make thick walls. Oak beams straddled the walls, and oak rafters held a high, long roof that looked golden when the thatch was first combed into place. The walls were painted with powdered lime in water, and one of the local men poured oxblood into the mix so that the walls were the color of a summer sky at sunset. The hall's great door faced east toward the Uisc and I paid a man from Exanceaster to carve the doorposts and lintels with writhing wolves, for the banner of Bebbanburg, my banner, is a wolf's head. Mildrith wanted the carving to show saints, but she got wolves. I paid the builders well, and when other men heard that I had silver they came looking for employment, and though they were there to build my hall I took only those who had experience fighting. I equipped them with spades, axes, adzes, weapons, and shields.

"You are making an army," Mildrith accused me. Her relief at my homecoming had soured quickly when it was apparent that I was no more a Christian than when I had left her.

"Seventeen men? An army?"

"We are at peace," she said. She believed that because the priests preached it, and the priests only said what they were told to say by the bishops, and the bishops took their orders from Alfred. A traveling priest sought shelter with us one night and he insisted that the war with the Danes was over.

"We still have Danes on the border," I said.

"God has calmed their hearts," the priest insisted, and told me that God had killed the Lothbrok brothers, Ubba, Ivar, and Halfdan, and that the rest of the Danes were so shocked by the deaths that they no longer dared to fight against Christians. "It is true, lord," the priest said earnestly. "I heard it preached in Cippanhamm, and the king was there and he praised God for the truth of it. We are to beat our swords into ard points and our spear blades into reaping hooks."

I laughed at the thought of melting Serpent-Breath into a tool to plow Oxton's fields, but then I did not believe the priest's nonsense. The Danes were biding their time, that was all, yet it did seem peaceful as the summer slid imperceptibly into autumn. No enemies crossed the frontier of Wessex and no ships harried our coasts. We threshed the corn, netted partridges, hunted deer on the hill, staked nets in the river, and practiced with our weapons. The women spun thread, gathered nuts, and picked mushrooms and blackberries. There were apples and pears, for this was the time of plenty, the time when the livestock was fattened before the winter slaughter. We ate like kings and, when my hall was finished, I gave a feast and Mildrith saw the ox head over the door and knew it was an offering to Thor, but said nothing.

Mildrith hated Iseult, which was hardly surprising, for I had told Mildrith that Iseult was a queen of the Britons and that I held her for the ransom that the Britons would offer. I knew no such ransom would ever come, and the story went some way to explaining Iseult's presence, but Mildrith resented that the British girl was given her own house. "She is a queen," I said.

"You take her hunting," Mildrith said resentfully.

I did more than that, but Mildrith chose to be

blind to much of it. Mildrith wanted little more than her church, her baby, and an unvarying routine. She had charge of the women who milked the cows, churned the butter, spun wool, and collected honey, and she took immense pride that those things were done well. If a neighbor visited there would be a flurry of panic as the hall was cleaned, and she worried much about those neighbors' opinions. She wanted me to pay Oswald's wergild. It did not matter to Mildrith that the man had been caught thieving, because to pay the wergild would make peace in the valley of the Uisc. She even wanted me to visit Odda the Younger. "You could be friends," she pleaded.

"With that snake?"

"And Wirken says you have not paid the tithe."

Wirken was the priest in Exanmynster, and I hated him. "He eats and drinks the tithe," I snarled. The tithe was the payment all landholders were supposed to make to the church, and by rights I should have sent Wirken part of my harvest, but I had not. Yet the priest was often at Oxton, coming when he thought I was hunting, and he ate my food and drank my ale and was growing fat on them.

"He comes to pray with us," Mildrith said.

"He comes to eat," I said.

"And he says the bishop will take the land if we don't pay the debt."

"The debt will be paid," I said.

"When? We have the money!" She gestured at the new hall. "When?" she insisted.

"When I want to," I snarled. I did not tell her when, or how, because if I had then Wirken the priest would know, and the bishop would know. It was not enough to pay the debt. Mildrith's father had foolishly donated part of our land's future produce to the church, and I wanted that burden taken away so the debt would not go on through eternity, and to do that I needed to surprise the bishop, and so I kept Mildrith ignorant, and inevitably those arguments would end with her tears. I was bored with her and she knew it. I found her beating Iseult's maid one day. The girl was a Saxon I had given to Iseult as a servant, but she also worked in the dairy and Mildrith was beating her because some cheeses had not been turned. I dragged Mildrith away, and that, of course, provoked another argument and Mildrith proved not to be so blind after all for she accused me of trying to whelp bastards on Iseult, which was true enough, but I reminded her that her own father had sired enough bastards, half a dozen of whom now worked for us. "You leave Iseult and her maid alone," I said, causing more tears. They were not happy days.

It was the time when Iseult learned to speak English, or at least the Northumbrian version of English for she learned it mostly from me. "You're my mon," she said. I was Mildrith's man and Iseult's mon. She said she had been born again on the day I came into Peredur's hall. "I had dreamed of you," she said, "tall and golden-haired."

"Now you don't dream?" I asked, knowing that her powers of scrying came from dreams.

"I do still dream," she said earnestly. "My brother speaks to me."

"Your brother?" I asked, surprised.

"I was born a twin," she told me, "and my brother came first and then, as I was born, he died. He went to the shadow world and he speaks to me of what he sees there."

"What does he see?"

"He sees your king."

"Alfred," I said sourly. "Is that good or bad?"

"I don't know. The dreams are shadowy."

She was no Christian. Instead she believed that every place and every thing had its own god or goddess: a nymph for a stream, a dryad for a wood, a spirit for a tree, a god for the fire and another for the sea. The Christian god, like Thor or Odin, was just one more deity among this unseen throng of powers, and her dreams, she said, were like eavesdropping on the gods. One day, as she rode beside me on the hills above the empty sea, she suddenly said that Alfred would give me power.

"He hates me," I told her. "He'll give me nothing."

"He will give you power," she said flatly. I stared at her and she gazed to where the clouds met the waves. Her black hair was unbound and the sea wind stirred it. "My brother told me," she said. "Alfred will give you power and you will take back your northern home and your woman will be a creature of gold."

"My woman?"

She looked at me and there was sadness in her face. "There," she said, "now you know," and she kicked back her heels and made the horse run along the ridgetop, her hair streaming, her eyes wet with tears. I wanted to know more, but she said she had told me what she had dreamed and I must be content.

At summer's end we drove the swine into the

forests to feed on the fallen beech nuts and acorns. I bought bags of salt because the killing time was coming and the meat of our pigs and cattle would have to be salted into barrels to feed us through the winter. Some of that food would come from the men who rented land at the edge of the estate, and I visited them all so they would know I expected payment of wheat, barley, and livestock, and to show them what would happen if they tried to cheat me I bought a dozen good swords from a smith in Exanceaster. I gave the swords to my men, and in the shortening days we practiced with them. Mildrith might not believe war was coming, but I did not think God had changed Danish hearts.

The late autumn brought heavy rain and the shire reeve to Oxton. The reeve was called Harald and he was charged with keeping the peace of Defnascir, and he came on horseback and with him were six other horsemen, all in mail coats and helmets, and all with swords or spears. I waited for him in the hall, making him dismount and come into the smoky shadows. He came cautiously, expecting an ambush. Then his eyes became accustomed to the gloom and he saw me standing by the central hearth. "You are summoned to the shire court," he told me.

His men had followed Harald into the hall. "You bring swords into my house?" I asked.

Harald looked around the hall and he saw my men armed with their spears and axes. I had seen the horsemen approaching and summoned my men and ordered them to arm themselves.

Harald had the reputation of being a decent man, sensible and fair, and he knew how weapons in a hall could lead to slaughter. "You will wait outside," he told his men, and I gestured for my men to put their weapons down. "You are summoned . . ." Harald began again.

"I heard you," I said.

"There is a debt to be paid," he said, "and a man's death to make good."

I said nothing. One of my hounds growled softly and I put a hand into its fur to silence it.

"The court will meet on All Saints' Day," Harald said, "at the cathedral."

"I shall be there," I said.

He took off his helmet to reveal a balding pate fringed with brown hair. He was at least ten years older than I, a big man, with two fingers missing from his shield hand. He limped slightly as he walked toward me. I calmed the hounds, waited.

"I was at Cynuit," he said to me, speaking softly.

"So was I," I said, "though men pretend I was not."

"I know what you did," he said.

"So do I."

He ignored my surliness. He was showing me sympathy, though I was too proud to show I appreciated it. "The ealdorman has sent men," he warned me, "to take this place once judgment is given."

There was a gasp behind me and I realized Mildrith had come into the hall. Harald bowed to her.

"The hall will be taken?" Mildrith asked.

"If the debt is not paid," Harald said, "the land will be given to the church." He stared up at the newly hewn rafters as if wondering why I would build a hall on land doomed to be given to God.

Mildrith came to stand beside me. She was plainly distressed by Harald's summons, but she made a great effort to compose herself. "I am sorry," she said, "about your wife."

A flicker of pain crossed Harald's face as he made the sign of the cross. "She was sick a long time, lady. It was merciful of God, I think, to take her."

I had not known he was a widower, nor did I care much. "She was a good woman," Mildrith said.

"She was," Harald said.

"And I pray for her."

"I thank you for that," Harald said.

"As I pray for Odda the Elder," Mildrith went on.

"God be praised, he lives." Harald made the sign of the cross again. "But he is feeble and in pain." He touched his scalp showing where Odda the Elder had been wounded.

"So who is the judge?" I asked harshly, interrupting the two.

"The bishop," Harald said.

"Not the ealdorman?"

"He is at Cippanhamm."

Mildrith insisted on giving Harald and his men ale and food. She and Harald talked a long time, sharing news of neighbors and family. They were both from Defnascir and I was not, and so I knew few of the folk they talked about, but I pricked up my ears when Harald said that Odda the Younger was marrying a girl from Mercia. "She's in exile here," he said, "with her family."

"Well born?" Mildrith asked.

"Exceedingly," Harald said.

"I wish them much joy," Mildrith said with evident sincerity. She was happy that day, warmed by Harald's company, though when he had gone she chided me for being churlish. "Harald is a good man," she insisted, "a kind man. He would have given you advice. He would have helped you!"

I ignored her, but two days later I went into Exanceaster with Iseult and all my men. Including Haesten I now had eighteen warriors and I had armed them, given them shields and leather coats, and I led them through the market that always accompanied the court's sittings. There were stilt walkers and jugglers, a man who ate fire, and a dancing bear. There were singers, harpists, storytellers, beggars, and pens of sheep, goats, cattle, pigs, geese, ducks, and hens. There were fine cheeses, smoked fish, bladders of lard, pots of honey, trays of apples, and baskets of pears. Iseult, who had not been to Exanceaster before, was amazed at the size of the city, and the life of it, and the seething closeness of its houses, and I saw folk make the sign of the cross when they saw her for they had heard of the shadow queen held at Oxton and they knew her for a foreigner and a pagan.

Beggars crowded at the bishop's gate. There was a crippled woman with a blind child, men who had lost arms or legs in the wars, a score of them, and I threw them some pence. Then, because I was on horseback, I ducked under the archway of the courtyard beside the cathedral where a dozen chained felons were awaiting their fate. A group of young monks, nervous of the chained men, were plaiting beehives, while a score of armed men were clustered around three fires. They eyed my followers suspiciously as a young priest, his hands flapping, hurried across the puddles. "Weapons are not to be brought into the precinct!" he told me sternly.

"They've got weapons," I said, nodding at the men warming themselves by the flames.

"They are the reeve's men."

"Then the sooner you deal with my business," I said, "the sooner my weapons will be gone."

He looked up at me, his face anxious. "Your business?"

"Is with the bishop."

"The bishop is at prayer," the priest said reprovingly, as though I should have known that. "And he cannot see every man who comes here. You can talk to me."

I smiled and raised my voice a little. "In Cippanhamm, two years ago," I said, "your bishop was friends with Eanflæd. She has red hair and works her trade out of the Corncrake tavern. Her trade is whoring."

The priest's hands were flapping again in an attempt to persuade me to lower my voice.

"I've been with Eanflæd," I said, "and she told me about the bishop. She said—"

The monks had stopped making beehives and were listening, but the priest cut me off by half shouting. "The bishop might have a moment free."

"Then tell him I'm here," I said pleasantly.

"You are Uhtred of Oxton?" he asked.

"No," I said. "I am Lord Uhtred of Bebbanburg."

"Yes, lord."

"Sometimes known as Uhtredærwe," I added mischievously. Uhtred the Wicked.

"Yes, lord," the priest said again and hurried away.

The bishop was called Alewold and he was really the Bishop of Cridianton, but that place had not been thought as safe as Exanceaster and so for years the Bishops of Cridianton had lived in the larger town, which, as Guthrum had shown, was not the wisest decision. Guthrum's

Danes had pillaged the cathedral and the bishop's house, which was still scantily furnished, and I discovered Alewold, sitting behind a table that looked as if it had once belonged to a butcher, for its hefty top was scored with knife cuts and stained with old blood. He looked at me indignantly. "You should not be here," he said snidely.

"Why not?"

"You have business before the court tomorrow."

"Tomorrow," I said, "you sit as a judge. Today you are a bishop."

He acknowledged that with a small nod. He was an elderly man with a heavy jowled face and a reputation as a severe judge. He had been with Alfred in Scireburnan when the Danes arrived in Exanceaster, which is why he was still alive, and, like all the bishops in Wessex, he was a fervent supporter of the king, and I had no doubt that Alfred's dislike of me was known to Alewold, which meant I could expect little clemency when the court sat.

"I am busy," Alewold said, gesturing at the parchments on the stained table. Two clerks shared the table and a half dozen resentful priests had gathered behind the bishop's chair.

"My wife," I said, "inherited a debt to the church."

Alewold looked at Iseult who alone had come into the house with me. She looked beautiful, proud, and wealthy. There was silver at her throat and in her hair, and her cloak was fastened with two brooches, one of jet and the other of amber. "Your wife?" the bishop asked snidely.

"I would discharge the debt," I said, ignoring his question, and I tipped a bag onto his butcher's table and the big silver plate we had taken from Ivar slid out. The silver made a satisfying noise as it thumped down and suddenly, in that small dark room ill lit by three rush lights and a small, wood-barred window, it seemed as if the sun had come out. The heavy silver glowed and Alewold just stared at it.

There are good priests. Beocca is one and Willibald another, but I have discovered in my long life that most churchmen preach the merits of poverty while they lust after wealth. They love money and the church attracts money like a candle brings moths. I knew Alewold was a greedy man, as greedy for wealth as he was for the delights of a red-haired whore in Cippanhamm, and he could not take his eyes from that plate. He reached out and caressed the thick rim as if he scarce believed what he was seeing, and then he pulled the plate toward him and examined the twelve apostles. "A pyx," he said reverently.

"A plate," I said casually.

One of the other priests leaned over a clerk's shoulder. "Irish work," he said.

"It looks Irish," Alewold agreed, then looked suspiciously at me. "You are returning it to the church?"

"Returning it?" I asked innocently.

"The plate was plainly stolen," Alewold said, "and you do well, Uhtred, to bring it back."

"I had the plate made for you," I said.

He turned the plate over, which took some effort for it was heavy, and once it was inverted he pointed to the scratches in the silver. "It is old," he said.

"I had it made in Ireland," I said grandly, "and doubtless it was handled roughly by the men who brought it across the sea."

He knew I was lying. I did not care. "There are silversmiths in Wessex who could have made you a pyx," one of the priests snapped.

"I thought you might want it," I said, then leaned forward and pulled the plate out of the bishop's hands, "but if you prefer West Saxon work," I went on, "then I can—"

"Give it back!" Alewold said and, when I made no move to obey, his voice became pleading. "It is a beautiful thing." He could see it in his church, or perhaps in his hall, and he wanted it. There was silence as he stared at it. If he had known that the plate existed, if I had told Mildrith of it, then he would have had a response ready, but as it was he was overwhelmed by desire for the heavy silver. A maid brought in a flagon and he waved her out of the room. She was, I noted, red-haired. "You had the plate made," Alewold said skeptically.

"In Dyflin," I said.

"Is that where you went in the king's ship?" the priest who had snapped at me asked.

"We patrolled the coast," I said, "nothing more."

"The value of the plate—" Alewold began, then stopped.

"Is far and above the debt Mildrith inherited," I said. That was probably not true, but it was close to the amount, and I could see Alewold did not care. I was going to get what I wanted.

The debt was discharged. I insisted on having that written down, and written three times, and I surprised them by being able to read and so discovering that the first scrap of parchment made no mention of the church yielding their rights to the future produce of my estate, but that was corrected and I let the bishop keep one copy while I took two. "You will not be arraigned for debt," the bishop said as he pressed his seal into the wax of the last copy, "but there is still the matter of Oswald's wergild."

"I rely on your good and wise judgment, bishop," I said, and I opened the purse hanging at my waist and took out a small lump of gold, making sure he could see there was more gold inside as I placed the small lump on the plate. "Oswald was a thief."

"His family will make oaths that he was not," the priest said.

"And I will bring men who will swear he was," I said. A trial relied heavily on oaths, but both sides would bring as many liars as they could muster, and judgment usually went to the better liars or, if both sides were equally convincing, to the side who had the sympathy of the onlookers. It was better, though, to have the sympathy of the judge. Oswald's family would have many supporters around Exanceaster, but gold is much the best argument in a law court.

And so it proved. To Mildrith's astonishment the debt was paid and Oswald's family denied two hundred shillings of wergild. I did not even bother to go to the court, relying on the persuasive power of gold, and sure enough the bishop peremptorily dismissed the demand for wergild, saying it was well known that Oswald had been a thief, and so I won. That did not make me any more popular. To the folk who lived in the Uisc's valley I was a Northumbrian interloper and, worse, it was known I was a pagan, but none dared confront me for I went nowhere beyond the estate without my men and my men went nowhere without their swords.

The harvest was in the storehouses. Now was the time for the Danes to come, when they could be sure to find food for their armies, but neither Guthrum nor Svein crossed the frontier. The winter came instead and we slaughtered the livestock, salted the meat, scraped hides, and made calves' foot jelly. I listened for the sound of church bells ringing at an unusual time, for that would have been a sign that the Danes had attacked, but the bells did not ring.

Mildrith prayed that the peace would continue and I, being young and bored, prayed it would not. She prayed to the Christian god and I took Iseult to the high woods and made a sacrifice to Hoder, Odin, and Thor and the gods were listening, for in the dark beneath the gallows tree, where the three spinners make our lives, a red thread was woven into my life. Fate is everything, and just after Yule the spinners brought a royal messenger to Oxton and he, in turn, brought me a summons. It seemed possible that Iseult's dream was true, and that Alfred would give me power for I was ordered to Cippanhamm to see the king. I was summoned to the witan.

FIVE

Mildrith was excited by the summons. The witan gave the king advice and her father had never been wealthy or important enough to receive such a summons, and she was overjoyed that the king wanted my presence. The witanegemot, as the meeting was called, was always held on the Feast of Saint Stephen, the day after Christmas, but my summons required me to be there on the twelfth day of Christmas and that gave Mildrith time to wash clothes for me. They had to be boiled and scrubbed and dried and brushed, and three women did the work and it took three days before Mildrith was satisfied that I would not disgrace her by appearing at Cippanhamm looking like a vagabond. She was not summoned, nor did she expect to accompany me, but she made a point of telling all our neighbors that I was to give counsel to the king. "You mustn't wear that," she told me, pointing to my Thor's hammer amulet.

"I always wear it," I said.

"Then hide it," she said, "and don't be belligerent!"

"Belligerent?"

"Listen to what others say," she said. "Be humble. And remember to congratulate Odda the Younger."

"For what?"

"He's to be married. Tell him I pray for them both." She was happy again, sure that by paying the church its debt I had regained Alfred's favor and her good mood was not even spoiled when I announced I would take Iseult with me. She bridled slightly at the news, then said that it was only right that Iseult should be taken to Alfred. "If she is a queen," Mildrith said, "then she belongs in Alfred's court. This isn't a fit place for her." She insisted on taking silver coins to the church in Exanceaster where she donated the money to the poor and gave thanks that I had been restored to Alfred's favor. She also thanked God for the good health of our son, Uhtred. I saw little of him, for he was still a baby and I have never had much patience for babies, but the women of Oxton constantly assured me that he was a lusty, strong boy.

We allowed two days for the journey. I took Haesten and six men as an escort for though the shire reeve's men patrolled the roads, there were plenty of wild places where outlaws preyed on travelers. We were in mail coats or leather tunics, with swords, spears, axes, and shields. We all rode. Iseult had a small black mare I had bought for her, and I had also given her an otter-skin cloak, and when we passed through villages folk would stare at her for she rode like a man, her black hair bound up with a silver chain. They would kneel to her, as well as to me, and call out for alms. She did not take her maid for I remembered how crowded every tavern and house had been in Exanceaster when the witan met, and I persuaded Iseult that we would be hard-pressed to find accommodation for ourselves, let alone a maid.

"What does the king want of you?" she asked as we rode up the Uisc valley. Rainwater puddled in the long furrows, gleaming in the winter sunshine, while the woods were glossy with holly leaves and bright with the berries of rowan, thorn, elder, and yew.

"Aren't you supposed to tell me that?" I asked her.

She smiled. "Seeing the future," she said, "is like traveling a strange road. Usually you cannot see far ahead, and when you can it is only a glimpse. And my brother doesn't give me dreams about everything."

"Mildrith thinks the king has forgiven me," I said.

"Has he?"

I shrugged. "Perhaps." I hoped so, not because I wanted Alfred's forgiveness, but because I wanted to be given command of the fleet again. I wanted to be with Leofric. I wanted the wind in my face and the sea rain on my cheek. "It's odd, though," I went on, "that he didn't want me there for the whole witanegemot."

"Maybe," Iseult suggested, "they discussed religious things at first?"

"He wouldn't want me there for that," I said.

"So that's it," she said. "They talk about their god, but at the end they will talk of the Danes, and that is why he summoned you. He knows he needs you."

"Or perhaps he just wants me there for the feast," I suggested.

"The feast?"

"The Twelfth Night feast," I explained, and that seemed to me the likeliest explanation; that

Alfred had decided to forgive me and, to show he now approved of me, would let me attend the winter feast. I secretly hoped that was true, and it was a strange hope. I had been ready to kill Alfred only a few months before, yet now, though I still hated him, I wanted his approval. Such is ambition. If I could not rise with Ragnar then I would make my reputation with Alfred.

"Your road, Uhtred," Iseult went on, "is like a bright blade across a dark moor. I see it clearly."

"And the woman of gold?"

She said nothing to that.

"Is it you?" I asked.

"The sun dimmed when I was born," she said, "so I am a woman of darkness and of silver, not of gold."

"So who is she?"

"Someone far away, Uhtred, far away," and she would say no more. Perhaps she knew no more, or perhaps she was guessing.

We reached Cippanhamm late on the eleventh day of Yule. There was still frost on the furrows and the sun was a gross red ball poised low above the tangling black branches as we came to the town's western gate. The city was full, but I was known in the Corncrake tavern where the redheaded whore called Eanflæd worked and she found us shelter in a half-collapsed cattle byre where a score of hounds had been kenneled. The hounds, she said, belonged to Huppa, Ealdorman of Thornsæta, but she reckoned the animals could survive a night or two in the yard. "Huppa may not think so," she said, "but he can rot in hell."

"He doesn't pay?" I asked her.

She spat for answer, then looked at me curiously. "I hear Leofric's here."

"He is?" I said, heartened by the news.

"I haven't seen him," she said, "but someone said he was here. In the royal hall. Maybe Burgweard brought him?" Burgweard was the new fleet commander, the one who wanted his ships to sail two by two in imitation of Christ's disciples. "Leofric had better not be here," Eanflæd finished.

"Why not?"

"Because he hasn't come to see me," she said indignantly, "that's why!" She was five or six years older than I with a broad face, a high forehead, and springy hair. She was popular, so much so that she had a good deal of freedom in the tavern that owed its profits more to her abilities than to the quality of the ale. I knew she was friendly with Leofric, but I suspected from her tone that she wanted to be more than friends. "Who's she?" she asked, jerking her head at Iseult.

"A queen," I said.

"That's another name for it, I suppose. How's your wife?"

"Back in Defnascir."

"You're like all the rest, aren't you?" She shivered. "If you're cold tonight bring the hounds back in to warm you. I'm off to work."

We were cold, but I slept well enough and, next morning, the twelfth after Christmas, I left my six men at the Corncrake and took Iseult and Haesten to the king's buildings that lay behind their own palisade to the south of the town where the river curled about the walls. A man expected to attend the witanegemot with retainers, though not usually with a Dane and a Briton, but Iseult wanted to see Alfred and I wanted to please her. Besides, there was the great feast that evening and, though I warned her that Alfred's feasts were poor things, Iseult still wanted to be there. Haesten, with his mail coat and sword, was there to protect her for I suspected she might not be allowed into the hall while the witanegemot debated and so might have to wait until evening for her chance to glimpse Alfred.

The gatekeeper demanded that we surrender our weapons, a thing I did with a bad grace, but no man, except the king's own household troops, could go armed in Alfred's presence. The day's talking had already begun, the gatekeeper told us, and so we hurried past the stables and past the big new royal chapel with its twin towers. A group of priests was huddled by the main door of the great hall and I recognized Beocca, my father's old priest, among them. I smiled in greeting, but his face, as he came toward us, was drawn and pale. "You're late," he said sharply.

"You're not pleased to see me?" I asked sarcastically.

He looked up at me. Beocca, despite his squint, red hair, and palsied left hand, had grown into a stern authority. He was now a royal chaplain, confessor, and a confidant to the king, and the responsibilities had carved deep lines on his face. "I prayed," he said, "never to see this day." He made the sign of the cross. "Who's that?" he asked, staring at Iseult.

"A queen of the Britons," I said.

"She's what?"

"A queen. She's with me. She wants to see Alfred."

I don't know whether he believed me, but he

seemed not to care. Instead he was distracted, worried, and, because he lived in a strange world of kingly privilege and obsessive piety, I assumed his misery had been caused by some petty theological dispute. He had been Bebbanburg's mass priest when I was a child and, after my father's death, he had fled Northumberland because he could not abide living among the pagan Danes. He had found refuge in Alfred's court where he had become a friend of the king. He was also a friend to me, a man who had preserved the parchments that proved my claim to the lordship of Bebbanburg, but on that twelfth day of Yule he was anything but pleased to see me. He plucked my arm, drawing me toward the door. "We must go in," he said, "and may God in his mercy protect you."

"Protect me?"

"God is merciful," Beocca said, "and you must pray for that mercy," and then the guards opened the door and we walked into the great hall. No one stopped Iseult and, indeed, there were a score of other women watching the proceedings from the edge of the hall.

There were also more than a hundred men there, though only forty or fifty comprised the witanegemot, and those thegns and senior churchmen were on chairs and benches set in a half circle in front of the dais where Alfred sat with two priests and with Ælswith, his wife, who was pregnant. Behind them, draped with a red cloth, was an altar on which stood thick candles and a heavy silver cross while all about the walls were platforms where, in normal times, folk slept or ate to be out of the fierce drafts. This day, though, the platforms were crammed with the followers of the thegns and noblemen of the witan and among them, of course, were a lot of priests and monks for Alfred's court was more like a monastery than a royal hall. Beocca gestured that Iseult and Haesten should join those spectators, then he drew me toward the half circle of privileged advisers.

No one noticed my arrival. It was dark in the hall, for little of the wintry sunshine penetrated the small high windows. Braziers tried to give some warmth, but failed, succeeding only in thickening the smoke in the high rafters. There was a large central hearth, but the fire had been taken away to make room for the witanegemot's circle of stools, chairs, and benches. A tall man in a blue cloak was on his feet as I approached. He was talking of the necessity of repairing bridges, and how local thegns were skimping the duty, and he suggested that the king appoint an official to survey the kingdom's roads. Another man interrupted to complain that such an appointment would encroach on the privileges of the shire ealdormen, and that started a chorus of voices, some for the proposal, most against, and two priests, seated at a small table beside Alfred's dais, tried to write down all the comments. I recognized Wulfhere, the Ealdorman of Wiltunscir, who yawned prodigiously. Close to him was Alewold, the Bishop of Exanceaster, who was swathed in furs. Still no one noticed me. Beocca had held me back, as if waiting for a lull in the proceedings before finding me a seat. Two servants brought in baskets of logs to feed the braziers, and it was then that Ælswith saw me and she leaned across and whispered in Alfred's ear. He had been paying close attention to the discussion, but now looked past his council to stare at me.

And a silence fell on that great hall. There had been a murmur of voices when men saw the king being distracted from the argument about bridges and they had all turned to look at me and then there was the silence that was broken by a priest's sneeze and a sudden odd scramble as the men closest to me, those sitting beside the cold stones of the hearth, moved to one side. They were not making way for me, but avoiding me.

Ælswith was smiling and I knew I was in trouble then. My hand instinctively went to my left side, but of course I had no sword so could not touch her hilt for luck. "We shall talk of bridges later," Alfred said. He stood. He wore a bronze circlet as a crown and had a fur-trimmed blue robe, matching the gown worn by his wife.

"What is happening?" I asked Beocca.

"You will be silent!" It was Odda the Younger who spoke. He was dressed in his war glory, in shining mail covered by a black cloak, in high boots and with a red-leather sword belt from which hung his weapons, for Odda, as commander of the king's troops, was permitted to go armed into the royal hall. I looked into his eyes and saw triumph there, the same triumph that was on the Lady Ælswith's pinched face, and I knew I had not been brought to receive the king's favor, but summoned to face my enemies.

I was right. A priest was called from the dark gaggle beside the door. He was a young man with a pouchy, scowling face. He moved briskly, as if the day did not have enough hours to complete his work. He bowed to the king, then took a parchment from the table where the two clerks sat and came to stand in the center of the witan's circle.

"There is an urgent matter," Alfred said, "which, with the witan's permission, we shall deal with now." No one there was likely to disagree so a low murmur offered approval of interrupting the more mundane discussions. Alfred nodded. "Father Erkenwald will read the charges," the king said, and took his throne again.

Charges? I was confused like a boar trapped between hounds and spears, and I seemed incapable of movement so I just stood there as Father Erkenwald unrolled the parchment and cleared his throat. "Uhtred of Oxton," he said, speaking in a high and precise voice, "you are this day charged with the crime of taking a king's ship without our king's consent, and with taking that ship to the country of Cornwalum and there making war against the Britons, again without our king's consent, and this we can prove by oaths." There was a small murmur in the hall, a murmur that was stilled when Alfred raised a thin hand. "You are further charged," Erkenwald went on, "with making an alliance with the pagan called Svein, and with his help you murdered Christian folk in Cornwalum, despite those folk living in peace with our king, and this also we can prove by oaths." He paused, and now there was complete silence in the hall. "And you are charged"—Erkenwald's voice was lower now, as though he could scarce believe what he was reading—"with joining the pagan Svein in an attack on our blessed king's realm by committing vile murder and impious church-robbery at Cynuit." This time there was no murmur, but a loud outburst of indignation and Alfred made no move to check it, so Erkenwald had to raise his voice to finish the indictment. "And this also," he was shouting now, and men hushed to listen, "we shall prove by oaths." He lowered the parchment, gave me a look of pure loathing, then walked back to the edge of the dais.

"He's lying," I snarled.

"You will have a chance to speak," a fierce-looking churchman sitting beside Alfred said. He was in monk's robes, but over them he wore a priest's half cape richly embroidered with crosses. He had a full head of white hair and a deep, stern voice.

"Who's that?" I asked Beocca.

"The most holy Æthelred," Beocca said softly

and, seeing I did not recognize the name, "Archbishop of Contwaraburg, of course."

The archbishop leaned over to speak with Erkenwald. Ælswith was staring at me. She had never liked me, and now she was watching my destruction and taking a great pleasure from it. Alfred, meanwhile, was studying the roof beams as though he had never noticed them before, and I realized he intended to take no part in this trial, for trial it was. He would let other men prove my guilt, but doubtless he would pronounce sentence, and not just on me, it seemed, because the archbishop scowled. "Is the second prisoner here?"

"He is held in the stables," Odda the Younger said.

"He should be here," the archbishop said indignantly. "A man has a right to hear his accusers."

"What other man?" I demanded.

It was Leofric, who was brought into the hall in chains, and there was no outcry against him because men perceived him as my follower. The crime was mine, Leofric had been snared by it, and now he would suffer for it, but he plainly had the sympathy of the men in the hall as he was brought to stand beside me. They knew him, he was of Wessex, while I was a Northumbrian interloper. He gave me a rueful glance as the guards led him to my side. "Up to our arses in it," he muttered.

"Quiet!" Beocca hissed.

"Trust me," I said.

"Trust you?" Leofric asked bitterly.

But I had glanced at Iseult and she had given me the smallest shake of her head, an indication, I reckoned, that she had seen the outcome of this day and it was good. "Trust me," I said again.

"The prisoners will be silent," the archbishop said.

"Up to our royal arses," Leofric said quietly.

The archbishop gestured at Father Erkenwald. "You have oath-takers?" he asked.

"I do, lord."

"Then let us hear the first."

Erkenwald gestured to another priest who was standing by the door leading to the passage at the back of the hall. The door was opened and a slight figure in a dark cloak entered. I could not see his face for he wore a hood. He hurried to the front of the dais and there bowed low to the king and went on his knees to the archbishop who held out a hand so that his heavy jeweled ring could be kissed. Only then did the man stand, push back his hood, and turn to face me.

It was the Ass. Asser, the Welsh monk. He stared at me as yet another priest brought him a gospel book on which he laid a thin hand. "I make oath," he said in accented English, still staring at me, "that what I say is truth, and God so help me in that endeavor and condemn me to the eternal fires of hell if I dissemble." He bent and kissed the gospel book with the tenderness of a man caressing a lover.

"Bastard," I muttered.

Asser was a good oath-taker. He spoke clearly, describing how I had come to Cornwalum in a ship that bore a beast head on its prow and another on its stern. He told how I had agreed to help King Peredur, who was being attacked by a neighbor assisted by the pagan Svein, and how I had betrayed Peredur by allying myself with the Dane. "Together," Asser said, "they made great slaughter, and I myself saw a holy priest put to death."

"You ran like a chicken," I said to him. "You couldn't see a thing."

Asser turned to the king and bowed. "I did run, lord king. I am a brother monk, not a warrior, and when Uhtred turned that hillside red with Christian blood I did take flight. I am not proud of that, lord king, and I have earnestly sought God's forgiveness for my cowardice."

Alfred smiled and the archbishop waved away Asser's remarks as if they were nothing. "And when you left the slaughter," Erkenwald asked, "what then?"

"I watched from a hilltop," Asser said, "and I saw Uhtred of Oxton leave that place in the company of the pagan ship. Two ships sailing westward."

"They sailed westward?" Erkenwald asked.

"To the west," Asser confirmed.

Erkenwald glanced at me. There was silence in the hall as men leaned forward to catch each damning word. "And what lay to the west?" Erkenwald asked.

"I cannot say," Asser said. "But if they did not go to the end of the world then I assume they turned about Cornwalum to go into the Sæfern Sea."

"And you know no more?" Erkenwald asked.

"I know I helped bury the dead," Asser said, "and I said prayers for their souls, and I saw the smoldering embers of the burned church, but what Uhtred did when he left the place of slaughter I do not know. I only know he went westward."

Alfred was pointedly taking no part in the proceedings, but he plainly liked Asser for, when the Welshman's testimony was done, he beckoned him to the dais and rewarded him with a coin and a moment of private conversation. The witan talked among themselves, sometimes glancing at me with the curiosity we give to doomed men. Lady Ælswith, suddenly so gracious, smiled on Asser.

"You have anything to say?" Erkenwald demanded of me when Asser had been dismissed.

"I shall wait," I said, "till all your lies are told."

The truth, of course, was that Asser had told the truth, and told it plainly, clearly, and persuasively. The king's councillors had been impressed, just as they were impressed by Erkenwald's second oath-taker.

It was Steapa Snotor, the warrior who was never far from Odda the Younger's side. His back was straight, his shoulders square, and his feral face with its stretched skin was grim. He glanced at me, bowed to the king, then laid a huge hand on the gospel book and let Erkenwald lead him through the oath, and he swore to tell the truth on pain of hell's eternal agony, and then he lied. He lied calmly in a flat, toneless voice. He said he had been in charge of the soldiers who guarded the place at Cynuit where the new church was being built, and how two ships had come in the dawn and how warriors streamed from the ships, and how he had fought against them and killed six of them, but there were too many, far too many, and he had been forced to retreat, but he had seen the attackers slaughter the priests and he had heard the pagan leader shout his name as a boast. "Svein, he was called."

"And Svein brought two ships?"

Steapa paused and frowned, as though he had trouble counting to two, then nodded. "He had two ships."

"He led both?"

"Svein led one of the ships," Steapa said. Then he pointed a finger at me. "And he led the other."

The audience seemed to growl and the noise was so threatening that Alfred slapped the arm of his chair and finally stood to restore quiet. Steapa seemed unmoved. He stood, solid as an oak, and though he had not told his tale as convincingly as Brother Asser, there was something very damning in his testimony. It was so matter-of-fact, so unemotionally told, so straightforward, and none of it was true.

"Uhtred led the second ship," Erkenwald said, "but did Uhtred join in the killing?"

"Join it?" Steapa asked. "He led it." He snarled those words and the men in the hall growled their anger.

Erkenwald turned to the king. "Lord king," he said, "he must die."

"And his land and property must be forfeited!" Bishop Alewold shouted in such excitement that a whirl of his spittle landed and hissed in the nearest brazier. "Forfeited to the church!"

The men in the hall thumped their feet on the ground to show their approbation. Ælswith nodded vigorously, but the archbishop clapped his hands for silence. "He has not spoken," he reminded Erkenwald, then nodded at me. "Say your piece," he ordered curtly.

"Beg for mercy," Beocca advised me quietly.

When you are up to your arse in shit there is only one thing to do. Attack, and so I admitted I had been at Cynuit, and that admission provoked some gasps in the hall. "But I was not there this summer," I went on. "I was there in the spring at which time I killed Ubba Lothbrokson, and there are men in this hall who saw me do it! Yet Odda the Younger claimed the credit. He took Ubba's banner, which I laid low, and he took it to his king and he claimed to have killed Ubba. Now, lest I spread the truth, which is that he is a coward and a liar, he would have me murdered by lies." I pointed to Steapa. "His lies."

Steapa spat to show his scorn. Odda the Younger was looking furious, but he said nothing and some men noted it. To be called a coward and a liar is to be invited to do battle, but Odda stayed still as a stump.

"You cannot prove what you say," Erkenwald said.

"I can prove I killed Ubba," I said.

"We are not here to discuss such things," Erkenwald said loftily, "but to determine whether you broke the king's peace by an impious attack on Cynuit."

"Then summon my crewmen," I demanded. "Bring them here, put them on oath, and ask what they did in the summer." I waited, and Erkenwald said nothing. He glanced at the king as if seeking help, but Alfred's eyes were momentarily closed. "Or are you in so much of a hurry to kill me," I went on, "that you dare not wait to hear the truth?"

"I have Steapa's sworn testimony," Erkenwald said as if that made any other evidence unnecessary. He was flustered.

"And you can have my oath," I said, "and Leofric's oath, and the oath of a crewman who is here." I turned and beckoned Haesten who looked frightened at being summoned, but at Iseult's urging came to stand beside me. "Put him on oath," I demanded of Erkenwald.

Erkenwald did not know what to do, but some men in the witan called out that I had the right to summon oath-takers and the newcomer must be heard, and so a priest brought the gospel book to Haesten. I waved the priest away. "He will swear on this," I said, and took out Thor's amulet.

"He's not a Christian?" Erkenwald demanded in astonishment.

"He is a Dane," I said.

"How can we trust the word of a Dane?" Erkenwald demanded.

"But our lord king does," I retorted. "He trusts the word of Guthrum to keep the peace, so why should this Dane not be trusted?"

That provoked some smiles. Many in the witan thought Alfred far too trusting of Guthrum and I felt the sympathy in the hall move to my side, but then the archbishop intervened to declare that the oath of a pagan was of no value. "None whatsoever," he snapped. "He must stand down."

"Then put Leofric under oath," I demanded, "and then bring our crew here and listen to their testimony."

"And you will all lie with one tongue," Erkenwald said, "and what happened at Cynuit is not the only matter on which you are accused. Do you deny that you sailed in the king's ship? That you went to Cornwalum and there betrayed Peredur and killed his Christian people? Do you deny that Brother Asser told the truth?"

"But what if Peredur's queen were to tell you that Asser lies?" I asked. "What if she were to tell you that he lies like a hound at the hearth?" Erkenwald stared at me. They all stared at me and I turned and gestured at Iseult who stepped forward, tall and delicate, the silver glinting at her neck and wrists. "Peredur's queen," I announced, "whom I demand that you hear under oath, and thus hear how her husband was planning to join the Danes in an assault on Wessex."

That was rank nonsense, of course, but it was the best I could invent at that moment, and Iseult, I knew, would swear to its truth. Quite why Svein would fight Peredur if the Briton planned to support him was a dangerously loose plank in the argument, but it did not really matter for I had confused the proceedings so much that no one was sure what to do. Erkenwald was speechless. Men stood to look at Iseult, who looked calmly back at them, and the king and the archbishop bent their heads together. Ælswith, one hand clapped to her pregnant belly, hissed advice at them. None of them wanted to summon Iseult for fear of what she would say, and Alfred, I suspect, knew that the trial, which had already become mired in lies, could only get worse.

"You're good, earsling," Leofric muttered, "you're very good."

Odda the Younger looked at the king, then at his fellow members of the witan, and he must have known I was slithering out of his snare for he pulled Steapa to his side. He spoke to him urgently. The king was frowning, the archbishop looked perplexed, Ælswith's blotched face showed fury, while Erkenwald seemed helpless. Then Steapa rescued them. "I do not lie!" he shouted.

He seemed uncertain what to say next, but he had the hall's attention. The king gestured to him, as if inviting him to continue, and Odda the Younger whispered in the big man's ear.

"He says I lie," Steapa said, pointing at me, "and I say I do not, and my sword says I do not." He stopped abruptly, having made what was probably the longest speech of his life, but it was enough. Feet drummed on the floor and men shouted that Steapa was right, which he was not, but he had reduced the whole tangled morass of lies and accusations to a trial by combat and they all liked that. The archbishop still looked troubled, but Alfred gestured for silence.

He looked at me. "Well?" he asked. "Steapa says his sword will support his truth. Does yours?"

I could have said no. I could have insisted on letting Iseult speak and then allowing the witan to advise the king which side had spoken the greater truth, but I was ever rash, ever impetuous, and the invitation to fight cut through the whole entanglement. If I fought and won, then Leofric and I were innocent of every charge.

I did not even think about losing. I just looked at Steapa. "My sword," I told him, "says I tell the truth, and that you are a stinking bag of wind, a liar from hell, a cheat and a perjurer who deserves death."

"Up to our arses again," Leofric said.

Men cheered. They liked a fight to the death, which was much better entertainment than listening to Alfred's harpist chant the psalms. Alfred hesitated, and I saw Ælswith look from me to Steapa, and she must have thought him the greater warrior for she leaned forward, touched Alfred's elbow, and whispered urgently.

And the king nodded. "Granted," he said. He sounded weary, as if he was dispirited by the lies and the insults. "You will fight tomorrow. Swords and shields, nothing else." He held up a hand to stop the cheering. "My lord Wulfhere?"

"Sire?" Wulfhere struggled to his feet.

"You will arrange the fight. And may God grant victory to the truth." Alfred stood, pulled his robe about him, and left.

And Steapa, for the first time since I had seen him, smiled.

"You're a damned fool," Leofric told me. He had been released from his chains and allowed to spend the evening with me. Haesten was there, as was Iseult and my men who had been brought from the town. We were lodged in the king's compound, in a cattle byre that stank of dung, but I did not notice the smell. It was Twelfth

Night so there was the great feast in the king's hall, but we were left out in the cold, watched there by two of the royal guards. "Steapa's good," Leofric warned me.

"I'm good."

"He's better," Leofric said bluntly. "He'll slaughter you."

"He won't," Iseult said calmly.

"Damn it, he's good!" Leofric insisted, and I believed him.

"It's that goddamned monk's fault," I said bitterly. "He went bleating to Alfred, didn't he?" In truth Asser had been sent by the king of Dyfed to assure the West Saxons that Dyfed was not planning war, but Asser had taken the opportunity of his embassy to recount the tale of the **Eftwyrd** and from that it was a small jump to conclude that we had stayed with Svein while he attacked Cynuit. Alfred had no proof of our guilt, but Odda the Younger had seen a chance to destroy me and so persuaded Steapa to lie.

"Now Steapa will kill you," Leofric grumbled, "whatever she says." Iseult did not bother to answer him. She was using handfuls of grubby straw to clean my mail coat. The armor had been fetched from the Corncrake tavern and given to me, but I would have to wait till morning to get my weapons, which meant they would not be newly sharpened. Steapa, because he served Odda the Younger, was one of the king's body-guards so he would have all night to put an edge on his sword. The royal kitchens had sent us food, though I had no appetite. "Just take it slow in the morning," Leofric told me.

"Slow?"

"You fight in a rage," he said, "and Steapa's always calm."

"So better to get in a rage," I said.

"That's what he wants. He'll fend you off and fend you off and wait till you're tired. Then he'll finish you off. It's how he fights."

Harald told us the same thing. Harald was the shire reeve of Defnascir, the widower who had summoned me to the court in Exanceaster, but he had also fought alongside us at Cynuit and that makes a bond, and sometime in the dark he splashed through the rain and mud and came into the light of the small fire that lit the cattle shed without warming it. He stopped in the doorway and gazed at me reproachfully. "Were you with Svein at Cynuit?" he asked.

"No," I said.

"I didn't think so." Harald came into the byre and sat by the fire. The two royal guards were at the door and he ignored them, and that was interesting. All of them served Odda, and the young ealdorman would not be pleased to hear that Harald had come to us, yet plainly Harald trusted the two guards not to tell, which suggested that there was unhappiness in Odda's ranks. Harald put a pot of ale on the floor. "Steapa's sitting at the king's table," he said.

"So he's eating badly," I said.

Harald nodded, but did not smile. "It's not much of a feast," he admitted. He stared into the fire for a moment, then looked at me. "How's Mildrith?"

"Well."

"She is a dear girl," he said, then glanced at Iseult's dark beauty before staring into the fire again. "There will be a church service at dawn," he said, "and after that you and Steapa will fight."

"Where?"

"In a field on the other side of the river," he said, then pushed the pot of ale toward me. "He's left-handed."

I could not remember fighting against a man who held his sword in his left hand, but nor could I see a disadvantage in it. We would both have our shields facing the other man's shield instead of his weapon, but that would be a problem to both of us. I shrugged.

"He's used to it," Harald explained, "and you're not. And he wears mail down to here"—he touched his calf—"and he has an iron strip on his left boot."

"Because that's his vulnerable foot?"

"He plants it forward," Harald said, "inviting attack, then chops at your sword arm."

"So he's a hard man to kill," I said mildly.

"No one's done it yet," Harald said gloomily.

"You don't like him?"

He did not answer at first, but drank ale, then passed the pot to Leofric. "I like the old man," he said, meaning Odda the Elder. "He's foul tempered, but he's fair enough. But the son?" He shook his head sadly. "I think the son is untested. Steapa? I don't dislike him, but he's like a hound. He only knows how to kill."

I stared into the feeble fire, looking for a sign from the gods in the small flames, but none came, or none that I saw. "He must be worried though," Leofric said.

"Steapa?" Harald asked. "Why should he be worried?"

"Uhtred killed Ubba."

Harald shook his head. "Steapa doesn't think

enough to be worried. He just knows he'll kill Uhtred tomorrow."

I thought back to the fight with Ubba. He had been a great warrior, with a reputation that glowed wherever Norsemen sailed, and I had killed him, but the truth was that he had put a foot into the spilled guts of a dying man and slipped. His leg had shot sideways, he had lost his balance, and I had managed to cut the tendons in his arm. I touched the hammer amulet and thought that the gods had sent me a sign after all. "An iron strip in his boot?" I asked.

Harald nodded. "He doesn't care how much you attack him. He knows you're coming from his left and he'll block most of your attacks with his sword. Big sword, heavy thing. But some blows will get by and he won't care. You'll waste them on iron. Heavy mail, helmet, boot, doesn't matter. It'll be like hitting an oak tree, and after a while you'll make a mistake. He'll be bruised and you'll be dead."

He was right, I thought. Striking an armored man with a sword rarely achieved much except to make a bruise because the edge would be stopped by mail or helmet. Mail cannot be chopped open by a sword, which was why so many men carried axes into battle, but the rules of trial by combat said the fight had to be with swords. A sword lunge would pierce mail, but Steapa was not going to make himself an easy target for a lunge. "Is he quick?" I asked.

"Quick enough," Harald said, then shrugged. "Not as quick as you," he added grudgingly, "but he isn't slow."

"What does the money say?" Leofric asked, though he surely knew the answer.

"No one's wagering a penny on Uhtred," Harald said.

"You should," I retorted.

He smiled at that, but I knew he would not take the advice. "The big money," he said, "is what Odda will give Steapa when he kills you. A hundred shillings."

"Uhtred's not worth it," Leofric said with rough humor.

"Why does he want me dead so badly?" I wondered aloud. It could not be Mildrith, I thought, and the argument over who had killed Ubba was long in the past, yet still Odda the Younger conspired against me.

Harald paused a long time before answering. He had his bald head bowed and I thought he was in prayer, but then he looked up. "You threaten him," he said quietly.

"I haven't even seen him for months," I protested, "so how do I threaten him?"

Harald paused again, choosing his words carefully. "The king is frequently ill," he said after the pause, "and who can say how long he will live? And if, God forbid, he should die soon, then the witan will not choose his infant son to be king. They'll choose a nobleman with a reputation made on the battlefield. They'll choose a man who can stand up to the Danes."

"Odda?" I laughed at the thought of Odda as king.

"Who else?" Harald asked. "But if you were to stand before the witan and swear an oath to the truth about the battle where Ubba died, they might not choose him. So you threaten him, and he fears you because of that."

"So now he's paying Steapa to chop you to bits," Leofric added gloomily.

Harald left. He was a decent man, honest and hardworking, and he had taken a risk by coming to see me, and I had been poor company for I did not appreciate the gesture he made. It was plain he thought I must die in the morning, and he had done his best to prepare me for the fight, but despite Iseult's confident prediction that I would live, I did not sleep well. I was worried, and it was cold. The rain turned to sleet in the night and the wind whipped into the byre. By dawn the wind and sleet had stopped and instead there was a mist shrouding the buildings and icy water dripping from the mossy thatch. I made a poor breakfast of damp bread and it was while I was eating that Father Beocca came and said Alfred wished to speak with me.

I was sour. "You mean he wants to pray with me?"

"He wants to speak with you," Beocca insisted and, when I did not move, he stamped his lamed foot. "It is not a request, Uhtred. It is a royal order!"

I put on my mail, not because it was time to arm for the fight, but because its leather lining offered some warmth on a cold morning. The mail was not very clean, despite Iseult's efforts. Most men wore their hair short, but I liked the Danish way of leaving it long and so I tied it behind with a lace and Iseult plucked the straw scraps from it. "We must hurry," Beocca said, and I followed him through the mud past the great hall and the newly built church to some smaller buildings made of timber that had still not weathered gray. Alfred's father had used Cippanhamm as a hunting lodge, but Alfred was expanding it. The church had been his first new building, and he had built that even before he repaired and extended the palisade, and that was an indication of his priorities. Even now, when the nobility of Wessex was gathered just a day's march from the Danes, there seemed to be more churchmen than soldiers in the place, and that was another indication of how Alfred thought to protect his realm. "The king is gracious," Beocca hissed at me as we went through a door, "so be humble."

Beocca knocked on another door, did not wait for an answer, but pushed it open and indicated I should step inside. He did not follow me, but closed the door, leaving me in a gloomy half darkness.

A pair of beeswax candles flickered on an altar and by their light I saw two men kneeling in front of the plain wooden cross that stood between the candles. The men had their backs to me, but I recognized Alfred by his fur-trimmed blue cloak. The second man was a monk. They were both praying silently and I waited. The room was small, evidently a private chapel, and its only furniture was the draped altar and a kneeling stool on which was a closed book.

"In the name of the father," Alfred broke the silence.

"And of the son," the monk said, and he spoke English with an accent and I recognized the voice of the Ass.

"And of the holy ghost," Alfred concluded, "amen."

"Amen," Asser echoed, and both men stood, their faces suffused with the joy of devout Christians who have said their prayers well, and Alfred blinked as though he were surprised to see me, though he must have heard Beocca's knocking and the sound of the door opening and closing.

"I trust you slept well, Uhtred?" he said.

"I trust you did, lord."

"The pains kept me awake," Alfred said, touching his belly. Then he went to one side of the room and hauled open a big pair of wooden shutters, flooding the chapel with a wan, misty light. The window looked onto a courtyard and I was aware of men out there. The king shivered, for it was freezing in the chapel. "It is Saint Cedd's feast day," he told me.

I said nothing.

"You have heard of Saint Cedd?" he asked me and, when my silence betrayed ignorance, he smiled indulgently. "He was an East Anglian, am I not right, brother?"

"The most blessed Cedd was indeed an East Angle, lord," Asser confirmed.

"And his mission was in Lundene," Alfred went on, "but he concluded his days at Lindisfarena. You must know that house, Uhtred?"

"I know it, lord," I said. The island was a short ride from Bebbanburg and not so long before I had ridden to its monastery with Earl Ragnar and watched the monks die beneath Danish swords. "I know it well," I added.

"So Cedd is famous in your homeland?"

"I've not heard of him, lord."

"I think of him as a symbol," Alfred said, "a man who was born in East Anglia, did his life's work in Mercia, and died in Northumbria." He brought his long, pale hands together so that the fingers embraced. "The Saxons of England, Uhtred, gathered together before God."

"And united in joyful prayer with the Britons," Asser added piously.

"I beseech Almighty God for that happy outcome," the king said, smiling at me, and by now I recognized what he was saying. He stood there, looking so humble, with no crown, no great necklace, no arm rings, nothing but a small garnet brooch holding the cloak at his neck, and he spoke of a happy outcome, but what he was really seeing was the Saxon people gathered under one king. A king of Wessex. Alfred's piety hid a monstrous ambition.

"We must learn from the saints," Alfred told me. "Their lives are a guide to the darkness that surrounds us, and Saint Cedd's holy example teaches that we must be united, so I am loath to shed Saxon blood on Saint Cedd's feast day."

"There need be no bloodshed, lord," I said.

"I am pleased to hear it," Alfred interjected.

"If the charges against me are retracted."

The smile went from his face and he walked to the window and stared into the misty courtyard and I looked where he looked and saw that a small display was being mounted for my benefit. Steapa was being armored. Two men were dropping a massive mail coat over his wide shoulders, while a third stood by with an outsized shield and a monstrous sword.

"I talked with Steapa last night," the king said, turning from the window, "and he told me there was a mist when Svein attacked at Cynuit. A morning mist like this one." He waved at the whiteness sifting into the chapel.

"I wouldn't know, lord," I said.

"So it is possible," the king went on, "that Steapa was mistaken when he thought he saw you." I almost smiled. The king knew Steapa had lied, though he would not say as much. "Father Willibald also spoke to the crew of the **Eft-wyrd**," the king went on, "and not one of them confirmed Steapa's tale."

The crew was still in Hamtun, so Willibald's report must have come from there and that meant the king had known I was innocent of the slaughter at Cynuit even before I was charged. "So I was falsely arraigned?" I said harshly.

"You were accused," the king corrected me, "and accusations must be proven or refuted."

"Or withdrawn."

"I can withdraw the charges," Alfred agreed. Steapa, outside the window, was making sure his mail coat was seated comfortably by swinging his great sword. And it was great. It was huge, a hammer of a blade. Then the king half closed the shutter, hiding Steapa. "I can withdraw the accusation about Cynuit," he said, "but I do not think Brother Asser lied to us."

"I have a queen," I said, "who says he does."

"A shadow queen," Asser hissed, "a pagan! A sorceress!" He looked at Alfred. "She is evil, lord," he said, "a witch! **Maleficos non patieris vivere!**"

"Thou shalt not permit a witch to live," Alfred translated for my benefit. "That is God's commandment, Uhtred, from the holy scriptures."

"Your answer to the truth," I sneered, "is to threaten a woman with death?"

Alfred flinched at that. "Brother Asser is a good Christian," he said vehemently, "and he tells the truth. You went to war without my orders. You used my ship, my men, and you behaved treacherously! You are the liar, Uhtred, and you are the cheat!" He spoke angrily, but managed to control his anger. "It is my belief," he went on, "that you have paid your debt to the church with goods stolen from other good Christians."

"Not true," I said harshly. I had paid the debt with goods stolen from a Dane.

"So resume the debt," the king said, "and we shall have no death on this blessed day of Saint Cedd."

I was being offered life. Alfred waited for my response, smiling. He was sure I would accept his offer because to him it seemed reasonable. He had no love for warriors, weapons, and killing. Fate decreed that he must spend his reign fighting, but it was not to his taste. He wanted to civilize Wessex, to give it piety and order, and two men fighting to the death on a winter's morning was not his idea of a well-run kingdom.

But I hated Alfred. I hated him for humiliating me at Exanceaster when he had made me wear a penitent's robe and crawl on my knees. Nor did I think of him as my king. He was a West Saxon and I was a Northumbrian, and I reckoned so long as he was king then Wessex had small chance of surviving. He believed God would protect him from the Danes, while I believed they had to be defeated by swords. I also had an idea how to defeat Steapa, just an idea, and I had no wish to take on a debt I had already paid, and I was young and I was foolish and I was arrogant and I was never able to resist a stupid impulse. "Everything I have said is the truth," I lied, "and I would defend that truth with my sword."

Alfred flinched from my tone. "Are you saying Brother Asser lied?" he demanded.

"He twists truth," I said, "like a woman wrings a hen's neck."

The king pulled the shutter open, showing me

the mighty Steapa in his gleaming war glory. "You really want to die?" he asked me.

"I want to fight for the truth, lord king," I said stubbornly.

"Then you are a fool," Alfred said, his anger showing again. "You are a liar, a fool, and a sinner." He strode past me, pulled open the door, and shouted at a servant to tell Ealdorman Wulfhere that the fight was to take place after all. "Go," he added to me, "and may your soul receive its just reward."

Wulfhere had been charged with arranging the fight, but there was a delay because the ealdorman had disappeared. The town was searched, the royal buildings were searched, but there was no sign of him until a stable slave nervously reported that Wulfhere and his men had ridden away from Cippanhamm before dawn. No one knew why, though some surmised that Wulfhere wanted no part in a trial by combat, which made little sense to me for the ealdorman had never struck me as a squeamish man. Ealdorman Huppa of Thornsæta was appointed to replace him, and so it was close to midday when my swords were brought to me and we were escorted down to the meadow that lay across the bridge that led from the town's eastern gate. A huge crowd had gathered on the river's far bank. There were cripples, beggars, jugglers, women selling pies, dozens of priests, excited children, and, of course, the assembled warriors of the West Saxon nobility, all of them in Cippanhamm for the meeting of the witan, and all eager to see Steapa Snotor show off his renowned skill.

"You're a damned fool," Leofric said to me.

"Because I insisted on fighting?"

"You could have walked away."

"And men would have called me a coward," I said. And that, too, was the truth, that a man cannot step back from a fight and stay a man. We make much in this life if we are able. We make children and wealth and amass land and build halls and assemble armies and give great feasts, but only one thing survives us. Reputation. I could not walk away.

Alfred did not come to the fight. Instead, with the pregnant Ælswith and their two children, and escorted by a score of guards and as many priests and courtiers, he had ridden westward. He was accompanying Brother Asser on the start of the monk's return journey to Dyfed, and the king was making a point that he preferred the company of the British churchman to watching two of his warriors fight like snarling hounds. But no one else in Wessex wanted to miss the battle. They were eager for it, but Huppa wanted everything to be orderly and so he insisted that the crowd push back from the damp ground beside the river to give us space. Eventually the folk were massed on a green bank overlooking the trampled grass and Huppa went to Steapa to enquire if he was ready.

He was ready. His mail shone in the weak sunlight. His helmet was glistening. His shield was a huge thing, bossed and rimmed with iron, a shield that must have weighed as much as a sack of grain and was a weapon in itself if he managed to hit me with it, but his chief weapon was his great sword that was longer and heavier than any I had seen.

Huppa, trailed by two guards, came to me. His feet squelched in the grass and I thought that the ground would prove treacherous. "Uhtred of Oxton," he said, "are you ready?"

"My name," I said, "is Uhtred of Bebbanburg."

"Are you ready?" he demanded, ignoring my correction.

"No," I said.

A murmur went through the folk nearest to

me, and the murmur spread, and after a few heartbeats the whole crowd was jeering me. They thought me a coward, and that thought was reinforced when I dropped my shield and sword and made Leofric help as I stripped off the heavy coat of mail. Odda the Younger, standing beside his champion, was laughing. "What are you doing?" Leofric asked me.

"I hope you put money on me," I said.

"Of course I didn't."

"Are you refusing to fight?" Huppa asked me.

"No," I said, and when I was stripped of my armor I took Serpent-Breath back from Leofric. Just Serpent-Breath. No helmet, no shield, just my good sword. Now I was unburdened. The ground was heavy, Steapa was armored, but I was light and I was fast and I was ready.

"I'm ready," I told Huppa.

He went to the meadow's center, raised an arm, dropped it, and the crowd cheered.

I kissed the hammer around my neck, trusted my soul to the great god Thor, and walked forward.

Steapa came steadily toward me, shield up, sword held out to his left. There was no trace of concern in his eyes. He was a workman at his trade and I wondered how many men he had killed, and he must have thought my death would be easy for I had no protection, not even a shield. And so we walked toward each other until, a dozen paces from him, I ran. I ran at him, feinted right toward his sword, and then broke hard to my left, still running, going past him now, and I was aware of the huge blade swinging fast after me as he turned, but then I was behind him, he was still turning, and I dropped to my knees, ducked, heard the blade go over my head, and I was up again, lunging.

The sword pierced his mail, drew blood from just behind his left shoulder, but he was quicker than I had expected and had already checked that first great swing and was bringing the sword back and his turn pulled Serpent-Breath free. I had scratched him.

I danced back two paces. I went left again and he charged me, hoping to crush me with the weight of his shield, but I ran back to the right, fending off the sword with Serpent-Breath and the crack of the blades was like the bell of doomsday, and I lunged again, this time aiming at his waist, but he stepped back quickly. I kept going to the right, my arm jarred by the clash of the swords. I went fast, making him turn, and I feinted a lunge, brought him forward, and went back to the left. The ground was boggy. I feared slipping, but speed was my weapon. I had to keep him turning, keep him swinging into empty air, and snatch what chances I could to use Serpent-Breath's point. Bleed him enough, I thought, and he would tire, but he guessed my tactics and started making short rushes to frustrate me, and each rush would be accompanied by the hiss of that huge sword. He wanted to make me parry and hoped he could break Serpent-Breath when the blades met. I feared the same. She was well made, but even the best sword can break.

He forced me back, trying to crowd me against the spectators on the bank so he could hack me to pieces in front of them. I let him drive me, then dodged to my right where my left foot slipped and I went down on that knee and the crowd, close behind me now, took in a great breath and a woman screamed because Steapa's huge sword was swinging like an ax onto my neck, only I had not slipped, merely pretended to, and I pushed off with my right foot, came out from under the blow and around his right flank, and he thrust the shield out, catching my shoulder with the rim, and I knew I would have a bruise there, but I also had a heartbeat of opportunity and I darted Serpent-Breath forward and her point punctured his mail again to scrape against the ribs of his back and he roared as he turned, wrenching my blade free of his mail, but I was already going backward.

I stopped ten paces away. He stopped, too, and watched me. There was a slight puzzlement on his big face now. There was still no worry there, just puzzlement. He pushed his left foot forward, as Harald had warned me, and he was hoping I would attack it and he would rely on the hidden iron strip in the boot to protect him while he thumped and hacked and bludgeoned me to death. I smiled at him and threw Serpent-Breath from my right hand into my left and held her there, and that was a new puzzle for him. Some men could fight with either hand, and perhaps I was one of them? He drew his foot back. "Why do they call you Steapa Snotor?" I asked. "You're not clever. You've got the brains of an addled egg."

I was trying to enrage him and hoped that anger would make him careless, but my insult bounced off him. Instead of rushing me in fury he came slowly, watching the sword in my left hand, and the men on the hill called for him to kill me and I suddenly ran at him, broke right, and he swung at me a little late, thinking I was going to go left at the last moment and I swept Serpent-Breath back and she caught his sword arm and I could feel her blade scraping through the rings of his mail, but she did not slice through them and then I was away from him and put her back into my right hand, turned, charged him, and swerved away at the last moment so that his massive swing missed me by a yard.

He was still puzzled. This was like a bull-baiting and he was the bull, and his problem was to get me in a place where he could use his greater strength and weight. I was the dog, and my job was to lure him, tease him, and bite him until he weakened. He had thought I would come with mail and shield and we would batter each other for a few moments until my strength faded and he could drive me to the ground with massive blows and chop me to scraps with the big sword, but so far his blade had not touched me. But nor had I weakened him. My two cuts had drawn blood, but they were mere scratches. So now he came forward again, hoping to herd me back to the river. A woman screamed from the top of the bank, and I assumed she was trying to encourage him, and the screaming grew louder and I just went back faster, making Steapa lumber forward, but I had slipped away to his right and was coming back at him, making him turn, and then he suddenly stopped and stared past me and his shield went down and his sword dropped, too, and all I had to do was lunge. He was there for the killing. I could thrust Serpent-Breath into his chest or throat, or ram her into his belly, but I did none of those things. Steapa was no fool at fighting and I guessed he was luring me and I did not take the bait. If I lunged, I thought, he would crush me between his shield and sword. He wanted me to think him defenseless so that I could come into range of his weapons, but instead I stopped and spread my arms, inviting him to attack me as he was inviting me to attack him.

But he ignored me. He just stared past my shoulder. And the woman's screaming was shrill now and there were men shouting, and Leofric was yelling my name, and the spectators were no longer watching us, but running in panic.

So I turned my back on Steapa and looked toward the town on its hill that was cradled by the river's bend.

And I saw that Cippanhamm was burning. Smoke was darkening the winter sky and the horizon was filled with men, mounted men, men with swords and axes and shields and spears and banners, and more horsemen were coming from the eastern gate to thunder across the bridge.

Because all Alfred's prayers had failed and the Danes had come to Wessex.

SIX

Steapa recovered his wits before I did. He stared openmouthed at the Danes crossing the bridge and then just ran toward his master, Odda the Younger, who was shouting for his horses. The Danes were spreading out from the bridge, galloping across the meadow with drawn swords and leveled spears. Smoke poured into the low wintry clouds from the burning town. Some of the king's buildings were alight. A riderless horse, stirrups flapping, galloped across the grass, then Leofric grabbed my elbow and pulled me northward beside the river. Most of the folk had gone south and the Danes had followed them, so north seemed to offer more safety. Iseult had my mail coat and I took it from her, leaving her to carry Wasp-Sting, and behind us the screaming rose as the Danes chopped into the panicked mass. Folk scattered. Escaping horsemen thumped past us, the hooves throwing up spadefuls of damp earth and grass with every step. I saw Odda the Younger swerve away with three other horsemen. Harald, the shire reeve, was one of them, but I could not see Steapa and for a moment I feared the big man was looking for me. Then I forgot him as a band of Danes turned north in pursuit of Odda. "Where are our horses?" I shouted at Leofric, who looked bemused and I remembered he had not traveled to Cippanhamm with me. The beasts were probably still in the yard behind the Corncrake tavern, which meant they were lost.

There was a fallen willow in a stand of leafless alders by the river and we paused there for breath, hidden by the willow's trunk. I pulled on the mail coat, buckled on my swords, and took my helmet and shield from Leofric. "Where's Haesten?" I asked.

"He ran," Leofric said curtly. So had the rest of my men. They had joined the panic and were gone southward. Leofric pointed northward. "Trouble," he said curtly. There was a score of Danes riding down our bank of the river, blocking our escape, but they were still some distance away, while the men pursuing Odda had vanished, so Leofric led us across the water meadow to a tangle of thorns, alders, nettles, and ivy. At its center was an old wattle hut, perhaps a herdsman's shelter, and though the hut had half collapsed, it offered a better hiding place than the willow and so the three of us plunged into the nettles and crouched behind the rotting timbers.

A bell was ringing in the town. It sounded like the slow tolling that announced a funeral. It stopped abruptly, started again, and then finally ended. A horn sounded. A dozen horsemen galloped close to our hiding place and all had black cloaks and black painted shields, the marks of Guthrum's warriors.

Guthrum. Guthrum the Unlucky. He called himself King of East Anglia, but he wanted to be King of Wessex and this was his third attempt to take the country and this time, I thought, his luck had turned. While Alfred had been celebrating the twelfth night of Yule, and while the witan met to discuss the maintenance of bridges and the punishment of malefactors, Guthrum had marched. The army of the Danes was in Wessex, Cippanhamm had fallen, and the great men of Alfred's kingdom had been surprised, scattered, or slaughtered. The horn sounded again and the dozen black-cloaked horsemen turned and rode toward the sound.

"We should have known the Danes were coming," I said angrily.

"You always said they would," Leofric said.

"Didn't Alfred have spies at Gleawecestre?"

"He had priests praying here instead," Leofric said bitterly, "and he trusted Guthrum's truce."

I touched my hammer amulet. I had taken it from a boy in Eoferwic. I had been a boy myself then, newly captured by the Danes, and my opponent had fought me in a whirl of fists and feet and I had hammered him down into the riverbank and taken his amulet. I still have it. I touch it often, reminding Thor that I live, but that day I touched it because I thought of Ragnar. The hostages would be dead, and was that why Wulfhere had ridden away at dawn? But how could he have known the Danes were coming? If Wulfhere had known, then Alfred would have known and the West Saxon forces would have been ready. None of it made sense, except that Guthrum had again attacked during a truce and the last time he had broken a truce he had showed that he was willing to sacrifice the hostages held to prevent just such an attack. It seemed certain he had done it again and so Ragnar would be dead and my world was diminished.

So many dead. There were corpses in the meadow between our hiding place and the river, and still the slaughter went on. Some of the Saxons had run back toward the town, discovered the bridge was guarded, and tried to escape northward and we watched them being ridden down by the Danes. Three men tried to resist, standing in a tight group with swords ready, but a Dane gave a great whoop and charged them with his horse, and his spear went through one man's mail, crushing his chest, and the other two were thrown aside by the horse's weight and immediately more Danes closed on them, swords and axes rose, and the horsemen spurred on. A girl screamed and ran in terrified circles until a Dane, long hair flying, leaned from his saddle and pulled her dress up over her head so she was blind and half naked. She staggered in the damp grass and a half dozen Danes laughed at her, then one slapped her bare rump with his sword and another dragged her southward, her screams muffled by the entangling dress. Iseult was shivering and I put a mail-clad arm around her shoulders.

I could have joined the Danes in the meadow. I spoke their language and, with my long hair and my arm rings, I looked like a Dane. But Haesten was somewhere in Cippanhamm and he might betray me, and Guthrum had no great love for me, and even if I survived then it would go hard with Leofric and Iseult. These Danes were in a rampant mood, flushed by their easy success and if a dozen decided they wanted Iseult then they would take her whether they thought I was a Dane or not. They were hunting in packs and so it was best to stay hidden until the frenzy had passed. Across the river, at the top of the low hill on which Cippanhamm was built, I could see the town's largest church burning. The thatched roof was whirling into the sky in great ribbons of flame and plumes of spark-riddled smoke.

"What in God's name were you doing back there?" Leofric asked me.

"Back there?" His question confused me.

"Dancing around Steapa like a gnat! He could have endured that all day!"

"I wounded him," I said, "twice."

"Wounded him? Sweet Christ, he's hurt himself worse when he was shaving!"

"Doesn't matter now, does it?" I said. I guessed Steapa was dead by now. Or perhaps he had escaped. I did not know. None of us knew what was happening except that the Danes had come. And Mildrith? My son? They were far away, and presumably they would receive warning of the Danish attack, but I had no doubt that the Danes would keep going deep into Wessex and there was nothing I could do to protect Oxton. I had no horse, no men, and no chance of reaching the south coast before Guthrum's mounted soldiers.

I watched a Dane ride past with a girl across his saddle. "What happened to that Danish girl you took home," I asked Leofric, "the one we captured off Wales?"

"She's still in Hamtun," he said, "and now that I'm not there she's probably in someone else's bed."

"Probably? Certainly."

"Then the bastard's welcome to her," he said. "She cries a lot."

"Mildrith does that," I said and then, after a pause, "Eanflæd was angry with you."

"Eanflæd? Angry with me! Why?"

"Because you didn't go to see her."

"How could I? I was in chains." He looked satisfied that the whore had asked after him. "Eanflæd doesn't cry, does she?"

"Not that I've seen."

"Good girl that. I reckon she'd like Hamtun."

If Hamtun still existed. Had a Danish fleet come from Lundene? Was Svein attacking across the Sæfern Sea? I knew nothing except that Wessex was suffering chaos and defeat. It began to rain again, a thin winter's rain, cold and stinging. Iseult crouched lower and I sheltered her with my shield. Most of the folk who had gathered to watch the fight by the river had fled south and only a handful had come our way, which meant there were fewer Danes near our hiding place, and those that were in the northern river meadows were now gathering their spoils. They stripped corpses of weapons, belts, mail, clothes, anything of value. A few Saxon men had survived, but they were being led away with the children and younger women to be sold as slaves. The old were killed. A wounded man was crawling on hands and knees and a dozen Danes tormented him like cats playing with an injured sparrow, nicking him with swords and spears, bleeding him to a slow death. Haesten was one of the tormentors. "I always liked Haesten," I said sadly.

"He's a Dane," Leofric said scornfully.

"I still liked him."

"You kept him alive," Leofric said, "and now he's gone back to his own. You should have killed him." I watched as Haesten kicked the wounded man who called out in agony, begging to be killed, but the group of young men went on jabbing him, laughing, and the first ravens came. I have often wondered if ravens smell blood, for the sky can be clear of them all day, but when a man dies they come from nowhere on their shining black wings. Perhaps Odin sends them, for the ravens are his birds, and now they flapped down to start feasting on eyes and lips, the first course of every raven feast. The dogs and foxes would soon follow.

"The end of Wessex," Leofric said sadly.

"The end of England," I said.

"What do we do?" Iseult asked.

There was no answer from me. Ragnar must be dead, which meant I had no refuge among the Danes, and Alfred was probably dead or else a fugitive, and my duty now was to my son. He was only a baby, but he was my son and he carried my name. Bebbanburg would be his if I could take it back, and if I could not take it back then it would be his duty to recapture the stronghold, and so the name Uhtred of Bebbanburg would go on till the last weltering chaos of the dying world.

"We must get to Hamtun," Leofric said, "and find the crew."

Except the Danes would surely be there already. Or else on their way. They knew where the power of Wessex lay, where the great lords had their halls, where the soldiers gathered, and Guthrum would be sending men to burn and kill and so disarm the Saxons' last kingdom.

"We need food," I said, "food and warmth."

"Light a fire here," Leofric grumbled, "and we're dead."

So we waited. The small rain turned to sleet. Haesten and his new companions, now that their victim was dead, wandered away, leaving the meadow empty but for the corpses and their attendant ravens. And still we waited, but Iseult, who was as thin as Alfred, was shivering uncontrollably and so, in the late afternoon, I took off my helmet and unbound my hair so it hung loose.

"What are you doing?" Leofric asked.

"For the moment," I said, "we're Danes. Just keep your mouth shut."

I led them toward the town. I would have preferred to wait until dark, but Iseult was too cold to wait longer, and I just hoped the Danes had calmed down. I might look like a Dane, but it was still dangerous. Haesten might see me, and if he told others how I had ambushed the Danish ship off Dyfed, then I could expect nothing but a slow death. So we went nervously, stepping past bloodied bodies along the riverside path. The ravens protested as we approached, flapped indignantly into the winter willows, and returned to their feast when we had passed. There were more corpses piled by the bridge where the young folk captured for slavery were being made to dig a grave. The Danes guarding them were drunk and none challenged us as we went across the wooden span and under the gate arch that was still hung with holly and ivy in celebration of Christmas.

The fires were dying now, damped by rain or else extinguished by the Danes who were ransacking houses and churches. I stayed in the narrowest alleys, edging past a smithy, a hide-dealer's shop, and a place where pots had been sold. Our boots crunched through the pottery shards. A young Dane was vomiting in the alley's entrance and he told me that Guthrum was in the royal compound where there would be a feast that night. He straightened up, gasping for breath, but was sober enough to offer me a bag of coins for Iseult. There were women screaming or sobbing in houses and their noise was making Leofric angry, but I told him to stay quiet. Two of us could not free Cippanhamm, and if the world had been turned upside down and it had been a West Saxon army capturing a Danish town, it would have sounded no different. "Alfred wouldn't allow it," Leofric said sullenly.

"You'd do it anyway," I said. "You've done it."

I wanted news, but none of the Danes in the street made any sense. They had come from Gleawecestre, leaving long before dawn, they had captured Cippanhamm, and now they wanted to enjoy whatever the town offered. The big church had burned, but men were raking through the smoking embers looking for silver. For lack of anywhere else to go we climbed the hill to the Corncrake tavern where we always drank and found Eanflæd, the redheaded whore, being held on a table by two young Danes while three others, none of them more than seventeen or eighteen, took turns raping her. Another dozen Danes were drinking peaceably enough, taking scant notice of the rape.

"You want her," one of the young men said, "you'll have to wait."

"I want her now," I said.

"Then you can jump in the shit pit," he said. He was drunk. He had a wispy beard and insolent eyes. "You can jump in the shit pit," he said again, evidently liking the insult, then pointed to Iseult, "and I'll have her while you drown." I hit him, breaking his nose and spattering his face with blood, and while he gasped I kicked him hard between the legs. He went down, whimpering, and I hit a second man in the belly while Leofric loosed all his day's frustration in a savage attack on another. The two who had been holding Eanflæd turned on us and one of them squealed when Eanflæd grabbed his hair and hooked sharp fingernails into his eyes. Leofric's opponent was on the floor and he stamped on the boy's throat and I head-slapped my boy until I had him by the door, then I thumped another in the ribs, rescued Eanflæd's victim, and broke his jaw, then went back to the lad who had threatened to rape Iseult. I ripped a silver loop from his ear, took off his one arm ring, and stole his pouch that clinked with coins. I dropped the silver into Eanflæd's lap, then kicked the groaning man between the legs, did it again, and hauled him out into the street.

"Go jump in a shit pit," I told him, then slammed the door. The other Danes, still drinking on the tavern's far side, had watched the fight with amusement and now gave us ironic applause.

"Bastards," Eanflæd said, evidently talking of the men we had driven away. "I'm sore as hell. What are you two doing here?"

"They think we're Danes," I said.

"We need food," Leofric said.

"They've had most of it," Eanflæd said, jerking her head at the seated Danes, "but there might be something left in the back." She tied her girdle. "Edwulf's dead." Edwulf had owned the tavern. "And thanks for helping me, you spavined bastards!" She shouted this at the Danes, who did not understand her and just laughed at her. Then she went toward the back room to find us food, but one of the men held out a hand to stop her.

"Where are you going?" he asked her in Danish.

"She's going past you," I called.

"I want ale," he said, "and you? Who are you?"

"I'm the man who's going to cut your throat if you stop her fetching food," I said.

"Quiet, quiet!" an older man said, then frowned at me. "Don't I know you?"

"I was with Guthrum at Readingum," I said, "and at Werham."

"That must be it. He's done better this time, eh?"

"He's done better," I agreed.

The man pointed at Iseult. "Yours?"

"Not for sale."

"Just asking, friend, just asking."

Eanflæd brought us stale bread, cold pork, wrinkled apples, and a rock-hard cheese in which red worms writhed. The older man carried a pot of ale to our table, evidently as a peace offering, and he sat and talked with me and I learned a little more of what was happening. Guthrum had brought close to three thousand men to attack Cippanhamm. Guthrum himself was now in Alfred's hall and half his men would stay in Cippanhamm as a garrison while the rest planned to ride either south or east in the morning. "Keep the bastards on the run, eh?" the man said, then frowned at Leofric. "He doesn't say much."

"He's dumb," I said.

"I knew a man who had a dumb wife. He was ever so happy." He looked jealously at my arm rings. "So who do you serve?"

"Svein of the White Horse."

"Svein? He wasn't at Readingum. Or at Werham."

"He was in Dyflin," I said, "but I was with Ragnar the Older then."

"Ah, Ragnar! Poor bastard."

"I suppose his son's dead now?" I asked.

"What else?" the man said. "Hostages, poor bastards." He thought for a heartbeat, then frowned again. "What's Svein doing here? I thought he was coming by ship?"

"He is," I said. "We're just here to talk to Guthrum."

"Svein sends a dumb man to talk to Guthrum?"

"He sent me to talk," I said, "and sent him," I jerked a thumb at the glowering Leofric, "to kill people who ask too many questions."

"All right, all right!" The man held up a hand to ward off my belligerence.

We slept in the stable loft, warmed by straw, and we left before dawn, and at that moment fifty West Saxons could have retaken Cippanhamm for the Danes were drunk, sleeping, and oblivious to the world. Leofric stole a sword, ax, and shield from a man snoring in the tavern. Then we walked unchallenged out of the western gate. In a field outside we found over a hundred horses, guarded by two men sleeping in a thatched hut, and we could have taken all the beasts, but we had no saddles or bridles and so, reluctantly, I knew we must walk. There were four of us now, because Eanflæd had decided to come with us. She had swathed Iseult in two big cloaks, but the British girl was still shivering.

We walked west and south along a road that twisted through small hills. We were heading for Baðum, and from there I could strike south toward Defnascir and my son, but it was clear the Danes were already ahead of us. Some must have ridden this way the previous day, for in the first village we reached there were no cocks crowing, no sound at all, and what I had taken for a morning mist was smoke from burned cottages. Heavier smoke showed ahead, suggesting the Danes might already have reached Baðum, a town they knew well for they had negotiated one of their truces there. Then, that afternoon, a horde of mounted Danes appeared on the road behind us and we were driven west into the hills to find a hiding place.

We wandered for a week. We found shelter in hovels. Some were deserted while others still had frightened folk, but every short winter's day was smeared with smoke as the Danes ravaged Wessex. One day we discovered a cow, trapped in its byre in an otherwise deserted homestead. The cow was with calf and bellowing with hunger, and that night we feasted on fresh meat. Next day we could not move for it was bitterly cold and a slanting rain slashed on an east wind and the trees thrashed as if in agony and the building that gave us shelter leaked and the fire choked us and Iseult just sat, eyes wide and empty, staring into the small flames.

"You want to go back to Cornwalum?" I asked her.

She seemed surprised I had spoken. It took her a few heartbeats to gather her thoughts. Then she shrugged. "What is there for me?"

"Home," Eanflæd said.

"Uhtred is home for me."

"Uhtred is married," Eanflæd said harshly.

Iseult ignored that. "Uhtred will lead men," she said, rocking back and forth, "hundreds of men. A bright horde. I want to see that."

"He'll lead you into temptation, that's all he'll

do," Eanflæd said. "Go home, girl, say your prayers, and hope the Danes don't come."

We kept trying to go southward and we made some small progress every day, but the bitter days were short and the Danes seemed to be everywhere. Even when we traveled across countryside far from any track or path, there would be a patrol of Danes in the distance, and to avoid them we were constantly driven west. To our east was the Roman road that ran from Baðum and eventually to Exanceaster, the main thoroughfare in this part of Wessex, and I supposed the Danes were using it and sending patrols out to either side of the road, and it was those patrols that drove us ever nearer the Sæfern Sea, but there could be no safety there, for Svein would surely have come from Wales.

I also supposed that Wessex had finally fallen. We met a few folk, fugitives from their villages and hiding in the woods, but none had any news, only rumor. No one had seen any West Saxon soldiers, no one had heard about Alfred, they only saw Danes and the ever-present smoke. From time to time we would come across a ravaged village or a burned church. We would see ragged ravens flapping black and follow them to find rotting bodies. We were lost and any hope I had of reaching Oxton was long gone, and I assumed Mildrith had fled west into the hills as the folk around the Uisc always did when the Danes came. I hoped she was alive, I hoped my son lived, but what future he had was as dark as the long winter nights.

"Maybe we should make our peace," I suggested to Leofric one night. We were in a shepherd's hut, crouched around a small fire that filled the low turf-roofed building with smoke. We had roasted a dozen mutton ribs cut from a sheep's half-eaten corpse. We were all filthy, damp, and cold. "Maybe we should find the Danes," I said, "and swear allegiance."

"And be made slaves?" Leofric answered bitterly.

"We'll be warriors," I said.

"Fighting for a Dane?" He poked the fire, throwing up a new burst of smoke. "They can't have taken all Wessex," he protested.

"Why not?"

"It's too big. There have to be some men fighting back. We just have to find them."

I thought back to the long-ago arguments in Lundene. Back then I had been a child with the Danes, and their leaders had argued that the best way to take Wessex was to attack its western heartland and there break its power. Others had wanted to start the assault by taking the old kingdom of Kent, the weakest part of Wessex and the part that contained the great shrine of Contwaraburg, but the boldest argument had won. They had attacked in the west and that first assault had failed, but now Guthrum had succeeded. Yet how far had he succeeded? Was Kent still Saxon? Defnascir?

"And what happens to Mildrith if you join the Danes?" Leofric asked.

"She'll have hidden," I spoke dully and there was a silence, but I saw Eanflæd was offended and I hoped she would hold her tongue.

She did not. "Do you care?" she challenged me.

"I care," I said.

Eanflæd scorned that answer. "Grown dull, has she?"

"Of course he cares." Leofric tried to be a peacemaker.

"She's a wife," Eanflæd retorted, still looking at me. "Men tire of wives," she went on and Iseult listened, her big dark eyes going from me to Eanflæd.

"What do you know of wives?" I asked.

"I was married," Eanflæd said.

"You were?" Leofric asked, surprised.

"I was married for three years," Eanflæd said, "to a man who was in Wulfhere's guard. He gave me two children, then died in the battle that killed King Æthelred."

"Two children?" Iseult asked.

"They died," Eanflæd said harshly. "That's what children do. They die."

"You were happy with him," Leofric asked, "your husband?"

"For about three days," she said, "and in the next three years I learned that men are bastards."

"All of them?" Leofric asked.

"Most." She smiled at Leofric, then touched his knee. "Not you."

"And me?" I asked.

"You?" She looked at me for a heartbeat. "I wouldn't trust you as far as I could spit," she said, and there was real venom in her voice, leaving Leofric embarrassed and me surprised. There comes a moment in life when we see ourselves as others see us. I suppose that is part of growing up, and it is not always comfortable. Eanflæd, at that moment, regretted speaking so harshly, for she tried to soften it. "I don't know you," she said, "except you're Leofric's friend."

"Uhtred is generous," Iseult said loyally.

"Men are usually generous when they want something," Eanflæd retorted.

"I want Bebbanburg," I said.

"Whatever that is," Eanflæd said, "and to get it you'd do anything. Anything."

There was silence. I saw a snowflake show at the half-covered door. It fluttered into the firelight and melted. "Alfred's a good man." Leofric broke the awkward silence.

"He tries to be good," Eanflæd said.

"Only tries?" I asked sarcastically.

"He's like you," she said. "He'd kill to get what he wants, but there is a difference. He has a conscience."

"He's frightened of the priests, you mean."

"He's frightened of God. And we should all be that. Because one day we'll answer to God."

"Not me," I said.

Eanflæd sneered at that, but Leofric changed the conversation by saying it was snowing, and after a while we slept. Iseult clung to me in her sleep and she whimpered and twitched as I lay awake, half dreaming, thinking of her words that

I would lead a bright horde. It seemed an un-
likely prophecy, indeed I reckoned her powers
must have gone with her virginity, and then I
slept, too, waking to a world made white. The
twigs and branches were edged with snow, but it
was already melting, dripping into a misty dawn.
When I went outside I found a tiny dead wren
just beyond the door and I feared it was a grim
omen.

Leofric emerged from the hut, blinking at the
dawn's brilliance. "Don't mind Eanflæd," he
said.

"I don't."

"Her world's come to an end."

"Then we must remake it," I said.

"Does that mean you won't join the Danes?"

"I'm a Saxon," I said.

Leofric half smiled at that. He undid his
breeches and had a piss. "If your friend Ragnar
was alive," he asked, watching the steam rise
from his urine, "would you still be a Saxon?"

"He's dead, isn't he?" I said bleakly. "Sacrificed to Guthrum's ambition."

"So now you're a Saxon?"

"I'm a Saxon," I said again, sounding more
certain than I felt, for I did not know what the
future held. How can we? Perhaps Iseult had

told the truth and Alfred would give me power and I would lead a shining horde and have a woman of gold, but I was beginning to doubt Iseult's powers. Alfred might already be dead and his kingdom was doomed, and all I knew at that moment was that the land stretched away south to a snow-covered ridgeline, and there it ended in a strange empty brightness. The skyline looked like the world's rim, poised above an abyss of pearly light. "We'll keep going south," I said. There was nothing else to do except walk toward the brightness.

We did. We followed a sheep track to the ridgetop and there I saw that the hills fell steeply away, dropping to the vast marshes of the sea. We had come to the great swamp, and the brightness I had seen was the winter light reflecting from the long meres and winding creeks.

"What now?" Leofric asked, and I had no answer. So we sat under the berries of a wind-bent yew and stared at the immensity of bog, water, grass, and reeds. This was the vast swamp that stretched inland from the Sæfern, and if I was to reach Defnascir I either had to go around it or try to cross it. If we went around it then we would have to go to the Roman road, and that was where the Danes were, but if we tried to cross the swamp we would face other dangers. I had heard a thousand stories of men being lost in its wet tangles. It was said there were spirits there, spirits that showed at night as flickering lights, and there were paths that led only to quicksand or to drowning pools, but there were also villages in the swamp, places where folk trapped fish and eels. The people of the swamp were protected by the spirits and by the sudden surges in the tide that could drown a road in an eyeblink. Now, as the last snows melted from the reed banks, the swamp looked like a great stretch of waterlogged land, its streams and meres swollen by the winter rains, but when the tide rose it would resemble an inland sea dotted with islands. We could see one of those islands not so far off, and there was a cluster of huts on that speck of higher ground; that would be a place to find food and warmth if we could ever reach it. Eventually we might cross the whole swamp, finding a way from island to island, but it would take far longer than a day, and we would have to find refuge at every high tide. I gazed at the long, cold stretches of water, almost black beneath the leaden clouds that came from the sea, and my spirits sank for I did not know where we were going, or why, or what the future held.

It seemed to get colder as we sat, and then a light snow began drifting from the dark clouds. Just a few flakes, but enough to convince me that we had to find shelter soon. Smoke was rising from the nearest swamp village, evidence that some folk still lived there. There would be food in their hovels and a meager warmth. "We have to get to that island," I said, pointing.

But the others were staring westward to where a flock of pigeons had burst from the trees at the foot of the slope. The birds rose and flew in circles. "Someone's there," Leofric said.

We waited. The pigeons settled in the trees higher up the hill. "Maybe it's a boar?" I suggested.

"Pigeons won't fly from a boar," Leofric said. "Boars don't startle pigeons, any more than stags do. There are folk there."

The thought of boars and stags made me wonder what had happened to my hounds. Had Mildrith abandoned them? I had not even told her where I had hidden the remains of the plunder we had taken off the coast of Wales. I had dug a hole in a corner of my new hall and buried the gold and silver down by the post stone, but it was not the cleverest hiding place and if there were Danes in Oxton then they were bound to delve into the edges of the hall floor, especially if a probing spear found a place where the earth had been disturbed. A flight of ducks flew overhead. The snow was falling harder, blurring the long view across the swamp.

"Priests," Leofric said.

There were a half dozen men off to the west. They were robed in black and had come from the trees to walk along the swamp's margin, plainly seeking a path into its tangled vastness, but there was no obvious track to the small village on its tiny island and so the priests came nearer to us, skirting the ridge's foot. One of them was carrying a long staff and, even at a distance, I could see a glint at its head and I suspected it was a bishop's staff, the kind with a heavy silver cross. Another three carried heavy sacks. "You think there's food in those bundles?" Leofric asked wistfully.

"They're priests," I said savagely. "They'll be carrying silver."

"Or books," Eanflæd suggested. "Priests like books."

"It could be food," Leofric said, though not very convincingly.

A group of three women and two children

now appeared. One of the women appeared to be wearing a swathing cloak of silver fur, while another carried the smaller child. The women and children were not far behind the priests, who waited for them, and then they all walked eastward until they were beneath us and there they discovered some kind of path twisting into the marshes. Five of the priests led the women into the swamp while the sixth man, evidently younger than the others, hurried back westward. "Where's he going?" Leofric asked.

Another skein of ducks flighted low overhead, skimming down the slope to the long meres of the swamp. Nets, I thought. There must be nets in the swamp villages and we could trap fish and wildfowl. We could eat well for a few days. Eels, duck, fish, geese. If there were enough nets we could even trap deer by driving them into the tangling meshes.

"They're not going anywhere," Leofric said scornfully, nodding at the priests who had stranded themselves a hundred paces out in the swamp. The path was deceptive. It had offered an apparent route to the village, but then petered out amid a patch of reeds where the priests hud-dled. They did not want to come back and did not want to go forward, and so they stayed where they were, lost and cold and despairing. They looked as though they were arguing.

"We must help them," Eanflæd said and, when I said nothing, she protested that one of the women was holding a baby. "We have to help them!" she insisted.

I was about to retort that the last thing we needed was more hungry mouths to feed, but her harsh words in the night had persuaded me that I had to do something to show her I was not as treacherous as she evidently believed, so I stood, hefted my shield, and started down the hill. The others followed, but before we were even halfway down I heard shouts from the west. The lone priest who had gone that way was now with four soldiers and they turned as horsemen came from the trees. There were six horsemen, then eight more appeared, then another ten, and I realized a whole column of mounted soldiers was streaming from the dead winter trees. They had black shields and black cloaks, so they had to be Guthrum's men. One of the priests stranded in the swamp ran back along the path and I saw he had a sword and was going to help his companions.

It was a brave thing for the lone priest to do,

but quite useless. The four soldiers and the single priest were surrounded now. They were standing back-to-back and the Danish horsemen were all around them, hacking down, and then two of the horsemen saw the priest with his sword and spurred toward him. "Those two are ours," I said to Leofric.

That was stupid. The four men were doomed, as was the priest if we did not intervene, but there were only two of us and, even if we killed the two horsemen, we would still face overwhelming odds, but I was driven by Eanflæd's scorn and I was tired of skulking through the winter countryside and I was angry. So I ran down the hill, careless of the noise I made as I crashed through brittle undergrowth. The lone priest had his back to the swamp now and the horsemen were charging at him as Leofric and I burst from the trees and came at them from their left side.

I hit the nearest horse's flank with my heavy shield. There was a scream from the horse and an explosion of wet soil, grass, snow, and hooves as man and beast went down sideways. I was also on the ground, knocked there by the impact, but I recovered first and found the rider tangled with his stirrups, one leg trapped under the struggling horse, and I chopped Serpent-Breath down hard. I cut into his throat, stamped on his face, chopped again, slipped in his blood, then left him and went to help Leofric who was fending off the second man who was still on horseback. The Dane's sword thumped on Leofric's shield, then he had to turn his horse to face me and Leofric's ax took the horse in the face and the beast reared, the rider slid backward, and I met his spine with Serpent-Breath's tip. Two down. The priest with the sword, not a half dozen paces away, had not moved. He was just staring at us. "Get back into the marsh!" I shouted at him. "Go! Go!" Iseult and Eanflæd were with us now and they seized the priest and hurried him toward the path. It might lead nowhere, but it was better to face the remaining Danes there than on the firm ground at the hill's foot.

And those black-cloaked Danes were coming. They had slaughtered the handful of soldiers, seen their two men killed, and now came for vengeance. "Come on!" I snarled at Leofric and, taking the wounded horse by the reins, I ran onto the small twisting path.

"A horse won't help you here," Leofric said.

The horse was nervous. Its face was wounded and the path was slippery, but I dragged it along the track until we were close to the small patch of land where the refugees huddled, and by now the Danes were also on the path, following us. They had dismounted. They could only come two abreast and, in places, only one man could use the track and in one of those places I stopped the horse and exchanged Serpent-Breath for Leofric's ax. The horse looked at me with a big brown eye. "This is for Odin," I said, and I swung the ax into its neck, chopping down through mane and hide, and a woman screamed behind me as the blood spurted bright and high in the dull day. The horse whinnied and tried to rear, and I swung again; this time the beast went down, thrashing hooves, blood, and water splashing. Snow turned red as I axed it a third time, finally stilling it, and now the dying beast was an obstacle athwart the track and the Danes would have to fight across its corpse. I took Serpent-Breath back.

"We'll kill them one by one," I told Leofric.

"For how long?" He nodded westward and I saw more Danes coming, a whole ship's crew of mounted Danes streaming along the swamp's edge. Fifty men? Maybe more, but even so they could only use the path in ones or twos and they would have to fight over the dead horse into

Serpent-Breath and Leofric's ax. He had lost his own ax, taken from him when he was brought to Cippanhamm, but he seemed to like his stolen weapon. He made the sign of the cross, touched the blade, then hefted his shield as the Danes came.

Two young men came first. They were wild and savage, wanting to make a reputation, but the first to come was stopped by Leofric's ax banging into his shield and I swept Serpent-Breath beneath the shield to slice his ankle and he fell, cursing, to tangle his companion, and Leofric wrenched the wide-bladed ax free and slashed it down again. The second man stumbled on the horse and Serpent-Breath took him under the chin, above his leather coat, and the blood ran down her blade in a sudden flood and now there were two Danish corpses added to the horse-flesh barricade. I was taunting the other Danes, calling them corpse worms, telling them I had known children who could fight better. Another man came, screaming in rage as he leaped over the horse, and he was checked by Leofric's shield and Serpent-Breath met his sword with a dull crack and his blade broke, and two more men were trying to get past the horse, struggling in water up to their knees and I rammed Serpent-Breath into the belly of the first, pushing her through his leather armor, left him to die, and swung right at the man trying to get through the water. Serpent-Breath's tip flicked across his face to spray blood into the thickening snowfall. I went forward, feet sinking, lunged again, and he could not move in the mire and Serpent-Breath took his gullet. I was screaming with joy because the battle calm had come, the same blessed stillness I had felt at Cynuit. It is a joy, that feeling, and the only other joy to compare is that of being with a woman.

It is as though life slows. The enemy moves as if he is wading in mud, but I was kingfisher fast. There is rage, but it is a controlled rage, and there is joy, the joy that the poets celebrate when they speak of battle, and a certainty that death is not in that day's fate. My head was full of singing, a keening note, high and shrill, death's anthem. All I wanted was for more Danes to come to Serpent-Breath and it seemed to me that she took on her own life in those moments. To think was to act. A man came across the horse's flank; I thought to slice at his ankle, knew he would drop his shield and so open his upper body to an attack, and before the thought was even coherent it was done and Serpent-Breath had taken one of his eyes. She had gone down and up, was already moving to the right to counter another man trying to get around the horse, and I let him get past the stallion's bloodied head, then scornfully drove him down into the water and there I stood on him, holding his head under my boot as he drowned. I screamed at the Danes, told them I was Valhalla's gatekeeper, that they had been weaned on coward's milk, and that I wanted them to come to my blade. I begged them to come, but five men were dead around the horse and the others were now wary.

I stood on the dead horse and spread my arms. I held the shield high to my left and the sword to my right, and my mail coat was spattered with blood, and the snow fell about my wolf-crested helmet, and all I knew was the young man's joy of slaughter. "I killed Ubba Lothbrokson!" I shouted at them. "I killed him! So come and join him! Taste his death! My sword wants you!"

"Boats," Leofric said. I did not hear him. The man I thought I had drowned was still alive and he suddenly reared from the marsh, choking and vomiting water, and I jumped down off the horse and put my foot on his head again.

"Let him live!" a voice shouted behind me. "I want a prisoner!"

The man tried to fight my foot, but Serpent-Breath put him down. He struggled again and I broke his spine with Serpent-Breath and he was still.

"I said I wanted a prisoner," the voice behind protested.

"Come and die!" I shouted at the Danes.

"Boats," Leofric said again, and I glanced behind and saw three punts coming through the marsh. They were long flat boats, propelled by men with poles, and they grounded on the other side of the huddled refugees who hurried aboard. The Danes, knowing Leofric and I had to retreat if we were to gain the safety of the boats, readied for a charge and I smiled at them, inviting them.

"One boat left," Leofric said. "Room for us. You'll have to run like hell."

"I'll stay here," I shouted, but in Danish. "I'm enjoying myself."

Then there was a stir on the path as a man came to the front rank of the Danes and the others edged aside to give him room. He was in chain mail and had a silvered helmet with a raven's wing at its crown, but as he came closer he took the helmet off and I saw the gold-tipped bone in his hair. It was Guthrum himself. The bone was one of his mother's ribs and he wore it out of love for her memory. He stared at me, his gaunt face sad, and then looked down at the men we had killed. "I shall hunt you like a dog, Uhtred Ragnarson," he said, "and I shall kill you like a dog."

"My name," I said, "is Uhtred Uhtredson."

"We have to run," Leofric hissed at me.

The snow whirled above the swamp, thick enough now so that I could hardly see the ridgetop from where we had glimpsed the pigeons circling. "You are a dead man, Uhtred," Guthrum said.

"I never met your mother," I called to him, "but I would have liked to meet her."

His face took on the reverent look that any mention of his mother always provoked. He seemed to regret that he had spoken so harshly to me for he made a conciliatory gesture. "She was a great woman," he said.

I smiled at him. At that moment, looking back, I could have changed sides so easily and Guthrum would have welcomed me if I had just given his mother a compliment, but I was a belligerent young man and the battle joy was on me.

"I would have spat in her ugly face," I told Guthrum, "and now I piss on your mother's soul, and tell you that the beasts of Niflheim are humping her rancid bones."

He screamed with rage and they all charged, some splashing through the shallows, all desperate to reach me and avenge the terrible insult, but Leofric and I were running like hunted boars, and we charged through the reeds and into the water and hurled ourselves onto the last punt. The first two were gone, but the third had waited for us and, as we sprawled on its damp boards, the man with the pole pushed hard and the craft slid away into the black water. The Danes tried to follow, but we were going surprisingly fast, gliding through the snowfall, and Guthrum was shouting at me and a spear was thrown, but the marshman poled again and the spear plunged harmlessly into the mud.

"I shall find you!" Guthrum shouted.

"Why should I care?" I called back. "Your men only know how to die!" I raised Serpent-Breath and kissed her sticky blade. "And your mother was a whore to dwarves!"

"You should have let that one man live," a voice said behind me, "because I wanted to question him." The punt only contained the one passenger besides Leofric and myself, and that one man was the priest who had carried a sword and now he was sitting in the punt's flat bow, frowning at me. "There was no need to kill that man," he said sternly and I looked at him with such fury that he recoiled. Damn all priests, I thought. I had saved the bastard's life and all he did was reprove me, and then I saw that he was no priest at all.

It was Alfred.

The punt slid over the swamp, sometimes gliding across black water, sometimes rustling through grass or reeds. The man poling it was a bent, dark-skinned creature with a massive beard, otter-skin clothes, and a toothless mouth. Guthrum's Danes were far behind now, carrying their dead back to firmer ground. "I need to know what they plan to do," Alfred complained to me. "The prisoner could have told us."

He spoke more respectfully. Looking back I realized I had frightened him, for the front of my mail coat was sheeted in blood and there was more blood on my face and helmet.

"They plan to finish Wessex," I said curtly. "You don't need a prisoner to tell you that."

"Lord," he said.

I stared at him.

"I am a king!" he insisted. "You address a king with respect."

"A king of what?" I asked.

"You're not hurt, lord?" Leofric asked Alfred.

"No, thank God. No." He looked at the sword he carried. "Thank God." I saw he was not wearing priest's robes, but a swathing black cloak. His long face was very pale. "Thank you, Leofric," he said, then looked up at me and seemed to shudder. We were catching up with the other two punts and I saw that Ælswith, pregnant and swathed in a silver fox-fur cloak, was in one. Iseult and Eanflæd were also in that punt whereas the priests were crowded onto the other, and I saw that Bishop Alewold of Exanceaster was one of them.

"What happened, lord?" Leofric asked.

Alfred sighed. He was shivering now, but he told his story. He had ridden from Cippanhamm with his family, his bodyguard, and a score of churchmen to accompany the monk Asser on the first part of his journey. "We had a service of thanksgiving," he said, "in the church at Soppan Byrg. It's a new church," he added earnestly to Leofric, "and very fine. We sang psalms, said prayers, and Brother Asser went on his way rejoicing." He made the sign of the cross. "I pray he's safe."

"I hope the lying bastard's dead," I snarled.

Alfred ignored that. After the church service they had all gone to a nearby monastery for a meal, and it was while they were there that the Danes had come. The royal group had fled, finding shelter in nearby woods while the monastery burned. After that they had tried to ride east into the heart of Wessex but, like us, they had constantly been headed off by patrolling Danes. One night, sheltering in a farm, they had been surprised by Danish troops who had killed some of Alfred's guards and captured all his horses and ever since they had been wandering, as lost as us, until they came to the swamp. "God knows what will happen now," Alfred said.

"We fight," I said. He just looked at me and I shrugged. "We fight," I said again.

Alfred stared across the swamp. "Find a ship," he said, but so softly that I hardly heard him. "Find a ship and go to Frankia." He pulled the cloak tighter around his thin body. The snow was thickening as it fell, though it melted as soon as it met the dark water. The Danes had vanished, lost in the snow behind. "That was Guthrum?" Alfred asked me.

"That was Guthrum," I said. "And he knew it was you he pursued?"

"I suppose so."

"What else would draw Guthrum here?" I asked. "He wants you dead. Or captured."

Yet, for the moment, we were safe. The island village had a score of damp hovels thatched with reeds and a few storehouses raised on stilts. The buildings were the color of mud, the street was mud, the goats and the people were mud-covered, but the place, poor as it was, could provide food, shelter, and a meager warmth. The men of the village had seen the refugees and, after a discussion, decided to rescue them. I suspect they wanted to pillage us rather than save our lives, but Leofric and I looked formidable and, once the villagers understood that their king was their guest, they did their clumsy best for him and his family. One of them, in a dialect I could scarcely understand, wanted to know the king's name. He had never heard of Alfred. He knew about the Danes, but said their ships had never reached the village, or any of the other settlements in the swamp. He told us the villagers lived off deer, goats, fish, eels, and wildfowl, and they had plenty of food, though fuel was scarce.

Ælswith was pregnant with her third child, while her first two were in the care of nurses.

There was Edward, Alfred's heir, who was three years old and sick. He coughed, and Ælswith worried about him, though Bishop Alewold insisted it was just a winter's cold. Then there was Edward's elder sister, Æthelflaed, who was now six and had a bright head of golden curls, a beguiling smile, and clever eyes. Alfred adored her, and in those first days in the swamp, she was his one ray of light and hope. One night, as we sat by a small, dying fire and Æthelflaed slept with her golden head in her father's lap, he asked me about my son.

"I don't know where he is," I said. There were only the two of us, everyone else was sleeping, and I was sitting by the door staring across the frost-bleached marsh that lay black and silver under a half-moon.

"You want to go and find him?" he asked earnestly.

"You truly want me to do that?" I asked. He looked puzzled. "These folk are giving you shelter," I explained, "but they'd as soon cut your throats. They won't do that while I'm here."

He was about to protest, then understood I probably spoke the truth. He stroked his daughter's hair. Edward coughed. He was in his mother's hut. The coughing had become worse, much worse, and we all suspected it was the whooping cough that killed small children. Alfred flinched at the sound. "Did you fight Steapa?" he asked.

"We fought," I said curtly. "The Danes came, and we never finished. He was bleeding, I was not."

"He was bleeding?"

"Ask Leofric. He was there."

He was silent a long time, then, softly, "I am still king."

Of a swamp, I thought, and said nothing.

"And it is customary to call a king 'lord,'" he went on.

I just stared at his thin, pale face that was lit by the dying fire. He looked so solemn, but also frightened, as if he was making a huge effort to hold on to the shreds of his dignity. Alfred never lacked for bravery, but he was not a warrior and he did not much like the company of warriors. In his eyes I was a brute: dangerous, uninteresting, but suddenly indispensable. He knew I was not going to call him lord, so he did not insist. "What do you notice about this place?" he asked.

"It's wet," I said.

"What else?"

I looked for the trap in the question and found none. "It can only be reached by punts," I said, "and the Danes don't have punts. But when they do have punts it'll need more than Leofric and me to fight them off."

"It doesn't have a church," he said.

"I knew I liked it," I retorted.

He ignored that. "We know so little of our own kingdom," he said in wonderment. "I thought there were churches everywhere." He closed his eyes for a few heartbeats, then looked at me plaintively. "What should I do?"

That morning I had told him to fight, but I could see no fight in him now, just despair. "You can go south," I said, thinking that was what he wanted to hear, "go south across the sea."

"To be another exiled Saxon king," he said bitterly.

"We hide here," I said, "and when we think the Danes aren't watching, we go to the south coast and find a ship."

"How do we hide?" he asked. "They know we're here. And they're on both sides of the swamp." The marshman had told us that a Danish fleet had landed at Cynuit, which lay at the swamp's western edge. That fleet, I assumed, was led by Svein and he would surely be wondering how to find Alfred. The king, I reckoned, was doomed, and his family, too. If Æthelflaed was lucky she would be raised by a Danish family, as I had been, but more probably they would all be killed so that no Saxon could ever again claim the crown of Wessex. "And the Danes will be watching the south coast," Alfred went on.

"They will," I agreed.

He looked out at the marsh where the night wind rippled the waters, shaking the long reflection of a winter moon. "The Danes can't have taken all Wessex," he said, then flinched because Edward was coughing so painfully.

"Probably not," I agreed.

"If we could find men," he said, then fell silent.

"What would we do with men?" I asked.

"Attack the fleet," he said, pointing west. "Get rid of Svein, if it is Svein at Cynuit, then hold the hills of Defnascir. Gain one victory and more men will come. We get stronger and one day we can face Guthrum."

I thought about it. He had spoken dully, as if he did not really believe in the words he had said, but I thought they made a perverse kind of sense. There were men in Wessex, men who were leaderless, but they were men who wanted a leader, men who would fight, and perhaps we could secure the swamp, then defeat Svein, then capture Defnascir, and so, piece by piece, take back Wessex. Then I thought about it more closely and reckoned it was a dream. The Danes had won. We were fugitives.

Alfred was stroking his daughter's golden hair. "The Danes will hunt us here, won't they?"

"Yes."

"Can you defend us?"

"Just me and Leofric?"

"You're a warrior, aren't you? Men tell me it was really you who defeated Ubba."

"You knew I killed Ubba?" I asked.

"Can you defend us?"

I would not be deflected. "Did you know I won your victory at Cynuit?" I demanded.

"Yes," he said simply.

"And my reward was to crawl to your altar? To be humiliated?" My anger made my voice too loud and Æthelflaed opened her eyes and stared at me.

"I have made mistakes," Alfred said, "and when this is all over, and when God returns Wessex to the West Saxons, I shall do the same. I shall put on the penitent's robe and submit myself to God."

I wanted to kill the pious bastard then, but Æthelflaed was watching me with her big eyes. She had not moved, so her father did not know she was awake, but I did, so instead of giving my anger a loose rein I cut it off abruptly. "You'll find that penitence helps," I said.

He brightened at that. "It helped you?" he asked.

"It gave me anger," I said, "and it taught me to hate. And anger is good. Hatred is good."

"You don't mean that," he said.

I half drew Serpent-Breath and little Æthelflaed's eyes grew wider. "This kills," I said, letting the sword slide back into its fleece-lined scabbard, "but anger and hate are what gives it the strength to kill. Go into battle without anger and hate and you'll be dead. You need all the blades, anger, and hate you can muster if we're to survive."

"But can you do it?" he asked. "Can you defend us here? Long enough to evade the Danes while we decide what to do?"

"Yes," I said. I had no idea whether I spoke the truth, indeed I doubted that I did, but I had

a warrior's pride so gave a warrior's answer.
Æthelflaed had not taken her eyes from me. She
was only six, but I swear she understood all that
we talked about.

"So I give you charge of that task," Alfred
said. "Here and now I appoint you as the de-
fender of my family. Do you accept that responsibility?"

I was an arrogant brute. Still am. He was chal-
lenging me, of course, and he knew what he was
doing even if I did not. I just bridled. "Of course
I accept it," I said, "yes."

"Yes what?" he asked.

I hesitated, but he had flattered me, given me
a warrior's responsibility, and so I gave him what
he wanted and what I had been determined not
to give to him. "Yes, lord," I said.

He held out his hand. I knew he wanted more
now. I had never meant to grant him this wish,
but I had called him "lord" and so I knelt to him
and, across Æthelflaed's body, I took his hand in
both mine.

"Say it," he demanded, and he put the crucifix that hung about his neck between our hands.

"I swear to be your man," I said, looking into
his pale eyes, "until your family is safe."

He hesitated. I had given him the oath, but I

had qualified it. I had let him know that I would not remain his man forever, but he accepted my terms. He should have kissed me on both cheeks, but that would have disturbed Æthelflaed and so he raised my right hand and kissed the knuckles, then kissed the crucifix. "Thank you," he said.

The truth, of course, was that Alfred was finished, but, with the perversity and arrogance of foolish youth, I had just given him my oath and promised to fight for him.

And all, I think, because a six-year-old stared at me. And she had hair of gold.

SEVEN

The kingdom of Wessex was now a swamp and, for a few days, it possessed a king, a bishop, four priests, two soldiers, the king's pregnant wife, two nurses, a whore, two children, one of whom was sick, and Iseult.

Three of the four priests left the swamp first. Alfred was suffering, struck by the fever and belly pains that so often afflicted him, and he seemed incapable of rousing himself to any decision, so I gathered the three youngest priests, told them they were useless mouths we could not afford to feed, and ordered them to leave the swamp and discover what was happening on dry ground. "Find soldiers," I told them, "and say the king wants them to come here." Two of the priests begged to be spared the mission, claiming they were scholars incapable of surviving the winter or of confronting the Danes or of enduring discomfort or of doing any real work, and Alewold, the Bishop of Exanceaster, supported them, saying that their joint prayers were needed to keep the king healthy and safe, so I reminded the bishop that Eanflæd was present.

"Eanflæd?" He blinked at me as though he had never heard the name.

"The whore," I said, "from Cippanhamm." He still looked ignorant. "Cippanhamm," I went on, "where you and she rutted in the Corncrake tavern and she says . . ."

"The priests will travel," he said hastily.

"Of course they will," I said, "but they'll leave their silver here."

"Silver?"

The priests had been carrying Alewold's hoard, which included the great pyx I had given him to settle Mildrith's debts. That hoard was my next weapon. I took it all and displayed it to the marshmen. There would be silver, I said, for the food they gave us and the fuel they brought us and the punts they provided and the news they told us, news of the Danes on the swamp's far side. I wanted the marshmen on our side, and the sight of the silver encouraged them, but Bishop Alewold immediately ran to Alfred and complained that I had stolen from the church. The king was too low in spirits to care, so Ælswith, his wife, entered the fray. She was a Mercian and Alfred had married her to tighten the bonds between Wessex and Mercia, though that did little good for us now because the Danes ruled Mercia. There were plenty of Mercians who would fight for a West Saxon king, but none would risk their lives for a king reduced to a soggy realm in a tidal swamp. "You will return the pyx!" Ælswith ordered me. She looked ragged, her greasy hair tangled, her belly swollen, and her clothes filthy. "Give it back now. This instant!"

I looked at Iseult. "Should I?"

"No," Iseult said.

"She has no say here!" Ælswith shrieked.

"But she's a queen," I said, "and you're not." That was one cause of Ælswith's bitterness, that the West Saxons never called the king's wife a queen. She wanted to be Queen Ælswith and had to be content with less. She tried to snatch back the pyx, but I tossed it on the ground and, when she reached for it, I swung Leofric's ax. The blade chewed into the big plate, mangling the silver crucifixion, and Ælswith squealed in alarm and backed away as I hacked again. It took several blows, but I finally reduced the heavy plate into shreds of mangled silver that I tossed onto the coins I had taken from the priests. "Silver for your help!" I told the marshmen.

Ælswith spat at me, then went back to her son. Edward was three years old and it was evident now that he was dying. Alewold had claimed it was a mere winter's cold, but it was plainly worse, much worse. Every night we would listen to the coughing, an extraordinary hollow racking sound from such a small child, and all of us lay awake, dreading the next bout, flinching from the desperate, rasping sound, and when the coughing fits ended we feared they would not start again. Every silence was like the coming of death, yet somehow the small boy lived, clinging on through those cold wet days in the swamp. Bishop Alewold and the women tried all they knew. A gospel book was laid on his chest and the bishop prayed. A concoction of herbs, chicken dung, and ash was pasted on his chest and the bishop prayed. Alfred traveled nowhere without his precious relics, and the toe ring of Mary Magdalene was rubbed on the child's chest and the bishop prayed, but Edward just became weaker and thinner. A woman of the swamp, who had a reputation as a healer, tried to sweat the cough from him, and when that did not work she attempted to freeze it from him, and when that did not work she tied a live fish to his chest and commanded the cough and the fever to flee to the fish, and the fish certainly died, but the boy went on coughing and the bishop prayed and Alfred, as thin as his sick son, was in despair. He knew the Danes would search for him, but so long as the child was ill he dared not move, and he certainly could not contemplate the long walk south to the coast where he might find a ship to carry him and his family into exile.

He was resigned to that fate now. He had dared to hope he might recover his kingdom, but the cold reality was more persuasive. The Danes held Wessex and Alfred was king of nothing, and his son was dying. "It is a retribution," he said. It was the night after the three priests had left and Alfred unburdened his soul to me and Bishop Alewold. We were outside, watching the moon silver the marsh mists, and there were tears on Alfred's face. He was not really talking to either of us, only to himself.

"God would not take a son to punish the father," Alewold said.

"God sacrificed his own son," Alfred said bleakly, "and he commanded Abraham to kill Isaac."

"He spared Isaac," the bishop said.

"But he is not sparing Edward," Alfred said, and flinched as the awful coughing sounded from the hut. He put his head in his hands, covering his eyes.

"Retribution for what?" I asked, and the bishop hissed in reprimand for such an indelicate question.

"Æthelwold," Alfred said bleakly. Æthelwold was his nephew, the drunken, resentful son of the old king.

"Æthelwold could never have been king," Alewold said. "He is a fool!"

"If I name him king now," Alfred said, ignoring what the bishop had said, "perhaps God will spare Edward?"

The coughing ended. The boy was crying now, a gasping, grating, pitiful crying, and Alfred covered his ears with his hands.

"Give him to Iseult," I said.

"A pagan!" Alewold warned Alfred. "An adulteress!" I could see Alfred was tempted by my suggestion, but Alewold was having the better of the argument. "If God will not cure Edward," the bishop said, "do you think he will let a witch succeed?"

"She's no witch," I said.

"Tomorrow," Alewold said, ignoring me, "is Saint Agnes's Eve. A holy day, lord, a day of miracles! We shall pray to Saint Agnes and she will surely unleash God's power on the boy." He raised his hands to the dark sky. "Tomorrow, lord, we shall summon the strength of the angels, we shall call heaven's aid to your son, and the blessed Agnes will drive the evil sickness from young Edward."

Alfred said nothing, just stared at the swamp's pools that were edged with a thin skim of ice that seemed to glow in the wan moonlight.

"I have known the blessed Agnes perform miracles!" the bishop pressed the king. "There was a child in Exanceaster who could not walk, but the saint gave him strength and now he runs!"

"Truly?" Alfred asked.

"With my own eyes," the bishop said, "I witnessed the miracle."

Alfred was reassured. "Tomorrow then," he said.

I did not stay to see the power of God unleashed. Instead I took a punt and went south to a place called Æthelingæg, which lay at the southern edge of the swamp and was the biggest of all the marsh settlements. I was beginning to learn the swamp. Leofric stayed with Alfred, to protect the king and his family, but I explored, discovering scores of trackways through the watery void. The paths were called beamwegs and were made of logs that squelched underfoot, but by using them I could walk for miles. There were also rivers that twisted through the low land, and the biggest of those, the Pedredan, flowed close to Æthelingæg, which was an island, much of it covered with alders in which deer and wild goats lived, but there was also a large village on the island's highest spot and the headman had built himself a great hall there. It was not a royal hall, not even as big as the one I had made at Oxton, but a man could stand upright beneath its beams and the island was large enough to accommodate a small army.

A dozen beamwegs led away from Æthelingæg, but none led directly to the mainland. It would be a hard place for Guthrum to attack, because he would have to thread the swamp, but Svein, who we now knew commanded the Danes at Cynuit, at the Pedredan's mouth, would find it an easy place to approach for he could bring his ships up the river and, just north of Æthelingæg, he could turn south onto the river Thon, which flowed past the island. I took the punt into the center of the Thon and discovered, as I had feared, that it was more than deep enough to float the Dane's beast-headed ships.

I walked back to the place where the Thon flowed into the Pedredan. Across the wider river was a sudden hill, steep and high, which stood in the surrounding marshland like a giant's burial mound. It was a perfect place to make a fort, and if a bridge could be built across the Pedredan, then no Danish ship could pass upriver.

I walked back to the village where I discovered that the headman was a grizzled and stubborn old man called Haswold who was disinclined to help. I said I would pay good silver to have a bridge made across the Pedredan, but Haswold declared the war between Wessex and the Danes did not affect him. "There is madness over there," he said, waving vaguely at the eastern hills. "There's always madness over there, but here in the swamp we mind our own business. No one minds us and we don't mind them." He stank of fish and smoke. He wore otter skins that were greasy with fish oil and his graying beard was flecked by fish scales. He had small cunning eyes in an old cunning face, and he also had a half dozen wives, the youngest of whom was a child who could have been his own granddaughter, and he fondled her in front of me as if her existence proved his manhood. "I'm happy," he said, leering at me, "so why should I care for your happiness?"

"The Danes could end your happiness."

"The Danes?" He laughed at that, and the laugh turned into a cough. He spat. "If the Danes come," he went on, "then we go deep into the swamp and the Danes go." He grinned at me and I wanted to kill him, but that would have done no good. There were fifty or more men in the village and I would have lasted all of a dozen heartbeats, though the man I really feared was a tall, broad-shouldered, stooping man with a puzzled look on his face. What frightened me about him was that he carried a long hunting bow, not one of the short fowling bows that many of the marshmen possessed, but a stag killer, as tall as a man, and capable of shooting an arrow clean through a mail coat. Haswold must have sensed my fear of the bow for he summoned the man to stand beside him. The man looked confused by the summons, but obeyed. Haswold pushed a gnarled hand under the young girl's clothes, then stared at me as he fumbled, laughing at what he perceived as my impotence. "The Danes come," he said again, "and we go deep into the swamp and the Danes go away." He thrust his hand deeper into the girl's goatskin dress and mauled her breasts. "Danes can't follow us, and if they do follow us, then Eofer kills them." Eofer was the archer and, hearing his name, he looked startled, then worried. "Eofer's my man," Haswold boasted. "He puts arrows where I tell him to put them." Eofer nodded.

"Your king wants a bridge made," I said, "a bridge and a fort."

"King?" Haswold stared about the village. "I know no king. If any man is king here, 'tis me." He cackled with laughter at that and I looked at the villagers and saw nothing but dull faces. None shared Haswold's amusement. They were not, I thought, happy under his rule and perhaps he sensed what I was thinking, for he suddenly became angry, thrusting his girl bride away. "Leave us!" he shouted at me. "Just go away!"

I went away, returning to the smaller island where Alfred sheltered and where Edward lay dying. It was nightfall and the bishop's prayers to Saint Agnes had failed. Eanflæd told me how

Alewold had persuaded Alfred to give up one of his most precious relics, a feather from the dove that Noah had released from the ark. Alewold cut the feather into two parts, returning one part to the king, while the other was scorched on a clean pan. When it was reduced to ash, the scraps were stirred into a cup of holy water, which Ælswith forced her son to drink. He had been wrapped in lambskin, for the lamb was the symbol of Saint Agnes who had been a child martyr in Rome.

But neither feather nor lambskin had worked. If anything, Eanflæd said, the boy was worse. Alewold was praying over him now. "He's given him the last rites," Eanflæd said. She looked at me with tears in her eyes. "Can Iseult help?"

"The bishop won't allow it," I said.

"He won't allow it?" she asked indignantly. "He's not the one who's dying!"

So Iseult was summoned, and Alfred came from the hut and Alewold, scenting heresy, came with him. Edward was coughing again, the sound terrible in the evening silence. Alfred flinched at the noise, then demanded to know if Iseult could cure his son's illness.

Iseult did not reply at once. Instead she

turned and gazed across the swamp to where the moon rose above the mists. "The moon gets bigger," she said.

"Do you know a cure?" Alfred pleaded.

"A growing moon is good," Iseult said dully, then turned on him. "But there will be a price."

"Whatever you want!" he said.

"Not a price for me," she said, irritated that he had misunderstood her. "But there's always a price. One lives? Another must die."

"Heresy!" Alewold intervened.

I doubt Alfred understood Iseult's last three words, or did not care what she meant. He only snatched the tenuous hope that perhaps she could help. "Can you cure my son?" he demanded.

She paused, then nodded. "There is a way," she said.

"What way?"

"My way."

"Heresy!" Alewold warned again.

"Bishop!" Eanflæd said warningly, and the bishop looked abashed and fell silent.

"Now?" Alfred demanded of Iseult.

"Tomorrow night," Iseult said. "It takes time. There are things to do. If he lives till nightfall tomorrow I can help. You must bring him to me at moonrise."

"Not tonight?" Alfred pleaded.

"Tomorrow," Iseult said firmly.

"Tomorrow is the Feast of Saint Vincent," Alfred said, as though that might help, and somehow the child survived that night. Next day, Saint Vincent's Day, Iseult went with me to the eastern shore where we gathered lichen, burdock, celandine, and mistletoe. She would not let me use metal to scrape the lichen or cut the herbs, and before any was collected we had to walk three times around the plants, which, because it was winter, were poor and shriveled things. She also made me cut thorn boughs, and I was allowed to use a knife for that because the thorns were evidently not as important as the lichen or herbs. I watched the skyline as I worked, looking for any Danes, but if they patrolled the edge of the swamp none appeared that day. It was cold, a gusting wind clutching at our clothes. It took a long time to find the plants Iseult needed, but at last her pouch was full and I dragged the thornbushes back to the island and took them into the hut where she instructed me to dig two holes in the floor. "They must be as deep as the child is tall," she said, "and as far apart from each other as the length of your forearm."

She would not tell me what the pits were for. She was subdued, very close to tears. She hung the celandine and burdock from a roof beam, then pounded the lichen and the mistletoe into a paste that she moistened with spittle and urine, and she chanted long charms in her own language over the shallow wooden bowl. It all took a long time and sometimes she just sat exhausted in the darkness beyond the hearth and rocked to and fro. "I don't know that I can do it," she said once.

"You can try," I said helplessly.

"And if I fail," she said, "they will hate me more than ever."

"They don't hate you," I said.

"They think I am a sinner and a pagan," she said, "and they hate me."

"So cure the child," I said, "and they will love you."

I could not dig the pits as deep as she wanted, for the soil became ever wetter and, just a couple of feet down, the two holes were filling with brackish water. "Make them wider," Iseult ordered me, "wide enough so the child can crouch in them." I did as she said, and then she made me join the two holes by knocking a passage in the damp earth wall that divided them. That had to be done carefully to ensure that an arch of soil remained to leave a tunnel between the holes. "It is wrong," Iseult said, not talking of my excavation, but of the charm she planned to work. "Someone will die, Uhtred. Somewhere a child will die so this one will live."

"How do you know that?" I asked.

"Because my twin died when I was born," she said, "and I have his power. But if I use it he reaches from the dark world and takes the power back."

Darkness fell and the boy went on coughing, though to my ears it sounded feebler now, as though there was not enough life left in his small body. Alewold was praying still. Iseult crouched in the door of our hut, staring into the rain, and when Alfred came close she waved him away.

"He's dying," the king said helplessly.

"Not yet," Iseult said, "not yet."

Edward's breath rasped. We could all hear it, and we all thought every harsh breath would be his last, and still Iseult did not move, and then at last a rift showed in the rain clouds and a feeble wash of moonlight touched the marsh and she told me to fetch the boy.

Ælswith did not want Edward to go. She wanted him cured, but when I said Iseult insisted on working her charms alone, Ælswith wailed that she did not want her son to die apart from his mother. Her crying upset Edward, who began to cough again. Eanflæd stroked his forehead. "Can she do it?" she demanded of me.

"Yes," I said and did not know if I spoke the truth.

Eanflæd took hold of Ælswith's shoulders. "Let the boy go, my lady," she said. "Let him go."

"He'll die!"

"Let him go," Eanflæd said, and Ælswith collapsed into the whore's arms and I picked up Alfred's son, who felt as light as the feather that had not cured him. He was hot, yet shivering, and I wrapped him in a wool robe and carried him to Iseult.

"You can't stay here," she told me. "Leave him with me."

I waited with Leofric in the dark. Iseult insisted we could not watch through the hut's entrance, but I dropped my helmet outside the door and, by crouching under the eaves, I could just see a reflection of what happened inside. The small rain died and the moon grew brighter.

The boy coughed. Iseult stripped him naked and rubbed her herb paste on his chest, and then she began to chant in her own tongue, an endless chant it seemed, rhythmic, sad, and so monotonous that it almost put me to sleep. Edward cried once, and the crying turned to coughing and his mother screamed from her hut that she wanted him back, and Alfred calmed her and then came to join us and I waved him down so that he would not shadow the moonlight before Iseult's door.

I peered at the helmet and saw, in the small reflected firelight, that Iseult, naked herself now, was pushing the boy into one of the pits and then, still chanting, she drew him through the earth passage. Her chanting stopped and, instead, she began to pant, then scream, then pant again. She moaned, and Alfred made the sign of the cross, and then there was silence and I could not see properly, but suddenly Iseult cried aloud, a cry of relief, as if a great pain was ended, and I dimly saw her pull the naked boy out of the second pit. She laid him on her bed and he was silent as she crammed the thornbushes into the tunnel of earth. Then she lay beside the boy and covered herself with my large cloak.

There was silence. I waited and waited, and still there was silence. And the silence stretched until I understood that Iseult was sleeping, and the boy was sleeping, too, or else he was dead, and I picked up the helmet and went to Leofric's hut. "Shall I fetch him?" Alfred asked nervously.

"No."

"His mother—" he began.

"Must wait till morning, lord."

"What can I tell her?"

"That her son is not coughing, lord."

Ælswith screamed that Edward was dead, but Eanflæd and Alfred calmed her, and we all waited, and still there was silence, and in the end I fell asleep.

I woke in the dawn. It was raining as if the world was about to end, a torrential gray rain that swept in vast curtains from the Sæfern Sea, a rain that drummed on the ground and poured off the reed thatch and made streams on the small island where the little huts crouched. I went to the door of Leofric's shelter and saw Ælswith watching from her doorway. She looked desperate, like a mother about to hear that her child had died, and there was nothing but silence from Iseult's hut, and Ælswith began to weep, the terrible tears of a bereaved mother, and then there was a strange sound. At first I could not hear properly, for the seething rain was loud, but then I realized the sound was laughter. A child's laughter, and a heartbeat later Edward, still naked as an egg, and all muddy from his rebirth through the earth passage, ran from Iseult's hut and went to his mother.

"Dear God," Leofric said.

Iseult, when I found her, was weeping and would not be consoled. "I need you," I told her harshly.

She looked up at me. "Need me?"

"To build a bridge."

She frowned. "You think a bridge can be made with spells?"

"My magic this time," I said. "I want you healthy. I need a queen."

She nodded. And Edward, from that day forward, thrived.

The first men came, summoned by the priests I had sent onto the mainland. They came in ones and twos, struggling through the winter weather and the swamp, bringing tales of Danish raids, and when we had two days of sunshine they came in groups of six or seven so that the island became crowded. I sent them out on patrol, but ordered none to go too far west for I did not want to provoke Svein, whose men were camped beside the sea. He had not attacked us yet, which was foolish of him, for he could have brought his ships up the rivers and then struggled through the marsh, but I knew he would attack us when he was ready, and so I needed to make our defenses. And for that I needed Æthelingæg.

Alfred was recovering. He was still sick, but he saw God's favor in his son's recovery and it never occurred to him that it had been pagan magic that caused the recovery. Even Ælswith was generous and, when I asked her for the loan of her silver fox-fur cloak and what few jewels she possessed, she yielded them without fuss. The fur cloak was dirty, but Eanflæd brushed and combed it.

There were over twenty men on our island now, probably enough to capture Æthelingæg from its sullen headman, but Alfred did not want the marshmen killed. They were his subjects, he said, and if the Danes attacked they might yet fight for us, which meant the large island and its village must be taken by trickery and so, a week after Edward's rebirth, I took Leofric and Iseult south to Haswold's settlement. Iseult was dressed in the silver fur and had a silver chain in her hair and a great garnet brooch at her breast. I had brushed her hair till it shone and in that winter's gloom she looked like a princess come from the bright sky.

Leofric and I, dressed in mail and helmets, did nothing except walk around Æthelingæg, but after a while a man came from Haswold and said the chieftain wished to talk with us. I think Haswold expected us to go to his stinking hut, but I demanded he come to us instead. He could have taken from us whatever he wanted, of course, for there were only the three of us and he had his men, including Eofer the archer, but Haswold had at last understood that dire things were happening in the world beyond the swamp and that those events could pierce even his watery fastness, and so he chose to talk. He came to us at the settlement's northern gate, which was nothing more than a sheep hurdle propped against decaying fish traps and there, as I expected, he gazed at Iseult as though he had never seen a woman before. His small cunning eyes flickered at me and back to her. "Who is she?" he asked.

"A companion," I said carelessly. I turned to look at the sudden steep hill across the river where I wanted the fort made.

"Is she your wife?" Haswold asked.

"A companion," I said again. "I have a dozen like her," I added.

"I will pay you for her," Haswold said. A score

of men were behind him, but only Eofer was armed with anything more dangerous than an eel spear.

I turned Iseult to face him; then I stood behind her and put my hands over her shoulders and undid the big garnet brooch. She shivered slightly and I whispered that she was safe and, when the brooch pin slid out of the heavy hide, I pulled her fur cloak apart. I showed her nakedness to Haswold and he dribbled into his fish-scaled beard and his dirty fingers twitched in his foul otter-skin furs, and then I closed the cloak and let Iseult fasten the brooch. "How much will you pay me?" I asked him.

"I can just take her," Haswold said, jerking his head at his men.

I smiled at that. "You could," I said, "but many of you will die before we die, and our ghosts will come back to kill your women and make your children scream. Have you not heard that we have a witch with us? You think your weapons can fight magic?"

None of them moved.

"I have silver," Haswold said.

"I don't need silver," I said. "What I want is a bridge and a fort." I turned and pointed to the hill across the river. "What is that hill called?"

He shrugged. "The hill," he said, "just the hill."

"It must become a fort," I said, "and it must have walls of logs and a gate of logs and a tower so that men can see a long way downriver. And then I want a bridge leading to the fort, a bridge strong enough to stop ships."

"You want to stop ships?" Haswold asked. He scratched his groin and shook his head. "Can't build a bridge."

"Why not?"

"Too deep." That was probably true. It was low tide now and the Pedredan flowed sullenly between steep and deep mud banks. "But I can block the river," Haswold went on, his eyes still on Iseult.

"Block the river," I said, "and build a fort."

"Give her to me," Haswold promised, "and you will have both."

"Do what I want," I said, "and you can have her, her sisters, and her cousins. All twelve of them."

Haswold would have drained the whole swamp and built a new Jerusalem for the chance to hump Iseult, but he had not thought beyond the end of his prick. But that was far enough for me, and I have never seen work done so quickly.

It was done in days. He blocked the river first and did it cleverly by making a floating barrier of logs and felled trees, complete with their tangling branches, all of them lashed together with goat-hide ropes. A ship's crew could eventually dismantle such a barrier, but not if they were being assailed by spears and arrows from the fort on the hill that had a wooden palisade, a flooded ditch, and a flimsy tower made of alder logs bound together with leather ropes. It was all crude work, but the wall was solid enough, and I began to fear that the small fort would be finished before enough West Saxons arrived to garrison it, but the three priests were doing their job and the soldiers still came, and I put a score of them in Æthelingæg and told them to help finish the fort.

When the work was done, or nearly done, I took Iseult back to Æthelingæg and I dressed her as she had been dressed before, only this time she wore a deerskin tunic beneath the precious fur, and I stood her in the center of the village and said Haswold could take her. He looked at me warily, then looked at her. "She's mine?" he asked.

"All yours," I said, and stepped away from her.

"And her sisters?" he asked greedily. "Her cousins?"

"I shall bring them tomorrow."

He beckoned Iseult toward his hut. "Come," he said.

"In her country," I said, "it is the custom for the man to lead the woman to his bed."

He stared at Iseult's lovely, dark-eyed face above the swathing silver cloak. I stepped farther back, abandoning her, and he darted forward, reaching for her, and she brought her hands out from under the thick fur and she was holding Wasp-Sting and its blade sliced up into Haswold's belly. She gave a cry of horror and surprise as she brought the blade up, and I saw her hesitate, shocked by the effort required to pierce a man's belly and by the reality of what she had done. Then she gritted her teeth and ripped the blade hard, opening him up like a gutted carp, and he gave a strange mewing cry as he staggered back from her vengeful eyes. His intestines spilled into the mud, and I was beside her then with Serpent-Breath drawn. She was gasping, trembling. She had wanted to do it, but I doubted she would want to do it again.

"You were asked," I snarled at the villagers,

"to fight for your king." Haswold was on the ground, twitching, his blood soaking his otter-skin clothes. He made a mewing noise and one of his filthy hands scrabbled among his own spilled guts. "For your king!" I repeated. "When you are asked to fight for your king it is not a request, but a duty! Every man here is a soldier and your enemy is the Danes and if you will not fight them, then you will fight against me!"

Iseult still stood beside Haswold, who jerked like a dying fish. I edged her away and stabbed Serpent-Breath down to slit his throat. "Take his head," she told me.

"His head?"

"Strong magic."

We mounted Haswold's head on the fort wall so that it stared toward the Danes, and in time eight more heads appeared there. They were the heads of Haswold's chief supporters, murdered by the villagers who were glad to be rid of them. Eofer, the archer, was not one of them. He was a simpleton, incapable of speaking sense, though he grunted and, from time to time, made howling noises. He could be led by a child, but when asked to use his bow he proved to have a terrible strength and uncanny accuracy. He was Æthelingæg's hunter, capable of dropping a full-grown boar at a hundred paces, and that was what his name meant: boar.

I left Leofric to command the garrison at Æthelingæg and took Iseult back to Alfred's refuge. She was silent and I thought her sunk in misery, but then she suddenly laughed. "Look!" She pointed at the dead man's blood matted and sticky in Ælswith's fur.

She still had Wasp-Sting. That was my short sword, a saxe, and it was a wicked blade in a close fight where men are so crammed together that there is no room to swing a long sword or an ax. She trailed the blade in the water, then used the hem of Ælswith's fur to scrub the diluted blood from the steel. "It is harder than I thought," she said, "to kill a man."

"It takes strength."

"But I have his soul now."

"Is that why you did it?"

"To give life," she said, "you must take it from somewhere else." She gave me back Wasp-Sting.

Alfred was shaving when we returned. He had been growing a beard, not for a disguise, but because he had been too low in spirits to bother about his appearance, but when Iseult and I reached his refuge he was standing naked to the waist beside a big wooden tub of heated water.

His chest was pathetically thin, his belly hollow, but he had washed himself, combed his hair, and was now scratching at his stubble with an ancient razor he had borrowed from a marshman. His daughter, Æthelflaed, was holding a scrap of silver that served as a mirror. "I am feeling better," he told me solemnly.

"Good, lord," I said. "So am I."

"Does that mean you've killed someone?"

"She did." I jerked my head at Iseult.

He gave her a speculative look. "My wife," he said, dipping the razor in the water, "was asking whether Iseult is truly a queen."

"She was," I said, "but that means little in Cornwalum. She was queen of a dung heap."

"And she's a pagan?"

"It was a Christian kingdom," I said. "Didn't Brother Asser tell you that?"

"He said they were not good Christians."

"I thought that was for God to judge."

"Good, Uhtred, good!" He waved the razor at me, then stooped to the silver mirror and scraped at his upper lip. "Can she foretell the future?"

"She can."

He scraped in silence for a few heartbeats. Æthelflaed watched Iseult solemnly. "So tell me," Alfred said, "does she say I will be king in Wessex again?"

"You will," Iseult said tonelessly, surprising me.

Alfred stared at her. "My wife," he said, "says that we can look for a ship now that Edward is better. Look for a ship, go to Frankia, and perhaps travel on to Rome. There is a Saxon community in Rome." He scraped the blade against his jawbone. "They will welcome us."

"The Danes will be defeated," Iseult said, still tonelessly, but without a quiver of doubt in her voice.

Alfred rubbed his face. "The example of Boethius tells me she's right," he said.

"Boethius?" I asked. "Is he one of your warriors?"

"He was a Roman, Uhtred," Alfred said in a tone that chided me for not knowing, "and a Christian and a philosopher and a man rich in book learning. Rich indeed!" He paused, contemplating the story of Boethius. "When the pagan Alaric overran Rome," he went on, "and all civilization and true religion seemed doomed, Boethius alone stood against the sinners. He suffered, but he won through, and we can take heart from him. Indeed we can." He pointed the razor at me. "We must never forget the example of Boethius, Uhtred, never."

"I won't, lord," I said, "but do you think book learning will get you out of here?"

"I think," he said, "that when the Danes are gone, I shall grow a proper beard. Thank you, my sweet." This last was to Æthelflaed. "Give the mirror back to Eanflæd, will you?"

Æthelflaed ran off and Alfred looked at me with some amusement. "Does it surprise you that my wife and Eanflæd have become friends?"

"I'm glad of it, lord."

"So am I."

"But does your wife know Eanflæd's trade?" I asked.

"Not exactly," he said. "She believes Eanflæd was a cook in a tavern. Which is truth enough. So we have a fort at Æthelingæg?"

"We do. Leofric commands there and has forty-three men."

"And we have twenty-eight here. The very hosts of Midian!" He was evidently amused. "So we shall move there."

"Maybe in a week or two."

"Why wait?" he asked.

I shrugged. "This place is deeper in the swamp. When we have more men, when we know we can hold Æthelingæg, that is the time for you to go there."

He pulled on a grubby shirt. "Your new fort can't stop the Danes?"

"It will slow them, lord. But they could still struggle through the marsh." They would find it difficult, though, for Leofric was digging ditches to defend Æthelingæg's western edge.

"You're telling me Æthelingæg is more vulnerable than this place?"

"Yes, lord."

"Which is why I must go there," he said. "Men can't say their king skulked in an unreachable place, can they?" He smiled at me. "They must say he defied the Danes. That he waited where they could reach him, that he put himself into danger."

"And his family?" I asked.

"And his family," he said firmly. He thought for a moment. "If they come in force they could take all the swamp, isn't that true?"

"Yes, lord."

"So no place is safer than another. But how large a force does Svein have?"

"I don't know, lord."

"Don't know?" It was a reproof, gentle enough, but still a reproof.

"I haven't gone close to them, lord," I explained, "because till now we've been too weak to resist them, and so long as they leave us undisturbed then so long do we leave them undisturbed. There's no point in kicking a wild bees' nest, not unless you're determined to get the honey."

He nodded acceptance of that argument. "But we need to know how many bees there are, don't we?" he said. "So tomorrow we shall take a look at our enemy. You and me, Uhtred."

"No, lord," I said firmly. "I shall go. You shouldn't risk yourself."

"That is exactly what I need to do," he said, "and men must know I do it for I am the king, and why would men want a king who does not share their danger?" He waited for an answer, but I had none. "So let's say our prayers," he finished. "Then we shall eat."

It was fish stew. It was always fish stew.

And next day we went to find the enemy.

There were six of us: the man who poled the punt, Iseult and I, two of the newly arrived household troops, and Alfred. I tried once again to make him stay behind, but he insisted. "If anyone should stay," he said, "it is Iseult."

"She comes," I said.

"Evidently." He did not argue, and we all climbed into a large punt and went westward, and Alfred stared at the birds, thousands of birds. There were coots, moorhens, dabchicks, ducks, grebes, and herons, while off to the west, white against the sullen sky, was a cloud of gulls.

The marshman slid us silent and fast through secret channels. There were times when he seemed to be taking us directly into a bank of reeds or grass, yet the shallow craft would slide through into another stretch of open water. The incoming tide rippled through the gaps, bringing fish to the hidden nets and basket traps. Beneath the gulls, far off to the west, I could see the masts of Svein's fleet that had been dragged ashore on the coast.

Alfred saw them, too. "Why don't they join Guthrum?"

"Because Svein doesn't want to take Guthrum's orders," I said.

"You know that?"

"He told me so."

Alfred paused, perhaps thinking of my trial in front of the witan. He gave me a rueful look. "What sort of man is he?"

"Formidable."

"So why hasn't he attacked us here?"

I had been wondering the same thing. Svein had missed a golden chance to invade the swamp and hunt Alfred down. So why had he not even tried? "Because there's easier plunder else-where," I suggested, "and because he won't do Guthrum's bidding. They're rivals. If Svein takes Guthrum's orders, then he acknowledges Guthrum as his king."

Alfred stared at the distant masts that showed as small scratches against the sky. Then I mutely pointed toward a hill that reared steeply from the western water flats and the marshman obedi-ently went that way, and when the punt grounded we clambered through thick alders and past some sunken hovels where sullen folk in dirty otter fur watched us pass. The marshman knew no name for the place, except to call it Brant, which meant steep, and it was steep. Steep and high, offering a view southward to where the Pedredan coiled like a great snake through the swamp's heart. And at the river's mouth, where sand and mud stretched into the Sæfern Sea, I could see the Danish ships.

They were grounded on the far bank of the Pedredan in the same place that Ubba had grounded his ships before meeting his death in battle. From there Svein could easily row to Æthelingæg, for the river was wide and deep, and he would meet no challenge until he reached the river barrier beside the fort where Leofric waited. I wanted Leofric and his garrison to have some warning if the Danes attacked, and this high hill offered a view of Svein's camp, but was far enough away so that it would not invite an attack from the enemy. "We should make a beacon here," I said to Alfred. A fire lit here would give Æthelingæg two or three hours' warning of a Danish attack.

He nodded but said nothing. He stared at the distant ships, but they were too far off to count. He looked pale, and I knew he had found the climb to the summit painful, so now I urged him downhill to where the hovels leaked smoke. "You should rest here, lord," I told him. "I'm going to count ships. But you should rest."

He did not argue and I suspected his stomach pains were troubling him again. I found a hovel that was occupied by a widow and her four children, and I gave her a silver coin and said her king needed warmth and shelter for the day, and I do not think she understood who he was, but she knew the value of a shilling and so Alfred went into her house and sat by the fire. "Give him broth," I told the widow, whose name was Elwide, "and let him sleep."

She scorned that. "Folk can't sleep while there's work!" she said. "There are eels to skin, fish to smoke, nets to mend, traps to weave."

"They can work," I said, pointing to the two household troops, and I left them all to Elwide's tender mercies while Iseult and I took the punt southward and, because the Pedredan's mouth was only three or four miles away and because Brant was such a clear landmark, I left the marshman to help skin and smoke eels.

We crossed a smaller river and then poled through a long mere broken by marram grass and by now I could see the hill on the Pedredan's far bank where we had been trapped by Ubba, and I told Iseult the story of the fight as I poled the punt across the shallows. The hull grounded twice and I had to push it into deeper water until I realized the tide was falling fast and so I tied the boat to a rotting stake. Then we walked across a drying waste of mud and sea lavender toward the Pedredan. I had grounded farther from the river than I had wanted, and it was a long walk into a cold wind, but we could see all we needed once we reached the steep bank at the river's edge. The Danes could also see us. I was not in mail, but I did have my swords, and the sight of me brought men to the farther shore, where they hurled insults across the swirling water. I ignored them. I was counting ships and saw twenty-four beast-headed boats hauled up on the strip of ground where we had defeated Ubba the year before. Ubba's burned ships were also there, their black ribs half buried in the sand where the men capered and shouted their insults.

"How many men can you see?" I asked Iseult.

There were a few Danes in the half-wrecked remnants of the monastery where Svein had killed the monks, but most were by the boats. "Just men?" she asked.

"Forget the women and children," I said. There were scores of women, mostly in the small village that was a small way upstream.

She did not know the English words for the bigger numbers, so she gave me her estimate by opening and closing her fingers six times. "Sixty?" I said, and nodded. "At most seventy. And there are twenty-four ships." She frowned, not understanding the point I made. "Twenty-four ships," I said, "means an army of what? Eight hundred? Nine hundred men? So those sixty or seventy men are the ship guards. And the others? Where are the others?" I asked the question of myself, watching as five of the Danes dragged a small boat to the river's edge. They planned to row across and capture us, but I did not intend to stay that long. "The others," I answered my own question, "have gone south. They've left their women behind and gone raiding. They're burning, killing, getting rich. They're raping Defnascir."

"They're coming," Iseult said, watching the five men clamber into the small boat.

"You want me to kill them?"

"You can?" She looked hopeful.

"No," I said, "so let's go."

We started back across the long expanse of mud and sand. It looked smooth, but there were runnels cutting through and the tide had turned and the sea was sliding back into the land with surprising speed. The sun was sinking, tangling with black clouds, and the wind pushed the flood up the Sæfern and the water gurgled and shivered as it filled the small creeks. I turned to see that the five Danes had abandoned their chase and gone back to the western bank where their fires looked delicate against the evening's fading light. "I can't see the boat," Iseult said.

"Over there," I said, but I was not certain I

was right because the light was dimming and our punt was tied against a background of reeds, and now we were jumping from one dry spot to another, and the tide went on rising and the dry spots shrank and then we were splashing through the water and still the wind drove the tide inland.

The tides are big in the Sæfern. A man could make a house at low tide, and by high it would have vanished beneath the waves. Islands appear at low tide, islands with summits thirty feet above the water, and at the high tide they are gone, and this tide was pushed by the wind and it was coming fast and cold and Iseult began to falter so I picked her up and carried her like a child. I was struggling and the sun was behind the low western clouds and it seemed now that I was wading through an endless chill sea, but then, perhaps because the darkness was falling, or perhaps because Hoder, the blind god of the night, favored me, I saw the punt straining against its tether.

I dropped Iseult into the boat and hauled myself over the low side. I cut the rope, then collapsed, cold and wet and frightened, and let the punt drift on the tide.

"You must get back to the fire," Iseult chided me. I wished I had brought the marshman now for I had to find a route across the swamp and it was a long, cold journey in the day's last light. Iseult crouched beside me and stared far across the waters to where a hill reared up green and steep against the eastern land. "Eanflæd told me that hill is Avalon," she said reverentially.

"Avalon?"

"Where Arthur is buried."

"I thought you believed he was sleeping."

"He does sleep," she said fervently. "He sleeps in his grave with his warriors." She gazed at the distant hill that seemed to glow because it had been caught by the day's last errant shaft of sunlight spearing from the west beneath the furnace-glowing clouds. "Arthur," she said in a whisper. "He was the greatest king who ever lived. He had a magic sword." She told me tales of Arthur, how he had pulled his sword from a stone, and how he had led the greatest warriors to battle, and I thought that his enemies had been us, the English Saxons, yet Avalon was now in England, and I wondered if, in a few years, the Saxons would recall their lost kings and claim they were great and all the while the Danes would rule us. When the sun vanished Iseult was singing softly in her own tongue, but she told me the song was about Arthur and how he had placed a ladder against the moon and netted a swath of stars to make a cloak for his queen, Guinevere. Her voice carried us across the twilit water, sliding between reeds, and behind us the fires of the Danish ship guards faded in the encroaching dark, and far off a dog howled and the wind sighed cold and a spattering of rain shivered the black mere.

Iseult stopped singing as Brant loomed. "There's going to be a great fight," she said softly and her words took me by surprise and I thought she was still thinking of Arthur and imagining that the sleeping king would erupt from his earthy bed in gouts of soil and steel. "A fight by a hill," she went on, "a steep hill, and there will be a white horse and the slope will run with blood and the Danes will run from the Sais."

The Sais were us, the Saxons. "You dreamed this?" I asked.

"I dreamed it," she said.

"So it is true?"

"It is fate," she said, and I believed her, and just then the bow of the punt scraped on the island's shore.

It was pitch dark, but there were fish-smoking fires on the beach, and by their dying light we found our way to Elwide's house. It was made of alder logs thatched with reeds and I found Alfred sitting by the central hearth where he stared absently into the flames. Elwide, the two soldiers, and the marshman were all skinning eels at the hut's farther end where three of the widow's children were plaiting willow withies into traps and the fourth was gutting a big pike.

I crouched by the fire, wanting its warmth to bring life to my frozen legs.

Alfred blinked as though he was surprised to see me. "The Danes?" he asked.

"Gone inland," I said. "Left sixty or seventy men as ship guards." I crouched by the fire, shivering, wondering if I would ever be warm again.

"There's food here," Alfred said vaguely.

"Good," I said, "because we're starving."

"No, I mean there's food in the marshes," he said. "Enough food to feed an army. We can raid them, Uhtred, gather men and raid them. But that isn't enough. I have been thinking. All day, I've been thinking." He looked better now, less pained, and I suspected he had wanted time to think and had found it in this stinking hovel. "I'm not going to run away," he said firmly. "I'm not going to Frankia."

"Good," I said, though I was so cold I was not really listening to him.

"We're going to stay here," he said, "raise an army, and take Wessex back."

"Good," I said again. I could smell burning. The hearth was surrounded by flat stones and Elwide had put a dozen oat bannocks on the stones to cook and the edges nearest the flames were blackening. I moved one of them, but Alfred frowned and gestured for me to stop for fear of distracting him. "The problem," he said, "is that I cannot afford to fight a small war."

I did not see what other war he could fight, but kept silent.

"The longer the Danes stay here," he said, "the firmer their grip. Men will start giving Guthrum their allegiance. I can't have that."

"No, lord."

"So they have to be defeated." He spoke grimly. "Not beaten, Uhtred, but defeated!"

I thought of Iseult's dream but said nothing. Then I thought how often Alfred had made peace with the Danes instead of fighting them, and still I said nothing.

"In spring," he went on, "they'll have new men and they'll spread through Wessex until, by summer's end, there'll be no Wessex. So we have to do two things." He was not so much telling me as just thinking aloud. "First," he held out

one long finger, "we have to stop them from dis-
persing their armies. They have to fight us here.
They have to be kept together so they can't send
small bands across the country and take estates."
That made sense. Right now, from what we
heard from the land beyond the swamp, the
Danes were raiding all across Wessex. They were
going fast, snatching what plunder they could
before other men could take it, but in a few
weeks they would start looking for places to live.
By keeping their attention on the swamp, Alfred
hoped to stop that process. "And while they look
at us," he said, "the fyrd must be gathered."

I stared at him. I had supposed he would stay
in the swamp until either the Danes overwhelmed us or we gained enough strength to
take back a shire, and then another shire, a
process of years, but his vision was much
grander. He would assemble the army of Wessex under the Danish noses and take everything
back at once. It was like a game of dice and he
had decided to take everything he had, little as it
was, and risk it all on one throw. "We shall make
them fight a great battle," he said grimly, "and
with God's help we shall destroy them."

There was a sudden scream. Alfred, as if startled from a reverie, looked up, but too late, be-

cause Elwide was standing over him, screaming that he had burned the oatcakes. "I told you to watch them!" she shouted and, in her fury, she slapped the king with a skinned eel. The blow made a wet sound as it struck and had enough force to knock Alfred sideways. The two soldiers jumped up, hands going to their swords, but I waved them back as Elwide snatched the burned cakes from the stones. "I told you to watch them!" she shrieked, and Alfred lay where he had fallen and I thought he was crying, but then I saw he was laughing. He was helpless with laughter, weeping with laughter, as happy as ever I saw him.

Because he had a plan to take back his kingdom.

Æthelingæg's garrison now had seventy-three men. Alfred moved there with his family and sent six of Leofric's men to Brant armed with axes and orders to make a beacon. He was at his best in those days, calm and confident, the panic and despair of the first weeks of January swept away by his irrational belief that he would regain his kingdom before summer touched the land. He was immensely cheered, too, by the arrival of Father Beocca who came limping from the landing stage, face beaming, to fall prostrate at the king's feet. "You live, lord!" Beocca said, clutching the king's ankles. "God be praised, you live!"

Alfred raised him and embraced him and both men wept, and next day, a Sunday, Beocca preached a sermon that I could not help hearing because the service was held in the open air, under a clear cold sky, and Æthelingæg's island was too small to escape the priest's voice. Beocca said how David, King of Israel, had been forced to flee his enemies, how he had taken refuge in the cave of Adullam, and how God had led him back into Israel and to the defeat of his enemies. "This is our Adullam!" Beocca said, waving his good hand at Æthelingæg's thatched roofs. "And this is our David!" He pointed to the king. "And God will lead us to victory!"

"It's a pity, father," I said to Beocca afterward, "that you weren't this belligerent two months ago."

"I rejoice," he said loftily, "to find you in the king's good graces."

"He's discovered the value," I said, "of murderous bastards like me, so perhaps he'll learn to distrust the advice of sniveling bastards like you who told him the Danes could be defeated by prayer."

He sniffed at that insult, then looked disapprovingly at Iseult. "You have news of your wife?"

"None."

Beocca had some news, though none of Mildrith. He had fled south in front of the invading Danes, getting as far as Dornwaraceaster in Thornsæta where he had found refuge with some monks. The Danes had come, but the monks had received warning of their approach and hid in an ancient fort that lay near the town. The Danes had sacked Dornwaraceaster, taking silver, coins, and women. Then they had moved eastward and shortly after that Huppa, Ealdorman of Thornsæta, had come to the town with fifty warriors. Huppa had set the monks and townspeople to mending the old Roman walls. "The folk there are safe for the moment," Beocca told me, "but there is not sufficient food if the Danes return and lay siege." Then Beocca had heard that Alfred was in the great swamps and Beocca had traveled alone, though on his last day of walking he had met six soldiers going to Alfred and so he had finished his journey with them. He brought no news of Wulfhere, but he had been told that Odda the Younger was somewhere on the upper reaches of Uisc in an ancient fort built by the old people. Beocca had seen no Danes on his journey. "They raid everywhere," he said gloomily, "but God be praised, we saw none of them."

"Is Dornwaraceaster a large place?" I asked.

"Large enough. It had three fine churches, three!"

"A market?"

"Indeed, it was prosperous before the Danes came."

"Yet the Danes didn't stay there?"

"Nor were they at Gifle," he said, "and that's a goodly place."

Guthrum had surprised Alfred, defeated the forces at Cippanhamm, and driven the king into hiding, but to hold Wessex he needed to take all her walled towns, and if Beocca could walk three days across country and see no Danes, then it suggested Guthrum did not have the men to hold all he had taken. He could bring more men from Mercia or East Anglia, but then those places might rise against their weakened Danish overlords, so Guthrum had to be hoping that more ships would come from Denmark. In the meantime, we learned, he had garrisons in Baðum, Readingum, Mærlebeorg, and Andefera, and doubtless he held other places, and Alfred suspected, rightly as it turned out, that most of eastern Wessex was in Danish hands, but great stretches of the country were still free of the enemy. Guthrum's men were making raids into those stretches, but they did not have sufficient force to garrison towns like Wintanceaster, Gifle, or Dornwaraceaster. In the early summer, Alfred knew, more ships would bring more Danes, so he had to strike before then, to which end, on the day after Beocca arrived, he summoned a council.

There were now enough men on Æthelingæg for a royal formality to prevail. I no longer found Alfred sitting outside a hut in the evening, but instead had to seek an audience with him. On the Monday of the council he gave orders that a large house was to be made into a church, and the family that lived there was evicted and some of the newly arrived soldiers were ordered to make a great cross for the gable and to carve new windows in the walls. The council itself met in what had been Haswold's hall, and Alfred had waited till we were assembled before making his entrance, and we had all stood as he came in and waited as he took one of the two chairs on the newly made dais. Ælswith sat beside him, her pregnant belly swathed in the silver fur cloak that was still stained with Haswold's blood.

We were not allowed to sit until the Bishop of Exanceaster said a prayer, and that took time, but at last the king waved us down. There were six priests in the half circle and six warriors. I sat beside Leofric, while the other four soldiers were newly arrived men who had served in Alfred's household troops. One of those was a gray-bearded man called Egwine who told me he had led a hundred men at Æsc's Hill and plainly thought he should now lead all the troops gathered in the swamp. I knew he had urged his case with the king and with Beocca who sat just below the dais at a rickety table on which he was trying to record what was said at the council. Beocca was having difficulties for his ink was ancient and faded, his quill kept splitting, and his parchments were wide margins torn from a missal, so he was unhappy, but Alfred liked to reduce arguments to writing.

The king formally thanked the bishop for his prayer, then announced, sensibly enough, that we could not hope to deal with Guthrum until Svein was defeated. Svein was the immediate threat for, though most of his men had gone south to raid Defnascir, he still had the ships with which to enter the swamp. "Twenty-four ships," Alfred said, raising an eyebrow at me.

"Twenty-four, lord," I confirmed.

"So, when his men are assembled, he can muster near a thousand men." Alfred let that figure linger awhile. Beocca frowned as his split quill spattered ink on his tiny patch of parchment.

"But two days ago," Alfred went on, "there were only seventy ship guards at the mouth of the Pedredan."

"Around seventy," I said. "There could be more we didn't see."

"Fewer than a hundred, though?"

"I suspect so, lord."

"So we must deal with them," Alfred said, "before the rest return to their ships." There was another silence. All of us knew how weak we were. A few men arrived every day, like the half dozen who had come with Beocca, but they came slowly, either because the news of Alfred's existence was spreading slowly, or else because the weather was cold and men do not like to travel on wet, cold days. Nor were there any thegns among the newcomers, not one. Thegns were noblemen, men of property, men who could bring scores of well-armed followers to a fight, and every shire had its thegns who ranked just below the reeve and ealdorman, who were themselves thegns. Thegns were the power of Wessex, but none had come to Æthelingæg. Some, we heard, had fled abroad, while others tried to protect their property. Alfred, I was certain, would have felt more comfortable if he had a dozen thegns about him, but instead he had me and Leofric and Egwine. "What are our forces now?" Alfred asked us.

"We have over a hundred men," Egwine said brightly.

"Of whom only sixty or seventy are fit to fight," I said. There had been an outbreak of sickness, men vomiting and shivering and hardly able to control their bowels. Whenever troops gather, such sickness seems to strike.

"Is that enough?" Alfred asked.

"Enough for what, lord?" Egwine was not quick-witted.

"Enough to get rid of Svein, of course," Alfred said, and again there was silence because the question was absurd.

Then Egwine straightened his shoulders. "More than enough, lord!"

Ælswith bestowed a smile on him.

"And how would you propose doing it?" Alfred asked.

"Take every man we have, lord," Egwine said, "every fit man, and attack them. Attack them!"

Beocca was not writing. He knew when he was hearing nonsense and he was not going to waste scarce ink on bad ideas.

Alfred looked at me. "Can it be done?"

"They'll see us coming," I said. "They'll be ready."

"March inland," Egwine said. "Come from the hills."

Again Alfred looked at me. "That will leave Æthelingæg undefended," I said, "and it will take at least three days, at the end of which our men will be cold, hungry, and tired, and the Danes will see us coming when we emerge from the hills, and that'll give them time to put on armor and gather weapons. And at best it will be equal numbers. At worst?" I just shrugged. After three or four days the rest of Svein's forces might have returned and our seventy or eighty men would be facing a horde.

"So how do you do it?" Alfred asked.

"We destroy their boats," I said.

"Go on."

"Without boats," I said, "they can't come up the rivers. Without boats, they're stranded."

Alfred nodded. Beocca was scratching away again. "So how do you destroy the boats?" the king asked.

I did not know. We could take seventy men to fight their seventy, but at the end of the fight, even if we won, we would be lucky to have twenty men still standing. Those twenty could burn the boats, of course, but I doubted we would survive that long. There were scores of Danish women at Cynuit and, if it came to a fight, they would join in and the odds were that we would be defeated. "Fire," Egwine said enthusiastically. "Carry fire in punts and throw the fire from the river."

"They are ship guards," I said tiredly, "and they'll be throwing spears and axes, sending arrows, and you might burn one boat, but that's all."

"Go at night," Egwine said.

"It's almost a full moon," I said, "and they'll see us coming. And if the moon is clouded we won't see their fleet."

"So how do you do it?" Alfred demanded again.

"God will send fire from heaven," Bishop Alewold said, and no one responded.

Alfred stood. We all got to our feet. Then he pointed at me. "You will destroy Svein's fleet," he said, "and I would know how you plan to do it by this evening. If you cannot do it then you"—he pointed to Egwine—"will travel to Defnascir, find Ealdorman Odda, and tell him to bring his forces to the river mouth and do the job for us."

"Yes, lord," Egwine said.

"By tonight," Alfred said to me coldly, and then he walked out.

He left me angry. He had meant to leave me angry. I stalked up to the newly made fort with Leofric and stared across the marshes to where the clouds heaped above the Sæfern. "How are we to burn twenty-four ships?" I demanded.

"God will send fire from heaven," Leofric said, "of course."

"I'd rather he sent a thousand troops."

"Alfred won't summon Odda," Leofric said. "He just said that to annoy you."

"But he's right, isn't he?" I said grudgingly. "We have to get rid of Svein."

"How?"

I stared at the tangled barricade that Haswold

had made from felled trees. The water, instead of flowing downstream, was coming upstream because the tide was on the flood and so the ripples ran eastward from the tangled branches. "I remember a story," I said, "from when I was a small child." I paused, trying to recall the tale, which, I assume, had been told to me by Beocca. "The Christian god divided a sea, isn't that right?"

"Moses did," Leofric said.

"And when the enemy followed," I said, "they were drowned."

"Clever," Leofric said.

"So that's how we'll do it," I said.

"How?"

But instead of telling him I summoned the marshmen and talked with them, and by that night I had my plan and, because it was taken from the scriptures, Alfred approved it readily. It took another day to get everything ready. We had to gather sufficient punts to carry forty men and I also needed Eofer, the simpleminded archer. He was unhappy, not understanding what I wanted, and he gibbered at us and looked terrified, but then a small girl, perhaps ten or eleven years old, took his hand and explained that he had to go hunting with us. "He trusts you?" I asked the child.

"He's my uncle," she said. Eofer was holding her hand and he was calm again.

"Does Eofer do what you tell him?"

She nodded, her small face serious, and I told her she must come with us to keep her uncle happy.

We left before the dawn. We were twenty marshmen, skilled with boats, twenty warriors, a simpleminded archer, a child, and Iseult. Alfred, of course, did not want me to take Iseult, but I ignored him and he did not argue. Instead he watched us leave, then went to Æthelingæg's church that now boasted a newly made cross of alder wood nailed to its gable.

And low in the sky above the cross was the full moon. She was low and ghostly pale, and as the sun rose she faded even more, but as the ten punts drifted down the river I stared at her and said a silent prayer to Hoder because the moon is his woman and it was she who must give us victory. Because, for the first time since Guthrum had struck in a winter's dawn, the Saxons were fighting back.

EIGHT

Before the Pedredan reaches the sea it makes a great curve through the swamp, a curve that is almost three-quarters of a circle and on the inside of the bank where the curve begins there was another tiny settlement: just a half dozen hovels built on stilts sunk into a slight rise in the ground. The settlement was called Palfleot, which means "the place with the stakes," for the folk who had once lived there had staked eel and fish traps in the nearby streams, but the Danes had driven those folk away and burned their houses, so that Palfleot was now a place of charred pilings and blackened mud. We landed there, shivering in the dawn. The tide was falling, exposing the great banks of sand and mud across which Iseult and I had struggled, while the wind was coming from the west, cold and fresh, hint-ing of rain, though for now there was a slanting sunlight throwing long shadows of marram grass and reeds across the marshes. Two swans flew south and I knew they were a message from the gods, but what their message was I could not tell.

The punts pushed away, abandoning us. They were now going north and east, following intricate waterways known only to the marshmen. We stayed for a while in Palfleot, doing nothing in particular, but doing it energetically so that the Danes, a long way off across the great bend in the river, would be sure to see us. We pulled down the blackened timbers and Iseult, who had acute eyesight, watched the place where the Danish ships' masts showed as scratches against the western clouds. "There's a man up a mast," she said after a while, and I stared, saw the man clinging to the mast top, and knew we had been spotted. The tide was falling, exposing more mud and sand, and now that I was sure we had been seen we walked across the drying expanse that was cradled by the river's extravagant bend.

As we drew closer I could see more Danes in their ships' rigging. They were watching us, but would not yet be worried for they outnumbered my few forces and the river lay between us and them, but whoever commanded in the Danish camp would also be ordering his men to arm themselves. He would want to be ready for whatever happened, but I also hoped he would be clever. I was laying a trap for him, and for the trap to work he had to do what I wanted him to do, but at first, if he was clever, he would do nothing. He knew we were impotent, separated from him by the Pedredan, and so he was content to watch as we closed on the river's bank opposite his grounded ships and then slipped and slid down the steep muddy bluff that the ebbing tide had exposed. The river swirled in front of us, gray and cold.

There were close to a hundred Danes watching now. They were on their grounded boats, shouting insults. Some were laughing for it seemed clear to them that we had walked a long way to achieve nothing, but that was because they did not know Eofer's skills. I called the big bowman's niece to my side. "What I want your uncle Eofer to do," I explained to the small girl, "is kill some of those men."

"Kill them?" She stared up at me with wide eyes.

"They're bad men," I said, "and they want to kill you."

She nodded solemnly, then took the big man

by the hand and led him to the water's edge where he sank up to his calves in the mud. It was a long way across the river and I wondered, pessimistically, if it was too far for even his massive bow, but Eofer strung the great stave and then waded into the Pedredan until he found a shallow spot, which meant he could go even farther into the river, and there he took an arrow from his sheaf, put it on the string, and hauled it back. He made a grunting noise as he released and I watched the arrow twitch off the cord. Then the fledging caught the air and the arrow soared across the stream and plunged into a group of Danes standing on the steering platform of a ship. There was a cry of anger as the arrow cut down. It did not hit any of the group, but Eofer's next arrow struck a man in his shoulder, and the Danes hurried back from their vantage point by the ship's sternpost. Eofer, who was compulsively nodding his shaggy head and making small animal noises, turned his aim to another ship. He had extraordinary strength. The distance was too great for any accuracy, but the danger of the long white-fledged arrows drove the Danes back and it was our turn to jeer them. One of the Danes fetched a bow and tried to shoot back, but his arrow sliced into the river twenty yards short and we taunted them, laughed at them, and capered up and down as Eofer's arrows slammed into ships' timbers. Only the one man had been wounded, but we had driven them backward and that was humiliating to them. I let Eofer loose twenty arrows. Then I waded into the river and took hold of his bow. I stood in front of him so the Danes could not see what I was doing.

"Tell him not to worry," I told the girl, and she soothed Eofer who was frowning at me and trying to remove his bow from my grasp.

I drew a knife and that alarmed him even more. He growled at me, then plucked the bow from my hand. "Tell him it's all right," I told the girl, and she soothed her uncle who then let me half sever the woven hemp bowstring. I stepped away from him and pointed at a group of Danes. "Kill them," I said.

Eofer did not want to draw the bow. Instead he fumbled under his greasy woolen cap and produced a second bowstring, but I shook my head and the small girl persuaded him he must use the half-severed cord and so he pulled it nervously back and, just before it reached the full draw, the string snapped and the arrow spun crazily into the sky to float away on the river.

The tide had turned and the water was rising. "We go!" I shouted to my men.

It was now the Danes' turn to jeer us. They thought we were retreating because our one bowstring had broken, and so they shouted insults as we clambered back up the muddy bluff, and then I saw two men running along the far beach and I hoped they were carrying the orders I wanted.

They were. The Danes, released from the threat of Eofer's terrible bow, were going to launch two of their smaller ships. We had stung them, laughed at them, and now they would kill us.

All warriors have pride. Pride and rage and ambition are the goads to a reputation, and the Danes did not want us to think we had stung them without being punished for our temerity. They wanted to teach us a lesson. But they also wanted more. Before we left Æthelingæg I had insisted that my men be given every available coat of mail. Egwine, who had stayed behind with the king, had been reluctant to give up his precious armor, but Alfred had ordered it and so sixteen of my men were dressed in chain mail. They looked superb, like an elite group of warriors, and the Danes would win renown if they defeated such a group and captured the precious armor. Leather offers some protection, but chain mail over leather is far better and far more expensive, and by taking sixteen coats of mail to the river's edge, I had given the Danes an irresistible lure.

And they snapped at it.

We were going slowly, deliberately seeming to struggle in the soft ground as we headed back toward Palfleot. The Danes were also struggling, shoving their two ships down the riverbank's thick mud, but at last the boats were launched and then, on the hurrying flood tide, the Danes did what I had hoped they would do.

They did not cross the river. If they had crossed, then they would merely have found themselves on the Pedredan's eastern bank and we would have been half a mile ahead and out of reach, so instead the commander did what he thought was the clever thing to do. He tried to cut us off. They had seen us land at Palfleot and they reckoned our boats must still be there, and so they rowed their ships upriver to find those boats and destroy them.

Except our punts were not at Palfleot. They had been taken north and east, so that they were waiting for us in a reed-fringed dike, but now was not the time to use them. Instead, as the Danes went ashore at Palfleot, we made a huddle on the sand, watching them, and they thought we were trapped, and now they were on the same side of the river as us and the two ships' crews outnumbered us by over two to one, and they had all the confidence in the world as they advanced from the burned pilings of Palfleot to kill us in the swamp.

They were doing exactly what I wanted them to do.

And we now retreated. We went back raggedly, sometimes running to open a distance between us and the confident Danes. I counted seventy-six of them and we were only thirty strong because some of my men were with the hidden punts, and the Danes knew we were dead men and they hurried across the sand and creeks, and we had to go faster, ever faster, to keep them away from us. It began to rain, the drops carried on the freshening west wind, and I kept looking into the rain until at last I saw a silver bar of light glint and spill across the swamp's edge and knew the incoming tide was beginning its long fast race across the barren flats.

And still we went back, and still the Danes pursued us, but they were tiring now. A few shouted at us, daring us to stand and fight, but others had no breath to shout, just a savage intent to catch and kill us, but we were slanting eastward now toward a line of buckthorn and reeds, and there, in a flooding creek, were our punts.

We dropped into the boats, exhausted, and the marshmen poled us back down the creek that was a tributary of the river Bru, which barred the northern part of the swamp, and the flat-bottomed craft took us fast south, against the current, hurrying us past the Danes who could only watch from a quarter mile away and do nothing to stop us, and the farther we went from them, the more isolated they looked in that wide, barren place where the rain fell and the tide seethed as it flowed into the creek beds. The wind-driven water was running deep into the swamp now, a tide made bigger by the full moon, and suddenly the Danes saw their danger and turned back toward Palfleot.

But Palfleot was a long way off, and we had already left the stream and were carrying the punts to a smaller creek, one that ran down to the Pedredan, and that stream took us to where the blackened pilings leaned against the weeping sky, and where the Danes had tied their two ships. The two craft were guarded by only four men, and we came from the punts with a savage shout and drawn swords and the four men ran. The other Danes were still out in the swamp, only now it was not a swamp but a tidal flat, and they were wading through water.

And I had two ships. We hauled the punts aboard, and then the marshmen, divided between the ships, took the oars, and I steered one and Leofric took the other, and we rowed against that big tide toward Cynuit where the Danish ships were now unguarded except for a few men and a crowd of women and children who watched the two ships come and did not know they were crewed by their enemy. They must have wondered why so few oars bit the water, but how could they imagine that forty Saxons would defeat nearly eighty Danes? And so none opposed us as we ran the ships into the bank, and there I led my warriors ashore. "You can fight us," I shouted at the few ship guards left, "or you can live."

I was in chain mail, with my new helmet. I was a warlord. I banged Serpent-Breath against the big shield and stalked toward them. "Fight if you want!" I shouted. "Come and fight us!"

They did not. They were too few and so they

retreated south and could only watch as we burned their ships. It took most of the day to ensure that the ships burned down to their keels, but burn they did, and their fires were a signal to the western part of Wessex that Svein had been defeated. He was not at Cynuit that day, but somewhere to the south, and as the ships burned I watched the wooded hills in fear that he would come with hundreds of men, but he was still far off and the Danes at Cynuit could do nothing to stop us. We burned twenty-three ships, including the **White Horse,** and the twenty-fourth, which was one of the two we had captured, carried us away as evening fell. We took good plunder from the Danish camp: food, rigging ropes, hides, weapons, and shields.

There were a score of Danes stranded on the low island of Palfleot. The rest had died in the rising water. The survivors watched us pass but did nothing to provoke us, and I did nothing to hurt them. We rowed on toward Æthelingæg and behind us, under a darkening sky, the water sheeted the swamp where white gulls cried above the drowned men and where, in the dusk, two swans flighted northward, their wings like drumbeats in the sky.

The smoke of the burned boats drifted to the

clouds for three days, and on the second day Egwine took the captured ship downstream with forty men and they landed on Palfleot and killed all the surviving Danes, except for six who were taken prisoner, and five of those six were stripped of their armor and lashed to stakes in the river at low tide so that they drowned slowly on the flood. Egwine lost three men in that fight, but brought back mail, shields, helmets, weapons, arm rings, and one prisoner who knew nothing except that Svein had ridden toward Exanceaster. That prisoner died on the third day, the day that Alfred had prayers said in thanks to God for our victory. For now we were safe. Svein could not attack us for he had lost his ships, Guthrum had no way of penetrating the swamp, and Alfred was pleased with me.

"The king is pleased with you," Beocca told me. Two weeks before, I thought, the king would have told me that himself. He would have sat with me by the water's edge and talked, but now a court had formed and the king was hedged with priests.

"He should be pleased," I said. I had been practicing weapon-craft when Beocca sought me out. We practiced every day, using stakes instead of swords, and some men grumbled that they did not need to play at fighting, and those I opposed myself and, when they had been beaten down to the mud, I told them they needed to play more and complain less.

"He's pleased with you," Beocca said, leading me down the path beside the river, "but he thinks you are squeamish."

"Me! Squeamish?"

"For not going to Palfleot and finishing the job."

"The job was finished," I said. "Svein can't attack us without ships."

"But not all the Danes drowned," Beocca said.

"Enough died," I said. "Do you know what they endured? The terror of trying to outrun the tide?" I thought of my own anguish in the swamp, the inexorable tide, the cold water spreading, and the fear gripping the heart. "They had no ships! Why kill stranded men?"

"Because they are pagans," Beocca said, "because they are loathed by God and by men, and because they are Danes."

"And only a few weeks ago," I said, "you believed they would become Christians and all our swords would be beaten into ard points to plow fields."

Beocca shrugged that off. "So what will Svein do now?" he wanted to know.

"March around the swamp," I said, "and join Guthrum."

"And Guthrum is in Cippanhamm." We were fairly certain of that. New men were coming to the swamp and they all brought news. Much of it was rumor, but many had heard that Guthrum had strengthened Cippanhamm's walls and was wintering there. Large raiding parties still ravaged parts of Wessex, but they avoided the bigger towns in the south of the country where West Saxon garrisons had formed. There was one such garrison at Dornwaraceaster and another at Wintanceaster, and Beocca believed Alfred should go to one of those towns, but Alfred refused, reckoning that Guthrum would immediately besiege him. He would be trapped in a town, but the swamp was too big to be besieged and Guthrum could not hope to penetrate the marshes. "You have an uncle in Mercia, don't you?" Beocca asked, changing the subject abruptly.

"Æthelred. He's my mother's brother, and an ealdorman."

He heard the flat tone of my voice. "You're not fond of him?"

"I hardly know him." I had spent some weeks in his house, just long enough to quarrel with his son who was also called Æthelred.

"Is he a friend of the Danes?"

I shook my head. "They suffer him to live and he suffers them."

"The king has sent messengers to Mercia," Beocca said.

I grimaced. "If he wants them to rise against the Danes, they won't. They'll get killed."

"He'd rather they brought men south in the springtime," Beocca said and I wondered how a few Mercian warriors were supposed to get past the Danes to join us, but said nothing. "We look to the springtime for our salvation," Beocca went on, "but in the meantime the king would like someone to go to Cippanhamm."

"A priest," I asked sourly, "to talk to Guthrum?"

"A soldier," Beocca said, "to gauge their numbers."

"So send me," I offered.

Beocca nodded, then limped along the riverbank where the willow fish traps had been exposed by the falling tide. "It's so different from Northumbria," he said wistfully.

I smiled at that. "You miss Bebbanburg?"

"I would like to end my days at Lindisfarena," he said. "I would like to say my dying prayer on that island." He turned and gazed at the eastern hills. "The king would go to Cippanhamm himself," he said, almost as an afterthought.

I thought I had misheard, then realized I had not. "That's madness," I protested.

"It's kingship," he said.

"Kingship?"

"The witan chooses the king," Beocca said sternly, "and the king must have the trust of the people. If Alfred goes to Cippanhamm and walks among his enemies, then folk will know he deserves to be king."

"And if he's captured," I said, "then folk will know he's a dead king."

"So you must protect him," he said. I said nothing. It was indeed madness, but Alfred was determined to show he deserved to be king. He had, after all, usurped the throne from his nephew, and in those early years of his reign he was ever mindful of that. "A small group will travel," Beocca said, "you, some other warriors, a priest, and the king."

"Why the priest?"

"To pray, of course."

I sneered at that. "You?"

Beocca patted his lamed leg. "Not me. A young priest."

"Better to send Iseult," I said.

"No."

"Why not? She's keeping the king healthy." Alfred was in sudden good health, better than he had been in years, and it was all because of the medicines that Iseult made. The celandine and burdock she had gathered on the mainland had taken away the agony in his arse, while other herbs calmed the pains in his belly. He walked confidently, had bright eyes, and looked strong.

"Iseult stays here," Beocca said.

"If you want the king to live," I said, "send her with us."

"She stays here," Beocca said, "because we want the king to live." It took me a few heart-beats to understand what he had said, and when I did realize his meaning I turned on him with such fury that he stumbled backward. I said nothing, for I did not trust myself to speak, or perhaps I feared that speech would turn to vio-lence. Beocca tried to look severe, but only looked fearful. "These are difficult times," he said plaintively, "and the king can only put his trust in men who serve God. In men who are bound to him by their love of Christ."

I kicked at an eel trap, sending it spinning over the bank into the river. "For a time," I said, "I almost liked Alfred. Now he's got his priests back and you're dripping poison into him."

"He—" Beocca began.

I turned on him, silencing him. "Who rescued the bastard? Who burned Svein's ships? Who, in the name of your luckless god, killed Ubba? And you still don't trust me?"

Beocca was trying to calm me now, making flapping gestures. "I fear you are a pagan," he said, "and your woman is assuredly a pagan."

"My woman healed Edward," I snarled. "Does that mean nothing?"

"It could mean," he said, "that she did the devil's work."

I was astonished into silence by that.

"The devil does his work in the land," Beocca said earnestly, "and it would serve the devil well if Wessex was to vanish. The devil wants the king dead. He wants his own pagan spawn all across England! There is a greater war, Uhtred. Not the fight between Saxon and Dane, but between God and the devil, between good and evil! We are part of it!"

"I've killed more Danes than you can dream of," I told him.

"But suppose," he said, pleading with me now, "that your woman has been sent by the devil? That the evil one allowed her to heal Edward so that the king would trust her? And then, when the king, in all innocence, goes to spy on the enemy, she betrays him!"

"You think she would betray him?" I asked sourly. "Or do you mean I might betray him?"

"Your love of the Danes is well known," Beocca said stiffly, "and you spared the men on Palfleot."

"So you think I can't be trusted?"

"I trust you," he said, without conviction. "But other men?" He waved his palsied hand in an impotent gesture. "But if Iseult is here—" He shrugged, not ending the thought.

"So she's to be a hostage," I said.

"A surety, rather."

"I gave the king my oath," I pointed out.

"And you have sworn oaths before, and you are known as a liar, and you have a wife and child, yet live with a pagan whore, and you love the Danes as you love yourself, and do you really think we can trust you?" This all came out in a bitter rush. "I have known you, Uhtred," he said, "since you crawled on Bebbanburg's rush floors. I baptized you, taught you, chastised you, watched you grow, and I know you better than any man alive and I do not trust you." Beocca stared at me belligerently. "If the king does not return, Uhtred, then your whore will be given to the dogs." He had delivered his message now, and he seemed to regret the force of it for he shook his head. "The king should not go. You're right. It's a madness. It is stupidity! It is"—he paused, searching for a word, and came upon one of the worst condemnations in his vocabulary—"it is irresponsible! But he insists, and if he goes then you must also go, for you're the only man here who can pass as a Dane. But bring him back, Uhtred, bring him back, for he is dear to God and to all Saxons."

Not to me, I thought, he was not dear to me. That night, brooding on Beocca's words, I was tempted to flee the swamp, to go away with Iseult, find a lord, give Serpent-Breath a new master, but Ragnar had been a hostage and so I had no friend among my enemies, and if I fled I would break my oath to Alfred and men would say Uhtred of Bebbanburg could never be trusted again and so I stayed. I tried to persuade Alfred not to go to Cippanhamm. It was, as Beocca had said, irresponsible, but Alfred insisted. "If I stay here," he said, "men will say I hid from the Danes. Others face them, but I hide? No. Men must see me, must know that I live, and know that I fight." For once Ælswith and I were in agreement, and we both tried to keep him in Æthelingæg, but Alfred would not be dissuaded. He was in a strange mood, suffused with happiness, utterly confident that God was on his side, and, because his sickness had abated, he was full of energy and confidence.

He took six companions. The priest was a young man called Adelbert who carried a small harp wrapped in leather. It seemed ridiculous to take a harp to the enemy, but Adelbert was famed for his music and Alfred blithely said that we should sing God's praises while we were among the Danes. The other four were all experienced warriors who had been part of his royal guard. They were called Osferth, Wulfrith, Beorth, and Egwine, the last of whom swore to Ælswith that he would bring the king home, which made Ælswith throw a bitter glance at me. Whatever favor I had gained by Iseult's cure of Edward had evaporated under the influence of the priests.

We dressed for war in mail and helmets, while Alfred insisted on wearing a fine blue cloak, trimmed with fur, which made him conspicuous, but he wanted folk to see a king. The best horses were selected, one for each of us and three spare mounts, and we swam them across the river, then followed log roads until we came at last to firm ground close to the island where Iseult said Arthur was buried. I had left Iseult with Eanflæd who shared quarters with Leofric.

It was February now. There had been a spell of fine weather after the burning of Svein's fleet and I had thought we should travel then, but Alfred insisted on waiting until the eighth day of February, because that was the Feast of Saint Cuthman, a Saxon saint from East Anglia, and Alfred reckoned that must be a propitious day. Perhaps he was right, for the day turned out wet and bitterly cold, and we were to discover that the Danes were reluctant to leave their quarters in the worst weather. We went at dawn and by midmorning we were in the hills overlooking the swamp, which was half hidden by a mist thickened by the smoke from the cooking fires of the small villages. "Are you familiar with Saint Cuthman?" Alfred asked me cheerfully.

"No, lord."

"He was a hermit," Alfred said. We were

riding north, keeping on the high ground with the swamp to our left. "His mother was crippled and so he made her a wheelbarrow."

"A wheelbarrow? What could a cripple do with a wheelbarrow?"

"No, no, no! He pushed her about in it! So she could be with him as he preached. He pushed her everywhere."

"She must have liked that."

"There's no written life of him that I know of," Alfred said, "but we must surely compose one. He could be a saint for mothers."

"Or for wheelbarrows, lord."

We saw our first evidence of the Danes just after midday. We were still on the high ground, but in a valley that sloped to the marshes we saw a substantial house with limewashed walls and thick thatch. Smoke came from the roof, while in a fenced apple orchard were a score of horses. No Dane would ever leave such a place unplundered, which suggested the horses belonged to them and that the farm was garrisoned. "They're there to watch the swamp," Alfred suggested.

"Probably." I was cold. I had a thick woolen cloak, but I was still cold.

"We shall send men here," Alfred said, "and teach them not to steal apples."

We stayed that night in a small village. The Danes had been there and the folk were frightened. At first, when we rode up the rutted track between the houses, they hid, thinking we were Danes, but when they heard our voices they crept out and stared at us as if we had just ridden down from the moon. Their priest was dead, killed by the pagans, so Alfred insisted that Adelbert hold a service in the burned-out remnants of the church. Alfred himself acted as precentor, accompanying his chanting with the priest's small harp. "I learned to play as a child," he told me. "My stepmother insisted, but I'm not very good."

"You're not," I agreed, which he did not like.

"There is never enough time to practice," he complained.

We lodged in a peasant's house. Alfred, reckoning that the Danes would have taken the harvest from wherever we visited, had laden the spare horses with smoked fish, smoked eels, and oatcakes, so we provided most of the food and, after we had eaten, the peasant couple knelt to me and the woman tentatively touched the skirt of my mail coat. "My children," she whispered, "there are two of them. My daughter is about seven years old and my boy is a little older. They are good children."

"What of them?" Alfred intervened.

"The pagans took them, lord," the woman said. She was crying. "You can find them, lord?" she said, tugging my mail. "You can find them and bring them back? My little ones? Please?"

I promised to try, but it was an empty promise for the children would have long gone to the slave market and, by now, would either be working on some Danish estate or, if they were pretty, sent overseas where heathen men pay good silver for Christian children.

We learned that the Danes had come to the village shortly after Twelfth Night. They had killed, captured, stolen, and ridden on southward. A few days later they had returned, going back northward, driving a band of captives and a herd of captured horses laden with plunder. Since then the villagers had seen no Danes except for the few on the swamp's edge. Those Danes, they said, caused no trouble, perhaps because they were so few and dared not stir up the enmity of the country about them. We heard the same tale in other villages. The Danes had come, they had pillaged, then had gone back north.

But on our third day we at last saw a force of the enemy riding on the Roman road that cuts straight westward across the hills from Baðum. There were close to sixty of them, and they rode hard in front of dark clouds and the gathering night. "Going back to Cippanhamm," Alfred said. It was a foraging party, and their pack-horses carried nets stuffed with hay to feed their warhorses, and I remembered my childhood winter in Readingum, when the Danes first invaded Wessex, and how hard it had been to keep horses and men alive in the cold. We had cut feeble winter grass and pulled down thatch to feed our horses that still became skeletal and weak. I have often listened to men declare that all that is needed to win a war is to assemble men and march against the enemy, but it is never that easy. Men and horses must be fed, and hunger can defeat an army much faster than spears. We watched the Danes go north, then turned aside to a half-ruined barn that offered us shelter for the night.

It began to snow that night, a relentless soft snow, silent and thick, so that by dawn the world was white under a pale blue sky. I suggested we waited till the snow had thawed before we rode further, but Egwine, who came from this part of the country, said we were only two or three hours south of Cippanhamm and Alfred was impatient. "We go," he insisted. "We go there, look at the town, and ride away."

So we rode north, our hooves crunching the newly fallen snow, riding through a world made new and clean. Snow clung to every twig and branch while ice skimmed the ditches and ponds. I saw a fox's trail crossing a field and thought that the spring would bring a plague of the beasts, for there would have been no one to hunt them, and the lambs would die bloodily and the ewes would bleat pitifully.

We came in sight of Cippanhamm before midday, though the great pall of smoke, made by hundreds of cooking fires, had shown in the sky all morning. We stopped south of the town, just where the road emerged from a stand of oaks, and the Danes must have noticed us, but none came from the gates to see who we were. It was too cold for men to stir themselves. I could see guards on the walls, though none stayed there long, retreating to whatever warmth they could find between their short forays along the wooden ramparts. Those ramparts were bright with round shields painted blue and white and blood-red and, because Guthrum's men were there, black. "We should count the shields," Alfred said.

"It won't help," I said. "They carry two or three shields each and hang them on the walls to make it look as if they have more men."

Alfred was shivering and I insisted we find some shelter. We turned back into the trees, following a path that led to the river, and a mile or so upstream we came across a mill. The millstone had been taken away, but the building itself was whole and it was well made, with stone walls and a turf roof held up by stout rafters. There was a hearth in a room where the miller's family had lived, but I would not let Egwine light a fire in case the trickle of smoke brought curious Danes from the town. "Wait till dark," I said.

"We'll freeze by then," he grumbled.

"Then you shouldn't have come," I snapped.

"We have to get closer to the town," Alfred said.

"You don't," I said. "I do." I had seen horses paddocked to the west of the walls and I reckoned I could take our best horse and ride about the town's western edge and count every horse I saw. That would give a rough estimate of the Danish numbers, for almost every man would have a horse. Alfred wanted to come, but I shook my head. It was pointless for more than one man to go, and sensible that the one man who did go should speak Danish, so I told him I would see him back in the mill before nightfall and then I rode north. Cippanhamm was built on a hill that was almost encircled by the river, so I could not ride clear around the town, but I went as close to the walls as I dared and stared across the river and saw no horses on its farther bank, which suggested that the Danes were keeping their beasts on the western side of the town. I went there, keeping in the snowy woods, and though the Danes must have seen me, they could not be bothered to ride into the snow to chase one man, and so I was able to find the paddocks where their horses shivered. I spent the day counting. Most of the horses were in fields beside the royal compound and there were hundreds of them. By late afternoon I had estimated that there were twelve hundred, and those were only the ones I could see, and the best horses would be in the town, but my reckoning was good enough. It would give Alfred an idea of how large Guthrum's force was. Say two thousand men? And elsewhere in Wessex, in the towns the Danes had occupied, there must be another thousand. That was a strong force, but not quite strong enough to capture all the kingdom. That would have to wait until spring when reinforcements would come from Denmark or from the three conquered kingdoms of England. I rode back to the watermill as dusk fell. There was a frost and the air was still. Three rooks flew across the river as I dismounted. I reckoned one of Alfred's men could rub my horse down; all I wanted was to find some warmth and it was plain Alfred had risked lighting a fire, for smoke was pouring out of the hole in the turf roof.

They were all crouched about the small fire and I joined them, stretching my hands to the flames. "Two thousand men," I said, "more or less."

No one answered.

"Didn't you hear me?" I asked, and looked around the faces.

There were five faces. Only five.

"Where's the king?" I asked.

"He went," Adelbert said helplessly.

"He did what?"

"He went to the town," the priest said. He was wearing Alfred's rich blue cloak and I assumed Alfred had taken Adelbert's plain garment.

I stared at him. "You let him go?"

"He insisted," Egwine said.

"How could we stop him?" Adelbert pleaded. "He's the king!"

"You hit the bastard, of course," I snarled. "You hold him down till the madness passes. When did he go?"

"Just after you left," the priest said miserably, "and he took my harp," he added.

"And when did he say he'd be back?"

"By nightfall."

"It is nightfall," I said. I stood and stamped out the fire. "You want the Danes to come and investigate the smoke?" I doubted the Danes would come, but I wanted the damned fools to suffer. "You." I pointed to one of the four soldiers. "Rub my horse down. Feed it."

I went back to the door. The first stars were bright and the snow glinted under a sickle moon.

"Where are you going?" Adelbert had followed me.

"To find the king, of course."

If he lived. And if he did not, then Iseult was dead.

I had to beat on Cippanhamm's western gate, provoking a disgruntled voice from the far side demanding to know who I was.

"Why aren't you up on the ramparts?" I asked in return.

The bar was lifted and the gate opened a few

inches. A face peered out, then vanished as I pushed the gate hard inward, banging it against the suspicious guard. "My horse went lame," I said, "and I've walked here."

He recovered his balance and pushed the gate shut. "Who are you?" he asked again.

"Messenger from Svein."

"Svein!" He lifted the bar and dropped it into place. "Has he caught Alfred yet?"

"I'll tell Guthrum that news before I tell you."

"Just asking," he said.

"Where is Guthrum?" I asked. I had no intention of going anywhere near the Danish chieftain for, after my insults to his dead mother, the best I could hope for was a swift death, and the likelihood was a very slow one.

"He's in Alfred's hall," the man said, and pointed south. "That side of town, so you've still farther to walk." It never occurred to him that any messenger from Svein would never ride alone through Wessex, that such a man would come with an escort of fifty or sixty men, but he was too cold to think, and besides, with my long hair and my thick arm rings I looked like a Dane. He retreated into the house beside the gate where his comrades were clustered around a hearth and I walked on into a town made strange. Houses were missing, burned in the first fury of the Danish assault, and the large church by the marketplace on the hilltop was nothing but blackened beams touched white by the snow. The streets were frozen mud, and only I moved there, for the cold was keeping the Danes in the remaining houses. I could hear singing and laughter. Light leaked past shutters or glowed through smoke holes in low roofs. I was cold and I was angry. There were men here who could recognize me, and men who might recognize Alfred, and his stupidity had put us both in danger. Would he have been mad enough to go back to his own hall? He must have guessed that was where Guthrum would be living and he would surely not risk being recognized by the Danish leader, which suggested he would be in the town rather than the royal compound.

I was walking toward Eanflæd's old tavern when I heard the roars. They were coming from the east side of town and I followed the sound, which led me to the nunnery by the river wall. I had never been inside the convent, but the gate was open and the courtyard inside was lit by two vast fires that offered some warmth to the men nearest the flames. And there were at least a hundred men in the courtyard, bellowing encouragement and insults at two other men who were fighting in the mud and melted snow between the fires. They were fighting with swords and shields, and every clash of blade against blade or of blade against wood brought raucous shouts. I glanced briefly at the fighters, then searched for faces in the crowd. I was looking for Haesten, or anyone else who might recognize me, but I saw no one, though it was hard to distinguish faces in the flickering shadows. There was no sign of any nuns and I assumed they had fled, were dead, or had been taken away for the conquerors' amusement.

I slunk along the courtyard wall. I was wearing my helmet and its faceplate was an adequate disguise, but some men threw me curious glances, for it was unusual to see a helmeted man off a battlefield. In the end, seeing no one I recognized, I took the helmet off and hung it from my belt. The nunnery church had been turned into a feasting hall, but there was only a handful of drunks inside, oblivious to the noise outside. I stole a half loaf of bread from one of the drunks and took it back outside and watched the fighting.

Steapa Snotor was one of the two men. He no longer wore his mail armor, but was in a leather coat, and he fought with a small shield and a long sword. Around his waist was a chain that led to the courtyard's northern side where two men held it and, whenever Steapa's opponent seemed to be in danger, they yanked on the chain to pull the huge Saxon off balance. He was being made to fight as Haesten had been fighting when I first discovered him, and doubtless Steapa's captors were making good money from fools who wanted to try their prowess against a captured warrior. Steapa's current opponent was a thin, grinning Dane who tried to dance around the huge man and slide his sword beneath the small shield, doing what I had done when I had fought Steapa, but Steapa was doggedly defending himself, parrying each blow and, when the chain allowed him, counterattacking fast. Whenever the Danes jerked him backward the crowd jeered and once, when the men yanked the chain too hard and Steapa turned on them, only to be faced by three long spears, the crowd gave him a great cheer. He whipped back to parry the next attack, then stepped backward, almost to the spear points, and the thin man followed fast, thinking he had Steapa at a disadvantage, but Steapa suddenly checked, slammed the shield down onto his opponent's blade, and brought his left hand around, sword hilt foremost, to hit the man on the head. The Dane went down, Steapa reversed the sword to stab, and the chain dragged him off his feet and the spears threatened him with death if he finished the job. The crowd liked it. He had won.

Money changed hands. Steapa sat by the fire, his grim face showing nothing, and one of the men holding the chain shouted for another opponent. "Ten pieces of silver if you wound him! Fifty if you kill him!"

Steapa, who probably did not understand a word, just stared at the crowd, daring another man to take him on, and sure enough a half-drunken brute came grinning from the crowd. Bets were made as Steapa was prodded to his feet. It was like a bull baiting, except Steapa was being given only one opponent at a time. They would doubtless have set three or four men on him, except that the Danes who had taken him prisoner did not want him dead so long as there were still fools willing to pay to fight him.

I was sidling around the courtyard's edge, still looking at faces. "Six pennies?" a voice said behind me and I turned to see a man grinning beside a door. It was one of a dozen similar doors, evenly spaced along the lime-washed wall.

"Six pennies?" I asked, puzzled.

"Cheap," he said, and he pushed back a small shutter on the door and invited me to look inside.

I did. A tallow candle lit the tiny room, which must have been where a nun had slept, and inside was a low bed and on the bed was a naked woman who was half covered by a man who had dropped his breeches. "He won't be long," the man said.

I shook my head and moved away from the shutter.

"She was a nun here," the man said. "Nice and young. Pretty, too. Screams like a pig usually."

"No," I said.

"Four pennies? She won't put up a fight. Not now she won't."

I walked on, convinced I was wasting my time. Had Alfred been and gone? More likely, I thought grimly, the fool had gone back to his hall and I wondered if I dared go there, but the thought of Guthrum's revenge deterred me. The new fight had started. The Dane was crouching low, trying to cut Steapa's feet from under him, but Steapa was swatting his blows easily enough and I sidled past the men holding his chains and saw another room off to my left, a large room, perhaps where the nuns had eaten, and a glint of gold in the light of its dying fire drew me inside.

The gold was not metal. It was the gilding on the frame of a small harp that had been stamped on so hard that it broke. I looked around the shadows and saw a man lying in a heap at the far end and went to him. It was Alfred. He was barely conscious, but he was alive and, so far as I could see, unwounded, but he was plainly stunned and I dragged him to the wall and sat him up. He had no cloak and his boots were gone. I left him there, went back to the church, and found a drunk to befriend. I helped him to his feet, put my arm around his shoulders, and persuaded him I was taking him to his bed, then took him through the back door to the latrine yard of the nunnery where I punched him three times in the belly and twice in the face, then carried his hooded cloak and tall boots back to Alfred.

The king was conscious now. His face was bruised. He looked up at me without showing any surprise, then rubbed his chin. "They didn't like the way I played," he said.

"That's because the Danes like good music," I said. "Put these on." I threw the boots beside him, draped him with the cloak, and made him pull the hood over his face. "You want to die?" I asked him angrily.

"I want to know about my enemies," he said.

"And I found out for you," I said. "There are roughly two thousand of them."

"That's what I thought," he said, then grimaced. "What's on this cloak?"

"Danish vomit," I said.

He shuddered. "Three of them attacked me," he sounded surprised. "They kicked and punched me."

"I told you, the Danes like good music," I said, helping him to his feet. "You're lucky they didn't kill you."

"They thought I was Danish," he said, then spat blood that trickled from his swollen lower lip.

"Were they drunk?" I asked. "You don't even look like a Dane."

"I pretended I was a musician who couldn't speak." He mouthed silently at me, then grinned bloodily, proud of his deception. I did not grin back and he sighed. "They were very drunk, but I need to know their mood, Uhtred. Are they confident? Are they readying to attack?" He paused to wipe more blood from his lips. "I could only find that out by coming to see them for myself. Did you see Steapa?"

"Yes."

"I want to take him back with us."

"Lord," I said savagely, "you are a fool. He's in chains. He's got half a dozen guards."

"Daniel was in a lion's den, yet he escaped. Saint Paul was imprisoned, yet God freed him."

"Then let God look after Steapa," I said. "You're coming back with me. Now."

He bent to relieve a pain his belly. "They punched me in the stomach," he said as he straightened. In the morning, I thought, he would have a rare black eye to display. He flinched as a huge cheer sounded from the courtyard and I guessed Steapa had either died or downed his last opponent. "I want to see my hall," Alfred said stubbornly.

"Why?"

"I'm a man who would look at his own home. You can come or stay."

"Guthrum's there! You want to be recognized? You want to die?"

"Guthrum will be inside, and I just want to look at the outside."

He would not be dissuaded and so I led him through the courtyard to the street, wondering if

I should simply pick him up and carry him away, but in his obdurate mood he would probably struggle and shout until men came to find out the cause of the noise. "I wonder what happened to the nuns," he said as we left the nunnery.

"One of them is being whored in there for pennies," I said.

"Oh, dear God." He made the sign of the cross and turned back and I knew he was thinking of rescuing the woman, so I dragged him onward. "This is madness!" I protested.

"It is a necessary madness," he said calmly, then stopped to lecture me. "What does Wessex believe? It thinks I am defeated, it thinks the Danes have won, it readies itself for the spring and the coming of more Danes. So they must learn something different. They must learn that the king lives, that he walked among his enemies, and that he made fools of them."

"That he got given a bloody nose and a black eye," I said.

"You won't tell them that," he said, "any more than you'll tell folk about that wretched woman who hit me with an eel. We must give men hope, Uhtred, and in the spring that hope will blossom into victory. Remember Boethius, Uhtred, remember Boethius! Never give up hope."

He believed it. He believed that God was protecting him, that he could walk among his enemies without fear or harm, and to an extent he was right, for the Danes were well supplied with ale, birch wine, and mead, and most were much too drunk to care about a bruised man carrying a broken harp.

No one stopped us going into the royal compound, but there were six black-cloaked guards at the hall door and I refused to let Alfred get close to them. "They'll take one look at your bloodied face," I said, "and finish what the others began."

"Then let me at least go to the church."

"You want to pray?" I asked sarcastically.

"Yes," he said simply.

I tried to stop him. "If you die here," I said, "then Iseult dies."

"That wasn't my doing," he said.

"You're the king, aren't you?"

"The bishop thought you would join the Danes," he said, "and others agreed."

"I have no friends left among the Danes," I said. "They were your hostages and they died."

"Then I shall pray for their pagan souls," he said, and pulled away from me and went to the church door where he instinctively pushed the hood off his head to show respect. I snatched it back over his hair, shadowing his bruises. He did not resist, but just pushed the door open and made the sign of the cross.

The church was being used to shelter more of Guthrum's men. There were straw mattresses, heaps of chain mail, stacks of weapons, and a score of men and women gathered around a newly made hearth in the nave. They were playing dice and none took any particular interest in our arrival until someone shouted that we should shut the door.

"We're leaving," I said to Alfred. "You can't pray here."

He did not answer. He was gazing reverently to where the altar had been, and where a half dozen horses were now tethered.

"We're leaving!" I insisted again.

And just then a voice hailed me. It was a voice full of astonishment and I saw one of the dice players stand and stare at me. A dog ran from the shadows and began to jump up and down, trying to lick me, and I saw the dog was Nihtgenga and that the man who had recognized me was Ragnar. Earl Ragnar, my friend.

Who I had thought was dead.

NINE

Ragnar embraced me. There were tears in both our eyes and for a moment neither of us could speak, though I retained enough sense to look behind me to make sure Alfred was safe. He was squatting beside the door, deep in the shadow of a bale of wool, with his cloak's hood drawn over his face. "I thought you were dead!" I said to Ragnar.

"I hoped you would come," he said at the same moment, and for a time we both talked and neither listened, and then Brida walked from the back of the church and I watched her, seeing a woman instead of a girl, and she laughed to see me and gave me a decorous kiss.

"Uhtred." She said my name as a caress. We had been lovers once, though we had been little more than children then. She was Saxon, but she had chosen the Danish side to be with Ragnar. The other women in the hall were hung with silver, garnet, jet, amber, and gold, but Brida wore no jewelry other than an ivory comb that held her thick black hair in a pile. "Uhtred," she said again.

"Why aren't you dead?" I asked Ragnar. He had been a hostage, and the hostages' lives had been forfeit the moment Guthrum crossed the frontier.

"Wulfhere liked us," Ragnar said. He put an arm around my shoulder and drew me to the central hearth where the fire blazed. "This is Uhtred," he announced to the dice players, "a Saxon, which makes him scum, of course, but he is also my friend and my brother. Ale." He pointed to jars. "Wine. Wulfhere let us live."

"And you let him live?"

"Of course we did! He's here. Feasting with Guthrum."

"Wulfhere? Is he a prisoner?"

"He's an ally!" Ragnar said, thrusting a pot into my hand and pulling me down beside the fire. "He's with us now." He grinned at me, and I laughed for the sheer joy of finding him alive. He was a big man, golden-haired, open-faced, and as full of mischief, life, and kindness as his father had been. "Wulfhere used to talk to Brida," Ragnar went on, "and through her to me. We liked each other. Hard to kill a man you like."

"You persuaded him to change sides?"

"Didn't need a great deal of persuasion," Ragnar said. "He could see we were going to win, and by changing sides he keeps his land, doesn't he? Are you going to drink that ale or just stare at it?"

I pretended to drink, letting some of the ale drip down my beard, and I remembered Wulfhere telling me that when the Danes came we must all make what shifts we could to survive. But Wulfhere? Alfred's cousin and the Ealdorman of Wiltunscir? He had changed sides? So how many other thegns had followed his example and now served the Danes?

"Who's that?" Brida asked. She was staring at Alfred. He was in shadow, but there was something oddly mysterious about the way he squatted alone and silent.

"A servant," I said.

"He can come by the fire."

"He cannot," I said harshly. "I'm punishing him."

"What did you do?" Brida called to him in English. His face came up and he stared at her, but the hood still shadowed him.

"Speak, you bastard," I said, "and I'll whip you till your bones show." I could just see his eyes in the hood's shadow. "He insulted me," I spoke in Danish again, "and I've sworn him to silence, and for every word he utters he receives ten blows of the whip."

That satisfied them. Ragnar forgot the strange hooded servant and told me how he had persuaded Wulfhere to send a messenger to Guthrum, promising to spare the hostages, and how Guthrum had warned Wulfhere when the attack would come to make sure that the ealdorman had time to remove the hostages from Alfred's revenge. That, I thought, was why Wulfhere had left so early on the morning of the attack. He had known the Danes were coming. "You call him an ally," I said. "Does that make him just a friend? Or a man who will fight for Guthrum?"

"He's an ally," Ragnar said, "and he's sworn to fight for us. At least he's sworn to fight for the Saxon king."

"The Saxon king?" I asked, confused. "Alfred?"

"Not Alfred, no. The true king. The boy who was the other one's son."

Ragnar meant Æthelwold, who had been heir to Alfred's brother, King Æthelred, and of course the Danes would want Æthelwold. Whenever they captured a Saxon kingdom they appointed a Saxon as king, and that gave their conquest a cloak of legality, though the Saxon never lasted long. Guthrum, who already called himself King of East Anglia, wanted to be King of Wessex, too, but by putting Æthelwold on the throne he might attract other West Saxons who could convince themselves they were fighting for the true heir. And once the fight was over and Danish rule established, Æthelwold would quietly be killed.

"But Wulfhere will fight for you?" I persisted.

"Of course he will! If he wants to keep his land," Ragnar said, then grimaced. "But what fighting? We just sit here like sheep and do nothing!"

"It's winter."

"Best time to fight. Nothing else to do." He wanted to know where I had been since Yule and I said I had been deep inside Defnascir. He assumed I had been making sure my family was safe, and he also assumed I had now come to

Cippanhamm to join him. "You're not sworn to Alfred, are you?" he asked.

"Who knows where Alfred is?" I evaded the question.

"You were sworn to him," he said reproachfully.

"I was sworn to him," I said, truthfully enough, "but only for a year, and that year has long ended." That was no lie; I just did not tell Ragnar I had sworn myself to Alfred once again.

"So you can join me?" he asked eagerly. "You'll give me your oath?"

I took the question lightly, though in truth it worried me. "You want my oath," I asked, "just so I can sit here like a sheep doing nothing?"

"We make some raids," Ragnar said defensively, "and men are guarding the swamp. That's where Alfred is. In the swamps. But Svein will dig him out." So Guthrum and his men had yet to hear that Svein's fleet was ashes beside the sea.

"So why are you just sitting here?" I asked.

"Because Guthrum won't divide his army," Ragnar said. I half smiled at that because I remembered Ragnar's grandfather advising Guthrum never to divide an army again. Guthrum had done that at Æsc's Hill and that had been the first victory of the West Saxons over the Danes. He had done it again when he abandoned Werham to attack Exanceaster, and the part of his army that went by sea was virtually destroyed by the storm. "I've told him," Ragnar said, "that we should split the army into a dozen parts. Take a dozen more towns and garrison them. All those places in southern Wessex, we should capture them, but he won't listen."

"Guthrum holds the north and east," I said, as if I was defending him.

"And we should have the rest! But instead we're waiting till spring in hope more men will join us. Which they will. There's land here, good land. Better than the land up north." He seemed to have forgotten the matter of my oath. I knew he would want me to join him, but instead he talked of what happened in Northumbria, how our enemies, Kjartan and Sven, thrived in Dunholm, and how that father and son dared not leave the fortress for fear of Ragnar's revenge. They had taken his sister captive and, so far as Ragnar knew, they held her still, and Ragnar, like me, was sworn to kill them. He had no news of Bebbanburg other than that my treacherous uncle still lived and held the fortress. "When we've finished with Wessex," Ragnar promised me, "we shall go north. You and I together. We'll carry swords to Dunholm."

"Swords to Dunholm," I said and raised my pot of ale.

I did not drink much, or if I did it seemed to have little effect. I was thinking, sitting there, that with one sentence I could finish Alfred forever. I could betray him; I could have him dragged in front of Guthrum and then watch as he died. Guthrum would even forgive me the insults to his mother if I gave him Alfred, and thus I could finish Wessex, for without Alfred there was no man about whom the fyrd would muster. I could stay with my friend Ragnar, I could earn more arm rings, I could make a name that would be celebrated wherever Northmen sailed their long ships, and all it would take was one sentence.

And I was so tempted that night in Cippanhamm's royal church. There is such joy in chaos. Stow all the world's evils behind a door and tell men that they must never, ever, open the door, and it will be opened because there is pure joy in destruction. At one moment, when Ragnar was bellowing with laughter and slapping my shoulder so hard that it hurt, I felt the words form on my tongue. That is Alfred, I would have said, pointing at him, and all my world would have changed and there would have been no more England. Yet, at the last moment, when the first word was on my tongue, I choked it back. Brida was watching me, her shrewd eyes calm, and I caught her gaze and I thought of Iseult. In a year or two, I thought, Iseult would look like Brida. They had the same tense beauty, the same dark coloring, and the same smoldering fire in the soul. If I spoke, I thought, Iseult would be dead, and I could not bear that. And I thought of Æthelflaed, Alfred's daughter, and knew she would be enslaved, and also knew that wherever the remnants of the Saxons gathered about their fires of exile my name would be cursed. I would be Uhtredærwe forever, the man who destroyed a people.

"What were you about to say?" Brida asked.

"That we have never known such a hard winter in Wessex."

She gazed at me, not believing my answer. Then she smiled. "Tell me, Uhtred," she spoke in English, "if you thought Ragnar was dead, then why did you come here?"

"Because I don't know where else to be," I said.

"So you came here? To Guthrum? Whom you insulted?"

So they knew about that. I had not expected them to know and I felt a surge of fear. I said nothing.

"Guthrum wants you dead," Brida said, speaking in Danish now.

"He doesn't mean it," Ragnar said.

"He does mean it," Brida insisted.

"Well, I won't let him kill Uhtred," Ragnar said. "You're here now!" He slapped me on the back again and glared at his men as if daring any of them to betray my presence to Guthrum. None of them moved, but they were nearly all of them drunk and some already asleep.

"You're here now," Brida said, "yet not so long ago you were fighting for Alfred and insulting Guthrum."

"I was on my way to Defnascir," I said, as if that explained anything.

"Poor Uhtred," Brida said. Her right hand fondled the black-and-white fur at the back of Nihtgenga's neck. "And I thought you'd be a hero to the Saxons."

"A hero? Why?"

"The man who killed Ubba?"

"Alfred doesn't want heroes," I said, loudly enough for him to hear, "only saints."

"So tell us about Ubba!" Ragnar demanded,

and so I had to describe Ubba's death and the Danes, who love a good story of a fight, wanted every detail. I told the tale well, making Ubba into a great hero who had almost destroyed the West Saxon army, and I said he had been fighting like a god, and told how he had broken our shield wall with his great ax. I described the burning ships, their smoke drifting over the battle slaughter like a cloud from the netherworld, and I said I had found myself facing Ubba in his victory charge. That was not true, of course, and the Danes knew it was not true. I had not just found myself opposing Ubba, but had sought him out. But when a story is told it must be seasoned with modesty and the listeners, understanding that custom, murmured approval. "I have never known such fear," I said, and I told how we had fought, Serpent-Breath against Ubba's ax, and how he had chopped my shield into firewood, and then I described, truthfully, how he had lost his footing in the spilled guts of a dead man. The Danes about the fire sighed with disappointment. "I cut the tendons of his arm," I said, chopping my left hand into the crook of my right elbow to show where I had cut him, "and then beat him down."

"He died well?" a man asked anxiously.

"As a hero," I said, and I told how I had put the ax back into his dying hand so that he would go to Valhalla. "He died very well," I finished.

"He was a warrior," Ragnar said. He was drunk now. Not badly drunk, but tired drunk. The fire was dying, thickening the shadows at the western end of the church where Alfred sat. More stories were told, the fire died, and the few candles guttered. Men were sleeping, and still I sat until Ragnar lay back and began to snore. I waited longer, letting the room go to sleep, and only then did I go back to Alfred. "We go now," I said. He did not argue.

No one appeared to notice as we went into the night, closing the door quietly behind us. "Who were you talking with?" Alfred asked me.

"Earl Ragnar."

He stopped, puzzled. "Wasn't he one of the hostages?"

"Wulfhere let them live," I said.

"He let them live?" he asked, astonished.

"And Wulfhere is now on Guthrum's side." I gave him the bad news. "He's here, in the hall. He's agreed to fight for Guthrum."

"Here?" Alfred could scarce believe what I said. Wulfhere was his cousin, he had married Alfred's niece, he was family. "He's here?"

"He's on Guthrum's side," I said harshly.

He just stared at me. "No." He mouthed the word, rather than said it. "And Æthelwold?" he asked.

"He's a prisoner," I said.

"A prisoner!" He asked the question sharply, and no wonder, for Æthelwold had no value to the Danes as a prisoner unless he had agreed to become their token king on the West Saxon throne.

"A prisoner," I said. It was not true, of course, but I liked Æthelwold and I owed him a favor. "He's a prisoner," I went on, "and there's nothing we can do about it, so let's get away from here." I pulled him toward the town, but too late, for the church door opened and Brida came out with Nihtgenga.

She told the dog to stay at her heels as she walked toward me. Like me she was not drunk, though she must have been very cold for she wore no cloak over her plain blue woolen dress. The night was brittle with frost, but she did not shiver. "You're going?" She spoke in English. "You're not staying with us?"

"I have a wife and child," I said.

She smiled at that. "Whose names you have not mentioned all evening, Uhtred. So what happened?" I gave no answer and she just stared at me, and there was something very unsettling in her gaze. "So what woman is with you now?" she asked.

"Someone who looks like you," I admitted.

She laughed at that. "And she would have you fight for Alfred?"

"She sees the future," I said, evading the question. "She dreams it."

Brida stared at me. Nihtgenga whined softly and she put down a hand to calm him. "And she sees Alfred surviving?"

"More than surviving," I said. "She sees him winning." Beside me Alfred stirred and I hoped he had the sense to keep his head lowered.

"Winning?"

"She sees a green hill of dead men," I said, "a white horse, and Wessex living again."

"Your woman has strange dreams," Brida said, "but you never answered my first question, Uhtred. If you thought Ragnar was dead, why did you come here?"

I had no ready answer so made none.

"Who did you expect to find here?" she asked.

"You?" I suggested glibly.

She shook her head, knowing I lied. "Why did you come?" I still had no answer and Brida smiled sadly. "If I was Alfred," she said, "I would send a man who spoke Danish to Cippanhamm, and that man would go back to the swamp and tell all he had seen."

"If you think that," I said, "then why don't you tell them?" I nodded toward Guthrum's black-cloaked men guarding the hall door.

"Because Guthrum is a nervous fool," she said savagely. "Why help Guthrum? And when Guthrum fails, Ragnar will take command."

"Why doesn't he command now?"

"Because he is like his father. He's decent. He gave his word to Guthrum and he won't break his word. And tonight he wanted you to give him an oath, but you didn't."

"I do not want Bebbanburg to be a gift of the Danes," I answered.

She thought about that, and understood it. "But do you think," she asked scornfully, "that the West Saxons will give you Bebbanburg? It's at the other end of Britain, Uhtred, and the last Saxon king is rotting in a swamp."

"This will give it to me," I said, pulling back my cloak to show Serpent-Breath's hilt.

"You and Ragnar can rule the north," she said.

"Maybe we will," I said. "So tell Ragnar that

when this is all finished, when all is decided, I shall go north with him. I shall fight Kjartan. But in my own time."

"I hope you live to keep that promise," she said, then leaned forward and kissed my cheek. Then, without another word, she turned and walked back to the church.

Alfred let out a breath. "Who is Kjartan?"

"An enemy," I said shortly. I tried to lead him away, but he stopped me.

He was staring at Brida who was nearing the church. "That is the girl who was with you at Wintanceaster?"

"Yes." He was talking of the time when I had first come to Wessex and Brida had been with me.

"And does Iseult truly see the future?"

"She has not been wrong yet."

He made the sign of the cross, then let me lead him back through the town that was quieter now, but he would not go with me to the western gate, insisting we return to the nunnery where, for a moment, we both crouched near one of the dying fires in the courtyard to get what warmth we could from the embers. Men slept in the nunnery church, but the courtyard was now deserted and quiet, and Alfred took a piece of half-burning wood and, using it as a torch, went to the row of small doors that led to the nuns' sleeping cells. One door had been fastened with two hasps and a short length of thick chain and Alfred paused there.

"Draw your sword," he ordered me.

When Serpent-Breath was naked he unwound the chain from the hasps and pushed the door inward. He entered cautiously, pushing the hood back from his face. He held the torch high, and in its light I saw the big man huddled on the floor.

"Steapa!" Alfred hissed.

Steapa was only pretending to be asleep and he uncoiled from the floor with wolflike speed, lashing out at Alfred, and I rammed the sword toward his breast, but then he saw Alfred's bruised face and he froze, oblivious of the blade. "Lord?"

"You're coming with us," Alfred said.

"Lord!" Steapa fell to his knees in front of his king.

"It's cold out there," Alfred said. It was freezing inside the cell as well. "You can sheath your sword, Uhtred." Steapa looked at me and seemed vaguely surprised to find I was the man he had been fighting when the Danes came. "The two of you will be friends," Alfred said sternly, and the big man nodded. "And we have one other person to fetch," Alfred said, "so come."

"One other person?" I asked.

"You spoke of a nun," Alfred said.

So I had to find the nun's cell, and she was still there, lying crushed against the wall by a Dane who was snoring flabbily. The flamelight showed a small, frightened face half hidden by the Dane's beard. His beard was black and her hair was gold, pale gold, and she was awake and, seeing us, gasped, and that woke the Dane who blinked in the flamelight and then snarled at us as he tried to throw off the thick cloaks serving as blankets. Steapa hit him and it was like the sound of a bullock being clubbed, wet and hard at the same time. The man's head snapped back and Alfred pulled the cloaks away and the nun tried to hide her nakedness. Alfred hurriedly put the cloaks back. He had been embarrassed and I had been impressed for she was young and very beautiful and I wondered why such a woman would waste her sweetness on religion. "You know who I am?" Alfred asked her. She shook her head. "I am your king," he said softly, "and you will come with us, sister."

Her clothes were long gone, so we swathed

her in the heavy cloaks. The Dane was dead by now, his throat cut by Wasp-Sting, and I had found a pouch of coins strung around his neck on a leather thong. "That money goes to the church," Alfred said.

"I found it," I said, "and I killed him."

"It is the money of sin," he said patiently, "and must be redeemed." He smiled at the nun. "Are there any other sisters here?" he asked.

"Only me," she said in a small voice.

"And now you are safe, sister." He straightened. "We can go."

Steapa carried the nun who was called Hild. She clung to him, whimpering, either from the cold or, more likely, from the memory of her ordeal.

We could have captured Cippanhamm that night with a hundred men. It was so bitterly cold that no guards stood on the ramparts. The gate sentries were in a house by the wall, crouched by the fire, and all the notice they took of the bar being lifted was to shout a bad-tempered question wanting to know who we were. "Guthrum's men," I called back, and they did not bother us further. A half hour later we were in the water mill, reunited with Father Adelbert, Egwine, and the three soldiers.

"We should give thanks to God for our deliverance," Alfred said to Father Adelbert, who had been aghast to see the blood and bruises on the king's face. "Say a prayer, father," Alfred ordered.

Adelbert prayed, but I did not listen. I just crouched by the fire, thought I would never be warm again, and then slept.

It snowed all next day. Thick snow. We made a fire, careless that the Danes might see the smoke, for no Dane was going to struggle through the bitter cold and deepening snow to investigate one small, far-off trickle of gray against a gray sky.

Alfred brooded. He spoke little that day, though once he frowned and asked me if it could really be true about Wulfhere. "We didn't see him with Guthrum," he added plaintively, desperately hoping that the ealdorman had not betrayed him.

"The hostages lived," I said.

"Dear God," he said, convinced by that argument, and leaned his head against the wall. He watched the snow through one of the small windows. "He's family!" he said after a while, then fell silent again.

I fed the horses the last of the hay we had

brought with us, then sharpened my swords for lack of anything else to do. Hild wept. Alfred tried to comfort her, but he was awkward and had no words, and oddly it was Steapa who calmed her. He talked to her softly, his voice a deep grumble, and when Serpent-Breath and Wasp-Sting were as sharp as I could make them, and as the snow sifted endlessly onto a silent world, I brooded like Alfred.

I thought of Ragnar wanting my oath. I thought of him wanting my allegiance.

The world began in chaos and it will end in chaos. The gods brought the world into existence, and they will end it when they fight among themselves, but in between the chaos of the world's birth and the chaos of the world's death is order, and order is made by oaths, and oaths bind us like the buckles of a harness.

I was bound to Alfred by an oath, and before I gave that oath I had wanted to bind myself to Ragnar, but now I felt affronted that he had even asked me. That was pride growing in me and changing me. I was Uhtred of Bebbanburg, slayer of Ubba, and while I would give an oath to a king, I was reluctant to make an oath to an equal. The oath-giver is subservient to the man who accepts the oath. Ragnar would have said I was a friend, he would be generous, he would treat me like a brother, but his assumption that I would give him an oath demonstrated that he still believed I was his follower. I was a lord of Northumbria, but he was a Dane, and to a Dane all Saxons are lesser men, and so he had demanded an oath. If I gave him an oath, then he would be generous but I would be expected to show gratitude, and I could only ever hold Bebbanburg because he allowed me to hold it. I had never thought it all through before, but suddenly, on that cold day, I understood that among the Danes I was as important as my friends, and without friends I was just another landless, masterless warrior. But among the Saxons I was another Saxon, and among the Saxons I did not need another man's generosity.

"You look thoughtful, Uhtred." Alfred interrupted my reverie.

"I was thinking, lord," I said, "that we need warm food." I fed the fire, then went outside to the stream where I knocked away the skim of ice and scooped water into a pot. Steapa had followed me outside, not to talk, but to piss, and I stood behind him. "At the witanegemot," I said, "you lied about Cynuit."

He tied the scrap of rope that served as a belt

and turned to look at me. "If the Danes had not come," he said in his growling voice, "I would have killed you."

I did not argue with that, for he was probably right. "At Cynuit," I said instead, "when Ubba died, where were you?"

"There."

"I didn't see you," I said. "I was in the thick of the battle, but I didn't see you."

"You think I wasn't there?" He was angry.

"You were with Odda the Younger?" I asked, and he nodded. "You were with him," I guessed, "because his father told you to protect him?" He nodded again. "And Odda the Younger," I said, "stayed a long way from any danger. Isn't that right?"

He did not answer, but his silence told me I was right. He decided he had nothing more to say to me so he started back toward the mill, but I pulled on his arm to stop him. He was surprised by that. Steapa was so big and so strong and so feared that he was unused to men using force on him, and I could see the slow anger burning in him. I fed it. "You were Odda's nursemaid," I sneered. "The great Steapa Snotor was a nursemaid. Other men faced and fought the Danes and you just held Odda's hand."

He just stared at me. His face, so tight-skinned and expressionless, was like an animal's gaze, nothing there but hunger and anger and violence. He wanted to kill me, especially after I used his nickname, but I understood something more about Steapa Snotor. He was truly stupid. He would kill me if he was ordered to kill me, but without someone to instruct him he did not know what to do, so I thrust the pot of water at him. "Carry that inside," I told him. He hesitated. "Don't stand there like a dumb ox!" I snapped. "Take it! And don't spill it." He took the pot. "It has to go on the fire," I told him, "and next time we fight the Danes you'll be with me."

"You?"

"Because we are warriors," I said, "and our job is to kill our enemies, not be nursemaids to weaklings."

I collected firewood, then went inside to find Alfred staring at nothing and Steapa sitting beside Hild who now seemed to be consoling him rather than being consoled. I crumbled oatcakes and dried fish into the water and stirred the mess with a stick. It was a gruel of sorts and tasted horrible, but it was hot.

That night it stopped snowing and next morning we went home.

Alfred need not have gone to Cippanhamm. Anything he learned there he could have discovered by sending spies, but he had insisted on going himself and he came back more worried than before. He had learned some good things, that Guthrum did not have the men to subjugate all Wessex and so was waiting for reinforcements, but he had also learned that Guthrum was trying to turn the nobility of Wessex to his side. Wulfhere was sworn to the Danes. Who else?

"Will the fyrd of Wiltunscir fight for Wulfhere?" he asked us.

Of course they would fight for Wulfhere. Most of the men in Wiltunscir were loyal to their lord, and if their lord ordered them to follow his banner to war, then they would march. Those men who were in the parts of the shire not occupied by the Danes might go to Alfred, but the rest would do what they always did, follow their lord. And other ealdormen, seeing that Wulfhere had not lost his estates, would reckon that their own future, and their family's safety, lay with the Danes. The Danes had ever worked that way.

Their armies were too small and too disorganized to defeat a great kingdom so they recruited lords of the kingdom, flattered them, even made them into kings, and only when they were secure did they turn on those Saxons and kill them.

So back in Æthelingæg Alfred did what he did best. He wrote letters. He wrote letters to all his nobility, and messengers were sent into every corner of Wessex to find ealdormen, thegns, and bishops, and deliver the letters. I am alive, the scraps of parchment said, and after Easter I shall take Wessex from the pagans, and you will help me. We waited for the replies.

"You must teach me to read," Iseult said when I told her about the letters.

"Why?"

"It is a magic," she said.

"What magic? So you can read psalms?"

"Words are like breath," she said. "You say them and they're gone. But writing traps them. You could write down stories, poems."

"Hild will teach you," I said, and the nun did, scratching letters in the mud. I watched them sometimes and thought they could have been taken for sisters except one had hair black as a raven's wing and the other had hair of pale gold.

So Iseult learned her letters and I practiced

the men with their weapons and shields until they were too tired to curse me, and we also made a new fortress. We restored one of the beamwegs that led south to the hills at the edge of the swamp, and where that log road met dry land we made a strong fort of earth and tree trunks. None of Guthrum's men tried to stop the work, though we saw Danes watching us from the higher hills, and by the time Guthrum understood what we were doing the fort was finished. In late February a hundred Danes came to challenge it, but they saw the thorn palisade protecting the ditch, saw the strength of the log wall behind the ditch, saw our spears thick against the sky, and rode away.

Next day I took sixty men to the farm where we had seen the Danish horses. They were gone, and the farm was burned out. We rode inland, seeing no enemy. We found newborn lambs slaughtered by foxes, but no Danes, and from that day on we rode ever deeper into Wessex, carrying the message that the king lived and fought, and some days we met Danish bands, but we only fought if we outnumbered them for we could not afford to lose men.

Ælswith gave birth to a daughter whom she and Alfred called Æthelgifu. Ælswith wanted to leave the swamp. She knew that Huppa of Thornsæta was holding Dornwaraceaster, for the ealdorman had replied to Alfred's letter saying that the town was secure and, as soon as Alfred demanded it, the fyrd of Thornsæta would march to his aid. Dornwaraceaster was not so large as Cippanhamm, but it had Roman walls and Ælswith was tired of living in the marshes, tired of the endless damp, of the chill mists, and she said her newborn baby would die of the cold, and that Edward's sickness would come back, and Bishop Alewold supported her. He had a vision of a large house in Dornwaraceaster, of warm fires and priestly comfort, but Alfred refused. If he moved to Dornwaraceaster then the Danes would immediately abandon Cippanhamm and besiege Alfred and starvation would soon threaten the garrison, but in the swamp there was food. In Dornwaraceaster Alfred would be a prisoner of the Danes, but in the swamp he was free, and he wrote more letters, telling Wessex he lived, that he grew stronger, and that after Easter but before Pentecost, he would strike the pagans.

It rained that late winter. Rain and more rain. I remember standing on the muddy parapet of the new fort and watching the rain just falling and falling. Mail coats rusted, fabrics rotted, and food went moldy. Our boots fell apart and we had no men skilled in making new ones. We slid and splashed through greasy mud, our clothes were never dry, and still gray swathes of rain marched from the west. Thatch dripped, huts flooded, the world was sullen. We ate well enough, though as more men came to Æthelingæg, the food became scarcer, but no one starved and no one complained except Bishop Alewold who grimaced whenever he saw another fish stew. There were no deer left in the swamp—all had been netted and eaten—but at least we had fish, eels, and wildfowl, while outside the swamp, in those areas the Danes had plundered, folk starved. We practiced with our weapons, fought mock battles with staves, watched the hills, and welcomed the messengers who brought news. Burgweard, the fleet commander, wrote from Hamtun saying that the town was garrisoned by Saxons but that Danish ships were off the coast. "I don't suppose he's fighting them," Leofric remarked glumly when he heard that news.

"He doesn't say so," I said.

"Doesn't want to get his nice ships dirty," Leofric guessed.

"At least he still has the ships."

A letter came from a priest in distant Kent saying that Vikings from Lundene had occupied Contwaraburg and others had settled on the Isle of Sceapig, and that the ealdorman had made his peace with the invaders. News came from Suth Seaxa of more Danish raids, but also a reassurance from Arnulf, Ealdorman of Suth Seaxa, that his fyrd would gather in the spring. He sent a gospel book to Alfred as a token of his loyalty, and for days Alfred carried the book until the rain soaked into the pages and made the ink run. Wiglaf, Ealdorman of Sumorsæte, appeared in early March and brought seventy men. He claimed to have been hiding in the hills south of Baðum and Alfred ignored the rumors that said Wiglaf had been negotiating with Guthrum. All that mattered was that the ealdorman had come to Æthelingæg and Alfred gave him command of the troops that continually rode inland to shadow the Danes and to ambush their forage parties. Not all the news was so encouraging. Wilfrith of Hamptonscir had fled across the water to Frankia, as had a score of other ealdormen and thegns.

But Odda the Younger, Ealdorman of Defnascir, was still in Wessex. He sent a priest who brought a letter reporting that the ealdorman was holding Exanceaster. "God be praised," the letter read, "but there are no pagans in the town."

"So where are they?" Alfred asked the priest. We knew that Svein, despite losing his ships, had not marched to join Guthrum, which suggested he was still skulking in Defnascir.

The priest, a young man who seemed terrified of the king, shrugged, hesitated, then stammered that Svein was close to Exanceaster.

"Close?" the king asked.

"Nearby," the priest managed to say.

"They besiege the town?" Alfred asked.

"No, lord."

Alfred read the letter a second time. He always had great faith in the written word and he was trying to find some hint of the truth that had escaped him in the first reading. "They are not in Exanceaster," he concluded, "but the letter does not say where they are. Nor how many they are. Nor what they're doing."

"They are nearby, lord," the priest said hopelessly. "To the west, I think."

"The west?"

"I think they're to the west."

"What's to the west?" Alfred asked me.

"The high moor," I said.

Alfred threw the letter down in disgust. "Maybe you should go to Defnascir," he told me, "and find out what the pagans are doing."

"Yes, lord," I said.

"It will be a chance to discover your wife and child," Alfred said.

There was a sting there. As the winter rains fell the priests hissed their poison into Alfred's ears and he was willing enough to hear their message, which was that the Saxons would only defeat the Danes if God willed it. And God, the priests said, wanted us to be virtuous. And Iseult was a pagan, as was I, and she and I were not married, while I had a wife, and so the accusation was whispered about the swamp that it was Iseult who stood between Alfred and victory. No one said it openly, not then, yet Iseult sensed it. Hild was her protector in those days, because Hild was a nun, a Christian, and a victim of the Danes, but many thought Iseult was corrupting Hild. I pretended to be deaf to the whispers until Alfred's daughter told me of them.

Æthelflaed was almost seven and her father's favorite child. Ælswith was fonder of Edward, and in those wet winter days she worried about her son's health and the health of her newborn child, which gave Æthelflaed a deal of freedom. She would stay at her father's side much of the time, but she also wandered about Æthelingæg where she was spoiled by soldiers and villagers. She was a bright ripple of sunlight in those rain-sodden days. She had golden hair, a sweet face, blue eyes, and no fear. One day I found her at the southern fort, watching a dozen Danes who had come to watch us. I told her to go back to Æthelingæg and she pretended to obey me, but an hour later, when the Danes had gone, I found her hiding in one of the turf-roofed shelters be-hind the wall. "I hoped the Danes would come," she told me.

"So they could take you away?"

"So I could watch you kill them."

It was one of the rare days when it was not raining. There was sunshine on the green hills and I sat on the wall, took Serpent-Breath from her fleece-lined scabbard, and began sharpening her two edges with a whetstone. Æthelflaed in-sisted on trying the whetstone and she laid the long blade on her lap and frowned in concentra-tion as she drew the stone down the sword. "How many Danes have you killed?" she asked.

"Enough."

"Mama says you don't love Jesus."

"We all love Jesus," I said evasively.

"If you loved Jesus," she said seriously, "then you could kill more Danes. What's this?" She had found the deep nick in one of Serpent-Breath's edges.

"It's where she hit another sword," I said. It had happened at Cippanhamm during my fight with Steapa and his huge sword had bitten deep into Serpent-Breath.

"I'll make her better," she said, and worked obsessively with the whetstone, trying to smooth the nick's edges. "Mama says Iseult is an aglæcwif." She stumbled over the word, then grinned in triumph because she had managed to say it. I said nothing. An aglæcwif was a fiend, a monster. "The bishop says it, too," Æthelflaed said earnestly. "I don't like the bishop."

"You don't?"

"He dribbles." She tried to demonstrate and managed to spit onto Serpent-Breath. She rubbed the blade. "Is Iseult an aglæcwif?"

"Of course not. She made Edward better."

"Jesus did that, and Jesus sent me a baby sister." She scowled because all her efforts had made no impression on the nick in Serpent-Breath.

"Iseult is a good woman," I said.

"She's learning to read. I can read."

"You can?"

"Almost. If she reads then she can be a Christian. I'd like to be an aglæcwif."

"You would?" I asked, surprised.

For answer she growled at me and crooked a small hand so that her fingers looked like claws. Then she laughed. "Are those Danes?" She had seen some horsemen coming from the south.

"That's Wiglaf," I said.

"He's nice."

I sent her back to Æthelingæg on Wiglaf's horse and I thought of what she had said and wondered, for the thousandth time, why I was among Christians who believed I was an offense to their god. They called my gods dwolgods, which meant false gods, so that made me Uhtredærwe, living with an aglæcwif and worshipping dwolgods. I flaunted it, though, always wearing my hammer amulet openly, and that night Alfred, as ever, flinched when he saw it. He had summoned me to his hall where I found him bent over a tafl board. He was playing against Beocca, who had the larger set of pieces. It seems a simple game, tafl, where one player has a king and a dozen other pieces, and the other has double the pieces, but no king, and then you move the pieces about the checkered board until one or other player has all his wooden pieces surrounded. I had no patience for it, but Alfred was fond of the game, though when I arrived he seemed to be losing and so was relieved to see me. "I want you to go to Defnascir," he said.

"Of course, lord."

"I fear your king is threatened, lord," Beocca said happily.

"Never mind," Alfred said irritably. "You're to go to Defnascir," he said, turning back to me, "but Iseult must stay here."

I bridled at that. "She's to be a hostage again?" I asked.

"I need her medicines," Alfred said.

"Even though they're made by an aglæcwif?"

He gave me a sharp look. "She is a healer," he said, "and that means she is God's instrument, and with God's help she will come to the truth. Besides, you must travel fast and don't need a woman for company. You will go to Defnascir and find Svein, and once you've found him you will instruct Odda the Younger to raise the fyrd. Tell him Svein must be driven from the shire, and once Odda has achieved that, he is to come here with his household troops. He commands my bodyguard. He should be here."

"You want me to give Odda orders?" I asked, partly in surprise, partly with scorn.

"I do," Alfred said, "and I order you to make your peace with him."

"Yes, lord," I replied.

He heard the sarcasm in my voice. "We are all Saxons, Uhtred, and now, more than ever, is the time to heal our wounds."

Beocca, realizing that defeating Alfred at tafl would not help the king's mood, was taking the pieces from the board. "A house divided against itself," he interjected, "will be destroyed. Saint Matthew said that."

"Praise God for that truth," Alfred said, "and we must be rid of Svein." That was a greater truth. Alfred wanted to march against Guthrum after Easter, but he could scarcely do that if Svein's forces were behind him. "You find Svein," the king told me, "and Steapa will accompany you."

"Steapa!"

"He knows the country," Alfred said, "and I have told him he is to obey you."

"It's best that two of you go," Beocca said earnestly. "Remember that Joshua sent two spies against Jericho."

"You're delivering me to my enemies," I said

bitterly, though when I thought about it I decided that using me as a spy made sense. The Danes in Defnascir would be looking out for Alfred's scouts, but I could speak the enemy's language and could pass for one of them and so I was safer than anyone else in Alfred's force. As for Steapa, he was from Defnascir, he knew the country, and he was Odda's sworn man, so he was best suited for carrying a message to the ealdorman.

And so the two of us rode south from Æthelingæg on a day of driving rain.

Steapa did not like me and I did not like him and so we had nothing to say to each other except when I suggested what path we take, and he never disagreed. We kept close to the large road, the road the Romans had made, though I went cautiously for such roads were much used by Danish bands seeking forage or plunder. This was also the route Svein must take if he marched to join Guthrum, but we saw no Danes. We saw no Saxons either. Every village and farm on the road had been pillaged and burned so that we journeyed through a land of the dead.

On the second day Steapa headed westward. He did not explain the sudden change of direction, but doggedly pushed up into the hills and I followed him because he knew the countryside and I supposed he was taking the small paths that would lead to the high bleakness of Dærentmora. He rode urgently, his hard face grim, and I called to him once that we should take more care in case there were Danish forage parties in the small valleys, but he ignored me. Instead, almost at a gallop, he rode down into one of those small valleys until he came in sight of a farmstead.

Or what had been a farmstead. Now it was wet ashes in a green place, a deep green place where narrow pastures were shadowed by tall trees on which the very first haze of spring was just showing. Flowers were thick along the pasture edges, but there were none where the few small buildings had stood. There were only embers and the black smear of ash in mud, and Steapa, abandoning his horse, walked among the ashes. He had lost his great sword when the Danes captured him at Cippanhamm, so now he carried a huge war ax and he prodded the wide blade into the dark piles.

I rescued his horse, tied both beasts to the scorched trunk of an ash that had once grown by the farmyard, and watched him. I said nothing, for I sensed that one word would release all his fury. He crouched by the skeleton of a dog and just stared at the fire-darkened bones for a few minutes, then reached out and stroked the bared skull. There were tears on Steapa's face, or perhaps it was the rain that fell softly from low clouds.

A score of people had once lived there. A larger house had stood at the southern end of the settlement and I explored its charred remains, seeing where the Danes had dug down by the old posts to find hidden coins. Steapa watched me. He was by one of the smaller patches of charred timbers and I guessed he had grown up there, in a slave hovel. He did not want me near him, and I pointedly stayed away, wondering if I dared suggest to him that we ride on. But he began digging instead, hacking the damp red soil with his huge war ax and scooping the earth out with bare hands until he had made a shallow grave for the dog. It was a skeleton now. There were still patches of fur on the old bones, but the flesh had been eaten away so that the ribs were scattered, so this had all happened weeks before. Steapa gathered the bones and laid them tenderly in the grave.

That was when the people came. You can ride through a landscape of the dead and see no one, but they will see you. Folk hide when enemies come. They go up into the woods and they wait there, and now three men came from the trees.

"Steapa," I said. He turned on me, furious that I had interrupted him, then saw I was pointing westward.

He gave a roar of recognition and the three men, who were holding spears, ran toward him. They dropped their weapons and they hugged the huge man, and for a time they all spoke together, but then they calmed down and I took one aside and questioned him. The Danes had come soon after Yule, he told me. They had come suddenly, before anyone was even aware that there were pagans in Defnascir. These men had escaped because they had been felling a beech tree in a nearby wood, and they had heard the slaughter. Since then they had been living in the forests, scared of the Danes who still rode about Defnascir in search of food. They had seen no Saxons.

They had buried the folk of the farm in a pasture to the south, and Steapa went there and knelt in the wet grass. "His mother died," the man told me. He spoke English with such a strange accent that I continually had to ask him to repeat himself, but I understood those three words. "Steapa was good to his mother," the man said. "He brought her money. She was no slave any more."

"His father?"

"He died long time back. Long time."

I thought Steapa was going to dig up his mother, so I crossed and stood in front of him. "We have a job to do," I said.

He looked up at me, his harsh face expressionless.

"There are Danes to kill," I said. "The Danes who killed folk here must be killed themselves."

He nodded abruptly, then stood, towering over me again. He cleaned the blade of his ax and climbed into his saddle. "There are Danes to kill," he said and, leaving his mother in her cold grave, we went to find them.

TEN

We rode south. We went cautiously, for folk said the Danes were still seen in this part of the shire, though we saw none. Steapa was silent until, in a river meadow, we rode past a ring of stone pillars, one of the mysteries left behind by the old people. Such rings stand all across England and some are huge, though this one was a mere score of lichen-covered stones, none taller than a man, standing in a circle some fifteen paces wide. Steapa glanced at them, then astonished me by speaking. "That's a wedding," he said.

"A wedding?"

"They were dancing," he growled, "and the devil turned them to stone."

"Why did the devil do that?" I asked cautiously.

"Because they wed on a Sunday, of course.

Folk never should wed on a Sunday, nèver! Everyone knows that." We rode on in silence, then, surprising me again, he began to talk about his mother and father and how they had been serfs of Odda the Elder. "But life was good for us," he said.

"It was?"

"Plowing, sowing, weeding, harvest, threshing."

"But Ealdorman Odda didn't live back there," I said, jerking my thumb toward Steapa's destroyed homestead.

"No! Not him!" Steapa was amused I should even ask such a question. "He wouldn't live there, not him! Had his own big hall. Still does. But he had a steward there. Man to give us orders. He was a big man! Very tall!"

I hesitated. "But your father was short?"

Steapa looked surprised. "How did you know that?"

"I just guessed."

"He was a good worker, my father."

"Did he teach you to fight?"

"He didn't, no. No one did. I just learned myself."

The land was less damaged the farther south we went. And that was strange, for the Danes had come this way. We knew that, for folk said the Danes were still in the southern part of the shire, but life suddenly seemed normal. We saw men spreading dung on fields, and other men ditching or hedging. There were lambs in the pastures. To the north the foxes had become fat on dead lambs, but here the shepherds and their dogs were winning that ceaseless battle.

And the Danes were in Cridianton.

A priest told us that in a village hard under a great oak-covered hill beside a stream. The priest was nervous because he had seen my long hair and arm rings and he presumed I was a Dane, and my northern accent did not persuade him otherwise, but he was reassured by Steapa. The two talked, and the priest gave his opinion that it would be a wet summer.

"It will," Steapa agreed. "The oak greened before the ash."

"Always a sign," the priest said.

"How far is Cridianton?" I broke into the conversation.

"A morning's walk, lord."

"You've seen the Danes there?" I asked.

"I seen them, lord, I have," he said.

"Who leads them?"

"Don't know, lord."

"They have a banner?" I asked.

He nodded. "It hangs on the bishop's hall, lord. It shows a white horse."

So it was Svein. I did not know who else it could have been, but the white horse confirmed that Svein had stayed in Defnascir rather than try to join Guthrum. I twisted in the saddle and looked at the priest's village that was unscarred by war. No thatch had been burned, no granaries emptied, and the church was still standing. "Have the Danes come here?" I asked.

"Oh yes, lord, they came. Came more than once."

"Did they rape? Steal?"

"No, lord. But they bought some grain. Paid silver for it."

Well-behaved Danes. That was another strange thing. "Are they besieging Exanceaster?" I asked. That would have made a sort of sense. Cridianton was close enough to Exanceaster to give most of the Danish troops shelter while the rest invested the larger town.

"No, lord," the priest said, "not that I know of."

"Then what are they doing?" I asked.

"They're just in Cridianton, lord."

"And Odda is in Exanceaster?"

"No, lord. He's in Ocmundtun. He's with Lord Harald."

I knew the shire reeve's hall was in Ocmundtun, which lay beneath the northern edge of the great moor. But Ocmundtun was also a long journey from Cridianton and no place to be if a man wanted to harry the Danes.

I believed the priest when he said Svein was at Cridianton, but we still rode there to see for ourselves. We used wooded, hilly tracks and came to the town at midafternoon and saw the smoke rising from cooking fires, then saw the Danish shields hanging from the palisade. Steapa and I were hidden in the high woods and could see men guarding the gate, and other men standing watch in a pasture where forty or fifty horses were grazing on the first of the spring grass. I could see Odda the Elder's hall where I had been reunited with Mildrith after the fight at Cynuit, and I could also see a triangular Danish banner flying above the larger hall that was the bishop's home. The western gate was open, though well guarded, and despite the sentries and the shields on the wall the town looked like a place at peace, not at war. There should be Saxons on this hill, I thought, Saxons watching the enemy, ready to attack. Instead the Danes

were living undisturbed. "How far to Ocmundtun?" I asked Steapa.

"We can make it by nightfall."

I hesitated. If Odda the Younger was at Ocmundtun, then why go there? He was my enemy
and sworn to my death. Alfred had given me a
scrap of parchment on which he had written
words commanding Odda to greet me peaceably, but what force did writing have against
hatred?

"He won't kill you," Steapa said, surprising
me again. He had evidently guessed my
thoughts. "He won't kill you," he said again.

"Why not?"

"Because I won't bide him killing you,"
Steapa said and turned his horse west.

We reached Ocmundtun at dusk. It was a
small town built along a river and guarded by a
high spur of limestone on which a stout palisade
offered a refuge if attackers came. No one was on
the limestone spur now and the town, which had
no walls, looked placid. There might be war in
Wessex, but Ocmundtun, like Cridianton, was
evidently at peace. Harald's hall was close to the
fort on its hill and no one challenged us as we
rode into the forecourt where servants recognized Steapa. They greeted him warily, but then

a steward came from the hall door and, seeing the huge man, clapped his hands twice in a sign of delight. "We heard you were taken by the pagans," the steward said.

"I was."

"They let you go?"

"My king freed me," Steapa growled as though he resented the question. He slid from his horse and stretched. "Alfred freed me."

"Is Harald here?" I asked the steward.

"My lord is inside." The steward was offended that I had not called the reeve "lord."

"Then so are we," I said, and led Steapa into the hall. The steward flapped at us because custom and courtesy demanded that he seek his lord's permission for us to enter the hall, but I ignored him.

A fire burned in the central hearth and dozens of rushlights stood on the platforms at the hall's edges. Boar spears were stacked against the wall on which hung a dozen deerskins and a bundle of valuable pine marten pelts. A score of men were in the hall, evidently waiting for supper, and a harpist played at the far end. A pack of hounds rushed to investigate us and Steapa beat them off as we walked to the fire to warm ourselves. "Ale," Steapa said to the steward.

Harald must have heard the noise of the hounds, for he appeared at a door leading from the private chamber at the back of the hall. He blinked when he saw us. He had thought the two of us were enemies, then he had heard that Steapa was captured, yet here we were, side by side. The hall fell silent as he limped toward us. It was only a slight limp, the result of a spear wound in some battle that had also taken two fingers of his sword hand. "You once chided me," he said, "for carrying weapons into your hall. Yet you bring weapons into mine."

"There was no gatekeeper," I said.

"He was having a piss, lord," the steward explained.

"There are to be no weapons in the hall," Harald insisted.

That was customary. Men get drunk in the hall and can do enough damage to one another with the knives we use to cut meat, and drunken men with swords and axes can turn a supper table into a butcher's yard. We gave the steward our weapons. I hauled off my mail coat and told the steward to hang it on a frame to dry, then have a servant clean its links.

Harald formally welcomed us when our weapons were gone. He said the hall was ours and that we should eat with him as honored guests. "I would hear your news," he said, beckoning a servant who brought us pots of ale.

"Is Odda here?" I demanded.

"The father is, yes. Not the son."

I swore. We had come here with a message for Ealdorman Odda, Odda the Younger, only to discover that it was the wounded father, Odda the Elder, who was in Ocmundtun. "So where is the son?" I asked.

Harald was offended by my brusqueness, but he remained courteous. "The ealdorman is in Exanceaster."

"Is he besieged there?"

"No."

"And the Danes are in Cridianton?"

"They are."

"And are they besieged?" I knew the answer to that, but wanted to hear Harald admit it.

"No," he said.

I let the ale pot drop. "We come from the king," I said. I was supposedly speaking to Harald, but I strode down the hall so that the men on the platforms could hear me. "We come from Alfred," I said, "and Alfred wishes to know why there are Danes in Defnascir. We burned their ships, we slaughtered their ship guards, and we drove them from Cynuit, yet you allow them to live here? Why?"

No one answered. There were no women in the hall, for Harald was a widower who had not remarried, and so the supper guests were all his warriors or else thegns who led men of their own. Some looked at me with loathing, for my words imputed cowardice to them, while others looked down at the floor. Harald glanced at Steapa as if seeking the big man's support, but Steapa just stood by the fire, his savage face showing nothing. I turned back to stare at Harald. "Why are there Danes in Defnascir?" I demanded.

"Because they are welcome here," a voice said behind me.

I turned to see an old man standing in the door. White hair showed beneath the bandage that swathed his head, and he was so thin and so weak that he had to lean on the door frame for support. At first I did not recognize him, for when I had last spoken to him he had been a big man, well built and vigorous, but Odda the Elder had taken an ax blow to the skull at Cynuit and he should have died from such a wound, yet somehow he had lived, and here he was, though now he was skeletal, pale, haggard, and feeble.

"They are here," Odda said, "because they are welcome. As are you, Lord Uhtred, and you, Steapa."

A woman was tending Odda the Elder. She had tried to pull him away from the door and take him back to his bed, but now she edged past him into the hall and stared at me. Then, seeing me, she did what she had done the very first time she saw me. She did what she had done when she came to marry me. She burst into tears.

It was Mildrith.

Mildrith was robed like a nun in a pale gray dress, belted with rope, over which she wore a large wooden cross. She had a close-fitting gray bonnet from which strands of her fair hair escaped. She stared at me, burst into tears, made the sign of the cross, and vanished. A moment later Odda the Elder followed her, too frail to stand any longer, and the door closed.

"You are indeed welcome here," Harald said, echoing Odda's words.

"But why are the Danes welcome here?" I asked.

Because Odda the Younger had made a truce. Harald explained it as we ate. No one in this part of Defnascir had heard how Svein's ships had been burned at Cynuit. They only knew that Svein's men, and their women and children, had marched south, burning and plundering, and Odda the Younger had taken his troops to Exanceaster, which he had prepared for a siege, but instead Svein had offered to talk. The Danes, quite suddenly, had stopped raiding. Instead they had settled in Cridianton and sent an embassy to Exanceaster, and Svein and Odda had made their private peace.

"We sell them horses," Harald said, "and they pay well for them. Twenty shillings a stallion, fifteen a mare."

"You sell them horses," I said flatly.

"So they will go away," Harald explained.

Servants threw a big birch log onto the fire. Sparks exploded outward, scattering the hounds who lay just beyond the ring of hearth stones.

"How many men does Svein lead?" I asked.

"Many," Harald said.

"Eight hundred?" I asked. "Nine?" Harald shrugged. "They came in twenty-four ships," I went on, "only twenty-four. So how many men can he have? No more than a thousand, and we killed a few, and others must have died in the winter."

"We think he has eight hundred," Harald said reluctantly.

"And how many men in the fyrd? Two thousand?"

"Of which only four hundred are seasoned warriors," Harald said. That was probably true. Most men of the fyrd are farmers, while every Dane is a sword warrior, but Svein would never have pitted his eight hundred men against two thousand. Not because he feared losing, but because he feared that in gaining victory he would lose a hundred men. That was why he had stopped plundering and made his truce with Odda, because in southern Defnascir he could recover from his defeat at Cynuit. His men could rest, feed, make weapons, and get horses. Svein was husbanding his men and making them stronger. "It was not my choice," Harald said defensively. "The ealdorman ordered it."

"And the king," I retorted, "ordered Odda to drive Svein out of Defnascir."

"What do we know of the king's orders?" Harald asked bitterly, and it was my turn to give him news, to tell how Alfred had escaped Guthrum and was in the great swamp.

"And sometime after Easter," I said, "we shall

gather the shire fyrds and we shall cut Guthrum into pieces." I stood. "There will be no more horses sold to Svein." I said it loudly so that every man in the big hall could hear me.

"But—" Harald began, then shook his head. He had doubtless been about to say that Odda the Younger, Ealdorman of Defnascir, had ordered the horses to be sold, but his voice trailed away.

"What are the king's orders?" I demanded of Steapa.

"No more horses," he thundered.

There was silence until Harald irritably gestured at the harpist who struck a chord and began playing a melancholy tune. Someone began singing, but no one joined in and his voice trailed away. "I must look to the sentinels," Harald said, and he threw me an inquisitive look that I took as an invitation to join him, and so I buckled on my swords and then walked with him down Ocmundtun's long street to where three spearmen stood guard beside a wooden hut. Harald talked to them for a moment, then led me farther east, away from the light of the sentinels' fire. A moon silvered the valley, lighting the empty road until the track vanished among trees. "I have thirty fighting men," Harald said suddenly.

He was telling me he was too weak to fight. "How many men does Odda have in Exanceaster?" I asked.

"A hundred? Hundred and twenty?"

"The fyrd should have been raised."

"I had no orders," Harald said.

"Did you seek any?"

"Of course I did." He was angry with me now. "I told Odda we should drive Svein away, but he wouldn't listen."

"Did he tell you the king ordered the fyrd raised?"

"No." Harald paused, staring down the moonlit road. "We heard nothing of Alfred, except that he'd been defeated and was hiding. And we heard the Danes were all across Wessex, and that more were gathering in Mercia."

"Odda didn't think to attack Svein when he landed?"

"He thought to protect himself," Harald said, "and sent me to the Tamur."

The Tamur was the river that divided Wessex from Cornwalum. "The Britons are quiet?" I asked.

"Their priests are telling them not to fight us."

"But priests or no priests," I said, "they'll cross the river if the Danes look like winning."

"Aren't they winning already?" Harald asked bitterly.

"We're still free men," I said.

He nodded at that. Behind us, in the town, a dog began howling and he turned as if the noise indicated trouble, but the howling stopped with a sharp yelp. He kicked a stone in the road. "Svein frightens me," he admitted suddenly.

"He's a frightening man," I agreed.

"He's clever," Harald said, "clever, strong, and savage."

"A Dane," I said drily.

"A ruthless man," Harald went on.

"He is," I agreed, "and do you think that after you have fed him, supplied him with horses and given him shelter, he will leave you alone?"

"No," he said, "but Odda believes that."

Then Odda was a fool. He was nursing a wolf cub that would tear him to shreds when it was strong enough. "Why didn't Svein march north to join Guthrum?" I asked.

"I wouldn't know."

But I knew. Guthrum had been in England for years now. He had tried to take Wessex before, and he had failed, but now, on the very brink of success, he had paused. Guthrum the Unlucky, he was called, and I suspected he had not changed. He was wealthy, led many men, but he was cautious. Svein, though, came from the Norsemen's settlements in Ireland and was a very different creature. He was younger than Guthrum, less wealthy than Guthrum, and led fewer men, but he was undoubtedly the better warrior. Now, bereft of his ships, he was weakened, but he had persuaded Odda the Younger to give him refuge and he gathered his strength so that when he did meet Guthrum he would not be a defeated leader in need of help, but a spear Dane of power. Svein, I thought, was a far more dangerous man than Guthrum, and Odda the Younger was only making him more dangerous.

"Tomorrow," I said, "we must start raising the fyrd. Those are the king's orders."

Harald nodded. I could not see his face in the darkness, but I sensed he was not happy, yet he was a sensible man and must have known that Svein had to be driven out of the shire. "I shall send the messages," he said, "but Odda might stop the fyrd assembling. He's made his truce with Svein and he won't want me breaking it. Folk will obey him before they obey me."

"And what of his father?" I asked. "Will they obey him?"

"They will," he said, "but he's a sick man. You saw that. It's a miracle he lives at all."

"Maybe because my wife nurses him?"

"Yes," he said, and fell silent. There was something odd in the air now, something unexpressed, a discomfort. "Your wife nurses him well," he finished awkwardly.

"He's her godfather," I said.

"So he is."

"It is good to see her," I said, not because I meant it, but because it was the proper thing to say and I could think of nothing else. "And it will be good to see my son," I added with more warmth.

"Your son," Harald said flatly.

"He's here, isn't he?"

"Yes." Harald flinched. He turned away to look at the moon and I thought he would say no more, but then he summoned his courage and looked back to me. "Your son, Lord Uhtred," he said, "is in the churchyard."

It took a few heartbeats for that to make sense, and then it did not make any sense at all, but left me confused. I touched my hammer amulet. "In the churchyard?"

"It is not my place to tell you."

"But you will tell me," I said, and my voice sounded like Steapa's growl.

Harald stared at the moon-touched river, silver white beneath the black trees. "Your son died," he said. He waited for my response, but I neither moved nor spoke. "He choked to death."

"Choked?"

"A pebble," Harald said. "He was just a baby. He must have picked the pebble up and swallowed it."

"A pebble?" I asked.

"A woman was with him, but . . ." Harald's voice trailed away. "She tried to save him, but she could do nothing. He died."

"On Saint Vincent's Day," I said.

"You knew?"

"No," I said, "I didn't know." But Saint Vincent's Day had been the day when Iseult drew Alfred's son, the Ætheling Edward, through the earth. And somewhere, Iseult had told me, a child must die so that the king's heir, the Ætheling, could live.

And it had been my child. Uhtred the Younger. Whom I had hardly known. Edward had been given breath and Uhtred had twitched and fought and gasped and died.

"I'm sorry," Harald said. "It was not my place to tell you, but you needed to know before you saw Mildrith again."

"She hates me," I said bleakly.

"Yes," he said, "she does." He paused. "I thought she would go mad with grief, but God has preserved her. She would like—"

"Like what?"

"To join the sisters at Cridianton. When the Danes leave. They have a nunnery there, a small house."

I did not care what Mildrith did. "And my son is buried here?"

"Under the yew tree"—he turned and pointed—"beside the church."

So let him stay there, I thought. Let him rest in his short grave to wait the chaos of the world's ending.

"Tomorrow," I said, "we raise the fyrd."

Because there was a kingdom to save.

Priests were summoned to Harald's hall and the priests wrote the summons for the fyrd. Most thegns could not read, and many of their priests would probably struggle to decipher the few words, but the messengers would tell them what the parchments said. They were to arm their men and bring them to Ocmundtun, and the wax seal on the summons was the authority for those orders. The seal showed Odda the Elder's badge of a stag. "It will take a week," Harald warned me, "for most of the fyrd to reach here, and the ealdorman will try to stop it happening at all."

"What will he do?"

"Tell the thegns to ignore it, I suppose."

"And Svein? What will he do?"

"Try to kill us."

"And he has eight hundred men who can be here tomorrow," I said.

"And I have thirty men," Harald said bleakly.

"But we do have a fortress," I said, pointing to the limestone ridge with its palisade.

I did not doubt that the Danes would come. By summoning the fyrd we threatened their safety, and Svein was not a man who would take a threat lightly, and so, while the messages were carried north and south, the townsfolk were told to take their valuables up to the fort beside the river. Some men were set to strengthening the palisade. Others took livestock up onto the moor so the beasts could not be taken by the Danes. Steapa went to every nearby settlement and demanded that men of fighting age go to

Ocmundtun with any weapon they possessed, so that by that afternoon the fort was manned by over eighty men. Few were warriors, most had no weapons other than an ax, but from the foot of the hill they looked formidable enough. Women carried food and water to the fort, and most of the town reckoned to sleep up there, despite the rain, for fear that the Danes would come in the night.

Odda the Elder refused to go to the fort. He was too sick, he said, and too feeble, and if he was supposed to die then he would die in Harald's hall. Harald and I tried to persuade him, but he would not listen. "Mildrith can go," he said.

"No," she said. She sat by Odda's bed, her hands clutched tight under the sleeves of her gray robe. She stared at me, challenge in her eyes, daring me to give her an order to abandon Odda and go to the fortress.

"I am sorry," I said to her.

"Sorry?"

"About our son."

"You were not a father to him," she accused me. Her eyes glistened. "You wanted him to be a Dane! You wanted him to be a pagan! You didn't even care for his soul!"

"I cared for him," I said, but she ignored that. I had not sounded convincing, even to myself.

"His soul is safe," Harald said gently. "He is in the Lord Jesus's arms. He is happy."

Mildrith looked at him and I saw how Harald's words had comforted her, though she still began crying. She caressed her wooden cross. Then Odda the Elder reached out and patted her arm. "If the Danes come, lord," I said to him, "I shall send men for you." I turned then and went from the sickroom. I could not cope with Mildrith crying or with the thought of a dead son. Such things are difficult, much more difficult than making war, and so I buckled on my swords, picked up my shield, and put on my splendid wolf-crested helmet so that, when Harald came from Odda's chamber, he checked to see me standing like a warlord by his hearth. "If we make a big fire at the eastern end of town," I said, "we'll see the Danes come. It will give us time to carry Lord Odda to the fort."

"Yes." He looked up at the great rafters of his hall, and perhaps he was thinking that he would never see it thus again, for the Danes would come and the hall would burn. He made the sign of the cross.

"Fate is inexorable," I told him. What else was

there to say? The Danes might come, the hall might burn, but they were small things in the balance of a kingdom, and so I went to order the fire that would illuminate the eastern road, but the Danes did not come that night. It rained softly all through the darkness, so that in the morning the folk in the fort were wet, cold, and unhappy. Then, in the dawn, the first men of the fyrd arrived. It might take days for the farther parts of the shire to receive their summons and to arm men and despatch them to Ocmundtun, but the nearer places sent men straight away so that by late morning there were close to three hundred beneath the fort. No more than seventy of those could be called warriors, men who had proper weapons, shields, and at least a leather coat. The rest were farm laborers with hoes or sickles or axes.

Harald sent foraging parties to find grain. It was one thing to gather a force, quite another to feed it, and none of us knew how long we would have to keep the men assembled. If the Danes did not come to us, then we would have to go to them and force them from Cridianton, and for that we would need the whole fyrd of Defnascir. Odda the Younger, I thought, would never allow that to happen.

Nor did he. For, as the rain ended and the noontime prayers were said, Odda himself came to Ocmundtun and he did not come alone, but rode with sixty of his warriors in chain mail and as many Danes in their war glory. The sun came out as they appeared from the eastern trees and it shone on mail and on spear points, on bridle chains and stirrup irons, on polished helmets and bright shield bosses. They spread into the pastures on either side of the road and advanced on Ocmundtun in a wide line, and at its center were two standards. One, the black stag, was the banner of Defnascir, while the other was a Danish triangle and displayed the white horse.

"There'll be no fight," I told Harald.

"There won't?"

"Not enough of them. Svein can't afford to lose men, so he's come to talk."

"I don't want to meet them here." He gestured at the fort. "We should be in the hall."

He ordered that the best armed men should go down to the town, and there we filled the muddy street outside the hall as Odda and the Danes came from the east. The horsemen had to break their line to enter the town, making a column instead, and the column was led by three men. Odda was in the center and he was flanked by two Danes, one of them Svein of the White Horse.

Svein looked magnificent, a silver-white warrior. He rode a white horse, wore a white woolen cloak, and his mail and boar-snouted helmet had been scrubbed with sand until they glowed silver in the watery sunlight. His shield bore a silvered boss around which a white horse had been painted. The leather of his bridle, saddle, and scabbard had been bleached pale. He saw me, but showed no recognition, just looked along the line of men barring the street and seemed to dismiss them as useless. His banner of the white horse was carried by the second horseman who had the same darkened face as his master, a face hammered by sun and snow, ice and wind.

"Harald." Odda the Younger had ridden ahead of the two Danes. He was sleek as ever, gleaming in mail, and with a black cloak draping his horse's rump. He smiled as though he welcomed the meeting. "You have summoned the fyrd. Why?"

"Because the king commanded it," Harald said.

Odda still smiled. He glanced at me, appeared not to notice I was present, then looked to the hall door where Steapa had just appeared. The big man had been talking with Odda the Elder, and now he stared at Odda the Younger with astonishment. "Steapa!" Odda the Younger said. "Loyal Steapa! How good to see you!"

"You too, lord."

"My faithful Steapa," Odda said, plainly pleased to be reunited with his erstwhile bodyguard. "Come here!" he commanded, and Steapa pushed past us and knelt in the mud by Odda's horse and reverently kissed his master's boot. "Stand," Odda said, "stand. With you beside me, Steapa, who can hurt us?"

"No one, lord."

"No one," Odda repeated, then smiled at Harald. "You said the king ordered the fyrd summoned? There is a king in Wessex?"

"There is a king in Wessex," Harald said firmly.

"There is a king skulking in the marshes!" Odda said, loudly enough for all Harald's men to hear. "He is the king of frogs, perhaps? A monarch of eels? What kind of king is that?"

I answered for Harald, only I answered in Danish. "A king who ordered me to burn Svein's boats. Which I did. All but one, which I kept and still have."

Svein took off his boar-snouted helmet and

looked at me and again there was no recognition. His gaze was like that of the great serpent of death that lies at the foot of Yggdrasil. "I burned the **White Horse**," I told him, "and warmed my hands on its flames." Svein spat for answer. "And the man beside you"—I spoke to Odda now, using English—"is the man who burned your church at Cynuit, the man who killed the monks. The man who is cursed in heaven, in hell, and in this world, yet now he is your ally?"

"Does that goat turd speak for you?" Odda demanded of Harald.

"These men speak for me," Harald said, indicating the warriors behind him.

"But by what right do you raise the fyrd?" Odda asked. "I am an ealdorman!"

"And who made you ealdorman?" Harald asked. He paused, but Odda gave no answer. "The king of frogs?" Harald asked. "The monarch of eels? If Alfred has no authority, then you have lost yours with his."

Odda was plainly surprised by Harald's defiance, and he was probably irritated by it, but he gave no sign of annoyance. He just went on smiling. "I do believe," he said to Harald, "that you have misunderstood what happens in Defnascir."

"Then explain to me," Harald said.

"I shall," Odda said, "but we shall talk with ale and food." He looked up at the sky. The brief sun was gone behind cloud and a chill wind was gusting the thatch of the street. "And we should talk under a roof," Odda suggested, "before it rains again."

There were matters to be agreed first, though that was done soon enough. The Danish horsemen would withdraw to the eastern end of the town while Harald's men would retreat to the fort. Each side could take ten men into the hall, and all of those men were to leave their weapons heaped in the street where they were to be guarded by six Danes and as many Saxons.

Harald's servants brought ale, bread, and cheese. There was no meat offered, for it was the season of Lent. Benches were placed on either side of the hearth. Svein crossed to our side of the fire as the benches were brought and at long last deigned to recognize me. "It was really you who burned the ships?" he asked.

"Including yours."

"The **White Horse** took a year and a day to build," he said, "and she was made of trees from which we'd hung Odin's sacrifices. She was a good ship."

"She's all ash on the seashore now," I said.

"Then one day I shall repay you," he retorted, and though he spoke mildly, there was a world of threat in his voice. "And you were wrong," he added.

"Wrong?" I asked. "Wrong to burn your ships?"

"There was no altar of gold at Cynuit."

"Where you burned the monks," I said.

"I burned them alive," he agreed, "and warmed my hands on their flames." He smiled at that memory. "You could join me again?" he suggested. "I shall forgive you burning my ship and you and I can fight side by side once more? I need good men. I pay well."

"I am sworn to Alfred."

"Ah." He nodded. "So be it. Enemies." He went back to Odda's benches.

"You would see your father before we talk?" Harald asked Odda, gesturing toward the door at the hall's end.

"I shall see him," Odda said, "when our friendship is repaired. And you and I must be friends." He said the last words loudly and they prompted men to sit on the benches. "You summoned the fyrd," he spoke to Harald, "because Uhtred brought you orders from Alfred?"

"He did."

"Then you did the right thing," Odda said, "and that is to be praised." Svein, listening to the translation that was provided by one of his own men, stared flatly at us. "And now you will do the right thing again," Odda continued, "and send the fyrd home."

"The king has ordered otherwise," Harald said.

"What king?" Odda asked.

"Alfred, who else?"

"But there are other kings in Wessex," Odda said. "Guthrum is King of East Anglia, and he is in Wessex, and some say Æthelwold will be crowned king before the summer."

"Æthelwold?" Harald asked.

"You'd not heard?" Odda asked. "Wulfhere of Wiltunscir has sided with Guthrum, and both Guthrum and Wulfhere have said Æthelwold will be King of Wessex. And why not? Is not Æthelwold the son of our last king? Should he not be king?"

Harald, uncertain, looked at me. He had not heard of Wulfhere's defection, and it was hard news for him. I nodded. "Wulfhere is with Guthrum," I said.

"So Æthelwold, son of Æthelred, will be king in Wessex," Odda said, "and Æthelwold has thousands of swords at his command. Ælfrig of Kent is with the Danes. There are Danes in Lundene, on Sceapig, and on the walls of Contwaraburg. All northern Wessex is in Danish hands. There are Danes here, in Defnascir. What, tell me, is Alfred king of?"

"Of Wessex," I said.

Odda ignored me, looking at Harald. "Alfred has our oaths," Harald said stubbornly.

"And I have your oath," Odda reminded him. He sighed. "God knows, Harald, no one was more loyal to Alfred than I. Yet he failed us! The Danes came and the Danes are here, and where is Alfred? Hiding! In a few weeks their armies will march! They will come from Mercia, from Lundene, from Kent! Their fleets will be off our coast. Armies of Danes and fleets of vikings! What will you do then?"

Harald shifted uneasily. "What will you do?" he retorted.

Odda gestured at Svein who, the question translated, spoke for the first time. I interpreted for Harald. Wessex is doomed, Svein said in his grating voice. By summer it will be swarming with Danes, with men newly come from the north, and the only Saxons who will live will be those men who aid the Danes now. Those who fight against the Danes, Svein said, will be dead, and their women will be whores and their children will be slaves and their homes will be lost and their names shall be forgotten like the smoke of an extinguished fire.

"And Æthelwold will be king?" I asked scornfully. "You think we will all bow to a whoring drunkard?"

Odda shook his head. "The Danes are generous," he said, and he drew back his cloak and I saw that he wore six golden arm rings. "To those who help them," he said, "there will be the reward of land, wealth, and honor."

"And Æthelwold will be king?" I asked again.

Odda again gestured at Svein. The big Dane seemed bored, but he stirred himself. "It is right," he said, "that Saxons should be ruled by a Saxon. We shall make a king here."

I scorned that. They had made Saxon kings in Northumbria and in Mercia and those kings were feeble, leashed to the Danes, and then I understood what Svein meant and I laughed aloud. "He's promised you the throne!" I accused Odda.

"I've heard more sense from a pig's fart," Odda retorted, but I knew I was right. Æthelwold was Guthrum's candidate for the throne of

Wessex, but Svein was no friend of Guthrum and would want his own Saxon as king. Odda.

"King Odda," I said jeeringly, then spat into the fire.

Odda would have killed me for that, but we met under the terms of a truce and so he forced himself to ignore the insult. He looked at Harald. "You have a choice, Harald," he said, "You can die or you can live."

Harald was silent. He had not known about Wulfhere, and the news had appalled him. Wulfhere was the most powerful ealdorman in Wessex, and if he thought Alfred was doomed, then what was Harald to think? I could see the shire reeve's uncertainty. His decency wanted him to declare loyalty to Alfred, but Odda had suggested that nothing but death would follow such a choice. "I . . ." Harald began, then fell silent, unable to say what he thought for he did not know his own mind.

"The fyrd is raised," I spoke for him, "at the king's orders, and the king's orders are to drive the Danes from Defnascir."

Odda spat into the fire for answer.

"Svein has been defeated," I said. "His ships are burned. He is like a whipped dog and you give him comfort." Svein, when that was translated, gave me a look like the stroke of a whip. "Svein," I went on as though he was not present, "must be driven back to Guthrum."

"You have no authority here," Odda said.

"I have Alfred's authority," I said, "and a written order telling you to drive Svein from your shire."

"Alfred's orders mean nothing," Odda said, "and you croak like a swamp frog." He turned to Steapa. "You have unfinished business with Uhtred."

Steapa looked uncertain for a heartbeat, then understood what his master meant. "Yes, lord," he said.

"Then finish it now."

"Finish what now?" Harald asked.

"Your king"—Odda said the last word sarcastically—"ordered Steapa and Uhtred to fight to the death. Yet both live! So your king's orders have not been obeyed."

"There is a truce!" Harald protested.

"Either Uhtred stops interfering in the affairs of Defnascir," Odda said forcefully, "or I shall have Steapa kill Uhtred. You want to know who is right? Alfred or me? You want to know who will be king in Wessex, Æthelwold or Alfred? Then put it to the test, Harald. Let Steapa and

Uhtred finish their fight and see which man God favors. If Uhtred wins then I shall support you, and if he loses?" He smiled. He had no doubt who would win.

Harald stayed silent. I looked at Steapa and, as on the first time I met him, saw nothing on his face. He had promised to protect me, but that was before he had been reunited with his master. The Danes looked happy. Why should they mind two Saxons fighting? Harald, though, still hesitated, and then the weary, feeble voice sounded from the doorway at the back of the hall. "Let them fight, Harald, let them fight." Odda the Elder, swathed in a wolf-skin blanket, stood at the door. He held a crucifix. "Let them fight," he said again, "and God will guide the victor's arm."

Harald looked at me. I nodded. I did not want to fight, but a man cannot back down from combat. What was I to do? Say that to expect God to indicate a course of action through a duel was nonsense? To appeal to Harald? To claim that everything Odda had said was wrong and that Alfred would win? If I had refused to fight I was granting the argument to Odda, and in truth he had half convinced me that Alfred was doomed, and Harald, I am sure, was wholly convinced. Yet there was more than mere pride making me fight in the hall that day. There was a belief, deep in my soul, that somehow Alfred would survive. I did not like him, I did not like his god, but I believed fate was on his side. So I nodded again, this time to Steapa. "I do not want to fight you," I said to him, "but I have given an oath to Alfred, and my sword says he will win and that Danish blood will dung our fields."

Steapa said nothing. He just flexed his huge arms, then waited as one of Odda's men went outside and returned with two swords. No shields, just swords. He had taken a pair of blades at random from the pile and he offered them to Steapa first, who shook his head, indicating that I should have the choice. I closed my eyes, groped, and took the first hilt that I touched. It was a heavy sword, weighted toward its tip. A slashing weapon, not a piercing blade, and I knew I had chosen wrong.

Steapa took the other and scythed it through the air so that the blade sang. Svein, who had betrayed little emotion so far, looked impressed, while Odda the Younger smiled. "You can put the sword down," he told me, "and thus yield the argument to me."

Instead I walked to the clear space beside the hearth. I had no intention of attacking Steapa, but would let him come to me. I felt weary and resigned. Fate is inexorable.

"For my sake," Odda the Elder spoke behind me, "make it fast."

"Yes, lord," Steapa said, and he took a step toward me and then turned as fast as a striking snake and his blade whipped in a slash that took Odda the Younger's throat. The sword was not as sharp as it could have been, so that the blow drove Odda down, but it also ripped his gullet open so that blood spurted a blade's length into the air, then splashed into the fire where it hissed and bubbled. Odda was on the floor rushes now, his legs twitching, his hands clutching at his throat that still pumped blood. He made a gargling noise, turned on his back, and went into a spasm so that his heels drummed against the floor and then, just as Steapa stepped forward to finish him, he gave a last jerk and was dead.

Steapa drove the sword into the floor, leaving it quivering there. "Alfred rescued me," he announced to the hall. "Alfred took me from the Danes. Alfred is my king."

"And he has our oaths," Odda the Elder added, "and my son had no business making peace with the pagans."

The Danes stepped back. Svein glanced at

me, for I was still holding a sword. Then he looked at the boar spears leaning against the wall, judging whether he could snatch one before I attacked him. I lowered the blade. "We have a truce," Harald said loudly.

"We have a truce," I told Svein in Danish.

Svein spat on the bloody rushes. Then he and his standard-bearer took another cautious backward pace.

"But tomorrow," Harald said, "there will be no truce, and we shall come to kill you."

The Danes rode from Ocmundtun. And next day they also went from Cridianton. They could have stayed if they wished. There were more than enough of them to defend Cridianton and make trouble in the shire, but Svein knew he would be besieged and, man by man, worn down until he had no force at all, and so he went north, going to join Guthrum, and I rode to Oxton. The land had never looked more beautiful, the trees were hazed with green, and bullfinches were feasting on the first tight fruit buds, while anemones, stitchwort, and white violets glowed in sheltered spots. Lambs ran from the buck hares in the pastures. The sun shimmered the wide sea-reach of the Uisc and the sky was full of lark song beneath which the foxes took lambs, magpies and jays feasted on other birds' eggs, and plowmen impaled crows at the edges of the fields to ensure a good harvest.

"There'll be butter soon," a woman told me. She really wanted to know if I was returning to the estate, but I was not. I was saying farewell. There were slaves living there, doing their jobs, and I assured them Mildrith would appoint a steward sooner or later. Then I went to the hall and I dug beside the post and found my hoard untouched. The Danes had not come to Oxton. Wirken, the sly priest of Exanmynster, heard I was at the hall and rode a donkey up to the estate. He assured me he had kept a watchful eye on the place, and doubtless he wanted a reward. "It belongs to Mildrith now," I told him.

"The Lady Mildrith? She lives?"

"She lives," I said curtly, "but her son is dead."

"God rest his poor soul," Wirken said, making the sign of the cross. I was eating a scrap of ham and he looked at it hungrily, knowing I broke the rules of Lent. He said nothing, but I knew he was cursing me for being a pagan.

"And the Lady Mildrith," I went on, "would live a chaste life now. She says she will join the sisters in Cridianton."

"There are no sisters in Cridianton," Wirken said. "They're all dead. The Danes saw to that before they left."

"Other nuns will settle there," I said. Not that I cared, for the fate of a small nunnery was none of my business. Oxton was no longer my business. The Danes were my business, and the Danes had gone north and I would follow them.

For that was my life. That spring I was twenty-one years old and for half my life I had been with armies. I was not a farmer. I watched the slaves tearing the couch grass from the home fields and knew the tasks of farming bored me. I was a warrior, and I had been driven from my home of Bebbanburg to the southern edge of England and I think I knew, as Wirken babbled on about how he had guarded the storehouses through the winter, that I was now going north again. Ever north. Back home.

"You lived off these storehouses all winter," I accused the priest.

"I watched them all winter, lord."

"And you got fat as you watched," I said. I climbed into my saddle. Behind me were two bags, ripe with money, and they stayed there as I rode to Exanceaster and found Steapa in The Swan. Next morning, with six other warriors from Ealdorman Odda's guard, we rode north. Our way was marked by pillars of smoke, for Svein was burning and plundering as he went, but we had done what Alfred had wanted us to do. We had driven Svein back to Guthrum, so that now the two largest Danish armies were united. If Alfred had been stronger he might have left them separate and marched against each in turn, but Alfred knew he had only one chance to take back his kingdom, and that was to win one battle. He had to overwhelm all the Danes and destroy them in one blow, and his weapon was an army that existed only in his head. He had sent demands that the fyrd of Wessex would be summoned after Easter and before Pentecost, but no one knew whether it would actually appear. Perhaps we would ride from the swamp and find no one at the meeting place. Or perhaps the fyrd would come, and there would be too few men. The truth was that Alfred was too weak to fight, but to wait longer would only make him weaker. So he had to fight or lose his kingdom.

So we would fight.

ELEVEN

"You will have many sons," Iseult told me. It was dark, though a half-moon was hazed by a mist. Somewhere to the northeast a dozen fires burned in the hills, evidence that a strong Danish patrol was watching the swamp. "But I am sorry about Uhtred," she said.

I wept for him then. I do not know why the tears had taken so long to come, but suddenly I was overwhelmed by the thought of his helplessness, his sudden smile, and the pity of it all. Both my half brothers and my half sister had died when they were babies and I do not remember my father crying, though perhaps he did. I do remember my stepmother shrieking in grief, and how my father, disgusted by the sound, had gone hunting with his hawks and hounds.

"I saw three kingfishers yesterday," Iseult said.

Tears were running down my cheeks, blurring the misted moon. I said nothing.

"Hild says the blue of the kingfisher's feathers is for the virgin and the red is for Christ's blood."

"And what do you say?"

"That your son's death is my doing."

"Wyrd bið ful āraed," I said. Fate is fate. It cannot be changed or cheated. Alfred had insisted I marry Mildrith so I would be tied to Wessex and would put roots deep into its rich soil, but I already had roots in Northumbria, roots twisted into the rock of Bebbanburg, and perhaps my son's death was a sign from the gods that I could not make a new home. Fate wanted me to go to my northern stronghold and until I reached Bebbanburg I would be a wanderer. Men fear wanderers for they have no rules. The Danes came as strangers, rootless and violent, and that, I thought, was why I was always happier in their company. Alfred could spend hours worrying about the righteousness of a law, whether it concerned the fate of orphans or the sanctity of boundary markers, and he was right to worry because folk cannot live together without law, or else every straying cow would lead to bloodshed, but the Danes hacked through the law with swords. It was easier that way, though once they had settled a land they started to make their own laws. "It was not your fault," I said. "You don't command fate."

"Hild says there is no such thing as fate," Iseult said.

"Then Hild is wrong."

"There is only the will of God," Iseult said, "and if we obey that we go to heaven."

"And if we choose not to," I said, "isn't that fate?"

"That's the devil," she said. "We are sheep, Uhtred, and we choose our shepherd, a good one or a bad one."

I thought Hild must have soured Iseult with Christianity, but I was wrong. It was a priest who had come to Æthelingæg while I had been in Defnascir who had filled her head with his religion. He was a British priest from Dyfed, a priest who spoke Iseult's native tongue and also knew both English and Danish. I was ready to hate him as I hated Brother Asser, but Father Pyrlig stumbled into our hut next morning booming that he had found five goose eggs and was dying of hunger. "Dying! That's what I am, dying of starvation!" He looked pleased to see me. "You're the famous Uhtred, eh? And Iseult tells me you hate Brother Asser? Then you're a friend of mine. Why Abraham doesn't take Asser to his bosom I do not know, except maybe Abraham doesn't want the little bastard clinging to his bosom. I wouldn't. It would be like suckling a serpent, it would. Did I say I was hungry?"

He was twice my age and a big man, big bellied and big-hearted. His hair stuck out in ungovernable clumps, he had a broken nose, only four teeth, and a broad smile. "When I was a child," he told me, "ever such a little child, I used to eat mud. Can you believe that? Do Saxons eat mud? Of course they do, and I thought I don't want to eat mud. Mud is for toads, it is. So eventually I became a priest. And you know why? Because I never saw a hungry priest! Never! Did you ever see a hungry priest? Nor me!" All this tumbled out without any introduction. Then he spoke earnestly to Iseult in her own tongue and I was sure he was pouring Christianity into her, but then he translated for me. "I'm telling her that you can make a marvelous dish with goose eggs. Break them up, stir them well, and add just a little crumbled cheese. So Defnascir is safe?"

"Unless the Danes send a fleet," I said.

"Guthrum has that in mind," Pyrlig said. "He

wants the Danes in Lundene to send their ships to the south coast."

"You know that?"

"I do indeed, I do indeed! He told me! I've just spent ten days in Cippanhamm. I speak Danish, see, because I'm clever, and so I was an ambassador for my king. How about that! Me, who used to eat mud, an ambassador! Crumble the cheese finer, my love. That's right. I had to discover, you see, how much money Guthrum would pay us to bring our spearmen over the hills and start skewering Saxons. Now that's a fine ambition for a Briton, skewering Saxons, but the Danes are pagans, and God knows we can't have pagans loose in the world."

"Why not?"

"It's just a fancy of mine," he said, "just a fancy." He stabbed his finger into a tiny pot of butter, then licked it. "It isn't really sour," he told Iseult, "not very, so stir it in." He grinned at me. "What happens when you put two bulls to a herd of cows?"

"One bull dies."

"There you are! Gods are the same, which is why we don't want pagans here. We're cows and the gods are bulls."

"So we get humped?"

He laughed. "Theology's difficult. Anyway, God is my bull so here I am, telling the Saxons about Guthrum."

"Did Guthrum offer you money?" I asked.

"He offered me the kingdoms of the world! He offered me gold, silver, amber, and jet! He even offered me women, or boys if I had that taste, which I don't. And I didn't believe a single promise he made. Not that it mattered. The Britons aren't going to fight anyway. God doesn't want us to. No! My embassy was all a pretense. Brother Asser sent me. He wanted me to spy on the Danes, see? Then tell Alfred what I saw, so that's what I'm doing."

"Asser sent you?"

"He wants Alfred to win. Not because he loves the Saxons—even Brother Asser isn't that curdled—but because he loves God."

"And will Alfred win?"

"If God has anything to do with it, yes," Pyrlig said cheerfully, then gave a shrug. "But the Danes are strong in men. A big army! But they're not happy, I can tell you that. And they're all hungry. Not starving, mind you, but pulling their belts tighter than they'd like, and now Svein's there so there'll be even less food. Their own fault, of course. Too many men in Cippanhamm! And too many slaves! They have scores of slaves. But he's sending the slaves to Lundene, to sell them there. They need some baby eels, eh? That'll fatten them up." The elvers were swarming into the Sæfern Sea and slithering up the shallow waterways of the swamp where they were being netted in abundance. There was no hunger in Æthelingæg, not if you gorged on elvers. "I caught three basketfuls yesterday," Pyrlig said happily, "and a frog. It had a face just like Brother Asser so I gave it a blessing and threw it back. Don't just stir the eggs, girl! Beat them! I hear your son died?"

"Yes," I answered stiffly.

"I am sorry," he said with genuine feeling, "I am truly sorry, for to lose a child is a desperate hard thing. I sometimes think God must like children. He takes so many to him. I believe there's a garden in heaven, a green garden where children play all the time. He's got two sons of mine up there, and I tell you, the youngest must be making the angels scream. He'll be pulling the girls' hair and beating up the other boys like they were goose eggs."

"You lost two sons?"

"But I kept three others and four daughters.

Why do you think I'm never home?" He grinned at me. "Noisy little things they are, children, and such appetites! Sweet Jesus, they'd eat a horse a day if they could! There are some folk who say priests shouldn't marry and there are times I think they're right. Do you have any bread, dearest?"

Iseult pointed to a net hanging from the roof. "Cut the mold off," she told me.

"I like to see a man obeying a woman," Father Pyrlig said as I fetched the loaf.

"Why's that?" I asked.

"Because it means I'm not alone in this sorry world. Good God, but that Ælswith was weaned on gall juice, wasn't she? Got a tongue in her like a starving weasel! Poor Alfred."

"He's happy enough."

"Good God, man, that's the last thing he is! Some folk catch God like a disease, and he's one of them. He's like a cow after winter, he is."

"He is?"

"You know when the late spring grass comes in? All green and new and rich? And you put the poor cow out to eat and she blows up like a bladder? She's nothing but shit and wind and then she gets the staggers and drops down dead if you don't take her off the grass for a while. That's

Alfred. He got too much of the good green grass of God, and now he's sick on it. But he's a good man, a good man. Too thin, he is, but good. A living saint, no less. Ah, good girl, let's eat." He scooped some of the eggs with his fingers, then passed the pot to me. "Thank God it's Easter next week," he said with his mouth full so that scraps of egg lodged in his huge beard, "and then we can eat meat again. I'm wasting away without meat. You know Iseult will be baptized at Easter?"

"She told me," I said shortly.

"And you don't approve? Just think of it as a good wash. Then maybe you won't mind so much."

I was not in Æthelingæg for Iseult's baptism, nor did I wish to be, for I knew Easter with Alfred would be nothing but prayers and psalms and priests and sermons. Instead I took Steapa and fifty men up into the hills, going toward Cippanhamm, for Alfred had ordered that the Danes were to be harried mercilessly in the next few weeks. He had decided to assemble the fyrd of Wessex close to Ascension Day, which was just six weeks away, and those were the weeks in which Guthrum would be hoping to revive his hungry horses on the spring grass, and so we rode to ambush Danish forage parties. Kill one forage party and the next must be protected by a hundred extra horsemen, and that wearies the horses even more and so requires still more forage. It worked for a while, but then Guthrum began sending his foragers north into Mercia where they were not opposed.

It was a time of waiting. There were two smiths in Æthelingæg now and, though neither had all the equipment they wanted, and though fuel for their furnaces was scarce, they were making good spear points. One of my jobs was to take men to cut ash poles for the spear shafts. Alfred was writing letters, trying to discover how many men the shires could bring to battle, and he sent priests to Frankia to persuade the thegns who had fled there to return. More spies came from Cippanhamm confirming that Svein had joined Guthrum and that Guthrum was strengthening his horses and raising men from the Danish parts of England. He was ordering his West Saxon allies like Wulfhere to arm their men, and warning his garrisons in Wintanceaster, Readingum, and Baðum that they must be ready to abandon their ramparts and march to his aid. Guthrum had his own spies and must have known Alfred was planning to assemble an army, and I dare say he welcomed that news for such an army would be Alfred's last hope and, should Guthrum destroy the fyrd, Wessex would fall, never to rise again.

Æthelingæg seethed with rumor. Guthrum, it was said, had five thousand men. Ships had come from Denmark and a new army of Norsemen had sailed from Ireland. The Britons were marching. The fyrd of Mercia was on Guthrum's side, and it was said the Danes had set up a great camp at Cracgelad on the river Temes where thousands of Mercian troops, both Danish and Saxon, were assembling. The rumors of Guthrum's strength crossed the sea and Wilfrith of Hamptonscir wrote from Frankia begging Alfred to flee Wessex. "Take ship to this coast," he wrote, "and save your family."

Leofric rarely rode on patrols with us but stayed in Æthelingæg, for he had been named commander of the king's bodyguard. He was proud of that, as he should have been, for he had been peasant born and he could neither read nor write, and Alfred usually insisted that his commanders were literate. Eanflæd's influence was behind the appointment, for she had become a confidante of Ælswith. Alfred's wife went nowhere without Eanflæd—even in church the onetime whore sat just behind Ælswith—and when Alfred held court, Eanflæd was always there. "The queen doesn't like you," Eanflæd told me one rare day when I found her alone.

"She's not a queen," I said. "Wessex doesn't have queens."

"She should be a queen," she said indignantly. "It would be right and proper." She was carrying a heap of plants and I noticed her forearms were a pale green. "Dyeing," she explained brusquely, and I followed her to where a great cauldron was bubbling on a fire. She threw in the plants and began stirring the mess in the pot. "We're making green linen," she said.

"Green linen?"

"Alfred must have a banner," she said indignantly. "He can't fight without a banner." The women were making two banners. One was the great green dragon flag of Wessex, while the other bore the cross of Christianity. "Your Iseult's working on the cross," Eanflæd told me.

"I know."

"You should have been at her baptism."

"I was killing Danes."

"But I'm glad she's baptized. Come to her senses, she has."

In truth, I thought, Iseult had been battered

into Christianity. For weeks she had endured the rancor of Alfred's churchmen, had been accused of witchcraft and of being the devil's instrument, and it had worn her down. Then came Hild with her gentler Christianity, and Pyrlig who spoke of God in Iseult's tongue, and Iseult had been persuaded. That meant I was the only pagan left in the swamp and Eanflæd glanced pointedly at my hammer amulet. She said nothing of it, instead asking me whether I truly believed we could defeat the Danes.

"Yes," I said confidently, though of course I did not know.

"How many men will Guthrum have?"

I knew the questions were not Eanflæd's but Ælswith's. Alfred's wife wanted to know if her husband had any chance of survival or whether they should take the ship we had captured from Svein and sail to Frankia. "Guthrum will lead four thousand men," I said, "at least."

"At least?"

"Depends how many come from Mercia," I said, then thought for a heartbeat, "but I expect four thousand."

"And Wessex?"

"The same," I said. I was lying. With enormous luck we could assemble three thousand, but I doubted it. Two thousand? Not likely, but possible. My real fear was that Alfred would raise his banner and no one would come, or that only a few hundred men would arrive. We could lead three hundred from Æthelingæg, but what could three hundred do against Guthrum's great army?

Alfred also worried about numbers, and he sent me to Hamptonscir to discover how much of the shire was occupied by the Danes. I found them well entrenched in the north, but the south of the shire was free of them and in Hamtun, where Alfred's fleet was based, the war ships were still drawn up on the beach. Burgweard, the fleet's commander, had over a hundred men in the town, all that was left of his crews, and he had them manning the palisade. He claimed he could not leave Hamtun for fear that the Danes would attack and capture the ships, but I had Alfred's scrap of parchment with his dragon seal on it, and I used it to order him to keep thirty men to protect the ships and bring the rest to Alfred.

"When?" he asked gloomily.

"When you're summoned," I said, "but it will be soon. And you're to raise the local fyrd, too. Bring them."

"And if the Danes come here?" he asked. "If they come by sea?"

"Then we lose the fleet," I said, "and we build another."

His fear was real enough. Danish ships were off the south coast again. For the moment, rather than attempt an invasion, they were being Vikings. They landed, raided, raped, burned, stole, and went to sea again, but they were numerous enough for Alfred to worry that a whole army might land somewhere on the coast and march against him. We were harassed by that fear and by the knowledge that we were few and the enemy numerous, and that the enemy's horses were fattening on the new grass.

"Ascension Day," Alfred announced on the day I returned from Hamtun.

That was the day we should be ready in Æthelingæg, and on the Sunday after, which was the Feast of Saint Monica, we would gather the fyrd, if there was a fyrd. Reports said the Danes were readying to march and it was plain they would launch their attack south toward Wintanceaster, the town that was the capital of Wessex, and to protect it, to bar Guthrum's road south, the fyrd would gather at Egbert's Stone. I had never heard of the place, but Leofric assured me it was an important spot, the place where King Egbert, Alfred's grandfather, had given judgments. "It isn't one stone," he said, "but three."

"Three?"

"Two big pillars and another boulder on top. The giants made it in the old days."

And so the summons were issued. Bring every man, the parchments instructed, bring every weapon, and say your prayers, for what is left of Wessex will meet at Egbert's Stone to carry battle to the Danes, and no sooner was the summons sent than disaster struck. It came just a week before the fyrd was to gather.

Huppa, Ealdorman of Thornsæta, wrote that forty Danish ships were off his coast and that he dared not lead the fyrd away from their threat. Worse, because the Danes were so numerous, he had begged Harald of Defnascir to lend him men.

That letter almost destroyed Alfred's spirits. He had clung to his dream of surprising Guthrum by raising an unexpectedly powerful army, but all his hopes were now shredding away. He had always been thin, but suddenly he looked haggard and he spent hours in the church, wrestling with God, unable to understand why the Almighty had so suddenly turned against him. And two days after the news of the

Danish fleet, Svein of the White Horse led three hundred mounted men in a raid against the hills on the edge of the swamp and, because scores of men from the Sumorsæte fyrd had gathered in Æthelingæg, Svein discovered and stole their horses. We had neither the room nor the forage to keep many horses in Æthelingæg itself, and so they were pastured beyond the causeway, and I watched from the fort as Svein, riding a white horse and wearing his white-plumed helmet and white cloak, rounded up the beasts and drove them away. There was nothing I could do to stop him. I had twenty men in the fort and Svein was leading hundreds.

"Why were the horses not guarded?" Alfred wanted to know.

"They were," Wiglaf, Ealdorman of Sumor-sæte, said, "and the guards died." He saw Alfred's anger, but not his despair. "We haven't seen a Dane here for weeks!" he pleaded. "How were we to know they'd come in force?"

"How many men died?"

"Only twelve."

"Only?" Alfred asked, wincing. "And how many horses lost?"

"Sixty-three."

On the night before Ascension Day Alfred

walked beside the river. Beocca, faithful as a hound, followed him at a distance, wanting to offer the king God's reassurance, but instead Alfred called to me. There was a moon, and its light shadowed his cheeks and made his pale eyes look almost white. "How many men will we have?" he asked abruptly.

I did not need to think about the answer. "Two thousand."

He nodded. He knew that number as well as I did.

"Maybe a few more," I suggested.

He grunted at that. We would lead three hundred and fifty men from Æthelingæg and Wiglaf, Ealdorman of Sumorsæte, had promised a thousand, though in truth I doubted if that many would come. The fyrd of Wiltunscir had been weakened by Wulfhere's defection, but the southern part of the shire should yield five hundred men, and we could expect some from Hamptonscir, but beyond that we would depend on whatever few men made it past the Danish garrisons that now ringed the heartland of Wessex. If Defnascir and Thornsæta had sent their fyrds, then we would have numbered closer to four thousand, but they were not coming.

"And Guthrum?" Alfred asked. "How many will he have?"

"Four thousand."

"More like five," Alfred said. He stared at the river that was running low between the muddy banks. The water rippled about the wicker fish traps. "So should we fight?"

"What choice do we have?"

He smiled at that. "We have a choice, Uhtred," he assured me. "We can run away. We can go to Frankia. I could become a king in exile and pray that God brings me back."

"You think God will?"

"No," he admitted. If he ran away, then he knew he would die in exile.

"So we fight," I said.

"And on my conscience," he said, "I will forever bear the weight of all those men who died in a hopeless cause. Two thousand against five thousand? How can I justify leading so few against so many?"

"You know how."

"So I can be king?"

"So that we are not slaves in our own land," I said.

He pondered that for a while. An owl flew low overhead, a sudden surprise of white feathers and the rush of air across stubby wings. It was an omen, I knew, but of what kind? "Perhaps we are being punished," Alfred said.

"For what?"

"For taking the land from the Britons?"

That seemed nonsense to me. If Alfred's god wanted to punish him for his ancestors having taken the land from the Britons, then why send the Danes? Why not send the Britons? God could resurrect Arthur and let his people have their revenge, but why send a new people to take the land? "Do you want Wessex or not?" I asked harshly.

He said nothing for a while, then gave a sad smile. "In my conscience," he said, "I can find no hope for this fight, but as a Christian I must believe we can win it. God will not let us lose."

"Nor will this," I said, and I slapped Serpent-Breath's hilt.

"So simple?" he asked.

"Life is simple," I said. "Ale, women, sword, and reputation. Nothing else matters."

He shook his head and I knew he was thinking about God and prayer and duty, but he did not argue. "So if you were I, Uhtred," he said, "would you march?"

"You've already made up your mind, lord," I said, "so why ask me?"

He nodded. A dog barked in the village and he turned to stare at the cottages and the hall and the church he had made with its tall alder cross. "Tomorrow," he said, "you will take a hundred horsemen and patrol ahead of the army."

"Yes, lord."

"And when we meet the enemy," he went on, still staring at the cross, "you will choose fifty or sixty men from the bodyguard. The best you can find. And you will guard my banners."

He did not say more, nor did he need to. What he meant was that I was to take the best warriors, the most savage men, the dangerous warriors who loved battle, and I was to lead them in the place where the fight would be hardest, for an enemy loves to capture his foe's banners. It was an honor to be asked and, if the battle was lost, an almost certain death sentence. "I shall do it gladly, lord," I said, "but ask a favor of you in return."

"If I can," he said guardedly.

"If you can," I said, "don't bury me. Burn my body on a pyre, and put a sword in my hand."

He hesitated, then nodded, knowing he had

agreed to a pagan funeral. "I never told you," he said, "that I am sorry about your son."

"So am I, lord."

"But he is with God, Uhtred, he is assuredly with God."

"So I'm told, lord, so I'm told."

And next day we marched. Fate is inexorable, and though numbers and reason told us we could not win, we dared not lose, and so we marched to Egbert's Stone.

We marched with ceremony. Twenty-three priests and eighteen monks formed our vanguard and chanted a psalm as they led Alfred's forces away from the fort guarding the southern trackway and east toward the heartland of Wessex.

They chanted in Latin so the words meant nothing to me, but Father Pyrlig had been given use of one of Alfred's horses and, dressed in a leather coat and with a great sword strapped to his side and with a stout-shafted boar spear on one shoulder, he rode alongside me and translated the words. " 'God,' " he said, " 'you have abandoned me, you have scattered us, you are angry with us, now turn to us again.' That sounds a reasonable request, doesn't it? You've kicked us in the face, so now give us a cuddle, eh?"

"It really means that?"

"Not the bit about kicks and cuddles. That was me." He grinned at me. "I do miss war. Isn't that a sin?"

"You've seen war?"

"Seen it? I was a warrior before I joined the church! Pyrlig the Fearless, they called me. I killed four Saxons in a day once. All by myself and I had nothing but a spear. And they had swords and shields, they did. Back home they made a song about me, but mind you, the Britons will sing about anything. I can sing you the song, if you like? It tells how I slaughtered three hundred and ninety-four Saxons in one day, but it's not entirely accurate."

"So how many did you kill?"

"I told you. Four." He laughed.

"So how did you learn English?"

"My mother was a Saxon, poor thing. She was taken in a raid on Mercia and became a slave."

"So why did you stop being a warrior?"

"Because I found God, Uhtred. Or God found me. And I was becoming too proud. Songs about yourself go to your head and I was wickedly proud of myself, and pride is a terrible thing."

"It's a warrior's weapon," I said.

"It is indeed," he agreed, "and that is why it is a terrible thing, and why I pray God purges me of it."

We were well ahead of the priests now, climbing toward the nearest hilltop to look north and east for the enemy, but the churchmen's voices followed us, their chant strong in the morning air. " 'Through God we shall do bravely,' " Father Pyrlig interpreted for me, " 'and God shall trample down our enemies.' Now there's a blessed thought for a fine morning, Lord Uhtred!"

"The Danes are saying their own prayers, father."

"But to what god, eh? No point in shouting at a deaf man, is there?" He curbed his horse at the hilltop and stared northward. "Not even a mouse stirring."

"The Danes are watching," I said. "We can't see them, but they can see us."

If they were watching, then what they could see was Alfred's three hundred and fifty men riding or walking away from the swamp, and in the distance another five or six hundred men who were the fyrd from the western part of Sumorsæte who had camped to the south of the swamp and now marched to join our smaller column. Most of the men from Æthelingæg were real soldiers, trained to stand in the shield wall, but we also had fifty of the marshmen. I had wanted Eofer, the strong bowman, to come with us, but he could not fight without his niece telling him what to do and I had no intention of taking a child to war and so we had left Eofer behind. A good number of women and children were following the column, though Alfred had sent Ælswith and his children south to Scireburnan under a guard of forty men. We could hardly spare those men, but Alfred insisted his family go. Ælswith was to wait in Scireburnan and, if news came that her husband was defeated and the Danes victorious, she was to flee south to the coast and find a ship that would take her to Frankia. She was also instructed to take with her whatever books she could find in Scireburnan, for Alfred reckoned the Danes would burn every book in Wessex and so Ælswith was to rescue the gospel books and saints' lives and church fathers and histories and philosophers and thus raise her son Edward to become a learned king in exile.

Iseult was with the army, walking with Hild

and with Eanflæd who had upset Ælswith by insisting on following Leofric. The women led packhorses, which carried the army's shields, food, and spare spears. Nearly every woman was equipped with some kind of weapon. Even Hild, a nun, wanted to take revenge on the Danes who had whored her and so carried a long, narrow-bladed knife. "God help the Danes," Father Pyrlig had said when he saw the women gather, "if that lot get among them."

He and I now trotted eastward. I had horsemen ringing the column, riding on every crest, staying in sight of one another, and ready to signal if they saw any sign of the enemy, but there was none. We rode or marched under a spring sky, through a land bright with flowers, and the priests and monks kept up their chanting, and sometimes the men behind, who followed Alfred's two standard-bearers, would start singing a battle song.

Father Pyrlig beat his hand in time to the singing, then gave me a big grin. "I expect Iseult sings to you, doesn't she?"

"She does."

"We Britons love to sing! I must teach her some hymns." He saw my sour look and laughed. "Don't worry, Uhtred, she's no Christian."

"She isn't?" I asked, surprised.

"Well, she is, for the moment. I'm sorry you didn't come to her baptism. It was cold, that water! Fair froze me!"

"She's baptized," I said, "but you say she's no Christian?"

"She is and she isn't," Pyrlig said with a grin. "She is now, see, because she's among Christians. But she's still a shadow queen, and she won't forget it."

"You believe in shadow queens?"

"Of course I do! Good God, man! She is one!" He made the sign of the cross.

"Brother Asser called her a witch," I said, "a sorceress."

"Well, he would, wouldn't he? He's a monk! Monks don't marry. He's terrified of women, Brother Asser, unless they're very ugly, and then he bullies them. But show him a pretty young thing and he goes all addled. And of course he hates the power of women."

"Power?"

"Not just tits, I mean. God knows tits are powerful enough, but the real thing. Power! My mother had it. She was no shadow queen, mind you, but she was a healer and a scryer."

"She saw the future?"

He shook his head. "She knew what was happening far off. When my father died she suddenly screamed. Screamed fit to kill herself because she knew what had happened. She was right, too. The poor man was cut down by a Saxon. But she was best as a healer. Folk came to her from miles around. It didn't matter that she was born a Saxon, they'd walk for a week to fetch the touch of her hand. Me? I got it for free! She banged me about, she did, and I dare say I deserved it, but she was a rare healer. And, of course, the priests don't like that."

"Why not?"

"Because we priests tell folk that all power comes from God, and if it doesn't come from God then it must be evil, see? So when folk are ill the church wants them to pray and to give the priests money. Priests don't like it when they don't understand things, and they don't like folk going to the women to be healed. But what else are folk to do? My mother's hand, God rest her Saxon soul, was better than any prayer! Better than the touch of the sacraments! I wouldn't stop folk going to see a healer. I'd tell them to!" He stopped talking because I raised my hand. I had seen movement on a hillside to the north, but it was only a deer. I dropped my hand and kicked the horse on. "Now your Iseult," Pyrlig went on, "she's been raised with the power and she won't lose it."

"Didn't the baptism wash it out of her?"

"Not at all! It just made her a bit colder and cleaner. Nothing wrong with a scrub once or twice a year." He laughed. "But she was frightened back there in the swamp. You were gone and all around were Saxons and they were spitting that she was a pagan, so what did you think she would do? She wants to be one of them, she wants folk to stop spitting at her, so she said she'd be baptized. And maybe she really is a Christian? I'd praise God for that mercy, but I'd rather praise him for making her happy."

"You don't think she is?"

"Of course she isn't! She's in love with you!" He laughed. "And being in love with you means living among the Saxons, doesn't it? Poor girl. She's like a beautiful young hind that finds herself living among grunting pigs."

"What a gift for words you have," I said.

He laughed, delighted with his insult. "Win your war, Lord Uhtred," he said, "then take her away from us priests and give her lots of children. She'll be happy, and one day she'll be truly wise. That's the women's real gift, to be wise, and not many men have it."

And my gift was to be a warrior, though there was no fighting that day. We saw no Danes, though I was certain they had seen us and that by now Guthrum would have been told that Alfred had at last come from the swamp and was marching inland. We were giving him the opportunity to destroy us, to finish Wessex, and I knew that the Danes would be readying to march on us.

We spent that night in an earthen fort built by the old people, and next morning went north and east through a hungry land. I rode ahead, going into the hills to look for the enemy, but again the world seemed empty. Rooks flew, hares danced, and cuckoos called from the woods that were thick with bluebells, but there were no Danes. I rode along a high ridge, gazing northward, and saw nothing, and when the sun was at its height I turned east. There were ten of us in my band and our guide was a man from Wiltunscir who knew the country and he led us toward the valley of the Wilig where Egbert's Stone stands.

A mile or so short of the valley we saw horse-

men, but they were to the south of us and we galloped across ungrazed pastureland to find it was
Alfred, escorted by Leofric, five soldiers, and
four priests. "Have you been to the stone?" Alfred called out eagerly as we closed on him.

"No, lord."

"Doubtless there are men there," he said, disappointed that I could not bring him news.

"I didn't see any Danes either, lord."

"It'll take them two days to organize," he said
dismissively. "But they'll come! They'll come!
And we shall beat them!" He twisted in his saddle to look at Father Beocca, who was one of the
priests. "Are you sore, father?"

"Mightily sore, lord."

"You're no horseman, Beocca, no horseman,
but it's not much farther. Not much farther,
then you can rest!" Alfred was in a feverish
mood. "Rest before we fight, eh! Rest and pray,
father, then pray and fight. Pray and fight!" He
kicked his horse into a gallop and we pounded
after him through a pink-blossomed orchard and
up a slope, then across a long hilltop where the
bones of dead cattle lay in the new grass. White
mayflower edged the woods at the foot of the hill
and a hawk slanted away from us, sliding across
the valley toward the charred remains of a barn.

"It's just across the crest, lord!" my guide shouted at me.

"What is?"

"Defereal, lord!"

Defereal was the name of the settlement in the valley of the river Wilig where Egbert's Stone waited, and Alfred now spurred his horse so that his blue cloak flapped behind him. We were all galloping, spread across the hilltop, racing to be the first over the crest to see the Saxon forces. Then Father Beocca's horse stumbled. He was, as Alfred said, a bad horseman, but that was no surprise for he was both lame and palsied, and when the horse tipped forward Beocca tumbled from the saddle. I saw him rolling in the grass and turned my horse back. "I'm not hurt," he shouted at me. "Not hurt! Not much. Go on, Uhtred, go on!"

I caught his horse. Beocca was on his feet now, limping as fast as he could to where Alfred and the other horsemen stood in a line gazing into the valley beyond. "We should have brought the banners," Beocca said as I gave him his reins.

"The banners?"

"So the fyrd knows their king has come," he said breathlessly. "They should see his banners on the skyline, Uhtred, and know he has come.

The cross and the dragon, eh? **In hoc signo!** Alfred will be the new Constantine, Uhtred, a warrior of the cross! **In hoc signo**, God be praised, God be praised, God indeed be mightily praised."

I had no idea what he meant, nor did I care.

For I had reached the hilltop and could stare down into the long lovely valley of the Wilig.

Which was empty.

Not a man in sight. Just the river and the willows and the water meadows and the alders and a heron flying and the grass bending in the wind and the triple stone of Egbert on a slope above the Wilig where an army was supposed to gather. And there was not one man there. Not one single man in sight. The valley was empty.

The men we had brought from Æthelingæg straggled into the valley, and with them now was the fyrd of Sumorsæte. Together they numbered just over a thousand men, and about half were equipped to fight in the shield wall while the rest were only good for shoving the front ranks forward or dealing with the enemy wounded or, more likely, dying.

I could not face Alfred's disappointment. He said nothing about it, but his thin face was pale and set hard as he busied himself with deciding where the thousand men should camp and where our few horses should be pastured. I rode up a high hill that lay to the north of the encampment, taking a score of men including Leofric, Steapa, and Father Pyrlig. The hill was steep, though that had not stopped the old people from making one of their strange graves high on the slope. The grave was a long mound and Pyrlig made a wide detour rather than ride past it. "Full of dragons, it is," he explained to me.

"You've seen a dragon?" I asked.

"Would I be alive if I had? No one sees a dragon and lives!"

I turned in the saddle and stared at the mound. "I thought folk were buried there?"

"They are! And their treasures! So the dragon guards the hoard. That's what dragons do. Bury gold and you hatch a dragon, see?"

The horses had a struggle to climb the steep slope, but at its summit we were rewarded by a stretch of firm turf that offered views far to the north. I had climbed the hill to watch for Danes. Alfred might believe that it would be two or three days before we saw them, but I expected their scouts to be close and it was possible that a war band might try to harass the men camping by the Wilig.

Yet I saw no one. To the northeast were great downs, sheep hills, while straight ahead was the lower ground where the cloud shadows raced across fields and over blossoming mayflower and darkened the bright green new leaves.

"So what happens now?" Leofric asked me.

"You tell me."

"A thousand men? We can't fight the Danes with a thousand men."

I said nothing. Far off, on the northern horizon, there were dark clouds.

"We can't even stay here!" Leofric said. "So where do we go?"

"Back to the swamp?" Father Pyrlig suggested.

"The Danes will bring more ships," I said, "and eventually they'll capture the swamp. If they send a hundred ships up the rivers, then the swamp is theirs."

"Go to Defnascir," Steapa growled.

And the same thing would happen there, I thought. We would be safe for a time in Defnascir's tangle of hills and woods, but the Danes would come and there would be a succession of little fights and bit by bit Alfred would be bled to death. And once the Danes across the sea knew that Alfred was pinned into a corner of Wessex, they would bring more ships to take the good land that he could not hold. And that, I thought, was why he had been right to try to end the war in one blow, because he dared not let Wessex's weakness become known.

Except we were weak. We were a thousand men. We were pathetic. We were dreams fallen to earth, and suddenly I began to laugh. "What is it?" Leofric asked.

"I was thinking that Alfred insisted I learn to read," I said, "and for what?"

He smiled, remembering. It was one of Alfred's rules that every man who commanded sizable bodies of troops must be able to read, though it was a rule he had ignored when he made Leofric commander of his bodyguard. It seemed funny at that moment. All that effort so I could read his orders and he had never sent me one. Not one. "Reading is useful," Pyrlig said.

"What for?"

He thought about it. The wind gusted, flapping his hair and beard. "You can read all those good stories in the gospel book," he suggested brightly, "and the saints' lives! How about those, eh? They're full of lovely things, they are. There was Saint Donwen! Beautiful woman she was, and she gave her lover a drink that turned him into ice."

"Why did she do that?" Leofric asked.

"Didn't want to marry him, see?" Pyrlig said, trying to cheer us up, but no one wanted to hear more about the frigid Saint Donwen so he turned and stared northward. "That's where they'll come from, is it?" he asked.

"Probably," I said, and then I saw them, or thought I did. There was a movement on the far hills, something stirring in the cloud shadow, and I wished Iseult was on the hilltop for she had remarkable eyesight, but she would have needed a horse to climb to that summit and there were no horses to spare for women. The Danes had thousands of horses, all the beasts they had captured from Alfred at Cippanhamm, and all the animals they had stolen across Wessex, and now I was watching a group of horsemen on that far hill. Scouts, probably, and they would have seen us. Then they were gone. It had been a glimpse, no more, and so far away that I could not be sure of what I had seen. "Or perhaps they won't come at all," I went on. "Perhaps they'll march around us. Capture Wintanceaster and everywhere else."

"The bastards will come," Leofric said grimly, and I thought he was probably right. The Danes would know we were here, they would want to destroy us, and after that all would be easy for them.

Pyrlig turned his horse as if to ride back down to the valley, then paused. "So it's hopeless, is it?" he asked.

"They'll outnumber us four or five to one," I said.

"Then we must fight harder!"

I smiled. "Every Dane who comes to Britain, father," I explained, "is a warrior. The farmers stay in Denmark, but the wild men come here. And us? We're nearly all farmers and it takes three or four farmers to beat down a warrior."

"You're warriors," he said, "all of you! You're warriors! You all know how to fight! You can inspire men, and lead men, and kill your enemies. And God is on your side. With God on your side, who can beat you, eh? You want a sign?"

"Give me a sign," I said.

"Then look," he said, and pointed down to the Wilig, and I turned my horse and there, in the afternoon sun, was the miracle we had wanted. Men were coming. Men in their hundreds. Men from the east and men from the south, men streaming down from the hills, men of the West Saxon fyrd, coming at their king's command to save their country.

"Now it's only two farmers to one warrior!" Pyrlig said cheerfully.

"Up to our arseholes," Leofric said.

But we were not alone any longer. The fyrd was gathering.

TWELVE

Most men came in large groups, led by their thegns, while others arrived in small bands, but together they swelled into an army. Arnulf, Ealdorman of Suth Seaxa, brought close to four hundred men and apologized that it could not be more, but there were Danish ships off his coast and he had been forced to leave some of his fyrd to guard the shore. The men of Wiltunscir had been summoned by Wulfhere to join Guthrum's army, but the reeve, a grim man named Osric, had scoured the southern part of the shire and over eight hundred men had ignored their ealdorman's summons and came to Alfred instead. More arrived from the distant parts of Sumorsæte to join Wiglaf's fyrd that now numbered a thousand men, while half that many came from Hamptonscir, including Burgweard's garrison in which were Eadric and Cenwulf, crewmen from the **Heahengel**, and both embraced me, and with them was Father Willibald, eager and nervous. Almost every man came on foot, weary and hungry, with their boots falling apart, but they had swords and axes and spears and shields, and by midafternoon there were close to three thousand men in the Wilig valley and more were still coming as I rode toward the distant hill where I thought I had seen the Danish scouts.

Alfred sent me and, at the last moment, Father Pyrlig had offered to accompany me and Alfred had looked surprised, appeared to think about it for a heartbeat, then nodded assent. "Bring Uhtred home safe, father," he had said stiffly.

I said nothing as we rode through the growing camp, but once we were on our own I gave Pyrlig a sour look. "That was all arranged," I said.

"What was?"

"You coming with me. He had your horse already saddled! So what does Alfred want?"

Pyrlig grinned. "He wants me to talk you into becoming a Christian, of course. The king has great faith in my powers of speech."

"I am a Christian," I said.

"Are you now?"

"I was baptized, wasn't I? Twice, as it happens."

"Twice! Doubly holy, eh? How come you got it twice?"

"Because my name was changed when I was a child and my stepmother thought heaven wouldn't recognize me under my old name."

He laughed. "So they washed the devil out of you the first time and slopped him back in the second?" I said nothing to that and Pyrlig rode in silence for a time. "Alfred wants me to make you a good Christian," he said after a while, "because he wants God's blessing."

"He thinks God will curse us because I'm fighting for him?"

Pyrlig shook his head. "He knows, Uhtred, that the enemy are pagans. If they win, then Christ is defeated. This isn't just a war over land, it's a war about God. And Alfred, poor man, is Christ's servant, so he will do all he can for his master, and that means trying to turn you into a pious example of Christian humility. If he can get you onto your knees, then it'll be easy to make the Danes grovel."

I laughed, as he had meant me to. "If it encourages Alfred," I said, "tell him I'm a good Christian."

"I planned to tell him that anyway," Pyrlig said, "just to cheer him up, but in truth I wanted to come with you."

"Why?"

"Because I miss this life. God, I miss it! I loved being a warrior. All that irresponsibility! I relished it. Kill and make widows, frighten children! I was good at it, and I miss it. And I was always good at scouting. We'd see you Saxons blundering away like swine and you never knew we were watching you. Don't worry, I'm not going to talk Christ into you, whatever the king wants."

Our job was to find the Danes, if they were near. Alfred had marched to the Wilig valley to block any advance Guthrum made into the heartland of Wessex, but he still feared that the Danes might resist the lure of destroying his small army and instead march around us to take southern Wessex, which would leave us stranded and surrounded by Danish garrisons. That uncertainty meant Alfred was desperate for news of the enemy, so Pyrlig and I rode north and east up the valley until we came to where a smaller river flowed south into the Wilig and we followed that lesser stream past a large village that had been reduced to ashes. The small river passed through good farmland, but there were no cattle, no sheep, and the fields were unplowed and thick with weeds. We went slowly, for the horses were tired and we were well north of our army now. The sun was low in the west, though it was early May so the days were lengthening. There were mayfly on the river and trout rising to them, and then a scuffling sound made us both pause, but it was only a pair of otter cubs scrabbling down to the water through the roots of a willow. Doves were nesting in the blackthorn, and warblers called from the riverbank, and somewhere a woodpecker drummed intermittently. We rode in silence for a while, turning away from the river to go into an orchard where wrynecks sang among the pink blossom.

Pyrlig curbed his horse under the trees and pointed at a muddy patch in the grass and I saw hoofprints sifted with fallen petals. The prints were fresh and there were a lot of them. "Bastards were here, weren't they?" he said. "And not so long ago."

I looked up the valley. There was no one in sight. The hills rose steeply on either side with thick woods on their lower slopes. I had the sudden uncomfortable feeling that we were being watched, that we were blundering and the wolves were close. "If I were a Dane," Pyrlig spoke softly, and I suspected he shared my discomfort, "I'd be over there." He jerked his head to the western trees.

"Why?"

"Because when you saw them, they saw us, and that's the way to where they saw us. Does that make sense?" He laughed wryly. "I don't know, Uhtred, I just think the bastards are over there."

So we went east. We rode slowly, as if we did not have a care in the world, but once we were in the woods we turned north. We both searched the ground for more hoofprints, but saw none, and the feeling of being watched had gone now, though we did wait for a long time to see if anyone was following us. There was only the wind in the trees. Yet I knew the Danes were near, just as a hall's hounds know when there are wolves in the nearby darkness. The hair on their necks stands up, they bare their teeth, they quiver.

We came to a place where the trees ended and we dismounted, tied the horses, and went to the wood's edge and just watched.

And at last we saw them.

Thirty or forty Danes were on the valley's farther side, above the woods, and they had plainly ridden to the top of the hills, looked southward, and were now coming back. They were scattered in a long line that was riding down into the woods. "Scouting party," Pyrlig said.

"They can't have seen much from that hilltop."

"They saw us," he said.

"I think so."

"But they didn't attack us?" He was puzzled. "Why not?"

"Look at me," I said.

"I get a treat every day."

"They thought I was a Dane," I said. I was not in mail and had no helmet, so my long hair fell free down my leather-clad back and my arms were bright with rings. "And they probably thought you were my performing bear," I added.

He laughed. "So shall we follow them?"

The only risk was crossing the valley, but if the enemy saw us, they would probably still assume I was a fellow Dane, so we cantered over the open ground, then rode up into the farther woods. We heard the Danes before we saw them. They were careless, talking and laughing, unaware that any Saxons were close. Pyrlig tucked his crucifix beneath his leather coat. Then we waited until we were sure the last of the Danes had passed before kicking the horses uphill to find their tracks and so follow them. The shadows were lengthening, and that made me think that the Danish army must be close for the scouting party would want to reach safety before dark, but as the hilly country flattened we saw that they had no intention of joining Guthrum's forces that evening. The patrolling Danes had their own camp, and as we approached it we were nearly caught by another group of mounted scouts who rode in from the east. We heard the newcomers and swerved aside into a thicket and watched a dozen men ride by, and then we dismounted and crept through the trees to see how many enemy were in the camp.

There were perhaps a hundred and fifty Danes in a small pasture. The first fires were being lit, suggesting they planned to spend the night where they were. "All scouting parties," Pyrlig suggested.

"Confident bastards," I said. These men had been sent ahead to explore the hills, and they felt safe to camp in the open countryside, sure that no Saxon would attack them. And they were right. The West Saxon army was a long way south and we had no war band in the area, and so the Danes would have a quiet night and, in the morning, their scouts would ride again to watch Alfred's movements.

"But if they're here," Pyrlig suggested, "then it means Guthrum is following them."

"Maybe," I said. Or perhaps Guthrum was marching well to the east or west and had sent these men to make sure that Alfred was ignorant of his movements.

"We should go back," Pyrlig said. "Be dark soon."

But I had heard voices and I held up a hand to silence him, and then went to my right, keeping to the places where the undergrowth was thickest, and heard what I thought I had heard. English. "They've got Saxons here," I said.

"Wulfhere's men?"

Which made sense. We were in Wiltunscir and Wulfhere's men would know this country, and who better to guide the Danes as they watched Alfred?

The Saxons were coming into the wood and we stayed behind some hawthorn bushes until we heard the sound of axes. They were cutting firewood. There seemed to be about a dozen of them. Most of the men who followed Wulfhere would probably be reluctant to fight Alfred, but some would have embraced their ealdorman's new cause and doubtless those were the men who had been dispatched to guide the Danish scouting parties. Wulfhere would only have sent men he could trust, fearing that less loyal men would desert to Alfred or just run away, so these Saxons were probably from the ealdorman's household troops, the warriors who would profit most from being on the winner's side in the war between the Danes and the West Saxons.

"We should get back to Alfred before it's dark," Pyrlig whispered.

But just then a voice sounded close and petulant. "I will go tomorrow," the voice said.

"You won't, lord," a man answered. There was the sound of splashing and I realized one of the two men had come to the bushes for a piss and the other had followed him. "You'll go nowhere tomorrow," the second man went on. "You'll stay here."

"I just want to see them!" the petulant voice pleaded.

"You'll see them soon enough. But not tomorrow. You'll stay here with the guards."

"You can't make me."

"I can do what I like with you, lord. You might

command here, but you take my orders all the same." The man's voice was hard and deep. "And my orders are that you're staying here."

"I'll go if I want," the first voice insisted weakly and was ignored.

Very slowly, so that the blade made no noise against the scabbard's throat, I drew Serpent-Breath. Pyrlig watched me, puzzled. "Walk away," I whispered to him, "and make some noise." He frowned in puzzlement at that, but I jerked my head and he trusted me. He stood and walked toward our horses, whistling softly, and immediately the two men followed. The one with the deep voice led. He was an old warrior, scar-faced and bulky. "You!" he shouted. "Stop!" And just then I stepped out from behind the hawthorn and swung Serpent-Breath once and her blade cut under his beard and into his throat, and cut so deep that I felt her scrape against his spine and the blood, sudden and bright in the spring dusk, sprayed across the leaf mold. The man went down like a felled ox. The second man, the petulant man, was following close behind and he was too astonished and much too scared to run away and so I seized his arm and pulled him down behind the bushes.

"You can't," he began, and I placed the flat of

Serpent-Breath's bloody blade against his mouth so that he whimpered with terror.

"Not a sound," I said to him, "or you're dead." Pyrlig came back then, sword drawn.

Pyrlig looked at the dead man whose breeches were still untied. He stooped to him and made the sign of the cross on his forehead. The man's death had been quick, and the capture of his companion had been quiet, and none of the woodcutters seemed to have taken alarm. Their axes went on thumping, the echoes rattling in the trees. "We're taking this one back to Alfred," I told Pyrlig. Then I moved Serpent-Breath to my captive's throat. "Make one sound," I said, pressing the blade into his skin, "and I'll gut you from your overused gullet to your overused crotch. Do you understand?"

He nodded.

"Because I'm doing you the favor I owe you," I explained, and smiled nicely.

Because my captive was Æthelwold, Alfred's nephew and the would-be king of the West Saxons.

The man I had killed was named Osbergh and he had been the commander of Wulfhere's household troops. His job on the day of his death was to make certain Æthelwold got into no trouble.

Æthelwold had a talent for misfortune. By rights he should have been the king of Wessex, though I daresay he would have been the last king for he was impetuous and foolish, and the twin solaces for having lost the throne to his uncle Alfred were ale and women. Yet he had ever wanted to be a warrior. Alfred had denied him the chance, for he dared not let Æthelwold make a name for himself on the battlefield. Æthelwold, the true king, had to be kept foolish so that no man saw in him a rival for Alfred's throne. It would have been far easier to have killed Æthelwold, but Alfred was sentimental about family. Or perhaps it was his Christian conscience. But for whatever reason, Æthelwold had been allowed to live and had rewarded his uncle's mercy by constantly making a fool of himself.

But in these last months he had been released from Alfred's leash and his thwarted ambition had been given encouragement. He dressed in mail and carried swords. He was a startling-looking man, handsome and tall, and he looked the part of the warrior, though he had no warrior's soul. He had pissed himself when I put Serpent-

Breath to his throat, and now that he was my captive he showed no defiance. He was submissive, frightened, and glad to be led.

He told us how he had pestered Wulfhere to be allowed to fight, and when Osbergh had brought a score of men to guide the Danes in the hills, he had been given notional charge of them. "Wulfhere said I was in command," Æthelwold said sullenly, "but I still had to obey Osbergh."

"Wulfhere was a damned fool to let you go so far from him," I said.

"I think he was tired of me," Æthelwold admitted.

"Tired of you? You were humping his woman?"

"She's only a servant! But I wanted to join the scouting parties, and Wulfhere said I could learn a lot from Osbergh."

"You've just learned never to piss into a hawthorn bush," I said, "and that's worth knowing."

Æthelwold was riding Pyrlig's horse and the Welsh priest was leading the beast by its reins. I had tied Æthelwold's hands. There was still a hint of light in the western sky, just enough to make our journey down the smaller river easy. I explained to Pyrlig who Æthelwold was, and the priest grinned up at him. "So you're a prince of Wessex, eh?"

"I should be king," Æthelwold said sullenly.

"No you shouldn't," I said.

"My father was! And Guthrum promised to crown me."

"And if you believed him," I said, "you're a damned fool. You'd be king as long as he needed you, then you'd be dead."

"Now Alfred will kill me," he said miserably.

"He ought to," I said, "but I owe you a favor."

"You think you can persuade him to let me live?" he asked eagerly.

"You'll do the persuading," I said. "You'll kneel to him, and you're going to say that you've been waiting for a chance to escape the Danes, and at last you succeeded, and you got away, found us, and have come to offer him your sword."

Æthelwold just stared at me.

"I owe you a favor," I explained, "and so I'm giving you life. I'll untie your hands, you go to Alfred, and you say you're joining him because that's what you've wanted to do ever since Christmas. You understand that?"

Æthelwold frowned. "But he hates me!"

"Of course he does," I agreed, "but if you kneel to him and swear you never broke your allegiance to him, then what can he do? He'll embrace you, reward you, and be proud of you."

"Truly?"

"So long as you tell him where the Danes are," Pyrlig put in.

"I can do that," Æthelwold said. "They're coming south from Cippanhamm. They marched this morning."

"How many?"

"Five thousand."

"Coming here?"

"They're going to wherever Alfred is. They reckon they'll have a chance to destroy him, and after that it's just a summer of women and silver." He said the last three words plaintively and I knew he had been relishing the prospect of plundering Wessex. "So how many men does Alfred have?" he asked.

"Three thousand," I said.

"Sweet Jesus," he said fearfully.

"You always wanted to be a warrior," I said, "and what name can you make for yourself fighting a smaller army?"

"Jesus Christ."

The last of the light went. There was no

moon, but by keeping the river on our left we knew we could not get lost and after a while we saw the glow of firelight showing over the loom of the hills and knew we were seeing Alfred's en-campment. I twisted in the saddle then and thought I saw another such glow far to the north. Guthrum's army.

"If you let me go," Æthelwold asked sulkily, "what's to stop me going back to Guthrum?"

"Absolutely nothing," I said, "except the cer-tainty that I'll hunt you down and kill you."

He thought about that for a short while. "You're sure my uncle will welcome me?"

Pyrlig answered for me. "With open arms!" he said. "It will be like the return of the prodigal son. You'll be welcomed by slaughtered calves and psalms of rejoicing. Just tell Alfred what you told us, about Guthrum marching toward us."

We reached the Wilig and the going was easy now, for the light of the campfires was much brighter. I cut Æthelwold free at the edge of the encampment, then gave him back his swords. He carried two, as I did, a long one and a short saxe. "Well, my prince," I said, "time to grovel, eh?"

We found Alfred at the camp's center. There was no pomp here. We did not have the animals to drag wagons loaded with tents or furniture, so

Alfred was seated on a spread cloak between two fires. He looked dispirited and later I learned that he had assembled the army in the twilight and made them a speech, but the speech, even Beocca admitted, had been less than successful. "It was more a sermon than a speech," Beocca told me glumly. Alfred had invoked God, spoken of Saint Augustine's doctrine of a righteous war, and talked about Boethius and King David, and the words had flown over the heads of the tired, hungry troops. Now Alfred sat with the leading men of the army, all of them eating stale hard bread and smoked eel. Father Adelbert, the priest who had accompanied us to Cippan-hamm, was playing a lament on a small harp. A bad choice of music, I thought. Then Alfred saw me and waved Adelbert to silence. "You have news?" he asked.

For answer I stood aside and bowed to Æthel-wold, gesturing him toward the king. "Lord," I said to Alfred, "I bring you your nephew."

Alfred stood. He was taken aback, especially as Æthelwold was plainly no prisoner for he wore his swords. Æthelwold looked good; indeed, he looked more like a king than Alfred. He was well made and handsome, while Alfred was much too thin and his face was so haggard that he looked many years older than his twenty-nine years. And of the two it was Æthelwold who knew how to behave at that moment. He un-buckled his swords and threw them with a great clatter at his uncle's feet. Then he went to his knees and clasped his hands and looked up into the king's face. "I have found you!" he said with what sounded like utter joy and conviction.

Alfred, bemused, did not know what to say, so I stepped forward. "We discovered him, lord," I said, "in the hills. He was searching for you."

"I escaped Guthrum," Æthelwold said. "God be praised, I escaped the pagan." He pushed his swords to Alfred's feet. "My blades are yours, lord king."

This extravagant display of loyalty gave Alfred no choice except to raise his nephew and em-brace him. The men around the fires applauded. Then Æthelwold gave his news, which was use-ful enough. Guthrum was on the march and Svein of the White Horse came with him. They knew where Alfred was and so they came, five thousand strong, to give him battle in the hills of Wiltunscir.

"When will they get here?" Alfred wanted to know.

"They should reach these hills tomorrow, lord," Æthelwold said.

So Æthelwold was seated beside the king and given water to drink, which was hardly a fit welcome for a prodigal prince and caused him to throw me a wry glance, and it was then that I saw Harald, shire reeve of Defnascir, among the king's companions. "You're here?" I asked, surprised.

"With five hundred men," he said proudly.

We had expected no men from either Defnascir or Thornsæta, but Harald, the shire reeve, had brought four hundred of his own fyrd and a hundred more from Thornsæta. "There's enough men left to protect the coast against the pagan fleet," he said, "and Odda insisted we help defeat Guthrum."

"How is Mildrith?"

"She prays for her son," Harald said, "and for all of us."

There were prayers after the meal. There were always prayers when Alfred was around, and I tried to escape them, but Pyrlig made me stay. "The king wants to talk with you," he said.

So I waited while Bishop Alewold droned, and afterward Alfred wanted to know whether Æthelwold had truly run away from the Danes.

"That's what he told me, lord," I said, "and I can only say we found him."

"He didn't run from us," Pyrlig offered, "and he could have run."

"So there's good in the boy," Alfred said.

"God be praised for that," Pyrlig said.

Alfred paused, gazing down into the glowing embers of a camp fire. "I spoke to the army tonight," he told us.

"I heard you did, lord," I said.

He looked up at me sharply. "What did you hear?"

"That you preached to them, lord."

He flinched at that, then seemed to accept the criticism. "What do they want to hear?" he asked.

"They want to hear," Pyrlig answered, "that you are ready to die for them."

"Die?"

"Men follow, kings lead," Pyrlig said. Alfred waited. "They don't care about Saint Augustine," Pyrlig went on. "They only care that their women and children are safe, that their lands are safe, and that they'll have a future of their own. They want to know that they'll win. They want to know the Danes are going to die. They want to hear that they'll be rich on plunder."

"Greed, revenge, and selfishness?" Alfred asked.

"If you had an army of angels, lord," Pyrlig went on, "then a rousing speech about God and Saint Augustine would doubtless fire their ardor, but you have to fight with mere men, and there's nothing quite like greed, revenge, and selfishness to inspire mortals."

Alfred frowned at that advice, but did not argue with it. "So I can trust my nephew?" he asked me.

"I don't know that you can trust him," I said, "but nor can Guthrum. And Æthelwold did seek you out, lord, so be content with that."

"I shall, I shall." He bade us good night, going to his hard bed.

The fires in the valley were dying. "Why didn't you tell Alfred the truth about Æthelwold?" I asked Pyrlig.

"I thought I would trust your judgment," he said.

"You're a good man."

"And that constantly astonishes me."

I went to find Iseult, then slept.

Next day the whole of the northern sky was dark with cloud, while over our army, and above the hills, was sunlight.

The West Saxon army, now almost three and

a half thousand strong, marched up the Wilig, then followed the smaller river that Pyrlig and I had explored the previous evening. We could see the Danish scouts on the hills and knew they would be sending messengers back to Guthrum.

I led fifty men to one of the hilltops. We were all mounted, all armed, all with shields and helmets, and we rode ready to fight, but the Danish scouts yielded the ground. There were only a dozen of them and they rode off the hill long before we reached the summit where a host of blue butterflies flickered above the springy turf. I gazed northward at the ominous dark sky and watched a sparrowhawk stoop. Down the bird went, and I followed its plunging fall and suddenly saw, beneath the folded wings and reaching claws, our enemy.

Guthrum's army was coming south.

The fear came then. The shield wall is a terrible place. It is where a warrior makes his reputation, and reputation is dear to us. Reputation is honor, but to gain that honor a man must stand in the shield wall where death runs rampant. I had been in the shield wall at Cynuit and I knew the smell of death, the stink of it, the uncertainty of survival, the horror of the axes and swords and spears, and I feared it. And it was coming.

I could see it coming, for in the lowlands north of the hills, in the green ground stretching long and level toward distant Cippanhamm, was an army. The great army, the Danes called it, the pagan warriors of Guthrum and Svein, the wild horde of wild men from beyond the sea.

They were a dark smear on the landscape. They were coming through the fields, band after band of horsemen, spread across the country, and because their leading men were only just emerging into the sunlight, it seemed as if their horde sprang from the shadowlands. Spears and helmets and mail and metal reflected the light, a myriad glints of broken sunlight that spread and multiplied as yet more men came from beneath the clouds. They were nearly all mounted.

"Jesus, Mary, and Joseph," Leofric said.

Steapa said nothing. He just glowered at them.

Osric, the shire reeve of Wiltunscir, made the sign of the cross. "Someone has to tell Alfred," he said.

"I'll go," Father Pyrlig offered.

"Tell him the pagans have crossed the Afen," Osric said. "Tell him they're heading toward"— he paused, trying to judge where the horde was going—"Ethandun," he finally said.

"Ethandun." Pyrlig repeated the name.

"And remind him there's a fort of the old people there," Osric said. This was his shire, his country, and he knew its hills and fields, and he sounded grim, doubtless wondering what would happen if the Danes found the old fortress and occupied it. "God help us," Osric said. "They'll be in the hills tomorrow morning, tell him."

"Tomorrow morning, at Ethandun," Pyrlig said, then turned his horse and spurred away.

"Where's the fort?" I asked.

Osric pointed. "You can see it." From this distance the ancient fastness looked like nothing more than green wrinkles on a far hilltop. All across Wessex there were such forts with their massive earthen walls, and this one was built at the top of the escarpment that climbed from the lowlands, a place guarding the sudden edge of the chalk downs. "Some of the bastards will get up there tonight," Osric said, "but most won't make it till morning. Let's just hope they ignore the fort."

We had all thought that Alfred would find a place where Guthrum must attack him, a slope made for defense, a place where our smaller numbers would be helped by the difficult ground, but the sight of that distant fort was a reminder that Guthrum might adopt the same tactics. He might find a place where it would be hard for us to attack him, and Alfred would have a grim choice then. To attack would be to court disaster, while to retreat would guarantee it. Our food would be exhausted in a day or two, and if we tried to withdraw south through the hills Guthrum would release a horde of horsemen against us. And even if the army of Wessex escaped unscathed, it would be a beaten army. If Alfred brought the fyrd together, then marched it away from the enemy, men would take it for a defeat and begin to slip away to protect their homes. We had to fight, because to decline battle was a defeat.

The army camped that evening to the north of the woods where I had found Æthelwold. He was in the king's entourage now and went with Alfred and his war leaders to the hilltop to watch the Danish army as it closed on the hills. Alfred looked a long time. "How far away are they?" he asked.

"From here," Osric answered, "four miles. From your army, six."

"Tomorrow, then," Alfred said, making the sign of the cross. The northern clouds were spreading, darkening the evening, but the slanting light reflected from spears and axes at the old people's fort. It seemed Guthrum had not ignored the place after all.

We went back down to the encampment to find yet more men arriving. Not many now, just small bands, but still they came, and one such band, travel weary and dusty, was mounted on horses and all sixteen men had chain mail and good helmets.

They were Mercians and they had ridden far to the east, crossed the Temes, then looped through Wessex, ever avoiding Danes, and so come to help Alfred. Their leader was a short young man, wide in the chest, round-faced, and with a pugnacious expression. He knelt to Alfred, then grinned at me, and I recognized my cousin, Æthelred.

My mother was a Mercian, though I never knew her, and her brother Æthelred was a power in the southern part of that country and I had spent a short time in his hall when I first fled from Northumbria. Back then I had quarreled with my cousin, called Æthelred like his father, but he seemed to have forgotten our youthful enmity and embraced me instead. The top of his head just came up to my collarbone. "We've come to fight," he told me, his voice muffled by my chest.

"You'll have a fight," I promised him.

"Lord." He let go of me and turned back to Alfred. "My father would have sent more men, but he must protect his land."

"He must," Alfred said.

"But he sent the best he has," Æthelred went on. He was young and bumptious, a little strut of a youth, but his confidence pleased Alfred, as did the gleaming silver crucifix hanging over Æthelred's chain mail. "Allow me to present Tatwine," my cousin went on, " the chief of my father's household troops."

I remembered Tatwine, a barrel of a man and a real fighter, whose arms were smothered in blotchy black marks, each made with a needle and ink and representing a man killed in battle. He gave me a crooked smile. "Still alive, lord?"

"Still alive, Tatwine."

"Be good to fight alongside you again."

"Good to have you here," I said, and it was. Few men are natural-born warriors, and a man like Tatwine was worth a dozen others.

Alfred had ordered the army to assemble again. He did it partly so the men could see their own numbers and take heart from that, and he did it, too, because he knew his speech the previous night had left men confused and uninspired. He would try again. "I wish he wouldn't," Leofric grumbled. "He can make sermons, but he can't make speeches."

We gathered at the foot of a small hill. The light was fading. Alfred had planted his two banners, the dragon and the cross, on the summit of the hill, but there was small wind so the flags stirred rather than flew. He climbed to stand between them. He was alone, dressed in a mail coat over which he wore the faded blue cloak. A group of priests began to follow him, but he waved them back to the hill's foot. Then he just stared at us huddled in the meadow beneath him and for a time he said nothing and I sensed the discomfort in the ranks. They wanted fire put into their souls and expected holy water instead.

"Tomorrow!" he said suddenly. His voice was high, but it carried clearly enough. "Tomorrow we fight! Tomorrow! The Feast of Saint John the Apostle!"

"Oh God," Leofric grumbled next to me, "up to our arseholes in more saints."

"John the Apostle was condemned to death!" Alfred said. "He was condemned to be boiled in oil! Yet he survived the ordeal! He was plunged into the boiling oil and he lived! He came from the cauldron a stronger man! And we shall do the same." He paused, watching us, and no one responded. We all just gazed at him, and he must have known that his homily on Saint John was not working, for he made an abrupt gesture with his right hand as if he was sweeping all the saints aside. "And tomorrow," he went on, "is also a day for warriors. A day to kill your enemies. A day to make the pagans wish they had never heard of Wessex!"

He paused again, and this time there were some murmurs of agreement.

"This is our land! We fight for our homes! For our wives! For our children! We fight for Wessex!"

"We do," someone shouted.

"And not just Wessex!" Alfred's voice was stronger now. "We have men from Mercia, men from Northumbria, men from East Anglia!" I knew of none from East Anglia and only Beocca and I were from Northumbria, but no one seemed to care. "We are the men of England," Alfred shouted, "and we fight for all Saxons."

Silence again. The men liked what they heard, but the idea of England was in Alfred's head, not theirs. He had a dream of one country, but it was too big a dream for the army in the meadow. "And why are the Danes here?" Alfred asked. "They want your wives for their pleasure, your children for their slaves, and your homes for their own, but they do not know us!" He said the last six words slowly, spacing them out, shouting each one distinctly. "They do not know our swords," he went on. "They do not know our axes, our spears, our fierceness! Tomorrow we teach them! Tomorrow we kill them! Tomorrow we hack them into pieces! Tomorrow we make the ground red with their blood and make them whimper! Tomorrow we shall make them call for our mercy!"

"None!" a man called out.

"No mercy!" Alfred shouted, and I knew he did not mean it. He would have offered every mercy to the Danes, he would have offered them the love of God and tried to reason with them, but in the last few minutes he had at last learned how to talk to warriors.

"Tomorrow," he shouted, "you do not fight for me! I fight for you! I fight for Wessex! I fight for your wives, for your children, and your homes! Tomorrow we fight and, I swear to you on my father's grave and on my children's lives, tomorrow we shall win!"

And that started the cheering. It was not, in all honesty, a great battle speech, but it was the best Alfred ever gave and it worked. Men stamped the ground and those who carried their shields beat them with swords or spears so that the twilight was filled with a rhythmic thumping as men shouted, "No mercy!" The sound echoed back from the hills. "No mercy, no mercy."

We were ready. And the Danes were ready.

That night it clouded over. The stars vanished one by one, and the thin moon was swallowed in the darkness. Sleep came hard. I sat with Iseult who was cleaning my mail while I sharpened both swords. "You will win tomorrow," Iseult said in a small voice.

"You dreamed that?"

She shook her head. "The dreams don't come since I was baptized."

"So you made it up?"

"I have to believe it," she said.

The stone scraped down the blades. All around me other men were sharpening weapons. "When this is over," I said, "you and I will go away. We shall make a house."

"When this is over," she said, "you will go north. Ever north. Back to your home."

"Then you'll come with me."

"Perhaps." She heaved the mail coat to start on a new patch, scrubbing it with a scrap of fleece to make the links shine. "I can't see my own future. It's all dark."

"You shall be the lady of Bebbanburg," I said, "and I shall dress you in furs and crown you with bright silver."

She smiled, but I saw there were tears on her face. I took it for fear. There was plenty of that in the camp that night, especially when men noticed the glow of light showing where the Danes had lit their fires in the nearby hills. We did sleep, but I was woken long before dawn by a small rain. No one slept through it, but all stirred and pulled on war gear.

We marched in the gray light. The rain came and went, spiteful and sharp, but always at our backs. Most of us walked, using our few horses to carry shields. Osric and his men went first, for they knew the shire. Alfred had said that the men of Wiltunscir would be on the right of the battle line, and with them would be the men of Suth Seaxa. Alfred was next, leading his bodyguard that was made of all the men who had come to him in Æthelingæg, and with him was Harald and the men of Defnascir and Thornsæta. Burgweard and the men from Hamptonscir would also fight with Alfred, as would my cousin Æthelred from Mercia, while on the left would be the strong fyrd of Sumorsæte under Wiglaf. Three and a half thousand men. The women came with us. Some carried their men's weapons; others had their own.

No one spoke much. It was cold that morning, and the rain made the grass slippery. Men were hungry and tired. We were all fearful.

Alfred had told me to collect fifty or so men to lead, but Leofric was unwilling to lose that many from his ranks, so I took them from Burgweard instead. I took the men who had fought with me in the **Heahengel** when she had been the **Fyrdraca**, and twenty-six of those men had come from Hamtun. Steapa was with us, for he had taken a perverse liking to me, and I had Father Pyrlig who was dressed as a warrior, not a priest. We were fewer than thirty men, but as we climbed past a green-mounded grave of the old folk, Æthelwold came to us. "Alfred said I could fight with you," he said.

"He said that?"

"He said I'm not to leave your side."

I smiled at that. If I wanted a man by my side it would be Eadric or Cenwulf, Steapa or Pyrlig, men I could trust to keep their shields firm. "You're not to leave my back," I said to Æthelwold.

"Your back?"

"And in the shield wall you stay close behind me. Ready to take my place."

He took that as an insult. "I want to be in the front," he insisted.

"Have you ever fought in a shield wall?"

"You know I haven't."

"Then you don't want to be in the front," I said, "and, besides, if Alfred dies, who'll be king?"

"Ah." He half smiled. "So I stay behind you?"

"You stay behind me."

Iseult and Hild were leading my horse. "If we lose," I told them, "you both get in the saddle and ride."

"Ride where?"

"Just ride. Take the money," I said. My silver and treasures, all I possessed, were in the horse's saddlebags. "Take it and ride with Hild."

Hild smiled at that. She looked pale and her fair hair was plastered tight to her scalp by the rain. She had no hat, and was dressed in a white shift belted with rope. I was surprised that she had come with the army, thinking she would have preferred to find a convent, but she had insisted on coming. "I want to see them dead," she told me flatly. "And the one called Erik I want to kill myself." She patted the long, narrow-bladed knife hanging from her belt.

"Erik is the one who—" I began, then hesitated.

"The one who whored me," she said.

"So he wasn't the one we killed that night?"

She shook her head. "That was the steersman of Erik's ship. But I'll find Erik, and I won't go back to a convent till I see him screaming in his own blood."

"Full of hate, she is," Father Pyrlig told me as we followed Hild and Iseult up the hill.

"Isn't that bad in a Christian?"

Pyrlig laughed. "Being alive is bad in a Christian! We say people are saints if they're good, but how few of us become saints? We're all bad! Some of us just try to be good."

I glanced at Hild. "She's wasted as a nun," I said.

"You do like them thin, don't you?" Pyrlig said, amused. "Now I like them meaty as well-fed heifers! Give me a nice dark Briton with hips like a pair of ale barrels and I'm a happy priest. Poor Hild. Thin as a ray of sunlight, she is, but I pity a Dane who crosses her path today."

Osric's scouts came back to Alfred. They had ridden ahead and seen the Danes. The enemy was waiting, they reported, at the edge of the escarpment, where the hills were highest and where the old people's fort stood. Their banners, the scouts said, were numberless. They had also seen Danish scouts, so Guthrum and Svein must have known we were coming.

On we went, ever higher, climbing into the chalk downs, and the rain stopped, but no sun appeared for the whole sky was a turmoil of gray and black. The wind gusted from the west. We passed whole rows of graves from the ancient days and I wondered if they contained warriors who had gone to battle as we did, and I wondered if in the thousands of years to come other men would toil up these hills with swords and shields. Of warfare there is no end, and I looked into the dark sky for a sign from Thor or Odin, hoping to see a raven fly, but there were no birds. Just clouds.

And then I saw Osric's men slanting away to the right. We were in a fold of the hills and they were going around the right-hand hill and, as we reached the saddle between the two low slopes, I saw the level ground and there, ahead of me, was the enemy.

I love the Danes. There are no better men to fight with, drink with, laugh with, or live with. Yet that day, as on so many others of my life, they were the enemy and they waited for me in a gigantic shield wall arrayed across the down. There were thousands of Danes, spear Danes and sword Danes, Danes who had come to make this land theirs, and we had come to keep it ours. "God give us strength," Father Pyrlig said when he saw the enemy who had begun shouting as we appeared. They clashed spears and swords against limewood shields, making a thunder on the hilltop. The ancient fort was the right wing of their army, and men were thick on the green turf walls. Many of those men had black shields and above them was a black banner, so that was where Guthrum was, while their left wing, which faced our right, was strung out on the open down and it was there I could see a triangular banner, supported by a small cross staff, showing a white horse. So Svein commanded their left, while to the Danish right, our left, the escarpment dropped to the river plains. It was a steep drop, a tumbling hill. We could not hope to outflank the Danes on that side, for no one could fight on such a slope. We had to attack straight ahead, directly into the shield wall and against the earthen ramparts and onto the spears and the swords and the war axes of our outnumbering enemy.

I looked for Ragnar's eagle-wing banner and thought I saw it in the fort, but it was hard to be certain, for every crew of Danes flew their standard, and the small flags were crowded together and the rain had started to fall again, obscuring the symbols, but off to my right, outside the fort and close to the bigger standard of the white horse, was a Saxon flag. It was a green flag with an eagle and a cross, which meant Wulfhere was there with that part of the Wiltunscir fyrd that had followed him. There were other Saxon banners in the enemy horde. Not many, maybe a score, and I guessed that the Danes had brought men from Mercia to fight for them. All the Saxon banners were in the open ground; none was inside the fort.

We were still a long way apart, much farther than a man could shoot an arrow, and none of us could hear what the Danes were shouting. Osric's men were making our right wing as Wiglaf led his Sumorsæte fyrd off to the left. We were making a line to oppose their line, but ours would inevitably be shorter. The odds were not quite two Danes to one Saxon, but it was close. "God help us," Pyrlig said, touching his crucifix.

Alfred summoned his commanders, gathering them under the rain-sodden banner of the dragon. The Danish thunder went on, the clattering of thousands of weapons against shields, as the king asked his army's leaders for advice.

Arnulf of Suth Seaxa, a wiry man with a short beard and a perpetual scowl, advised attack. "Just attack," he said, waving at the fort. "We'll lose some men on the walls, but we'll lose men anyway."

"We'll lose a lot of men," my cousin Æthelred warned. He only led a small band, but his status as the son of a Mercian ealdorman meant he had to be included in Alfred's council of war.

"We do better defending," Osric growled. "Give a man land to defend and he stands, so let the bastards come to us." Harald nodded agreement.

Alfred cast a courteous eye on Wiglaf of Sumorsæte who looked surprised to be consulted. "We shall do our duty, lord," he said, "do our duty whatever you decide." Leofric and I were present, but the king did not invite our opinion so we kept silent.

Alfred gazed at the enemy, then turned back to us. "In my experience," he said, "the enemy expect something of us." He spoke pedantically, in the same tone he used when he was discussing theology with his priests. "They want us to do certain things. What are those things?"

Wiglaf shrugged, while Arnulf and Osric looked bemused. They had both expected something fiercer from Alfred. Battle, for most of us, was a hammering rage, nothing clever, a killing orgy, but Alfred saw it as competition of wisdom, or perhaps as a game of tafl that took cleverness to win. That, I am sure, was how he saw our two armies, as tafl pieces on their checkered board.

"Well?" he asked.

"They expect us to attack!" Osric said uncertainly.

"They expect us to attack Wulfhere," I said.

Alfred rewarded me with a smile. "Why Wulfhere?"

"Because he's a traitor and a bastard and a piece of whore-begotten goat shit," I said.

"Because we do not believe," Alfred corrected me, "that Wulfhere's men will fight with the same passion as the Danes. And we're right, they won't. His men will pull back from killing fellow Saxons."

"But Svein is there," I said.

"Which tells us?" he asked.

The others stared at him. He knew the answer, but he could never resist being a teacher, and so he waited for a response. "It tells us," I supplied it again, "that they want us to attack their left, but they don't want their left to break. That's why Svein is there. He'll hold us and they'll launch an assault out of the fort to hit the flank of our attack. That breaks the right of our army and then the whole damned lot come and kill the rest of us."

Alfred did not respond, but looked worried, suggesting that he agreed with me. The other men turned and looked at the Danes, as if some magical answer might suggest itself, but none did.

"So do as Lord Arnulf suggests," Harald said. "Attack the fort."

"The walls are steep," Wiglaf warned. The Ealdorman of Sumorsæte was a man of sunny disposition, frequent laughter, and casual generosity, but now, with his men arrayed opposite the fort's green ramparts, he was downcast.

"Guthrum would dearly like us to assail the fort," the king observed.

This caused some confusion for it seemed, according to Alfred, that the Danes wanted us to attack their right just as much as they wanted us to attack their left. The Danes, meanwhile, were jeering us for not attacking at all. One or two ran toward our lines and screamed insults, and their whole shield wall was still banging weapons in a steady, threatening rhythm. The rain made the colors of the shields darker. The colors were black and red and blue and brown and dirty yellow.

"So what do we do?" Æthelred asked plaintively.

There was silence and I realized that Alfred, though he understood the problem, had no answer to it. Guthrum wanted us to attack and probably did not care whether we went against Svein's seasoned warriors on the left of the enemy line or against the steep, slippery ditches in front of the fort's walls. And Guthrum must also have known that we dared not retreat because his men would pursue and break us like a horde of wolves savaging a frightened flock.

"Attack their left," I said.

Alfred nodded as though he had already come to that conclusion. "And?" he invited me.

"Attack it with every man we've got," I said. There were probably two thousand men outside the fort and at least half of those were Saxons. I thought we should assault them in one violent rush, and overwhelm them by numbers. Then the weakness of the Danish position would be revealed, for they were on the very lip of the escarpment and once they were forced over the edge they had nowhere to go but down the long, precipitous slope. We could have destroyed those two thousand men, then re-formed our lines for the harder task of attacking the three thousand inside the fort.

"Employ all our men?" Alfred asked. "But then Guthrum will attack our flank with every man he has."

"Guthrum won't," I said. "He'll send some men to attack our flank, but he'll keep most of his troops inside the fort. He's cautious. He won't abandon the fort, and he won't risk much to save Svein. They don't like each other."

Alfred thought about it, but I could see he did not like the gamble. He feared that while we attacked Svein the other Danes would charge from the fort and overwhelm our left. I still think he should have taken my advice, but fate is inexorable and he decided to imitate Guthrum by being cautious. "We will attack on our right," he said, "and drive off Wulfhere's men, but we must be ready for their counterstroke and so our left stays where it is."

So it was decided. Osric and Arnulf, with the men of Wiltunscir and Suth Seaxa, would give battle to Svein and Wulfhere on the open land to the east of the fort, but we suspected that some Danes would come from behind the ramparts to attack Osric's flank and so Alfred would take his own bodyguard to be a bulwark against that assault. Wigulf, meanwhile, would stay where he was, which meant a third of our men were doing nothing. "If we can defeat them," Alfred said, "then their remnant will retreat into the fort and we can besiege it. They have no water there, do they?"

"None," Osric confirmed.

"So they're trapped," Alfred said as though the whole problem was neatly resolved and the battle as good as won. He turned to Bishop Alewold. "A prayer, bishop, if you would be so kind."

Alewold prayed, the rain fell, the Danes went

on jeering, and I knew the awful moment, the clash of the shield walls, was close. I touched Thor's hammer, then Serpent-Breath's hilt, for death was stalking us. God help me, I thought, touching the hammer again, Thor help us all, for I did not think we could win.

THIRTEEN

The Danes made their battle thunder and we prayed. Alewold harangued God for a long time, mostly begging him to send angels with flaming swords, and those angels would have been useful, though none appeared. It would be up to us to do the job.

We readied for battle. I took my shield and helmet from the horse that Iseult led, but first I teased out a thick hank of her black hair. "Trust me," I said to her, because she was nervous, and I used a small knife to cut the tress. I tied one end of the hair to Serpent-Breath's hilt and made a loop with the other end. Iseult watched. "Why?" she asked.

"I can put the loop over my wrist." I showed her. "Then I can't lose the sword. And your hair will bring me luck."

Bishop Alewold was angrily demanding that the women go back. Iseult stood on tiptoe to buckle my wolf-crested helmet in place. Then she pulled my head down and kissed me through the gap in the faceplate. "I shall pray for you," she said.

"So will I," Hild said.

"Pray to Odin and Thor," I urged them, then watched as they led the horse away. The women would hold the horses a quarter mile behind our shield wall and Alfred insisted they went that far back so that no man was tempted to make a sudden dash for a horse and gallop away.

It was time to make the shield wall, and that is a cumbersome business. Some men offer to be in the front rank, but most try to be behind, and Osric and his battle leaders were shoving and shouting as they tried to settle the men. "God is with us!" Alfred was shouting at them. He was still mounted and rode down Osric's slowly forming shield wall to encourage the fyrd. "God is with us!" he shouted again. "We cannot lose! God is with us!" The rain fell harder. Priests were walking down the lines offering blessings and adding to the rain by throwing handfuls of holy water at the shields. Osric's fyrd was mostly five ranks thick, and behind them was a scatter of men with spears. Their job, as the two sides met, was to hurl the spears over their comrades' heads, and the Danes would have similar spear-throwers readying their own weapons. "God is with us!" Alfred shouted. "He is on our side! Heaven watches over us! The holy saints pray for us! The angels guard us! God is with us!" His voice was already hoarse. Men touched amulets for luck, closed their eyes in silent prayer, and tugged at buckles. In the front rank they obsessively touched their shields against their neighbors' shields. The right-hand edge of every man's shield was supposed to overlap the next shield so that the Danes were confronted with a solid wall of iron-reinforced limewood. The Danes would make the same wall, but they were still jeering us, daring us to attack. A young man stumbled from the back of Osric's fyrd and vomited. Two dogs ran to eat the vomit. A spear-thrower was on his knees, shaking and praying.

Father Beocca stood beside Alfred's standards with his hands raised in prayer. I was in front of the standards with Steapa to my right and Pyrlig to my left. "Bring fire on them, oh most holy Lord!" Beocca wailed. "Bring fire on them and strike them down! Punish them for their iniquities." His eyes were closed tight and his face raised to the rain so that he did not see Alfred gallop back to us and push through our ranks. The king would stay mounted so he could see what happened, and Leofric and a dozen other men were also on horseback so that their shields could protect Alfred from thrown spears and axes.

"Forward!" Alfred shouted.

"Forward!" Leofric repeated the order because the king's voice was so hoarse.

No one moved. It was up to Osric and his men to begin the advance, but men are ever reluctant to go against an enemy shield wall. It helps to be drunk. I have been in battles where both sides struggled in a reeking daze of birch wine and ale, but we had little of either and our courage had to be summoned out of sober hearts and there was not much to be found on that cold wet morning.

"Forward!" Leofric shouted again, and this time Osric and his commanders took up the shout and the men of Wiltunscir shuffled a few paces forward and the Danish shields clattered into the wall and locked together and the sight of that **skjaldborg** checked the advance. That is what the Danes call their shield wall, the **skjaldborg** or shield fort. The Danes roared mockery, and two of their younger warriors strutted out of their line to taunt us and invite a duel. "Stay in the wall!" Leofric roared.

"Ignore them!" Osric shouted.

Horsemen rode from the fort, perhaps a hundred of them, and they trotted behind the **skjaldborg** that was formed of Svein's warriors and Wulfhere's Saxons. Svein joined the horsemen. I could see his white horse, the white cloak, and the white horsetail plume. The presence of the horsemen told me that Svein expected our line to break and he wanted to ride our fugitives down just as his riders had slaughtered Peredur's broken Britons at Dreyndynas. The Danes were full of confidence, and so they should have been, for they outnumbered us and they were all warriors, while our ranks were filled with men more used to the plow than the sword.

"Forward!" Osric shouted. His line quivered, but did not advance more than a yard.

Rain dripped from the rim of my helmet. It ran down inside the faceplate, worked itself inside my mail coat, and ran in shivers down my chest and belly.

"Strike them hard, lord!" Beocca shouted. "Slaughter them without mercy! Break them in pieces!"

Pyrlig was praying, at least I think he was praying, for he was speaking in his own tongue, but I heard the word **duw** repeated over and over and I knew, from Iseult, that **duw** was the Britons' word for god. Æthelwold was behind Pyrlig. He was supposed to be behind me, but Eadric had insisted on being at my back, so Æthelwold would protect Pyrlig instead. He was chattering incessantly, trying to cover his nervousness, and I turned on him. "Keep your shield up," I told him.

"I know, I know."

"You protect Pyrlig's head, understand?"

"I know!" He was irritated that I had given him the advice. "I know," he repeated petulantly.

""Forward! Forward!" Osric called. Like Alfred he was on horseback and he went up and down behind his line, sword drawn, and I thought he would jab the blade at his men to goad them onward. They went a few paces and the Danish shields came up again and the lime-wood made a knocking sound as the **skjaldborg** was made and once again our line faltered. Svein and his horsemen were now at the very far flank, but Osric had placed a group of picked warriors there, ready to guard the open end of his line.

"For God! For Wiltunscir!" Osric shouted. "Forward!"

Alfred's men were on the left of Osric's fyrd where we were bent slightly back, ready to receive the expected flank attack from the fort. We went forward readily enough, but then we were mostly warriors and knew we could not advance in front of Osric's more nervous troops. I almost stepped into a scrap of the ground where, astonishingly, three leverets lay low and quivering. I stared at them and hoped that the men behind me would avoid the little beasts and knew they would not. I do not know why hares leave their young in the open, but they do and there they lay, three sleek leverets in a hollow of the downs, doubtless the first things to die in that day of wind and rain.

"Shout at them!" Osric called. "Tell them they're bastards! Call them sons of whores! Say they're shit from the north! Shout at them!" He knew that was one way to get men moving. The Danes were screaming at us, calling us women, saying we had no courage, and no one in our ranks was shouting back, but Osric's men started now and the wet sky was filled with the noise of weapons banging on shields and men calling insults.

I had hung Serpent-Breath on my back. In the crush of battle a sword is easier to draw over the shoulder than from the hip, and the first stroke can then be a vicious downward hack. I carried Wasp-Sting in my right hand. Wasp-Sting was a saxe, a short sword, a stout blade for stabbing, and in the press of men heaving against an enemy shield wall a short sword can do more damage than a long blade. My shield, iron-rimmed, was held on my left forearm by two leather loops. The shield had a metal boss the size of a man's head, a weapon in itself. Steapa, to my right, had a long sword, not as long as the one with which he had fought me at Cippanhamm, but still a hefty blade, though in his big hand it looked almost puny. Pyrlig carried a boar spear, short and stout and with a wide blade. He was saying the same phrase over and over. "**Ein tad, yr hwn wyt yn y nefoedd, sancteiddier dy enw.**" I learned later it was the prayer Jesus had taught his disciples. Steapa was muttering that the Danes were bastards. "Bastards," he said, then, "God help me, bastards." He kept saying it. Over and over. "Bastards, God help me, bastards." My mouth was suddenly too dry to speak, and my stomach felt sour and my bowels loose.

"Forward! Forward!" Osric called and we shuffled on, shields touching, and we could see the enemies' faces now. We could see men's unkempt beards and yellow-toothed snarls, see their scarred cheeks, pocked skin, and broken noses. My faceplate meant I could only see directly ahead. Sometimes it is better to fight without a faceplate, to see the attacks coming from the side, but in the clash of shield walls a faceplate is useful. The helmet was lined with leather. I was sweating. Arrows flicked from the Danish line. They did not have many bowmen and the arrows were scattered, but we raised shields to protect our faces. None came near me, but we were bent back from the line to watch the fort's green walls that were rimmed with men, thick with sword Danes, and I could see Ragnar's eagle-wing banner there and I wondered what would happen if I found myself face-to-face with him. I could see the axes and spears and swords, the blades that sought our souls. Rain drummed on helmets and shields.

The line paused again. Osric's shield wall and Svein's **skjaldborg** were only twenty paces apart now and men could see their immediate foes, could see the face of the man they must kill or the man who would kill them. Both sides were screaming, spitting anger and insults, and the spear-throwers had their first missiles hefted.

"Keep close!" someone shouted.

"Shields touching!"

"God is with us!" Beocca called.

"Forward!" Another two paces, more of a shuffle forward than stepping.

"Bastards," Steapa said. "God help me, bastards."

"Now!" Osric screamed. "Now! Forward and kill them! Forward and kill them! Go! Go! Go!" And the men of Wiltunscir went. They let out a great war shout, as much to hearten themselves as to frighten the enemy, and suddenly, after so long, the shield wall went forward fast, men screaming, and the spears came over the Danish line and our own spears were hurled back and then came the clash, the real battle thunder as shield wall met **skjaldborg**. The shock of the collision shook our whole line so that even my troops, who were not yet engaged, staggered. I heard the first screams, the clangor of blades, the thump of metal driving into shield wood, the grunting of men, and then I saw the Danes coming over the green ramparts, a flood of Danes charging us, intent on hacking into the flank of our attack, but that was why Alfred had put us on the left of Osric's force.

"Shields!" Leofric roared.

I hoisted my shield, touched Steapa's and Pyrlig's shields, then crouched to receive the charge. Head down, body covered by wood, legs braced, Wasp-Sting ready. Behind us and to our right Osric's men fought. I could smell blood and shit. Those are the smells of battle. Then I forgot Osric's fight for the rain was in my face, and the Danes were coming at a run, no shield wall formed, just a frenzied charge intent on winning the battle in one furious assault. There were hundreds of them, and then our spear-throwers let their missiles go.

"Now!" I shouted, and we stepped one pace forward to meet the charge and my left arm was crushed into my chest as a Dane hit me, shield against shield, and he slammed an ax down and I rammed Wasp-Sting forward, past his shield, into his flank, and his ax buried itself in Eadric's shield that was above my head. I twisted Wasp-Sting's blade, pulled her free, and stabbed again. I could smell ale on the Dane's sour breath. His face was a grimace. He yanked his ax free. I stabbed again and twisted the saxe's tip into mail or bone, I could not tell which. "Your mother was a piece of pig shit," I told the Dane, and he screamed in rage and tried to bring the ax down onto my helmet, but I ducked and shoved forward, and Eadric protected me with his shield, and Wasp-Sting was red now, warm and sticky with blood, and I ripped her upward.

Steapa was screaming incoherently, his sword slashing left and right, and the Danes avoided him. My enemy stumbled, went down onto his knees, and I hit him with the shield boss, breaking his nose and teeth, then shoved Wasp-Sting into his bloody mouth. Another man immediately took his place, but Pyrlig buried his boar spear in the newcomer's belly.

"Shields!" I shouted, and Steapa and Pyrlig instinctively lined their shields with mine. I had no idea what happened elsewhere on the hilltop. I only knew what happened within Wasp-Sting's reach.

"Back one! Back one!" Pyrlig called, and we stepped back one pace so that the next Danes, taking the place of the men we had wounded or killed, would trip over the fallen bodies of their comrades, and then we stepped forward as they came so that we met them when they were off balance. That was how to do it, the way of the

warrior, and we in Alfred's immediate force were
his best soldiers. The Danes had charged us
wildly, not bothering to lock shields in the belief
that their fury alone would overwhelm us. They
had been drawn, too, by the sight of Alfred's
banners and the knowledge that should those
twin flags topple, then the battle was as good as
won, but their assault hit our shield wall like an
ocean wave striking a cliff, and it shattered there.
It left men on the turf and blood on the grass,
and now the Danes at last made a proper shield
wall and came at us more steadily.

I heard the enemy shields touching, saw the
Danes' wild eyes over the round rims, saw their
grimaces as they gathered their strength. Then
they shouted and came to kill us.

"Now!" I shouted and we thrust forward to
meet them.

The shield walls crashed together. Eadric was
at my back, pressing me forward, and the art of
fighting now was to keep a space between my
body and my shield with a strong left arm, and
then to stab under the shield with Wasp-Sting.
Eadric could fight over my shoulder with his
sword. I had space to my right for Steapa was
left-handed, which meant his shield was on his
right arm, and he kept moving it away from me

to give his long sword room to strike. That gap, no wider than a man's foot is long, was an invitation to the Danes, but they were scared of Steapa and none tried to burst through the small space. His height alone made him distinctive, and his skull-tight face made him fearsome. He was bellowing like a calf being gelded, half shriek and half belligerence, inviting the Danes to come and be killed. They refused. They had learned the danger of Pyrlig, Steapa, and me, and they were cautious. Elsewhere along Alfred's shield wall there were men dying and screaming, swords and axes clanging like bells, but in front of me the Danes hung back and merely jabbed with spears to keep us at bay. I shouted that they were cowards, but that did not goad them onto Wasp-Sting, and I glanced left and right and saw that all along Alfred's line we were holding them. Our shield wall was strong. All that practice in Æthelingæg was proving itself, and for the Danes the fight grew ever more difficult for they were attacking us, and to reach us they had to step over the bodies of their own dead and wounded. A man does not see where he treads in battle for he is watching the enemy, and some Danes stumbled, and others slipped on the rain-slicked grass, and when they were off balance we struck hard, spears and swords like snake tongues, making more bodies to trip the enemy.

We of Alfred's household troops were good. We were steady. We were beating the Danes, but behind us, in Osric's larger force, Wessex was dying.

Because Osric's shield wall unraveled.

Wulfhere's men did it. They did not break Osric's shield wall by fighting it, but by trying to join it. Few of them wanted to fight for the Danes and, now that the battle was joined, they shouted at their countrymen that they were no enemy and wanted to change sides, and the shield wall opened to let them through, and Svein's men went for the gaps like wildcats. One after the other those gaps widened as sword Danes burst through. They cut Wulfhere's men down from behind; they prized open Osric's ranks and spread death like a plague. Svein's Vikings were warriors among farmers, hawks among pigeons, and all of Alfred's right wing shattered. Arnulf saved the men of Suth Seaxa by leading them to the rear of our ranks, and they were safe enough there, but Osric's fyrd was broken, harried, and driven away east and south.

The rain had stopped and a cold damp wind

scoured the edge of the downs now. Alfred's men, reinforced by Arnulf's four hundred and a dozen or so of Osric's fugitives, stood alone as the Wiltunscir fyrd retreated. They were being driven away from us, and Svein and his horsemen were panicking them. The fyrd had been eight hundred strong, ranked firm, and now they were shattered into small groups that huddled together for protection and tried to fend off the galloping horsemen who thrust with their long spears. Bodies lay all across the turf. Some of Osric's men were wounded and crawled south as if there might be safety where the women and horses were gathered around a mounded grave of the old folk, but the horsemen turned and speared them, and the unmounted Danes were making new shield walls to attack the fugitives. We could do nothing to help, for we were still fighting Guthrum's men who had come from the fort and, though we were winning that fight, we could not turn our backs on the enemy. So we thrust and hacked and pushed, and slowly they went backward, and then they realized that they were dying man by man, and I heard the Danish shouts to go back to the fort, and we let them go. They retreated from us, walking backward, and when they saw we would not follow, they turned and ran to the green walls. They left a tide line of corpses, sixty or seventy Danes on the turf, and we had lost no more than twenty men. I took a silver chain off one corpse, two arm rings from another, and a fine bone-handled knife with a knob of amber in its hilt from a third.

"Back!" Alfred called.

It was not till we retreated to where we had begun the fight that I realized the disaster on our right. We had been the center of Alfred's army, but now we were its right wing, and what had been our strong right flank was splintered chaos. Many of Osric's men had retreated to where the women and horses waited, and they made a shield wall there, which served to protect them, but most of the fyrd had fled farther east and was being carved into smaller and smaller groups.

Svein at last hauled his men back from the pursuit, but by then nearly all our right wing was gone. Many of those men lived, but they had been driven from the field and would be reluctant to come back and take more punishment. Osric himself had survived, and he brought the two hundred men who had retreated to the women and horses back to Alfred, but that was all he had left. Svein formed his men again, facing us, and I could see him haranguing them. "They're coming for us," I said.

"God will protect us," Pyrlig said. He had blood on his face. A sword or ax had pierced his helmet and cut open his scalp so that blood was crusted thick on his left cheek.

"Where was your shield?" I demanded of Æthelwold.

"I've got it," he said. He looked pale and frightened.

"You're supposed to protect Pyrlig's head," I snarled at him.

"It's nothing." Pyrlig tried to calm my anger.

Æthelwold looked as if he would protest, then suddenly jerked forward and vomited. I turned away from him. I was angry, but I was also disappointed. The bowel-loosening fear was gone, but the fighting had seemed halfhearted and ineffective. We had seen off the Danes who had attacked us, but we had not hurt them so badly that they would abandon the fight. I wanted to feel the battle rage, the screaming joy of killing, and instead all seemed ponderous and difficult.

I had looked for Ragnar during the fight, fearing having to fight my friend, and when the Danes had gone back to the fort I saw he had been engaged farther down the line. I could see him now, on the rampart, staring at us. Then I looked right, expecting to see Svein lead his men in an assault on us, but instead I saw Svein galloping to the fort and I suspected he went to demand reinforcements from Guthrum.

The battle was less than an hour old, yet now it paused. Some women brought us water and moldy bread while the wounded sought what help they could find. I wrapped a rag around Eadric's left arm where an ax blade had gone through the leather of his sleeve. "It was aimed at you, lord," he said, grinning at me toothlessly.

I tied the rag into place. "Does it hurt?"

"Bit of an ache," he said, "but not bad. Not bad." He flexed his arm, found it worked, and picked up his shield. I looked again at Svein's men, but they seemed in no hurry to resume their attack. I saw a man tip a skin of water or ale to his mouth. Just ahead of us, among the line of dead, a man suddenly sat up. He was Danish and had plaited black hair that had been tied in knots and decorated with ribbons. I had thought he was dead, but he sat up and stared at us with a look of indignation and then, seemingly, yawned. He was looking straight at me, his mouth open, and then a flood of blood rimmed and spilled over his lower lip to soak his beard. His eyes rolled white and he fell backward. Svein's men were still not moving. There were some eight hundred of them arrayed in their line. They were still the left wing of Guthrum's army, but that wing was much smaller now that it had been shorn of Wulfhere's men, and so I turned and pushed through our ranks to find Alfred. "Lord!" I called, getting his attention. "Attack those men!" I pointed to Svein's troops. They were a good two hundred paces from the fort and, for the moment at least, without their leader because Svein was still inside the ramparts. Alfred looked down on me from his saddle and I urged him to attack with every man in the center division of our army. The Danes had the escarpment at their back and I reckoned we could tip them down that treacherous slope. Alfred listened to me, looked at Svein's men, then shook his head dumbly. Beocca was on his knees, hands spread wide and face screwed tight in an intensity of prayer.

"We can drive them off, lord," I insisted.

"They'll come from the fort," Alfred said, meaning that Guthrum's Danes would come to help Svein's men.

Some would, but I doubted enough would

come. "But we want them out of the fort," I insisted. "They're easier to kill in open ground, lord."

Alfred just shook his head again. I think, at that moment, he was almost paralyzed by the fear of doing the wrong thing, and so he chose to do nothing. He wore a plain helmet with a nasal, no other protection for his face, and he looked sickly pale. He could not see an obvious opportunity, and so he would let the enemy make the next decision.

It was Svein who made it. He brought more Danes out of the fort, three or four hundred of them. Most of Guthrum's men stayed behind the ramparts, but those men who had made the first attack on Alfred's bodyguard now streamed onto the open downland where they joined Svein's troops and made their shield wall. I could see Ragnar's banner among them.

"They're going to attack, aren't they?" Pyrlig said. The rain had washed much of the blood from his face, but the split in his helmet looked gory. "I'm all right," he said, seeing me glance at the damage. "I've had worse from a row with the wife. But those bastards are coming, aren't they? They want to keep killing us from our right."

"We can beat them, lord," I called back to

Alfred. "Put all our men against them. All of them!"

He seemed not to hear.

"Bring Wiglaf's fyrd across, lord!" I appealed to him.

"We can't move Wiglaf," he said indignantly.

He feared that if he moved the Sumorsæte fyrd from its place in front of the fort, then Guthrum would lead all his men out to assault our left flank, but I knew Guthrum was far too cautious to do any such thing. He felt safe behind the turf ramparts and he wanted to stay safe while Svein won the battle for him. Guthrum would not move until our army was broken; then he would launch an assault. But Alfred would not listen. He was a clever man, perhaps as clever as any man born, but he did not understand battle. He did not understand that battle is not just about numbers, it is not about moving tafl pieces, and it is not even about who has the advantage in ground, but about passion and madness and a screaming, ungovernable rage.

And so far I had felt none of those things. We in Alfred's household troops had fought well enough, but we had merely defended ourselves. We had not carried slaughter to the enemy, and it is only when you attack that you win. Now, it seemed, we were to defend ourselves again, and Alfred stirred himself to order me and my men to the right of his line. "Leave the standards with me," he said, "and make sure our flank is safe."

There was honor in that. The right end of the line was where the enemy might try to wrap around us and Alfred needed good men to hold that open flank, and so we formed a tight knot there. Far off across the down I could see the remnants of Osric's fyrd. They were watching us. Some of them, I thought, would return if they thought we were winning, but for the moment they were too full of fear to rejoin Alfred's army.

Svein rode his white horse up and down the face of his shield wall. He was shouting at his troops, encouraging them. Telling them we were weaklings who needed only one push to topple.

" 'And I looked,' " Pyrlig said to me, " 'and I saw a pale horse, and the rider's name was death.' " I just stared in astonishment. "It's in the gospel book, " he explained sheepishly, "and it just came to mind."

"Then put it out of your mind," I said harshly, "because our job is to kill him, not fear him." I turned to tell Æthelwold to make certain he kept his shield up, but saw he had taken a new place in the rear rank. He was better there, I decided, so let him alone. Svein was shouting that we were lambs waiting to be slaughtered, and his men had begun beating weapons against their shields. There were just over a thousand men in Svein's ranks now, and they would be assaulting Alfred's division, which numbered about the same, but the Danes still had the advantage, for every man in their shield wall was a warrior, while over half our men were from the fyrds of Defnascir, Thornsæta, and Hamptonscir. If we had brought Wiglaf's fyrd to join us we could have overwhelmed Svein, but by the same token he could have swamped us if Guthrum had the courage to leave the fort. Both sides were being cautious. Neither was willing to throw everything into the battle for fear of losing everything.

Svein's horsemen were on his left flank, opposite my men. He wanted us to feel threatened by the riders, but a horse will not charge into a shield wall. It will sheer away, and I would rather face horsemen than foot soldiers. One horse was tossing its head and I could see blood on its neck. Another horse was lying dead out where the corpses lay in the cold wind, which was bringing the first ravens from the north. Black wings in a dull sky. Odin's birds.

"Come and die!" Steapa suddenly shouted. "Come and die, you bastards! Come on!"

His shout prompted others along our line to call insults to the Danes. Svein turned, apparently surprised by our sudden defiance. His men had started forward, but stopped again, and I realized, with surprise, that they were just as fearful as we were. I had always held the Danes in awe, reckoning them the greatest fighting men under the sky. Alfred, in a moment of gloom, once told me it took four Saxons to beat one Dane, and there was truth in that, but it was not a binding truth, and it was not true that day, for there was no passion in Svein's men. There was unhappiness there, a reluctance to advance, and I reckoned that Guthrum and Svein had quarreled. Or perhaps the cold, damp wind had quelled everyone's ardor. "We're going to win this battle!" I shouted, and surprised myself by shouting it.

Men looked at me, wondering if I had been sent a vision by my god.

"We're going to win!" I was hardly aware of speaking. I had not meant to make a speech, but I made one anyway. "They're frightened of us!" I called out. "They're scared! Most of them are skulking in the fort because they daren't come out to face Saxon blades! And those men," I gestured at Svein's ranks with Wasp-Sting, "know they're going to die! They're going to die!" I took a few paces forward and spread my arms to get the Danes' attention. I held my shield out to the left and Wasp-Sting to the right. "You're going to die!" I shouted it in Danish, loud as I could, then in English. "You're going to die!"

And all Alfred's men took up that shout. "You're going to die! You're going to die!"

Something odd happened then. Beocca and Pyrlig claimed that the spirit of God wafted through our army, and maybe that did happen, or else we suddenly began to believe in ourselves. We believed we could win and as the chant was shouted at the enemy, we began to go forward, step by step, beating swords against shields and shouting that the enemy would die. I was ahead of my men, taunting the enemy, screaming at them, dancing as I went, and Alfred called me back to the ranks. Later, when all was done, Beocca told me that Alfred called me repeatedly, but I was capering and shouting, out ahead on the grass where the corpses lay, and I did not hear him. And Alfred's men were following me and he did not call them back though he had not ordered them forward.

"You bastards!" I screamed, "you goat turds! You fight like girls!" I do not know what insults I shouted that day, only that I shouted them and that I went ahead, on my own, asking just one of them to come and fight me man-to-man.

Alfred never approved of those duels between the shield walls. Perhaps, sensibly, he disapproved because he knew he could not have fought one himself, but he also saw them as dangerous. When a man invites an enemy champion to a fight, man on man, he invites his own death, and if he dies he takes the heart from his own side and gives courage to the enemy, and so Alfred ever forbade us to accept Danish challenges, but on that cold wet day one man did accept my challenge.

It was Svein himself. Svein of the White Horse, and he turned the white horse and spurred toward me with his sword in his right hand. I could hear the hooves thumping, see the clods of wet turf flying behind, see the stallion's mane tossing, and I could see Svein's boar-masked helmet above the rim of his shield. Man and horse coming for me, and the Danes were jeering and just then Pyrlig shouted at me. "Uhtred! Uhtred!"

I did not turn to look at him. I was too busy

sheathing Wasp-Sting and was about to pull Serpent-Breath from her scabbard, but just then Pyrlig's thick-shafted boar spear skidded beside me in the wet grass, and I understood what he was trying to tell me. I left Serpent-Breath on my shoulder and snatched up the Briton's spear just as Svein closed on me. All I could hear was the thunder of hooves, see the white cloak spreading, the bright shine of the lofted blade, the tossing horsehair plume, white eyes on the horse, teeth bared, and then Svein twitched the stallion to his left and cut the sword at me. His eyes were glitters behind the eyepieces of his helmet as he leaned to kill me, but as his sword came I threw myself into his horse and rammed the spear into the beast's guts. I had to do it one-handed, for I had my shield on my left arm, but the wide blade pierced hide and muscle, and I was screaming, trying to drive it deeper, and then Svein's sword struck my lifted shield like a hammer blow and his right knee struck my helmet so that I was thrown hard back to sprawl on the grass. I had let go of the spear, but it was well buried in the horse's belly and the animal was screaming and shaking, bucking and tossing, and thick blood was pouring down the spear's shaft that banged and bounced along the grass.

The horse bolted. Svein somehow stayed in the saddle. There was blood on the beast's belly. I had not hurt Svein, I had not touched him, but he was fleeing from me, or rather his white horse was bolting in pain, and it ran straight at Svein's own shield wall. A horse will instinctively swerve away from a shield wall, but this horse was blinded by pain, and then, just short of the Danish shields, it half fell. It slid on the wet grass and skidded hard into the **skjaldborg**, breaking it open. Men scattered from the animal. Svein tumbled from the saddle, and then the horse somehow managed to get back on its feet, and it reared and screamed. Blood was flying from its belly, and its hooves were flailing at the Danes, and now we were charging them at the run. I was on my feet, Serpent-Breath in my right hand, and the horse was thrashing and twisting, and the Danes backed away from it, and that opened their shield wall as we hit them.

Svein was just getting to his feet as Alfred's men arrived. I did not see it, but men said Steapa's sword took Svein's head off in one blow, a blow so hard that the helmeted head flew into the air. Perhaps that was true, but what was certain was that the passion was on us now: the blinding, seething passion of battle. The blood lust, the killing rage, and the horse was doing the work for us, breaking the Danish shield wall apart so all we had to do was ram into the gaps and kill.

And so we killed. Alfred had not meant this to happen. He had expected to wait for the Danish attack and hoped we would resist it, but instead we had thrown off his leash and were doing his work, and he had the wit to send Arnulf's men out to the right because my men were among the enemy. The horsemen had tried to come around our rear, but the men of Suth Seaxa saw them off with shields and swords, then guarded the open flank as all Alfred's men from Æthelingæg and all Harald's men from Defnascir and Thornsæta joined the slaughter. My cousin was there, with his Mercians, and he was a stout fighter. I watched him parry, stab, put down a man, take on another, kill him, and go on steadily. We were making the hilltop rich with Danish blood because we had the fury and they did not, and the men who had fled the field, Osric's men, were coming back to join the fight.

The horsemen went. I did not see them go, though their tale will be told. I was fighting, screaming, shouting at Danes to come and be killed, and Pyrlig was beside me, holding a sword now, and the whole left-hand side of Svein's shield wall had broken and its survivors were making small groups, and we attacked them. I charged one group with the shield, using its boss to slam a man back, and stabbing with Serpent-Breath, feeling her break through mail and leather. Leofric appeared from somewhere, ax swinging, and Pyrlig was ramming his sword's tip into a man's face, and for every Dane there were two Saxons and the enemy stood no chance. One man shouted for mercy and Leofric broke his helmet apart with the ax so that blood and brains oozed onto the jagged metal. I kicked the man aside and plunged Serpent-Breath into a man's groin so that he screamed like a woman in childbirth. The poets often sing of that battle, and for once they get something right when they tell of the sword joy, the blade song, the slaughter. We tore Svein's men to bloody ruin, and we did it with passion, skill, and savagery. The battle calm was on me at last and I could do no wrong. Serpent-Breath had her own life and she stole it from the Danes who tried to oppose me, but those Danes were broken and running and all the left wing of Svein's vaunted troops was defeated.

And there was suddenly no enemy near me

except for the dead and injured. Alfred's nephew, Æthelwold, was jabbing his sword at one of the wounded Danes. "Either kill him," I snarled, "or let him live." The man had a broken leg and had an eye hanging down his bloody cheek and he was no danger to anyone.

"I have to kill one pagan," Æthelwold said. He prodded the man with the sword tip and I kicked his blade aside and would have helped the wounded man except it was then that I saw Haesten.

He was at the hill's edge, a fugitive, and I shouted his name. He turned and saw me, or saw a blood-drenched warrior in mail and a wolf-crested helmet, and he stared at me. Then perhaps he recognized the helmet, for he fled. "Coward!" I shouted at him. "You treacherous, bastard coward! You swore me an oath! I made you rich! I saved your rotten life!"

He turned then, half grinned at me, and waved his left arm on which hung the splintered remnants of a shield. Then he ran to what remained of the right-hand side of Svein's shield wall, and that was still in good order, its shields locked tight. There were five or six hundred men there, and they had swung back, then retreated toward the fort, but now they checked because

Alfred's men, having no one left to kill, were turning on them. Haesten joined the Danish ranks, pushing through the shields, and I saw the eagle-wing banner above them and knew that Ragnar, my friend, was leading those survivors.

I paused. Leofric was shouting at men to form a shield wall and I knew this attack had lost its fury, but we had damaged them. We had killed Svein and a good number of his men, and the Danes were now penned back against the fort. I went to the hill's edge, following a trail of blood on the wet grass, and saw that the white horse had bolted over the down's lip and now lay, its legs grotesquely cocked in the air and its white pelt spattered with blood, a few yards down the slope.

"That was a good horse," Pyrlig said. He had joined me on the edge of the hill. I had thought this crest was the top of the escarpment, but the land was tangled here, as though a giant had kicked the hillside with a massive boot. The ground fell away to make a steep valley that suddenly climbed to a farther crest that was the real edge of the downs. The steep valley sloped up to the fort's eastern corner, and I wondered whether it would offer a way into the fastness. Pyrlig was still staring at the dead horse. "You know what we say at home?" he asked me. "We say that a good horse is worth two good women, that a good woman is worth two good hounds, and that a good hound is worth two good horses."

"You say what?"

"Never mind." He touched my shoulder. "For a Saxon, Uhtred, you fight well. Like a Briton."

I decided the valley offered no advantage over a direct assault and turned away to see that Ragnar was retreating step by step toward the fort. I knew this was the moment to attack him, to keep the battle anger alive and the slaughter fresh, but our men were plundering the dead and the dying and none had the energy to renew the assault, and that meant we would have the harder task of killing Danes protected by a rampart. I thought of my father, killed in an attack on a wall. He had not shown much liking for me, probably because I had been a small child when he died, and now I would have to follow him into the death trap of a well-protected wall. Fate is inexorable.

Svein's banner of the white horse had been captured and a man was waving it toward the Danes. Another had Svein's helmet on the tip of a spear, and at first I thought it was Svein's head, then I saw it was only the helmet. The white horsetail plume was pink now. Father Willibald was holding his hands to heaven, saying a prayer of thanks, and that was premature, I thought, for all we had done was break Svein's men; Guthrum's troops still waited for us behind their walls. And Ragnar was there, too, safe in the fort. Its walls made a semicircle jutting into the downs, ending at the escarpment's lip. They were high walls, protected by a ditch. "It'll be a bastard crossing those ramparts," I said.

"Maybe we won't have to," Pyrlig answered.

"Of course we have to."

"Not if Alfred can talk them out of there," Pyrlig said, and he pointed and I saw that the king, accompanied by two priests and by Osric and Harald, was approaching the fort. "He's going to let them surrender," Pyrlig said.

I could not believe this was the time to talk. This was the killing time, not a place for negotiations. "They won't surrender," I said. "Of course they won't! They still think they can beat us."

"Alfred will try to persuade them," Pyrlig said.

"No." I shook my head. "He'll offer them a truce." I spoke angrily. "He'll offer to take hostages. He'll preach to them. It's what he always does." I thought about going to join him, if for nothing else than to add some sourness to his reasonable suggestions, but I could not summon the effort. Three Danes had gone to talk to him, but I knew they would not accept his offer. They were not beaten; far from it. They still had more men than we did and they had the walls of the fort, and the battle was still theirs to win.

Then I heard the shouts. Shouts of anger and screams of pain, and I turned and saw that the Danish horsemen had reached our women, and the women were screaming and there was nothing we could do.

The Danish horsemen had expected to slaughter the broken remnants of Alfred's shield wall, but instead it had been Svein's men who had been broken and the riders, out on Svein's left flank, had retreated into the downs. They must have thought to circle about our army and rejoin Guthrum from the west, and on the way they had seen our women and horses and smelled easy plunder.

Yet our women had weapons, and there were a few wounded men there, and together they had resisted the horsemen. There was a brief flurry of killing. Then the Danish riders, with nothing to show for their attack, rode away westward. It had taken a few moments, nothing more, but Hild had snatched up a spear and run at a horseman, screaming hate for the horrors the Danes had inflicted on her in Cippanhamm, and Eanflæd, who saw it all, said that Hild sank the spear in a Dane's leg and the man had chopped down with his sword, and Iseult, who had gone to help Hild, had parried the blow with another sword, and a second Dane caught her from behind with an ax, and then a rush of screaming women drove the Danes away. Hild lived, but Iseult's skull had been broken open and her head almost split into two. She was dead.

"She has gone to God," Pyrlig told me when Leofric brought us the news. I was weeping, but I did not know whether it was sorrow or anger that consumed me. I could say nothing. Pyrlig held my shoulders. "She is with God, Uhtred."

"Then the men who sent her there must go to hell," I said. "Any hell. Freeze or burn, the bastards!"

I pulled away from Pyrlig and strode toward Alfred. I saw Wulfhere then. He was a prisoner, guarded by two of Alfred's bodyguards, and he brightened when he saw me as though he thought I was a friend, but I just spat at him and walked on past.

Alfred frowned when I joined him. He was escorted by Osric and Harald, and by Father Beocca and Bishop Alewold, none of whom spoke Danish, but one of the Danes was an English speaker. There were three of them, all strangers to me, but Beocca told me their spokesman was called Hrothgar Ericson and I knew he was one of Guthrum's chieftains. "They attacked the women," I told Alfred. The king just stared at me, perhaps not understanding what I had said. "They attacked the women!" I repeated.

"He's whimpering," the Danish interpreter said to his two companions, "that the women were attacked."

"If I whimper," I turned on the man in fury, "then you will scream." I spoke in Danish. "I shall pull your guts out of your arsehole, wrap them around your filthy neck, and feed your eyeballs to my hounds. Now if you want to translate, you shriveled bastard, translate properly, or else go back to your vomit."

The man blinked but said nothing. Hrothgar, resplendent in mail and silvered helmet, half smiled. "Tell your king," he said, "that we might agree to withdraw to Cippanhamm, but we shall want hostages."

I turned on Alfred. "How many men does Guthrum still have?"

He was still unhappy that I had joined him, but he took the question seriously. "Enough," he said.

"Enough to hold Cippanhamm and a half dozen other towns. We break them now."

"You are welcome to try," Hrothgar said when my words were translated.

I turned back to him. "I killed Ubba," I said, "and I put Svein down, and next I shall cut Guthrum's throat and send him to his whore-mother. We'll try."

"Uhtred." Alfred did not know what I had said, but he had heard my tone and he tried to calm me.

"There's work to be done, lord," I said. It was anger speaking in me, a fury at the Danes and an equal fury at Alfred who was once again offering the enemy terms. He had done it so often. He would beat them in battle and immediately make a truce because he believed they would become Christians and live in brotherly peace. That was his desire, to live in a Christian Britain devoted to piety, but on that day I was right. Guthrum was not beaten, he still outnumbered us, and he had to be destroyed.

"Tell them," Alfred said, "that they can surrender to us now. Tell them they can lay down their weapons and come out of the fort."

Hrothgar treated that proposal with the scorn it deserved. Most of Guthrum's men had yet to fight. They were far from defeated, and the green walls were high and the ditches were deep, and it was the sight of those ramparts that had prompted Alfred to speak with the enemy. He knew men must die, many men, and that was the price he had been unwilling to pay a year before when Guthrum had been trapped in Exanceaster, but it was a price that had to be paid. It was the price of Wessex.

Hrothgar had nothing more to say, so he turned away. "Tell Earl Ragnar," I called after him, "that I am still his brother."

"He will doubtless see you in Valhalla one day," Hrothgar called back, then waved a negligent hand to me. I suspected that the Danes had never intended to negotiate a truce, let alone a surrender, but when Alfred offered to talk they had accepted because it gave them time to organize their defenses.

Alfred scowled at me. He was plainly annoyed that I had intervened, but before he could say anything Beocca spoke. "What happened to the women?" he asked.

"They fought the bastards off," I said, "but Iseult died."

"Iseult," Alfred said, and then he saw the tears in my eyes and did not know what to say. He flinched, stuttered incoherently, then closed his eyes as if in prayer. "I am glad," he said after he had collected his thoughts, "that she died a Christian."

"Amen," Beocca said.

"I would rather she was a live pagan," I snarled, and then we went back to our army and Alfred again summoned his commanders.

There was really no choice. We had to assault the fort. Alfred talked for a time about establishing a siege, but that was not practical. We would have to sustain an army on the summit of the downs and, though Osric insisted the enemy had no springs inside the fort, neither did we have springs close by. Both armies would be thirsty, and we did not have enough men to stop Danes going down the steep embankment at night to fetch water. And if the siege lasted longer than a week, then men of the fyrd would begin to slip home to look after their fields, and Alfred would be tempted to mercy, especially if Guthrum promised to convert to Christianity.

So we urged an assault on Alfred. There could be nothing clever. Shield walls must be made and men sent against the ramparts, and Alfred knew that every man in the army must join the attack. Wiglaf and the men of Sumorsæte would attack on the left, Alfred's men in the center, while Osric, whose fyrd had gathered again and was now reinforced by the men who had deserted from Guthrum's army, would assault on the right. "You know how to do it," Alfred said, though without any enthusiasm for he knew he was ordering us into a feast of death. "Put your best men in the center, let them lead, and make the others press behind and on either side."

No one said anything. Alfred offered a bitter smile. "God has smiled on us so far," he said, "and he will not desert us."

Yet he had deserted Iseult. Poor, fragile Iseult, shadow queen and lost soul, and I pushed into the front rank because the only thing I could do for her now was to take revenge. Steapa, as smothered in blood as I was, pushed into the rank beside me. Leofric was to my left and Pyrlig was now behind me. "Spears and long swords," Pyrlig advised us, "not those short things."

"Why not?" Leofric asked.

"You climb that steep wall," he said, "and all you can do is go for their ankles. Bring them down. I've done it before. You need a long reach and a good shield."

"Jesus help us," Leofric said. We were all fearful, for there is little in warfare as daunting as an assault on a fortress. If I had been in my senses I would have been reluctant to make that attack, but I was filled with a keening sorrow for Iseult and nothing except revenge filled my mind. "Let's go," I said, "let's go."

But we could not go. Men were collecting spears thrown in the earlier fighting, and the bowmen were being brought forward. Whenever we attacked we wanted a shower of spears to precede us and a plague of stinging arrows to annoy the enemy, but it took time to array the spearmen and archers behind the men who would make the assault.

Then, ominously for our archers, it began to rain again. Their bows would still work, but water weakened the strings. The sky became darker as a great belly of black cloud settled over the down and the rain started to drum on helmets. The Danes were lining the ramparts, clashing their weapons against shields, as our army curled about their fastness.

"Forward!" Alfred shouted, and we went toward the ramparts, but stopped just out of bowshot. Rain beaded the rim of my shield. There was a new, bright scar in the iron there, a blade strike, but I had not been aware of the blow. The Danes mocked us. They knew what was coming, and they probably welcomed it. Ever since Guthrum had climbed the escarpment and discovered the fort, he had probably imagined Alfred's men assaulting its walls and his men cutting the enemy down as we struggled up the steep banks. This was Guthrum's battle now. He had placed his rival, Svein, and his Saxon ally, Wulfhere, outside the fort, and doubtless he had hoped they could destroy a good part of our army before the assault on the ramparts, but it would not matter much to Guthrum that those men had been destroyed themselves. Now his own men would fight the battle he had always envisaged.

"In the name of God!" Alfred called, then said no more for suddenly a clap of thunder crashed, a vast sound that consumed the heavens and was so loud that some of us flinched. A crack of light-ning splintered white inside the fort. The rain pelted now, a cloudburst that hammered and soaked us, and more thunder rolled away in the distance. Perhaps we thought that noise and sav-age light was a message from God for suddenly the whole army started forward. No one had given a command unless Alfred's invocation was an order. We just went.

Men were shouting as they advanced. They were not calling insults, but just making a noise to give themselves courage. We did not run, but walked, because the shields had to be kept close. Then another bellow of thunder deafened us, and the rain seemed to have a new and vicious intensity. It seethed on the dead and the living, and we were close now, very close, yet the rain was so thick it was hard to see the waiting Danes. Then I saw the ditch, already flooding, and the bows sounded and the spears flew and we were splashing down the ditch's side and Danish spears were thumping into us. One stuck in my shield, fell away, and I stumbled on its shaft, half sprawled in the water, then recovered and began the climb.

Not all the army tried to cross the ditch. Many men's courage faltered at the brink, but a dozen or more groups went into the attack. We were what the Danes call the **svinfylkjas**, the swine wedges, the elite warriors who try to pierce the **skjaldborg** like a boar trying to gouge the hunter with its tusks. But this time we not only had to gouge the **skjaldborg**, but cross the rain-flooded ditch and clamber up the bank.

We held our shields over our heads as we splashed through the ditch. Then we climbed, but the wet bank was so slippery that we constantly fell back, and the Danish spears kept coming, and someone pushed me from behind and I was crawling up the bank on my knees, the shield over my head, and Pyrlig's shield was covering my spine and I heard a thumping above me and thought it was thunder. Except the shield kept banging against my helmet and I knew a Dane was hacking at me, trying to break through the limewood to drive his ax or sword into my spine, and I crawled again, lifted the shield's lower edge, and saw boots. I lunged with Serpent-Breath, tried to stand, felt a blow on my leg, and fell again. Steapa was roaring beside me. There was mud in my mouth, and the rain hammered at us. I could hear the crash of blades sinking in shields and I knew we had failed, but I tried to stand again and lunged with Serpent-Breath and on my left Leofric gave a shrill cry and I saw blood streaming into the grass. The blood was instantly washed away by the rain, and another peal of thunder crashed overhead as I slithered back to the ditch.

The bank was scarred where we had tried to climb; the grass had been gouged down to the white chalk. We had failed utterly and the Danes were screaming defiance. Then another rush of men splashed through the ditch and the banging of blades and shields began again. I climbed a second time, trying to dig my boots into the chalk, and my shield was raised so I did not see the Danes coming down to meet me, and the first I knew was when an ax struck the shield so hard that the boards splintered, and a second ax gave me a glancing blow on the helmet and I fell backward and would have lost Serpent-Breath if it had not been for the loop of Iseult's hair about my wrist. Steapa managed to seize a Danish spear and pulled its owner down the bank where a half dozen Saxons hacked and stabbed in fury so that the ditch was churning with water, blood, and blades, and someone shouted for us to go again, and I saw it was Alfred, dismounted, coming to cross the ditch, and I roared for my men to protect him.

Pyrlig and I managed to get in front of the king and we stayed there, protecting him as we tried to climb that blood-fouled bank a third time. Pyrlig was screaming in his native tongue, I was cursing in Danish, and somehow we got halfway up and stayed on our feet. Someone, perhaps it was Alfred, was pushing me from behind. Rain hammered us, soaked us. A peal of thunder shook the heavens and I swung Serpent-Breath, trying to hack the Danish shields aside, then swung again, and the shock of the blade striking a shield boss jarred up my arm. A Dane, all beard and wide eyes, lunged a spear at me. I lunged back with the sword, shouted Iseult's name, tried to climb, and the spear Dane slammed his spear forward again. The blade struck my helmet's forehead and my head snapped back, and another Dane hit me on the side of the head and all the world went drunken and dark. My feet slid and I was half aware of falling down into the ditch water. Someone pulled me clear and dragged me back to the ditch's far side, and there I tried to stand, but fell again.

The king. The king. He had to be protected and he had been in the ditch when I had last seen him, and I knew Alfred was no warrior. He was brave, but he did not love the slaughter as a warrior loves it. I tried to stand again, and this time succeeded, but blood squelched in my right boot and flowed over the boot top when I put my weight on that leg. The ditch bottom was thick with dead and dying men, half drowned by the flood, but the living had fled from the ditch and the Danes were laughing at us. "To me!" I shouted. There had to be one last effort. Steapa and Pyrlig closed on me, and Eadric was there, and I was groggy and my head was filled with a ringing sound and my arm seemed feeble, but we had to make that last effort. "Where's the king?" I asked.

"I threw him out of the ditch," Pyrlig said.

"Is he safe?"

"I told the priests to hold him down. Told them to hit him if he tried to go again."

"One more attack," I said. I did not want to make it. I did not want to clamber over the bodies in the ditch and try to climb that impossible wall, and I knew it was stupid, knew I would probably die if I went again, but we were warriors and warriors will not be beaten. It is reputation. It is pride. It is the madness of battle. I began beating Serpent-Breath against my half-broken shield, and other men took up the rhythm, and the Danes, so close, were inviting us to come and be killed, and I shouted that we were coming. "God help us," Steapa said.

"God help us," Pyrlig echoed.

I did not want to go. I was frightened, but I feared being called a coward more than I feared the ramparts, and so I screamed at my men to slaughter the bastards, and then I ran. I jumped over the corpses in the ditch, lost my footing on the far side, fell on my shield, and rolled aside so that no Dane could plunge a spear into my unprotected back. I hauled myself up and my helmet had skewed in the fall so that the faceplate half-blinded me, and I fumbled it straight with my sword hand as I began to climb and Steapa was there, and Pyrlig was with me, and I waited for the first hard Danish blow.

It did not come. I struggled up the bank, the shield over my head, and I expected the death blow, but there was silence and I lifted the shield and thought I must have died for all I saw was the rain-filled sky. The Danes had gone. One moment they had been sneering at us, calling us women and cowards, and boasting how they would slice open our bellies and feed our guts to the ravens, and now they were gone. I clambered to the top of the wall and saw a second ditch and second wall beyond, and the Danes were scrambling up that inner rampart and I supposed that they intended to make a defense there, but instead they vanished over its top and Pyrlig grabbed my arm and pulled me on. "They're running!" he shouted. "By God, the bastards are running!" He had to shout to make himself heard over the rain.

"On! On!" someone shouted and we ran into the second flooded ditch and up over the undefended inner bank and I saw Osric's men, the fyrd of Wiltunscir that had been defeated in the opening moments of the fight, had managed to cross the fort's walls. We learned later that they had gone into the valley where the white horse lay dead, and in the blinding rain they had made it to the fort's eastern corner, which, because Guthrum thought it unapproachable, was only lightly defended. The rampart was lower there, hardly more than a grassy ridge on the valley's slope, and they had flooded over the wall and so got behind the other defenders.

Who now ran. If they had stayed, then they would have been slaughtered to a man, so they fled across the fort's wide interior, and some were slow to realize that the battle was lost and those we trapped. I just wanted to kill for Iseult's sake, and I put two fugitives down, hacking them with Serpent-Breath with such fury that she cut through mail, leather, and flesh to bite as deep as an ax. I was screaming my anger, wanting more victims, but we were too many and the trapped Danes were too few. The rain kept falling and the thunder bellowed as I looked about for enemies to kill, and then I saw one last group of them, back-to-back, fighting off a swarm of Saxons, and I ran toward them and suddenly saw their banner. The eagle's wing. It was Ragnar.

His men, outnumbered and overwhelmed, were dying. "Let him live!" I shouted. "Let him live!" And three Saxons turned toward me and they saw my long hair and my arm rings bright on my mailed sleeves, and they must have thought I was a Dane for they ran at me, and I fended off the first with Serpent-Breath. The second hammered my shield with his ax, and the third circled behind me and I turned fast, scything Serpent-Breath, shouted that I was a Saxon, but they did not hear me. Then Steapa slammed into them and they scattered, and Pyrlig grabbed my arm, but I shook him off and ran toward Ragnar who was snarling at the ring of enemies, inviting any one of them to try to kill him. His banner had fallen and his crewmen were dead, but he looked like a war god in his shining mail and with his splintered shield and his long sword and his defiant face, and then the ring began to close. I ran, shouting, and he turned toward me, thinking I had come to kill him, and he raised his sword and I brushed it aside with my shield, threw my arms around him, and drove him to the turf.

Steapa and Pyrlig guarded us. They fended off the Saxons, telling them to look for other victims, and I rolled away from Ragnar who sat up and looked at me with astonishment. I saw that his shield hand was bloody. A blade, cutting through the limewood, had sliced into his palm, hacking down between the fingers so that it looked as though he had two small hands instead of one. "I must bind that wound," I said.

"Uhtred," he just said, as if he did not really believe it was me.

"I looked for you," I told him, "because I did not want to fight you."

He flinched as he shook the shattered remnants of the shield away from his wounded hand. I could see Bishop Alewold running across the fort in mud-spattered robes, waving his arms and shouting that God had delivered the pagans into our hands. "I told Guthrum to fight outside the fort," Ragnar said. "We would have killed you all."

"You would," I agreed. By staying in the fort Guthrum had let us defeat his army piece by piece, but even so it was a miracle that the day was ours.

"You're bleeding," Ragnar said. I had taken a spear blade in the back of my right thigh. I have the scar to this day.

Pyrlig cut a strip of cloth from a dead man's jerkin and used it to bind Ragnar's hand. He wanted to bandage my thigh, but the bleeding had lessened and I managed to stand, though the pain, which I had not felt ever since the wound had been given, suddenly struck me. I touched Thor's hammer. We had won. "They killed my woman," I told Ragnar. He said nothing, but just stood beside me and, because my thigh was agony and I suddenly felt weak, I put an arm about his shoulders. "Iseult, she was called," I said, "and my son is dead, too." I was glad it was raining or else the tears on my face would have shown. "Where's Brida?"

"I sent her down the hill," Ragnar told me. We were limping together toward the fort's northern ramparts.

"And you stayed?"

"Someone had to stay as a rear guard," he said bleakly. I think he was crying, too, because of the shame of the defeat. It was a battle Guthrum could not lose, yet he had.

Pyrlig and Steapa were still with me, and I could see Eadric stripping a dead Dane of his mail, but there was no sign of Leofric. I asked Pyrlig where he was, and Pyrlig gave me a pained look and shook his head.

"Dead?" I asked.

"An ax," he said, "in the spine." I was numb, too numb to speak, for it did not seem possible that the indestructible Leofric was dead, but he was, and I wished I could give him a Danish funeral, a fire funeral, so that the smoke of his corpse would rise to the halls of the gods. "I'm sorry," Pyrlig said.

"The price of Wessex," I said, and then we climbed the northern ramparts that were crowded with Alfred's soldiers.

The rain was lessening, though it still fell in great swaths across the plain below. It was as if we stood on the rim of the world, and ahead of us was an immensity of cloud and rain, while beneath us, on the long steep slope, hundreds of Danes scrambled to the foot of the escarpment where their horses had been left. "Guthrum," Ragnar said bitterly.

"He lives?"

"He was the first to run," he said. "Svein told him we should fight outside the walls," he went on, "but Guthrum feared defeat more than he ever wanted victory."

A cheer sounded as Alfred's banners were carried across the captured fort to the northern ramparts. Alfred, mounted again, and with a bronze circlet about his helmet, rode with the flags. Beocca was on his knees giving thanks, while Alfred had a dazed smile and a look of disbelief, and I swear he wept as his standards were rammed into the turf at the world's edge. The dragon and the cross flew above his kingdom that had almost been lost, but had been saved so that there was still one Saxon king in England.

But Leofric was dead and Iseult was a corpse and a hard rain fell across the land we had rescued.

Wessex.

HISTORICAL NOTE

The Westbury white horse is cut into the chalk of the escarpment beneath Bratton Camp on the edge of the Wiltshire Downs. From the north it can be seen for miles. The present horse, a handsome beast, is over a hundred feet long and almost two hundred feet high and was cut in the 1770s, making it the oldest of Wiltshire's ten white horses, but local legend says that it replaced a much older horse that was blazoned into the chalk hillside after the battle of Ethandun in 878.

I should like to think that legend is true, but no historian can be certain of the location of the battle of Ethandun where Alfred met Guthrum's Danes, though Bratton Camp, above the village of Edington, is the prime candidate. Bratton Camp is an Iron Age fortress that still stands just above the Westbury white horse. John Peddie, in his useful book, **Alfred, Warrior King**, places Ethandun at Bratton Camp, and Edgar's Stone at Kingston Deverill in the Wylye valley, and I am persuaded by his reasoning.

There is no debate about the location of Æthelingæg. That is now Athelney, in the Somerset Levels, near Taunton, and if Bratton Camp is substantially unaltered since 878, the levels are changed utterly. Today, mostly thanks to the medieval monks who diked and drained the land, they make a wide, fertile plain, but in the ninth century they were a vast swamp mingled with tidal flats, an almost impenetrable marsh into which Alfred retreated after the disasters at Chippenham.

That disaster was the result of his generosity in agreeing to the truce that allowed Guthrum to leave Exeter and retreat to Gloucester in Danish-held Mercia. That truce was secured by Danish hostages, but Guthrum, just as he had broken the truce arranged at Wareham in 876, again proved untrustworthy and, immediately after Twelfth Night, attacked and captured Chippenham, thus precipitating the greatest crisis of Alfred's long reign. The king was defeated and most of his country taken by the Danes. Some great nobles, Wulfhere, the Ealdorman of Wilt-shire, among them, defected to the enemy, and Alfred's kingdom was reduced to the watery wastes of the Somerset Levels. Yet in the spring, just four months after the disaster at Chippen-ham, Alfred assembled an army, led it to Ethandun, and there defeated Guthrum. All that happened. What, sadly, did not probably happen is the burning of the cakes. That story, how a peasant woman struck Alfred after he allowed her cakes to burn, is the most famous folktale at-tached to Alfred, but its source is very late and thus very unreliable.

Alfred, Ælswith, Wulfhere, Æthelwold, and Brother (later Bishop) Asser all existed, as did Guthrum. Svein is a fictional character. The great Danish enemies before Guthrum had been the three Lothbrok brothers, and the defeat of the last of them at the battle of Cynuit occurred while Alfred was at Athelney. For fictional rea-sons I moved that Saxon victory forward a year, and it forms the ending of **The Last Kingdom**, the novel that precedes **The Pale Horseman**, which meant I had to invent a character, Svein, and a skirmish, the burning of Svein's ships, to replace Cynuit.

The two primary sources for Alfred's reign are

the Anglo-Saxon Chronicle and Bishop Asser's life of the king, and neither, alas, tells us much about how Alfred defeated Guthrum at Ethandun. Both armies, by later standards, were small, and it is almost certain that Guthrum considerably outnumbered Alfred. The West Saxon fyrd that won Ethandun was mostly drawn from Somerset, Wiltshire, and western Hampshire, suggesting that all eastern Wessex, and most of the north of the country, had been subdued by the Danes. We know the fyrd of Devonshire was intact (it had won the victory at Cynuit), as was the fyrd of Dorset, yet neither is mentioned as part of Alfred's army, suggesting that they were held back to deter a seaborne attack. The lack of the fyrds from those two powerful shires, if indeed they were absent, only confirms what a remarkable victory Alfred won.

The Saxons had been in Britain since the fifth century. By the ninth century they ruled almost all of what is now England, but then the Danes came and the Saxon kingdoms crumbled. **The Last Kingdom** tells of the defeat of Northumbria, Mercia, and East Anglia, and **The Pale Horseman** describes how Wessex almost followed those northern neighbors into history's oblivion. For a few months in early 878 the idea of England, its culture and language, were reduced to a few square miles of swamp. One more defeat and there would probably never have been a political entity called England. We might have had a Daneland instead, and this novel would probably have been written in Danish. Yet Alfred survived, he won, and that is why history awarded him the honorific "the Great." His successors were to finish his work. They were to take back the three northern kingdoms and so, for the first time, unite the Saxon lands into one kingdom called England, but that work was begun by Alfred the Great.

Yet in 878, even after the victory at Ethandun, that must have seemed an impossible dream. It is a long way from Ethandun's white horse to the bleak moors north of Hadrian's Wall, so Uhtred and his companions must campaign again.